Ruth Padel is a prizewinning poet, Fellow of the Royal Society of Literature and Zoological Society of London. She has also written a range of non-fiction, including a highly acclaimed book on tiger conservation – *Tigers in Red Weather* – for which she explored tiger forests in Asia and India. She writes and presents radio programmes on writers, scientists and composers such as Tennyson, Darwin and Elgar, and her latest poetry collection is a much-praised biography in lyric poems of her great-great-grandfather Charles Darwin. Ruth was born and lives in London but is currently Resident Poet at Christ's College, Cambridge. This is her first novel.

'The prose is beautiful, and the sexy charming husband is a frightful and fascinating creation'
The Times

'Padel brings a poet's intensity to her prose . . . her narrative spirals like a tropical plant, luxuriant with metaphor and imagery'
Spectator

'Gripping and wonderfully original'
Gillian Beer

'Mystery in the wordless world of animals watching humans'
TLS

'A spell-binding read, luminous and true'
Oxford Times

'Magical. The wildlife is conjured up exquisitely. When the naturalist confronts a king cobra, there has been little in literature to match it since D.H. Lawrence's poem "The Snake"'
Time Out Mumbai

'A nature lover's delight, surprisingly readable. Compelling, acute, lyrical, and wonderfully pulse-quickening moments. She has done for the forests of Karnataka and Bengal what Amitav Ghosh did for the Sundarbans in *The Hungry Tide*'
India Today

Also by Ruth Padel

POETRY

Alibi
Summer Snow
Angel
Fusewire
Rembrandt Would Have Loved You
Voodoo Shop
The Soho Leopard
Darwin – A Life in Poems

NON-FICTION

In and Out of the Mind
Whom Gods Destroy
I'm a Man: Sex, Gods and Rock 'n' Roll
52 Ways of Looking at a Poem
The Poem and the Journey
Tigers in Red Weather
Silent Letters of the Alphabet

EDITIONS

Alfred Lord Tennyson, Selected Poems with Introduction
Sir Walter Ralegh, Selected Poems with Introduction

WHERE THE SERPENT LIVES

Ruth Padel

ABACUS

First published in Great Britain in 2010 by Little, Brown
This paperback edition published in 2011 by Abacus

5 7 9 10 8 6 4

A CIP catalogue record for this book
is available from the British Library.

ISBN 978-0-349-12232-8

Typeset in Palatino by M Rules
Printed and bound in Great Britain by
Clays Ltd, St Ives plc

Papers used by Abacus are from well-managed forests
and other responsible sources.

MIX
Paper from
responsible sources
FSC® C104740

Abacus
An imprint of
Little, Brown Book Group
100 Victoria Embankment
London EC4Y 0DY

An Hachette UK Company
www.hachette.co.uk

www.littlebrown.co.uk

For the Master and Fellows, staff and students of
Christ's College, Cambridge

Many warm thanks for reading and criticism to Gwen Burnyeat, Shekar Dattari, Nicola Lane, Nicholas de Lange, Elaine Feinstein, Pedro Ferreira, Eva Hoffman, Aamer Hussein, Vivek Nanda, Michèle Roberts, Mandana Ruane and members of Kindlings. Also to my agent Patrick Walsh and my editors Antonia Hodgson and Jenny Parrott.

Many thanks also to people who gave advice on snakes: Jennifer Daltry, Shekar Dattari (especially on milking cobras), Richard Griffiths and Romulus Whittaker. On what it feels like to step on a king cobra in twilit jungle and be head-butted, thanks to Jeremy Holden. I apologise for introducing an Olive Oriental Slender Snake to north-east Bengal. Warm thanks to Martin Tuck, carpenter at Christ's College, Cambridge, for practical tuition on handling snakes.

Warm thanks also for other information to Leonor and Zoran Stjepic, Bettina Jonic, Andy Fisher of the Metropolitan Police Wildlife Unit, Girish Karnad (for his help and also for his play *Naga-Mandala*) and Sunetra Gupta.

Many thanks to the Society of Authors for an unexpected travel bursary, the Calouste Gulbenkian Foundation for a grant for research in Karnataka in 2005, and the British Council for a Darwin Now Award 2009, which enabled me to go snake-catching with the Irula south of Chennai, explore king cobra territory in Bhadra Forest with the Wildcats, visit Agumbe Rainforest Research Station to learn about their research on king cobras, and go out with trackers into prime king cobra territory. Many thanks for all these projects also to Rom Whitaker, his research and his help, Dr Ullas Karanth and his unique organization Wildlife First, Gowri Shankar, Education Officer at Agumbe Research Station and king cobra rescuer supreme; and also to Sharmila Chandrashegram, Base Manager P. Prashanth and Vipul Ramanuj for looking after me at Agumbe.

Finally, many warm thanks to the Leverhulme Foundation and Christ's College, Cambridge, for a Leverhulme-funded artist's residency at Charles Darwin's old college, which bought me time to write a final draft while allowing me to take part in the life of a delightful community of teachers, scholars and students.

They will charge us with having culpably allowed the destruction of some of those records of Creation we had it in our power to conserve. And, while professing to regard every living thing as the direct handiwork and best evidence of a Creator, yet, with a strange inconsistency, seeing many of them perish irrevocably from the face of the earth.

Alfred Russel Wallace

This is where the serpent lives, the bodiless.
His head is air. Beneath his tip at night
Eyes open and fix on us in every sky.

Or is this another wriggling out of the egg,
Another image at the end of the cave,
Another bodiless for the body's slough?

This is where the serpent lives. This is his nest,
These fields, these hills, these tinted distances,
And the pines above and along and beside the sea.

Wallace Stevens, 'The Auroras of Autumn'

CONTENTS

CONTENTS

NEST

1

Wednesday 9 March 2005, Karnataka, India, 4.30 p.m.; 11.00 a.m., UK

Rainforest, in the dry season. If you had looked closely at those black zigzag lines under green bamboo, you would have seen they were not the shadows of overlapping leaves but edges between the charcoal-grey scales of her head. You could have admired the bronze shadows in each honey-flame iris, the pearl-pale ring encircling each black pupil, and maybe have seen the whole of her – a dark knot on a double-decked mound of dead bamboo leaves, high as a man's thigh.

The only movement was a luminous ant exploring the underside of a leaf, and a few mites, like red full stops, sampling her interstitial skin.

Suddenly, far off, there was a rasping cry, a leopard calling cubs, maybe. She part-spread her hood. She had no external ear, she would not have heard us talking beside her, but this low-frequency call hit the side of her skull, travelled from her skin into jaw muscle and quadrate bone, and flicked her inner ear. She dabbed out her tongue. The prongs, two tubes of glistening black shading to grey-pink, waved in different directions, tasting the air, decoding scents and calling them into cavities in her mouth, lined with nerve endings. To her, as to all snakes, taste and smell were one.

A small brown babbler flew to a lower branch, displacing a leaf, and her eyes were on it before it reached the ground. She was on guard. But she was very thirsty. Making a tumulus and laying thirty eggs in it is hard work.

She was young and this was her first time. Evolution had not let her down, a million years of it had been at work in her as she made the incubation chamber. Her eggs required specific heat and humidity for two months and they'd get it, no problem. She was not one degree out. But she needed water.

Afternoon light shone through the translucent flanges either side of her head and on the gold horizontal throat scales. Her throat would have seemed curiously thin and flat, like a twist of sugar-paper, if you'd looked at her from the side.

And someone was looking. A slight, bespectacled man, utterly silent, whose palms were hot and rather wet. Her heart had three chambers. He knew that, he was a biologist. His own had four and he wanted the blood to keep going safely through them all. Which it would stop doing, if it came into contact with one drop of the neuro-toxin being manufactured, twenty feet away, by salivary glands in her head.

Some people call king cobras aggressive. But aggressive, Richard would tell you, is only interpretation. He'd say active defensive, him-self. Anyway, each king is different. Snakes, Richard sometimes said to his wife (she'd heard it before but she'd laugh and listen again), are like beings from outer space, a totally different intelligence. Their brains and emotions are not large or complex, but they do have them and king cobras have them in spades.

Richard had watched this female frothing fallen leaves into a heap, muscling sideways like a TV cable brushing the studio floor. Female kings, he'd tell you, are the only snake to make a nest. They sit over the eggs for two months, not leaving even to eat. If they leave, humid-ity and temperature change. The eggs start to discolour within an hour. But this female was young; she might behave differently.

She did. Dark coils flowed over each other as she unwound. Nine foot of ivory chevrons disappeared like a yanked rope into the under-growth. She could only have left for water and Richard knew where the stream was. This was his chance. Five minutes, maybe ten. He stepped forward, putting each foot down slow, to press snappable veins of any dry leaf deep into the loam. He was thirty-seven and a field zoologist. His research permit from the chief wildlife warden allowed him to walk in the forest, measure and observe, but not remove anything, even king cobra scat.

*

4

Richard's relations with the director of this South Indian national park were strained. The last director was devoted to the forest. Richard's research, and the kings themselves, had flourished. The new one had arrived six months ago. He resented being sent into the sticks from an office job in Mangalore, knew nothing about wildlife and at once began selling protected trees to a saw mill. Richard had been agonised to see forest he had worked in for fifteen years dwindling. There are hundreds of wonderful directors in India, he emailed his wife despairingly, and they've sent us a tosser.

He had not pointed out that what the director had done was illegal.

'Cutting those trees,' he said carefully in the state language, Kannada, over the desk where he had held so many ardent conversations with the previous director, 'destroys wild animals that depend on the trees.'

'I am trained in forest management,' said the new director in English, even more carefully, in a voice like granite. 'You are not.' He must have phoned the forest minister at once, for someone tried cancelling Richard's permit on the grounds that he was interfering in forest policy. That failed, so the director turned to local journalists. A paragraph in the *Mangalore Times* said Richard was smuggling king cobra skins. What else would an Englishman be doing in the national forest but making money? And why king cobras? All cobras are messengers from god. King cobras, those mystical, deep-forest dwellers, are doubly divine.

Richard was protected by friends in the state, but how long could this go on? He was a scientist, no diplomat. He simply believed that the more we know about king cobras, the better we can protect them. And just now, knowledge meant taking precise measurements in a vacant nest.

The eggs were soft, like tennis balls. No leeches, but a few mites. More must be sucking her blood. But she'd looked OK – shiny, not anaemic. Out with the humidity gauge. Ninety per cent. Brilliant. Thermometer: 27.8. Perfect. Well done, young mum. Hurry home now.

He heard a rustle. Oh God, was she back already? No, just a tree shrew, staring from a branch. But it was definitely time to go.

Where a small stream leaked over the path, he saw a paw mark filling with water. Leopard, in the last fifteen minutes. You never saw leopards but they were always around. He heard human voices, ducked under bushes and saw five men. They must belong to the village inside the park. Those villagers wanted to move to a settlement, already built to their requirements, outside the park. They'd be close to schools there, and to work. But the new director had not released the funds to move them so here they stayed, decimating the wildlife.

Three carried mattocks and bags. Two had guns. All were thin: the villagers were very poor. Hunting was their traditional livelihood. It was illegal here now this was a sanctuary. The animals were supposed to be protected. But with better medicine there were more children, so fewer wild animals every year. The previous year poachers all over India had killed or maimed a hundred forest guards.

When they'd gone, Richard began slowly to straighten, but above him came a low roary growl and he froze. He was one of the few people in the world who knew what that growl was.

King cobras do not hiss like other snakes: they expel air through holes in their trachea. Now he saw a hood, towering above him. Her golden throat, black-edged like a mourning card, was two feet from his nose. She must have been rearing up to see over the bushes and he'd alarmed her by standing up himself.

In that electric moment when human meets king cobra eye to eye, each is liable to confuse the other's motive. Keep still, he thought. Be very still. He knew the biology all too well. She could force into his tissues 0.7 millilitres of citron-tinged venom, enough to kill an elephant; or twenty people. Running was hopeless. He'd still be in her range six feet away and she could charge amazingly fast. No eye contact. Let her gaze. She would do what she decided. He thought of Irena. Irena in the kitchen, laughing. Irena's narrow body smooth in the dark, hair tickling his shoulder.

Then, treacherously, that dark hair became red-gold curls. Oh no, not now . . . A face formed in front of him. Pale, perfect cheekbones he had never touched, a wide soft mouth, ringlets of tangerine hair which for twenty years he'd longed to run his fingers through. He shifted slightly, the snake growled again and his vision faded.

The forest was utterly still, but for the thud of his still healthy heart. The leech wriggling over his shoe might be surprised in a minute by what was happening to the blood it was so keen to reach.

Every snake venom is a unique cocktail of enzymes, polypeptides and glycoproteins which act on different systems of the body: nerves, breath, muscles and blood. Neurotoxin, the main component in cobra venom, would bind instantly to receptors on the surface of his muscle cells, block communication between his nerves and muscles, severing the impulses that made his muscles contract. Meanwhile, tissues round the bite would swell and necrotise, haemorrhagin would crumble his capillaries and his own blood would circulate to the rest of his body the proteins causing all this havoc.

The park did not stock king cobra antivenin, which was only made in Thailand. Anyway, he would never reach the guard post. Within minutes, those neurotoxins would stun his nervous system and slow his breathing. Paralysis would follow, as the textbooks said, very fast.

Looking down at his feet like a boy confessing to a broken rule, Richard stood immobile for what seemed a very long time. He concentrated, as only a scientist or poet can, on precise names for the leaves he was looking at. He felt her eyes upon him. He was in the hands of the living god, of neurosynapses in a reptile brain.

When he looked up she was gone.

Wednesday 9 March, Primrose Hill, London, 11.30 a.m.; 5.00 p.m., India

Picturing herself as a small jungle animal peering from the shadows, Rosamund Fairfax walks out of her house into a garden.

Rosamund never asked to go through life with a zoo in her head. She has never told anybody she can only make sense of human existence by recoding it all, herself included, as animal. Not Irena, not Tyler. She shared more of her inner self with Russel when he was little than with anyone else, but she never told him either.

There is, or used to be, an outside Rosamund, warm and sparkly. But she is afraid there is something quite different inside. A wild shy unlovable animal. The Madagascan Cryptic Frog looks more like dead leaves than a lot of leaves do and Rosamund sympathises. She often feels like a pile of dead leaves herself.

She doesn't know these animals in real life. The zoo in her head is a dead zoo, placed there by her father, whom she hasn't seen for thirteen years. Father cared a lot about her mind, and her mind is where the wildlife stays. She has no idea that every move she makes, in this pewtery light of March, is being monitored from the back fence where a pregnant vixen is curled up under the brambles.

Since Rosamund and Tyler put a conservatory on the end of their kitchen, the local foxes have watched them cook and eat through a transparent wall. Foxes listen to all they do, with hearing keen as a spike through the heart.

Rosamund's nose and hands are mauve with cold. She hates gardening in gloves, she likes feeling stems and roots. She has high cheekbones and pale skin. Even at thirty-seven, in a raw wind with no make-up, she has a frail grace which makes being human seem appealing and easy. At school and college she used to be surrounded by admirers. She told jokes, she was a star on the dance floor. Now she has a husband and son but feels alone all the time and scuttles through her days on mental paths like vole runs through a field. This garden is where she feels safe.

Last year she did a course in design at the Chelsea Physic Garden. Tyler bought her the course for her birthday, slapping the brochure on the table like a winning hand at poker.

'Stop you sitting on your fanny all day,' he said, which was very unfair since it was he who stopped her working when she had Russel. But when did Tyler ever do fair?

She is proud of her diploma, the only qualification she has. She studied biology for three years at university, which pleased her biologist father, but dropped out before the fourth year which did not please Father at all.

There is a story behind that, but not thinking about it helps her stay safe. Not thinking is how her solitary jungle self keeps going. She sees this as a Rusty Spotted Cat – one of Asia's smallest wild cats, Father used to say, which slips through the undergrowth trying not to be seen by larger predators.

She hasn't done what her course was meant for and launched her own garden design business. Her design file (*Costing, Axonometric Drawing, Theory*) lies quilted with dust on a kitchen shelf. She tells herself she will start, soon. She did design a patio garden for friends of Tyler's but they wanted mirrors, decking and stones, Japanese style, and in Rosamund's opinion a garden is made of living things. She likes getting her hands dirty, breathing the leaves.

No one else comes here now. Russel stays in his room, Tyler lights the odd cigarette out here now he's forbidden to smoke in the house, and loves their summer parties. Yes, amazingly large, for London. Quarter of an acre, actually. So lucky.

There's an enormous mortgage somewhere. Rosamund pictures it as an exotic pet fed by Tyler in the basement and paraded in an iron collar. I'm loaded, Tyler says. I make more money than anyone I know. He is a music promoter, specialising in girl bands. Doing shockingly well these days, he will say with a self-deprecating smile.

Tyler billowed into her life in her second year of college, seven years older than her, broad shoulders and twinkling smiles, convinced that the world came into existence for him to enjoy. In the lavish appreciating that is Tyler's great gift, Rosamund's Rusty Spotted self vanished as if it had never been. She felt human for the very first time. You're everything, he said, I've ever loved.

That was eighteen years ago and Rusty Spotted is back now with a vengeance. For ten years, Rosamund has slept alone in a carved walnut bed, originally their guest bed. For our fab friends, said Tyler, to cavort in when they stay. No one cavorts in it now. Rosamund has covered it in vintage Edwardian lawn and sleeps there in a night-dress that covers her completely, throat to ankle.

Today, in her mud-coloured cargo pants, mole-brown jumper and cracked waxed jacket, Rosamund blends into this chilly garden like its resident divinity. Her hair spills out under her woolly cap like gold leaf scraped into curls by a knife. Her mouth is full and wide as if made to do nothing but laugh. A cold sore has erupted on her lip.

Two flowerbeds wing away either side of the bare rose arch and a path curves onwards towards the shed, their Heidi Home, which has hearts cut in its eaves, a porch covered in brambles and one corner marbled by Bono's territorial dribbles.

This is pruning time, before the garden wakes up. But where to start?

She looks at emerald leaves cascading over the fence by the house. You'd never know there are camellias in there. That jasmine is nice and green now when everything is brown, but it has to go. She advances on it with secateurs.

The vixen watches from the brambles. The woman is carrying something. Some things she carries are edible and get left on odorous heaps behind the shed. But instead she begins attacking the best thing about this territory, from the fox point of view: its cover. For ten years, an outsize dog has prevented foxes denning here. The dog is slowing and stiffening now. Any fox could mark the tremor in the back legs. The vixen has decided to have her cubs here. The Heidi Home used to stand on solid ground. Rosamund and Tyler think it still does, but the foxes have dug a hole beneath.

Marching to the rescue of her camellias, Rosamund untwists long green whips of jasmine, which pile up round her boots. She likes pruning, you can't be a gardener without it, but she hates to hurt living cells. Snip, snip. The secateurs get into a rhythm. When did she plant this jasmine? The summer they came, fifteen years ago when she was pregnant. The first thing she planted, clumsily, not having done it since she was little. Trying to recreate the magic, the garden she grew up in.

Cutting into the hardened spaghetti of jasmine fronds she sees a demon mask looking at her, crooked and sly like the eyes she saw on her ninth birthday, the one day she went into forest with Father.

But no. This is only a funny-shaped knot. She throws it behind her and snips on.

She hadn't wanted to go into forest. The garden was what she loved as a child. She felt so alive, slipping out in early morning alone. She loved the rustly silence, tendrils dancing in the wind that came before the rains, the dreamtangle of flowers over her head, the little orange paths between islands of coarse grass, the hundreds of

10

different shapes of leafs, bronze, red, peppermint, all kinds of green. Some two-tone with paler undersides, like sweets the cook brought from the bazaar.

In the mornings, that garden had a Light Side and Dark Side. Where the trees were close together, one path disappeared in deep black shadow and was deliciously scary. Once she had seen a mongoose there, a calm brown little presence, silent and comforting. And there was a bush covered in bees, the Buzzing Bush, which she always ran past, fast as she could.

But when Father came round the garden with her, drilling her in scientific names for butterflies and birds, expounding the anatomy of lizards, all that magic vanished. With him there, she felt two opposite uncomfortable things. She lost touch with the mystery, but she also felt threatened by a different mystery, the frightening out-of-controlness which hung round Father like a dangerous smell. To which, long ago, she had given the name of Jungle.

She snips on. Maybe she had never given Father credit for simply trying to show her things *he* loved. But things never were simple with Father. There was always something frightening beneath, as if all his knowing things, names, behaviour, explanations, was his way of not thinking about other more important things, unspoken. She resented the explaining, though she never dared show it.

And yet, how funny, when Russel was little she had found herself explaining things to him just as Father had to her.

Forest was Father's place. Whenever he asked her to come with him into it she hung back. But just before her ninth birthday he insisted. She was old enough now, it was a privilege. He prepared her beforehand. 'Make no sound, Rosamund. Put your feet down slowly. If in danger, freeze.' When they got there, there was forest all round her and above, and she was so damn quiet that, following Father round a corner through bushes miles higher than she was, she came right smack face to face with a wild dog, a dhole.

She knew what it was from *The Jungle Book*. Even the tiger will turn aside for the dhole. Amber eyes stared into hers. She heard a distant whistle. Suddenly Father was beside her.

'There are more,' he whispered. 'They hunt in packs and the pack

11

is calling. Very rare, now. We shall retreat, Rosamund. Slowly. Keep your face towards him.'

When they got home she ran to her room and refused to go into forest again, the only time she defied Father openly as a child. Father knew everything and was always right, but he made her feel that everything, she herself, was all wrong.

She's cut off most of the green leaves now. They'll grow back. Snipping on into a maze of brown, she sees something like an arrow-head in the heart of the tangle. One of Russel's toys, chucked in the air years ago, mourned briefly and forgotten? No. A tiny skeleton, neck and skull hanging, beak pointing down. And above it an old nest, a blackbird's.

The birds she grew up with, and their Latin names – Father made sure she knew those – were tropical. Some native only to South India. But when Russel was little she learned the British ones. Together they collected eggshells, feathers, nests. They had a clock that chimed in the song of different birds, a garden table for the birds themselves.

Such heaven, being the mum of a five-year-old whom it was so easy to make happy.

Rosamund peers at the skeleton. It died here and she had never known it had lived. Blackbirds did nest here once. She remembers showing Russel the parents flying in and out. This chick must have fallen head first and got caught by the very fronds the parents had chosen to protect it.

Rosamund gathers up the severed stems, drops them on the compost heap and retreats to the house. Not quite steadily, observes the watching vixen. Rosamund usually ripples slightly when she moves, as if accompanied by a loving little wind. But her walk is jerky now and her face shiny with tears.

Wednesday 9 March, Western Ghats, Karnataka, 5.45 p.m.; 12.15 p.m., UK

He must report those poachers. Richard looked gloomily at the closed door of the green bungalow, the Forest Department head-quarters. Once, this was his second home. But the new director

12

resented scientists and suspected them of spying on the way he ran the forest. Poaching had tripled since he was appointed. Elephants had been found dead with their tusks cut off. A tiger had been electrocuted: someone had rerouted the perimeter fence across its trail just as the director had diverted the anti-poaching budget into his own pocket.

Ranjay, a ranger Richard liked, came out of the door with a pile of files tied together with pink ribbon.

'Is Mr Sreenivasan in, Ranjay?'

'Gone home,' said Ranjay, not meeting his eyes. So quickly did morale disappear when the man at the top changed.

'Can I leave a note? I saw poachers in the eastern sector.'

'I will tell him.'

Richard wanted to leave something in writing, but didn't want to look as if he disbelieved Ranjay. Ranjay needed to keep his job.

'Is there a patrol tonight? I saw pug marks, I could pinpoint the place . . .'

'I'll tell him.'

Richard gave up.

'Thanks.'

He got into his Gypsy Jeep. Stars were coming out in quick black velvet, the instant Indian night he loved, when animals were most active; and so were the poachers. He drove up the track, resting his mind with relief on the forest either side of him. This was the buffer zone between the sanctuary and human dwellings. Animals frequented it at night. He saw two jackals and a spotted deer, a chital, which stamped her foot in alarm. Her *tapetum lucidum*, that bright carpet of reflective cells at the back of her retina, glittered in the headlights.

Richard stopped by a wall of pale rock, closed the jeep door silently, walked across the track and stood in forest, letting the trees take him over. The sky was purple, latticed with black leaves. Keep them safe, he told the shushing forest. The cobra, deer, leopard. Let them live.

He stood a long time. Gradually a scene gathered, like figures flushing up on a negative. A shadowy bed, gold hair spread on a pillow, eyes like Botticelli's Venus, welcoming and shining. He touched her hair, ran fingers down her throat to her breast. Her nipple, big and fat as a thumb, stood up under his fingers. The shock went through him like brandy. Her breast fitted his hand as his hand had fitted the leopard's paw mark. She was life itself, the truth of all this tangle, shadow, whisker, leaf.

He heard a whistle and stamp and the vision stopped as if someone had pressed pause. That chital, alarmed again. Why? He inched his head around and saw the deer looking at his Gypsy. The rock face he'd parked beside was moving. He held his breath. Had it seen him, heard him, winded him? He'd never been so close. The chital scudded off. An enormous bull elephant was on the track, gazing into night. His tusks, lit by the headlamps, gleamed like new-poured cream. Then, soundless as he came, he was gone.

Thursday 10 March, Primrose Hill, London, 1.00 a.m.; 6.30 a.m., India

Rosamund presses the remote and the screen goes black with a sigh. Tyler has sacked this telly from the living room and installed a plasma screen, but the old one staggers on here, at the conservatory end of the kitchen.

She's cold. She never draws the curtains, she likes to feel part of the garden. She's not usually up this late. Should she put the heating back on? No, she'll go to bed in a moment.

Bono snores in his basket. She watches white fur riffling up and down as he breathes. Rays from the table lamp glow on patches of buttery walls, on Mexican rugs and Korean scrolls brought back by Tyler from work trips abroad. The house is full of these things. They are Tyler's guilt offerings, some beautiful, some kitsch. She knows when he's had a good time by the glitz of the bring-back. That russet-brown Indian wall hanging for instance, painted with curly white mazes and stick men. 'Made of cow poo, old fellow,' Tyer told Russel impressively, when he nailed it up. 'From Jaipur.' Who did he go there with?

Rosamund had minded India most. India was her place. Only it wasn't; she'd been desperate to get away. There were things she'd loved there, the garden, the dancing, but India was also betrayal. Every time she thought of Father's bungalow she felt a familiar hollow in her stomach. India was where she'd grown up wrong.

Rosamund stands and sees her reflection stand too, in the glass. She stares, the phantom stares back, the past rifts open and she sees herself in a mirror, not as a child but sixteen years ago, the last moment before she knew what Tyler really was, in a pub toilet one Sunday lunchtime. Strand-on-the-Green. She was washing her hands, thinking of Tyler on top of her the night before, whispering. She was living with him by then, had chucked the degree and was doing PR at his office. It was the end of the eighties and everything was gold. Or it was for them.

Gazing now into blackness, she remembers coming in through the pub garden, weaving through tables towards Tyler's friends and feeling Tyler's hand rubbing her buttocks. His friends had someone with them, a girl called Autumn, with an improbably large bust. F cup at least, maybe G. EVIAN, said red letters on the straining T-shirt. Autumn looked up, and the V and I shifted moltenly. Tyler flashed his instant intimacy smile, and brought out his most Tylery voice.

'Well hullo! See you've brought along the water of life!'

Autumn bridled, as women always did. Bridle away, Rosamund thought as she went off for a pee. She came back, saw bee-coloured lager sparkling in glasses, saw Autumn glowing at Tyler like chosen bride at risen god and Tyler taking his hand off Autumn's thigh just one second too late. Standing in her kitchen now, Rosamund still remembers the shock, an 'Oh' of pain, a stun-gun.

It happens so quick. As soon as she feels betrayed, or rejected, there's nothing.

She remembers Tyler's hand with its bitten nails holding a chair for her. 'I miss you,' he whispered, 'every second you're absent from my side!' He didn't address another word to Autumn and Rosamund began doubting what she'd seen. Bewick's swans mate for ever. Impossible to imagine him with any other swan.

I doubted myself, she thinks now, not him. He must have got Autumn's phone number before I came back from the loo.

Next time it was a drink with Liza in marketing. As they left,

Rosamund had seen Tyler's fingers kneading Liza's silky blue buttock in the mirror. Again the kick of jealous panic. Again the disbelief.

'Hey,' she'd said later. 'What was that with Liza?' He'd looked deep in her eyes. 'I was being *galant*. You're the only one, darling. My great love!'

He took such trouble, at first. But then the excuses changed. 'I'll make it up to you.' 'You're a very understanding woman.' How that phrase made her feel fulfilled. Tyler had coaxed her out of the jungle, turned her into a human being. She thought she was discovering how to be a woman. But what did loving him turn out to be? Getting mortally wounded, that's what. Forgiving him and getting clobbered worse. Tyler feels so *entitled*.

His real name is Peter Vere d'Abney-Fairfax. She caught sight of his birth certificate when they moved in.

'Peter Vere – what on earth's this?'

'M' darkest secret.' He took it from her and put his head on one side with a boyish twinkle. 'No one else knows I changed my name. Just you, sweetie. Don't tell anyone, ever.'

That night, their first night in this house, she'd asked more about his parents.

'I went to Harrow, actually,' he whispered. 'God's sake, you witch, why am I telling you? Never live it down if it got out. At least I left before the end.'

She got the feeling he'd been asked to go. He'd grown up in Surrey. His mum, he called her The Lady, had died when he was eight. Motherlessness: they had that in common. There was some mystery about his dad, Tyler shied away from talking about him. He'd been in the navy, some business, there had been trouble about drink, and also money. Tyler had spent a lot of time in school.

'Didn't do uni, never felt the need. Rock music! That was where it was all happening,' he whispered in the dark, head on her breast. At some point his dad had died, he'd inherited the house, sold it, changed his name. There was a lot, she felt, to be ashamed of. It seemed sweet and vulnerable then. She remembers stroking his thick hair, over and over. No one else knew. Only her.

16

Now, when she hears him putting on his Tyler voice to impress, like pulling on a pair of carefully torn jeans, his street persona sets her teeth on edge. Plus he'd romance a rhinoceros if there was nothing else on offer.

Even this conservatory was built on making-it-up-to-you money, after she walked into the bathroom at one of their own parties and found Tyler kissing a friend of theirs, a Chinese-American called Daisy. Tyler's jaw, wide like a bullfrog's, was gobbling Daisy's lips. His hand scumbled, a bird-eating spider in Daisy's oyster-coloured blouse. Sharply, like a bell rope she expected not to work, Rosamund had tugged the plait of black hair down Daisy's back. Daisy shrieked and slapped her. Tyler looked up mid-gobble and explained he was looking for Daisy's contact lens, it had slipped on to the white of her eye. Daisy yelled about lawsuits, Rosamund screamed for Daisy to get out *now*, and Tyler hissed that she was wrecking a fab party making a scene about fuck all.

Rosamund shivers. Whatever she felt then is a blur now. Afterwards she felt ashamed. But so, apparently, did Tyler. 'Let's add a conservatory, Rosie, to this tired old kitchen.'

She sighs. She's terrified how angry she'd be if she let herself feel. Maybe her inner self isn't a Rusty Spotted Cat at all. Maybe it's an ambush predator. A Gaboon viper, the world's heaviest viperid. There it is on the ground, just by Tyler's foot. Squamous, deadly, disguised as dappled leaves.

But Tyler depends on her. *And* runs her bath on Saturday evening, filling it with bubbles, bringing sherry. Weekends are truce time. They watch films; he cooks. He also brings Chanel scent, a Fendi bag, atonements for whatever it is he can't give.

She plugs in the kettle. Instead of a sleeping pill, she'll try camomile tea. She chooses the mug from Down House with a sequence of black figures, each a little straighter: ape becoming man, each figure more erect. She went there, to Darwin's home, with Russel's class when he was seven and bought this as a memento.

She listens to water coming to boil. What Tyler really loves is seeing himself new. A hero to an unending sequence of new faces.

The flashpoint came one Sunday when Russel was four. She'd

woken early. Tyler was asleep, he'd stayed up watching TV. She'd kissed him and thrust her feet into the embroidered slippers he'd given her for Christmas. She still wears them now, ten years later. The silk has frayed to spiky whiskers.

She went into the front room to draw the curtains. Russel would get up and watch cartoons, Tyler still smoked in the house and she didn't want Russel breathing smoke. On the floor by the sofa were two empty tumblers. On the sofa, where Russel cuddled up with her to watch *The Snowman*, was a dark stain, the size and shape of an earwig. And on the air, a smell of not just smoke but sex.

Marta, the Hungarian help, must have come home when Tyler was watching telly.

A live-in au pair was supposed to free Rosamund for her own life. Tyler had complained Marta had the sex appeal of a double-decker and there was hair on her upper lip. 'Doesn't she know about Immac?' But so what? He did it because he *could*.

Rosamund remembers sitting in the kitchen, watching morning sun creep across the lawn, longing for the jungle she inhabited before she met Tyler, where she expected nothing and no one could hurt.

At breakfast, Russel had kept up a relentless four-year-old burble. Can pythons play football? Do lady pythons wear lipstick? Why not? Why don't pythons wear lipstick? Tyler had flipped sausages on to Russel's plate and said they were baby pythons. Marta cut up Russel's fried bread avoiding everyone's eye and Rosamund sat on a cinder of a planet saying to herself, Don't upset Russel.

After breakfast Tyler played football with Russel and Rosamund moved her things to the spare room.

'What the fuck?' said Tyler.

'I've had enough.' She brushed past him, arms full of winter jumpers that smelt like old straw.

Afterwards, walking round in a fog of self-pity, Rosamund couldn't forgive Marta. She knew Marta was a victim too, but her forgiveness quota was all used up. She asked Marta to find somewhere else.

How does Tyler live with who he is? There have been other terrible scenes. China shatters on the floor and *she* ends up in the wrong.

18

Yet Tyler can still make her laugh, even make her feel sorry for him because he's hurt her. 'I don't deserve you. Poor me!' Or he breaks down, real tears shining in his eyes. 'It'll never happen again.' The hero, collapsed in her forgiving arms.

But once, when Russel was nine, he tried new tactics. That row had been over someone called Sara who'd interviewed him for *Cosmopolitan*. In the middle of it he'd dropped to his knees, buried his face in Rosamund's thighs and whispered, 'What's happened to us, Rosie? Let's have another baby. Start again.' He still has that power to make the world anew. Or he did five years ago. She wasn't going to let him into her room, so she'd climbed fearfully back into the bed she'd left. The sex was nice, though a bit awkward. Tyler had almost been shy.

You can live without sex, she thinks now, looking at the apes on the mug, but not without love. In those days she was pouring love into Russel so she hadn't missed it from Tyler, not really. When Tyler fell asleep she had retired to her room. They had managed a few weeks of this, then the rows came back, the visits ceased. And then . . .

But she won't think about the bad time. She'd told no one. Irena had been on tour in Canada. Rosamund had taken anti-depressants for a year after and has used sleeping pills ever since.

She carries her tea to the table. Is Russel asleep? When she went up earlier to say goodnight he was hunched in his attic by the open window, staring at the screen.

'Doin' my homework.'

'Turn it off, darling. Time to sleep.'

Should she check now? Teenagers make you feel everything you do is wrong. 1.30. She revolves the mug, inhaling the straw smell of camomile, watching bent ape turn into hairy man, and hears Tyler's key in the door.

Damn. She should have gone to bed. He must be standing in the hall like an animal that belongs to the night. She hears him pad softly towards the kitchen. She's in shadow. He won't expect her to be here. She often leaves this lamp on for him. The door opens. Bono doesn't wake because he's deaf and fast asleep. Tyler doesn't look up, he's aiming at the fridge.

Tyler is forty-four, but in the fridge's bluish glow he looks like an ageing caveman, his jowls underlit by the witch-light of the fridge. The rock god she married has vanished. The locks that crackled with electricity are thinning on top. As he peers in she sees the beginning of a little tonsure, like a monk. He is a lone troll, further back in the Darwin sequence even than *homo erectus*, reaching into a cave for its food. He extracts a half-eaten shepherd's pie. Then some extra sense makes him look round.

'Spying on me, young lady? Didn't think you'd still be up. Why don't you draw the curtains, you weirdo? Fancy a finger of malt?'

He opens the cupboard where he keeps the Tiffany tumblers which appeared after Christmas. 'Little treat to myself,' he'd said airily. Who were they really from?

'Dash of m' charming Laphroaig?'

He puts a glass before her, heaps a plate and sits opposite. In her throat is the ashy scorch of malt.

'Where were you tonight?'

'Cold shepherd's pie!' he says, the same moment. 'Always the way. Poor me! I slave to keep this show on the road, come home starving and what do I get?'

'You're never here at suppertime! Who were you with?'

'Darling, the search for love is endless!' He drains his malt and shoots her a wary stare like a merchant appraising an emerald. 'Fancy another slug?'

This is their life. For a moment she feels fine.

'Anything passable on telly?' Tyler holds his glass to the light and squints at it lazily. Rosamund hears a roaring in her ears, the whoosh of patience flying through the window. She scrapes back her chair, which squawks on the tiles. Bono lifts his head.

'*TV?!* It's not fair, Tyler! You know I'd like to go out and have fun too! You spend all day with gorgeous girls then go dancing, boozing, what do I know, while I sit here alone because of Russel, getting old. It's not *fair!*'

She begins to cry. She can't confront, it never works and then self-pity kicks in. She's become a victim before she even starts. She cries harder at this thought, but something inside her wonders, Will he play the outraged innocent or soothing spouse?

'Sweetheart . . .' he murmurs, in a voice drenched in concern. He's gone for option B. 'Look, darling, you've woken Bono.'

He pours another measure and puts a hand on her shoulder. 'Why don't you try Botox? Iron out the wrinkles?' Rosamund tries hard to stay as she used to be. Gold-red hair is easy, but her face! The face he used to say wouldn't just launch but fucking burn a thousand fucking ships. 'Or,' he is kneading her shoulder, 'the knife? For that sag at the corners of the mouth? I'll pay.'

She stands up, spins round and throws her tumbler. Awkwardly, she doesn't want to hit his face. It grazes his shoulder and shatters on the tiles into crystals like coloured sugar.

'Rosie! You fucking terrorist!'

She wants to run out of the house, out of her life. But Bono is rising stiffly to his feet.

'Bono's paws!' This has happened before. 'Hold him.' She scampers to the door, turns on the overhead light, finds a dustpan. Tyler cuddles Bono while she falls to her knees, tears pouring down her cheeks, to brush up the shards.

Next morning, she walks into the kitchen and finds Russel lying all over Bono's basket. Two giants, overflowing the basket they used to fit in together, when they were little. Bono, breathing stertorously, has his head on Russel's arm.

'Boiled eggs or scrambles?' She worries that Russel is anorexic.

'I'm good thanks.' It comes out 'fanks'. Tyler complains about Russel's new voice. 'That fucking school! He doesn't use T at all. He puts H in front of the letter aitch. Never had one in my day.'

Tyler covers up his public school background but reserves the right to it. Sometimes she hears him on the phone pulling rank as an Old Harrovian. She knows he minds that Russel has done exactly what he did with his voice, moved from posh to street. But Russel has done it for real.

'You must have some protein, darling,' she says. 'Maybe fried?'

Russel's silence is hard and glistening, like chrome. He ratchets himself up with a heave, a giraffe emerging from a gully. His head is bald with a blush of fuzz. She has no idea what colour his hair would be now, if allowed to grow. His eyebrows, Tyler's eyebrows, look like black lipstick slashed on his white forehead. He comes over as a dingy ghost; he only ever wears white. He is taller than Rosamund. Another two inches and he'll be up with Tyler.

'You're so big,' she says, hugging him, and he lets her. Happy suddenly, she hunts the fridge for eggs. TV voices start up behind her, loud and pleased with themselves. She watches threads of albumen harden like viscose. Tyler never shows for weekday breakfast. He will rise late and race to the office, scattering chaos as he goes.

'I'm seeing Irena today,' she says and puts down the plates. Slowly, as if the act were a favour to any egg, Russel levers white off one of the yolks.

Thursday 10 March, Parliament Square, London, 8.55 a.m.

Anka walked round Parliament Square. She carried a British passport in her scarlet bag but she'd been born in north-east Croatia. She did not speak English exactly properly, she'd had no time to learn it when she came sixteen years ago and now was too late. Sixteen years! Nearly half her life.

Nothing here looked like a law court. These houses of the British Parliament bristled against the blue sky like a pincushion. She examined her letter again.

Anka had grown up on the great Pannonian Plain. Her mother's hand was tattooed, like all the older village women's hands, with a cross. Her parents ran a market garden. Anka's life had been morning Mass, evening Mass, picking peppers, plucking feathers and reaching up to harvest the corn-heads of blond silk. She'd expected to marry at seventeen like all village girls, but when she was thirteen the teacher told her parents a gift like hers must be used for the glory of God, so she went to Zagreb Conservatoire. (Only, said her mother, if you go to Mass every day. And Anka did.) Then there was a music scholarship to London. Two years later Croatia was at war, her father and brothers had disappeared and her London singing teacher helped her get asylum. Then citizenship. Since Independence in 1995 she had returned to Croatia on short visits but never told that she too had a daughter now; and no husband.

She found Middlesex Guildhall behind a statue of Abraham Lincoln at the side of Parliament Square in a narrow street called Broad Sanctuary. Upstairs, she entered the crowded jurors' room and pressed a plastic flange on the water machine. She had to look after her voice. Water fell into a small plastic cone. She held the chill little pyramid in her palm till she finished, then threw it away and sat in the only empty chair beside a small plump man with curly hair and very black glasses. He wore an expensive-looking dark suit with white stripes and was hammering a laptop in angry spasms as if he hated every letter.

'Court six,' a woman shouted, and read out twelve numbers. Twelve people left. Anka went back to worrying about her boyfriend.

Her boyfriend was not her daughter's father, but she'd been with him five years and saw him twice a week. Never weekends, never a whole night. But she had her daughter, and friends, and work. This year she'd been asked to sing on Croatia Day. Life was very full, really. She was not jealous of his wife, he stayed with her for the children.

'You're my big love,' he said. 'The only one. My saviour.' He'd said often, though less often now, that Anka had rescued him from a dungeon of short stupid affairs. He worked with so many girls.

And he kept changing arrangements! She had not seen him in six days. She was seeing him tonight because he had cancelled Monday. *And* she'd see him tomorrow. Two days running. Almost like living together.

Thursday 10 March, Shad Thames, London, 12.05 p.m.; 5.35 p.m., India

Beside the khaki sparkle of the Thames, Rosamund sees Irena waving, in an enormous jacket like a child wearing its father's coat, from the door of a restaurant. She talks to Irena all the time on the phone but they don't often meet. When Irena's in London she must stay elsewhere: Tyler feels uncomfortable looking into Irena's clear eyes. Maybe he suspects she knows too much about him. While Irena, Rosamund thinks, fails to make allowances for Tyler.

She stoops to kiss Irena, who is five inches shorter.

'You look gorgeous, Ros!'

Rosamund hugs her. She has camouflaged the cold sore with concealer. Irena doesn't dress up herself but is always appreciative. Today, after pressing toast into Russel's hand and seeing him off to school, Rosamund picked out an indigo trouser suit dotted with red and a scarlet poloneck. She loves red.

'Are you working in town?' Rosamund holds Irena at arm's length like a doll. She has known these hazel eyes, and mouth like a curling leaf, since their first day at King's College, upriver. She has watched this face lengthen and feather lines wing away from Irena's eyes. Her own changes are all loss but Irena's seem to be Irena becoming more herself.

Irena lives in Devon. With Richard when he's in England, alone when he isn't. Like a disguised princess in a fairytale, Irena lives in a wood, in a cottage built by her parents out of an old barn.

At college, Rosamund was fascinated by Irena's parents. They were teachers and folk musicians. She longed to meet them but never did because, by the end of her and Irena's first year at college, they had died. Tyler, when she described them, called them the sandals and ginger-beer brigade. Not the real thing. Tyler was swinging up the music-business ladder then like a young gorilla. It worried Rosamund that he laughed at Irena's parents. Maybe there were different sorts of real thing.

Irena takes Rosamund's arm. Protectively, though she is the short one.

'I'm part-timing in the education department at the Globe.' Irena takes temporary jobs till the next acting part comes along. 'Let's go in, it's freezing.' She propels Rosamund into a bar full of people laughing and flirting before going back to their Docklands offices. Rosamund's picture of those offices is vague. What's it like, working surrounded by people? She thinks of her garden design file on its shelf.

In the old days, when Rosamund walked into restaurants heads used to turn like sunflowers to the sun. It's different now.

Irena has reserved a table by the window.

'You look great,' Irena says again and orders mineral water and pea casserole. Rosamund chooses Campari and sea bass with saffron. Beside them, the river gleams like a restless animal.

They first met in a student hostel. Staring in from opposite doors at a cement-floored cell between their two rooms, they saw each other's horror and burst out laughing. The wet room! Everyone called it the shit-shower-and-shave room because you could do all three at once.

Irena showed Rosamund an England she hadn't known. Rosamund had grown up in India till she was twelve, then gone to boarding school in Hertfordshire. Irena was utterly unlike the girls at school. Cross-legged on Rosamund's carpet, she played tapes by people Rosamund had never heard of, and read poems to her. 'Listen to this,' she urged after their first Christmas ball. '"When you dance, I wish you a wave of the sea." That's how *you* make people feel, Ros, when you dance.' When Rosamund told Irena what her father did, she read her a poem about a snake who fell in love. 'She changes to a woman to seduce the guy. Listen, Ros, this is you too. "Put her new lips to his, and gave afresh / The life she had so tangled in her mesh."'

Those words became their mantra. Seeing Rosamund with a new man, Irena would murmur, 'Tangled in her mesh.' They'd giggle, and the man would look suspicious and baffled. The joke stopped when Rosamund met Tyler.

Rosamund was the theatrical one then. She played Helen of Troy in *Doctor Faustus*, a non-speaking part, but she looked wonderful. She hung out in the theatre bar while Irena studied in the library. Everyone thought Rosamund would go on TV and Irena would be a librarian. But then Irena went to Guildhall to study voice and Rosamund went to live with Tyler, having dropped out before her fourth-year of biology. Other girls mistrusted her perfect figure, gold locks and the way men flocked around her while Irena followed her own road and was happy to see Rosamund go hers. Rosamund used to think of being with Irena as time out from important things. Now she knows Irena's friendship *was* the important thing.

'God it's good to see you.' Rosamund watches a rainbow from the window's bevelled edge stripe Irena's throat. Irena is wearing a child's watch on her tiny wrist. Rosamund knows that when Richard's away Irena is aware, every second, of the time difference with India. 'When's Richard back?'

'Easter. This is on me, Ros. The Globe's asked me to play Emilia in *Othello* this summer. Will you bring my godson?'

'Of course. Fantastic. Russel will come for *you*.'

'Will you bring him to Devon at Easter? Can you all come? Richard's coming back the week before.'

'Love to.'

Rosamund looks at Irena's face, unusually flushed, and remembers it after that devastating phone call at the bottom of the hostel stairwell. They were revising for exams, the end of their first year, and suddenly Irena's dad had throat cancer. Not now, Rosamund remembers thinking wildly. Some other time. Not now.

Irena had rushed down to Devon. 'He's turned his face to the wall,' she said when she got back. 'A singer who can't sing.' She went down two weeks later for the funeral. Irena's mother insisted she come back and do the exams. She was a teacher, after all. After the exams, Irena phoned home and got no reply. Then a letter came, Rosamund remembers Irena opening it, from one of their Devon neighbours. That weekend while they were revising, Irena's mum had died too. An aspirin, swallowed without water, had lodged in her stomach and developed into a cyst, which burst just like that. 'No,' Rosamund had cried, hugging Irena. Her own mother died when she was two. With Irena's waif-body shaking in her arms, she almost envied this grief for a mother Irena had known. All summer, feeling needed for the first time in her life, Rosamund stayed with Irena in her empty cottage. It rained, Irena walked in the woods and Rosamund tackled next year's biology reading by the fire.

Irena is alone a lot, Rosamund thinks now, sipping Campari, feeling its bitterness shoot through the soft skin under her arms. She'd hate that. Tyler still turns on his six-cylinder charm when he wants. He can be such fun. But Irena has always felt loved. Perhaps that's why she's OK with *alone*.

The slice of orange bumps Rosamund's lip. Her cold sore is stinging. The concealer must be gone by now.

'What about you?' says Irena and Rosamund describes last night's quarrel. 'Then he told me to get a facelift,' she finishes, feeling eased by the telling, 'or Botox!' She hasn't mentioned throwing the glass. 'He can't imagine what *I* feel.'

'It's called narcissism,' says Irena. 'Like a disease. Why do you *stay* with him? He's stopped you doing anything of your own. Finishing college, working . . .'

'I helped in Russel's nursery school.'

'Russel was fourteen last November. Pick a day, pack, I'll organise some out-of-work actors to help. You can do garden design, look after Russel, live a life.'

'I belong with Tyler.' Can't she mention a row without having to do things about it afterwards? 'Something about him makes me feel . . .'

'Feel what?'

'Safe.'

'That's mad.'

'I know.'

'It's the opposite of true.'

'Call it an affliction – like piles.' They giggle. 'Tyler's my life. Something in me says it's my fault.'

'Tell it to shut up. You know what he gets up to.'

'Not exactly.' Now she's got the sympathy, she can think Irena's too hard on Tyler.

'You stopped shagging him ten years ago, more than half Russel's life. You've lived for nearly twenty years with someone with the morals of a black mamba.'

Rosamund giggles again. Irena has made snake jokes ever since she knew about Rosamund's dad.

'And he's brainwashed you into thinking how he behaves is normal. Out every night? It's monstrous. Pathological.'

Above the fuss-splash of cutlery and talk they hear guitar slides on the hi-fi. And a husky female voice, *'Touch me, tell me who I am . . .'*

'Oh, that song. Gorgeous!'

'Is she one of Tyler's?'

You are my earth and sky.
You're everything I ever loved.

'God no, he'd call it folksy and groan. They play it in my Pilates class.' Rosamund watches Irena listen, head on one side.

Light me a candle when I die
To say I'm everything you ever loved.

'Don't you like the tune?'

'Tune's beautiful. Lovely voice. Who is she?'

'Shadiyah. Lebanese or something.'

'She could do opera or blues. But she's not using her voice properly. And I *hate* the words.'

'Your ruffled quail look.' Irena gets cross about strange things. 'It's only a pop song.'

'It starts out fine, but turns fake,' says Irena, elbows on the table like an argumentative boy. Like Russel, as he used to be. 'Why do you like it?'

'I thought you would too. It's like the songs you used to sing.' Irena's mouth twitches.

'What?' They know each other so well.

'Some people prefer instant coffee to real.' Rosamund bursts out laughing. Women at the next table turn and smile. 'Now you look like you used to, Ros. Fun, that's what you need, not bloody Botox.'

Has she too opted for fake by staying with Tyler? Sometimes, Rosamund thinks, Irena overdoes the morality.

A girl in a pink apron brings coffee. The soundtrack changes to 'The Londonderry Air'.

'St Patrick's Day,' they say together and laugh again. I shall cry in a minute, thinks Rosamund.

'That's not till next week.' says Rosamund.

'They're gearing up for it.'

In her second year, Rosamund had dragged Irena to a St Patrick's Day party and her quiet friend talked for the first time to the thin, bespectacled biologist whom Rosamund had casually asked along

28

too, like chucking a bone to a puppy. Richard had adored Rosamund from their first day in the lab. She let him set her dissections straight but never dreamed of going out with him. Plus it was a bit embarrassing, frankly, when he asked her to marry him. But Irena took Richard seriously. She said she liked the way he talked about science.

'You don't know about science,' said Rosamund. She didn't go on about science like Irena did about poetry but biology, after all, was her thing.

'I liked how he felt about it,' Irena said. But she'd only got together with Richard later, when she was at Guildhall, Richard was slogging away at fourth-year biology and Rosamund was living with Tyler.

'A week to go,' says Irena. 'St Patrick's Day. Two years since Blair persuaded Parliament to go to war.' She changed her voice. '"I *do* believe*! I do believe we must hold firm!"'

'Brilliant, Irena. Blair's voice exactly.'

'Doing what actors do, believing himself into his part I knew he was lying.' Rosamund watches Irena tilt her water glass so bubbles float up the side. Maybe she lives her own life underwater. But why does she always look for what's wrong with her? What *is* wrong with her? 'Believing you must be right, simply because you're you, is the most dangerous lying of all. "To back away would leave Iraq's people in pitiless terror." That's what Blair said, and pitiless terror is exactly what they've got now. Thanks to him.'

Rosamund fiddles with a lump of sugar. She never worries about the world like Irena. There's too much to contend with inside.

'All this is threatened too,' Irena waves at the intricate iron undersling of Tower Bridge, 'by what he said then. It can't last, our beautiful selfish civilisation.' Rosamund stares at a black barge. Irena lives outside London but somehow makes it hers by loving it. Maybe her own ways of loving are as false as Tyler's. 'We've no idea what we do to other people. If we smash up another country illegally, people will smash *us* up. It's all in Shakespeare. Violence breeds violence. There'll be something worse than 9/11, here.'

'You're not usually so doom-laden.'

Irena wriggles her shoulders. She's wearing a pale yellow shirt with paler embroidery. If Rosamund wore it she'd look washed out. It looks lovely on Irena.

Easter will be tricky. Irena bugs Tyler because she won't flirt, and he calls Richard an anorak. She'll say Russel needs to see his god-mother.

As often happens, Irena picks up her thought.

'I haven't seen Russel in so long.'

Thursday 10 March, Parliament Square, London, 12.55 p.m.

Anka asked a man in a straw hat for a prawn sandwich.

'Pepper, *signorina*? Hot, for beautiful girl like you?'

She smiled.

'*Eccola!*'

She walked round Parliament Square watching shadows sink into the paving stones. Her mobile buzzed.

'How the hell *are* you, sweet thing?' She smiled as if he could see her. 'How's jury service? Any good murders?'

Anka had a good ear. Perfect, her singing teacher had said. She could copy the music of English fine. But her grammar, Helen said, was crap.

'Is nothing. Is waiting. You, *dragi*?' Croatian endearments made him seem more hers.

'Rushed off my feet, sweetie. But I'll be there tonight, I swear. Seven-thirty. Can't wait. Oh, Anka . . .'

'Yes?' She loved the slow melt in his voice when he was going to say beautiful things. Things she repeated to herself, like songs.

'I love you beyond all the world!'

Dark-edged clouds chase blue from the sky as Rosamund passes the fat black metal barriers outside the Houses of Parliament. Is this city really under threat? For her, the city itself is threat enough, teeming with women ready to open up to Tyler's prowling charm. What's he up to now? That question lies under her life like a sewer. He's not pathological, she just can't believe a word he says.

These barriers are like climbing blocks for toddlers only black and with armed police attached. They're supposed to be temporary like the concrete blast blocks round the American Embassy, which mess up the traffic back to Bond Street. Everywhere, London is promising it will get back to normal; and doesn't.

There's a man sitting on the grass surrounded by placards. YOU LIE, KIDS DIE! BLIAR! SERIAL KILLER, NATION KILLER! GENO-CIDE OF IRAQ'S INFANT INNOCENTS! Even Rosamund knows the prime minister is furious about this. He can invade Iraq but cannot legally remove the Parliament Square protester. Stopping beside a tall girl with black hair, eating a sandwich, she reads the pro-tester's placards. The man grins at them both and holds up his thumb. They both smile. Then Rosamund walks on to Whitehall and climbs to the top of a bus.

Irena has never gone on so hard about leaving Tyler. But she can't. Because of Tyler she's cut herself off from everything. Well, from Father, who is Russel's last grandparent. Tyler's parents died before Rosamund met him and the only time Tyler and Father met was at her wedding, which was also Russel's first birthday. Rosamund was sitting in the front room with Russel when she looked up and saw Father before her, crackling like an electric pylon. Tyler must have tossed out some crass remark in the kitchen.

'Rosamund, that is a dangerous man. Take your son and come away. Now.'

Tyler was behind him, furious.

'You've done enough damage in her life.'

Father looked at her as if she had stabbed him. She said nothing. He walked to the door.

'This is an aggressive act,' he said, and was gone. Tyler bent over her and looked in her eyes.

'Shall I go after him?'

'No.' She felt safe then, with Tyler's arm round her and Russel's padded bottom on her knee. She had a protector. When the guests left, Tyler held Russel up to watch his mum wash the glasses.

'Sad old tosser,' he said. 'How did such a weak man tyrannise you so long, sweetheart, with his gaucheness and weirdo ideas?'

31

But Russel, as he grew, was fascinated by the photo taken that day of himself on Father's knee.

'Your grandfather's a famous scientist,' Rosamund told him. 'He lives in India. He studies snakes. He's a herpetologist.'

Russel fastened on that word like a terrier. 'Herpetologist,' he went round shouting. 'Herpetologist.' He adored the bricks her father had made for Rosamund when *she* was little. She would find him holding the bricks, talking to them.

These bricks had stayed forgotten with a Cambridge neighbour of Father's. When Russel was born, Tyler put a notice in *The Times*. ('Chap's got to do things properly when he has a son.') A woman wrote to him at work, wanting to give the bricks back. Russel connected them with India, herpetologists and snakes. He built mazy palaces for imaginary snakes which he called Cold Layers and giggled when Tyler called them his Cold Stares.

Rosamund smiles fondly. It hasn't all been bad. But surely this bus has stayed stopped for a very long time?

'Broken down,' the driver shouts up. 'Hang on to your tickets and get the next.'

People shuffle on to the pavement and mill resentfully in the drizzle. Rosamund squeezes on to the next bus and stands holding a yellow pole, looking up to where it ends in a triangular silver flange. The two screws bolting it to the ceiling are eyes of a small accusing elephant blowing a yellow trumpet.

Two people leave and Rosamund sits by a window.

'Don't understand,' says a loud voice. A man, standing by the empty seat next to her, blocking the aisle, is tossing these words over his shoulder. 'Say it in English. You want to say something, say it in *English*!' Chewing gum, as if masticating all languages not English, he stares into space, keeping his back to the first of the incoming passengers, a woman in a sari. He has unshaved cheeks and a high tight forehead and is eyeballing the passengers in front of him, daring them to challenge his rudeness. They look at the woman, at the empty seat, and look away. The woman whispers to her friend. Both wear coloured saris. Rosamund's whole being loathes the man but like everyone she says nothing. I don't stand up for my feelings, she thinks. I'm a doormat. Suddenly the guy scoots up the stairs. He wants to sit down, but not by Rosamund. She's witnessed his squalid little triumph. He knows what she's feeling and is glad of it, but wants to get away.

Rosamund pats the seat and smiles but the woman sticks to her friend and more people get on. Rosamund pats the empty seat again. The woman points at a pink bundle in the luggage rack. Rosamund stands up, offering her own seat too if she wants to bring her bundle. The woman pats her arm and stays standing. She doesn't care about the man, simply about her bundle. I'm the one, thinks Rosamund, who's jolted by the rudeness. And that's our city, too.

Thursday 10 March, Mangalore, Karnataka, 8.00 p.m.; 2.30 p.m., UK

Richard switched off his engine. Hot metal began cooling in the Mangalore night as he walked up an iron staircase.

'Richard? Come.'

Richard took off his shoes and dropped into an armchair. Girish put on a CD and stood listening, head on one side. He was astoundingly handsome, looking much younger than thirty-seven. He made wildlife films; Richard had collaborated with him on many of them. Now, though, Girish had abandoned mainstream wildlife films. They suggested the forests and animals were fine and would live for ever. City people, he said, had a million TV channels and weren't interested in nature anyway. He only made films now for forest officers, and politicians who ought to know about wildlife and didn't. He seemed to Richard a man of no bonds except to the forest. He sometimes turned up at restaurants with beautiful women, usually dancers, but lived alone, always free to go on a forest expedition, and was happiest sitting in a hide with insects crawling up his back, waiting for a frog to jump into a river.

Moths flickered round the lamp. Richard sighed. Everything here was shabby, real and beautiful. If love for a country starts with one person, like the first stone taken out of a quarry into daylight, Girish was that love. He had given Richard his own exasperated passion for this country and was a devotee of South Indian music.

'Eighteen beats to a bar,' he'd explained once, after taking Richard to watch a famous dancer. Richard had seen the same rapt concentration on his face while filming a tiger. 'You reach enlightenment by appreciating beauty – of the world, of divinity which created the world, of nature, and of the ancient arts. Like dance, which the gods created and help us recreate.'

They had been walking through humid, mosquitoey night.

'Dancing is a kind of praying, really. *Lead me from the unreal to the real.*' They passed pie-dogs asleep on the road like scones on a baking tray. 'But where the dance really happens, in sculpture, dance or sex, is your own heart.'

Richard had gazed hard, embarrassed, at their reflection in the window of a sandal shop.

Girish handed him a glass of tea. For years, all over south India, the two of them had walked in jungle together, scratched their groins together when the ticks dug in and faced the same suspicious forest officers.

'I saw poachers in the forest. Sreenivasan wasn't in. He won't send any patrols. The more I protest, the more he restricts what *I* do. He'd rather stop my research than stop the poaching. There was a tusker in the buffer zone; he may not last the night.'

'You can't fight all our battles, Richard. You could lose your visa.'

'I'm going back anyway for a while. Chennai and Delhi, then London.'

'Ask Kellar's advice, in Chennai.'

Kellar was a herpetology legend, an internationally renowned zoologist who, forty years before had given up a Cambridge chair for field research and now advised a Snake Centre in Chennai. Girish had grown up in Chennai and Kellar was his mentor. But to Richard, Kellar was father of the girl who had bewitched him twenty years ago. On his first day in the lab, Richard had seen Rosamund's luminous beauty and fell plummetingly in love, as if he had fallen through the bottom of his own self. Five years later, reading Kellar's scientific papers as a graduate, he fell in love again with a mind thinking out of its box, with Kellar's whole approach to science. Kellar was why he had turned to field zoology.

He'd first met Kellar at Rosamund's wedding. Now they were colleagues, but science was one thing, life another. Richard's friendship with Rosamund made him feel more awkward with Kellar, not less.

A voice flowed round them on a ripple of plucked strings.

'What's the language?' Richard knew Hindi and some Kannada. He envied Indian friends their three or four Indian languages as well as English.

'Bengali.' Girish listened dreamily. 'A love song, by Tagore.'

'Irena'd like that. She's keen on poetry.'

The question Girish never asked, being far too tactful, was why didn't Irena ever come to India? She can't afford the time. Actors have to take work when it comes. That's what Richard would have said, but never needed to.

'There's a Yakshagana play tomorrow in the hills at a Shiva shrine,' said Girish. 'Like to go?'

Thursday March 10, Primrose Hill, London, 3.30 p.m.; 9.00 p.m., India

Rosamund walks round the square to their battlemented house. Inside, Bono rises stiffly to greet her. When she is out he sleeps here in the hall, having angled himself with Euclidean geometry to spot the door the minute it opens. They progress through to the kitchen and she lets him out on to the lawn where he humps into a white question-mark. The willow boughs are clouded in green fuzz as if a dragon has breathed benignly upon them.

It should all be wonderful. A primrose house kept spotless by Maria, to whom Rosamund gives Russel's castoffs for her children in Bolivia. A kitchen speckled with silvery light. On the side a photo of Russel aged two, laughing with Tyler. She used to imagine a candy-striped parasol of happiness bobbing over Russel's head then. He had Tyler's animal charm and his own sunniness. All one winter he refused to eat spaghetti because it was wiggly, unless Daddy fed it to him. Now he barely looks at Tyler from one week to the next.

Bono rests his shaggy chin on her knee and pants smelly breath at her, his eyes sclerotic with cataracts. Her one achievement in fourteen years, apart from the garden, has been training this creature, Russel's third birthday present. People used to laugh when he slammed the door on command with his shaggy, saucer paws.

'*Isn't* he clever? Big as a donkey. What breed is he?'

'Grand Griffon Vendéen,' four-year-old Russel would say, with his gold curls under the dog's chin.

'From the Vendée region of France,' six-year-old Russel said, holding his dad's hand. 'We go there sometimes.'

'Descended from the Italian St Hubert hound,' he explained at nine. 'Developed to hunt wild boar in medieval France.'

Now, if forced to explain Bono, Russel hunches his shaved head back in its hood like a tortoise and mutters, 'French.'

Bono, too, has changed. He is thinner, as if his strength had descended into his paws and he might tear, like paper. But still two foot high at the withers, still that sheepy whiteness with a touch of blue like snow at twilight. Bono the smelly, brown patch over his right eye, brown stripe over his nose as if he's constantly pulling off a knitted muzzle, and ears in which grass seeds get stuck every summer. All the grass seeds in Britain seem in competition to pierce the eardrum of a Grand Griffon Vendéen.

'They're programmed to fall into tangled grass, like his fur, and work their way into earth,' explains the vet.

Bono has loved them all equally for eleven years. The only thing that ever went wrong was when Tyler drove into a car wash with Russel and Bono. Rosamund got back a scratched hysterical little boy, a rolling-eyed hyperventilating dog and a furious husband.

'They both went mad. My charming son. Pandemonium, screaming – fuck it, he's old enough to control himself.'

Tyler must have panicked, as he did when *he* lost control. He must have hit Bono to stop him scrabbling. In vain – the soft car ceiling was in ribbons and Russel was sobbing. Mainly, Rosamund suspected, because Dad had been angry with Bono.

But they had had wonderful holidays: Cornwall, Wales, with dog, boy and Dad ecstatic all day, fishing, biking, surfing. Then, four years ago, Russel turned against his dad and now seems to let Bono do the loving for him.

Bono sleeps most of the day, rather noisily. But he still barges his bottom against the lot of them, desiring unity with his huge, pack-loyal heart.

The front door bangs. Russel comes into the kitchen, drops his rucksack on the floor, lolls softly against the table and cuddles Bono.

'He really is deaf. He didn't hear you at all.'

Silence.

'School OK? Tea? Toast?'

"m good.'

'Lot of homework?'

Russel picks up his rucksack and disappears to the living room. Bono follows. She hears the TV.

'Supper at seven,' she calls

Russel seems to live behind an invisible drawbridge with boiling oil optional. 'Safe, man,' she hears him say when his phone rings, and he closes the nearest door. At weekends he vanishes into the night with friends she doesn't know.

Rosamund fiddles with a biro. How about an ad for corner-shop windows? Surely someone in Primrose Hill needs a garden makeover.

Thursday 10 March, Kilburn, London, 5.00 p.m.; 10.30 p.m., India

'What's this stuff in the fridge, Mum?'

Helen's dark hair was long and her lips were like ripe plums. Anka's boyfriend had noticed that when he first saw her. 'Fab mouth,' he had muttered, almost to himself. 'Gorgeously tacky.' Anka had felt jolted. Helen had been seven. She wanted him to love Helen's spark and personality.

'Fish eggs, my little aubergine,' she said now, slicing tomatoes. Round the walls were posters for concerts she'd sung in. From her prize poster Josef Haydn looked down, music score in one elegant hand and sausages of grey wig over his ears. 'Who's *that*?' her boyfriend had asked, the first time he came. 'Holding a cigar like a Spanish roué weighing up a tart?' 'Is not cigar,' Anka had said indignantly. 'Is Papa Haydn.'

'*Black eggs,*' Helen said now in disgust. 'Yuk.'

'Is caviar. Lampfish row, from Budgeons. Would you like, with toast, for your supper?'

'What about yours?'

'You forget, you are going to Katya? Budimir will come seven o'clock to fetch you.'

Helen fiddled with the magnets on the fridge. One fell to the floor and she bent to pick it up. She looked heavy in her school blouse. She worried so much how she looked. That was the age. She hated Anka saying she looked gorgeous. She had the largest breasts in her class and hated that too. She hunched, to hide them. Her friend Katya, small for thirteen, worried about being skinny. Helen was twelve but looked sixteen. They never argued. Better than sisters, Helen said.

'Mum?'

'*Andele moj?*'

'Why can't we go to Croatia like Katya?' Helen had gone with Katya and her parents, Lasta and Budimir, to Korčula last year, to Lasta's parents' summer house. Budimir and Lasta came from the coast, not inland, not a village like her. They were safely in England before the Serbian war, had met at medical school and spoke beautiful English. Helen had been in Katya's playgroup. Now the girls met every morning at King's Cross and went to school in Lisson Street, next to Edgware Road.

'Katya has a great time with her *baka*. I know all your family died in the war but can't *we* go to Croatia, too?'

She had called her Helen because Helena was a Croatian name, but Helen did not know her grandmother was still alive. Anka felt bad about that. But what would her mother, to whom church was everything, say about an illegitimate child?

Helen's father had played in an Australian rock band and Anka had known him only a few weeks. He had gone back to Sydney and died, she read in the papers, of a drug overdose. He never knew Anka was pregnant. When Helen was a baby, Anka had lived by singing Croatian folk tunes to English words in the Underground, accompanying herself on guitar with Helen beside her on a blanket. But then she had one big success. She might not speak English exactly perfectly but she did seem able to find English words to go with her tunes. So now Helen went to a good school. Katya's school.

'When's supper?'

'Fifteen minutes. You have time, for practise.'

'Homework,' said Helen and disappeared.

Helen thought Anka's boyfriend was just a friend. It was difficult, now Helen was older, to keep love secret. Sleepovers with Katya would not be the answer for ever. But Anka did not want Helen to say, If he's your boyfriend, why don't you ever see him at weekends? She did not want Helen to know he was married, with a little girl of his own.

When the pepper stew was ready, she knocked on Helen's door then pushed it open. Helen was reading *Honey* magazine on the bed. Anka burst out laughing.

'Doh, Mum. I've finished my homework.'

On the mantelpiece were the *Puddle Lane* books from which Helen had learnt to read her good English. On the shelves were Barbie dolls, rows of coloured nail polish bottles and pebbles that Katya and Helen had spent hours painting with nail polish.

'Supper, *dragi*. Budimir comes, half in an hour.'

Hours later, alone in her black silk blouse with plunge neckline, Anka was gazing despairingly at Papa Haydn when the phone rang in the living room.

'I'll be a bit longer I'm afraid, sweetie. Held up with these guys from China. We're developing that market. It's doing my head in.'

'But . . .'

'You know I'd rather smash my heart into splinters of glass than stand you up.' She looked at the twisted phone wire. 'Ten-thirty, how's that? I'll be pawing at the door, my face a mask of lust. With some lovely lovely Burgundy.'

'OK.' What else could she say?

'Going out?' Rosamund sees a shadow in the unlit hall. 'Done your homework?'

Russel mumbles and eases the rucksack on his shoulder.

'What?'

'Well easy.'

'What was it?'

'Maths.'

In maths and biology, Russel seems to sail through on no work. The struggles are with history and English.

'Back by twelve, OK?' He opens the door on the orange-purple night. 'Bye, darling. Have a good time.'

If she'd known he was going out ... You stay in so they have someone at home, then they go out and leave you. Should she ring someone, suggest a film? But most people are couples and have things to do.

She goes upstairs, hears Bono turning in a circle behind her, scraping an imaginary hole for his stiff bones, and opens Tyler's bedroom door.

Tyler, say the maroon stripes. They look like old-fashioned pyjamas. Tyler re-papered the room when she moved out. On his floor is a mosaic of dirty socks; the duvet is half-off the brass bed. When she first met him his Soho flat had fur up the side of the bath, empty champagne bottles down the stairs and a mirror over this same brass bed.

Something in this room makes her remember opening the door to Father's empty study long ago, peeping in when he wasn't there, at the armchair where she sat to be read to, lectured at and ticked off for unknown crimes. When she knew what she was supposed to feel guilty about, she said sorry. 'You're a devil, aren't you?' Father would say, almost admiringly. 'Glad we understand each other now.'

That was their closeness. She grew up with rules she never understood. The people who looked after her had learnable rules – what to eat when, never use the left hand. But she couldn't second-guess

Father's rules so the safest thing was not even to feel. Once she admitted being a devil and said sorry, she could escape to the kitchen where Parvati the cook would give her a honey cake and teach her new dance steps.

She never told Father about Parvati's lessons. Anything she loved would vanish, she felt, if she let on she yearned for it.

Abandoning Tyler's chaos, Rosamund takes a sleeping pill from the bathroom cabinet. In her bedroom, the red curtain over the alcove hides clothes she hardly ever wears. She doesn't want to give up being the person who might wear that gypsy dress, this golden skirt. On the chest of drawers is a photo of her mother in 1969. Mini-skirt, Mary Quant fringe and spiky black eyelashes.

Rosamund strips off the sweatshirt and jeans she changed into when she came home. Her ribs show. Her breasts are tiny, who'd want those? Her whole body seems to be trying not to be. Forcing herself to feel unconnected to Tyler has cast her out from her own body. She pulls on the nightdress and climbs into her walnut bed.

Thursday 10 March, Kilburn, London, 10.45 p.m.

How had she put up with this, all these years? Helen could have stayed.

The doorbell rang.

'Oh, Anka!' She was in his arms. His tongue, tasting of wine, was inside her mouth, his hands all over her hips, rubbing her nipples, pushing back her collar, lips gulping her skin. 'God, darling, it's been so *long*.'

She curled her legs around his waist. He carried her into the bedroom, flung her across the bed and dropped his face to her thighs, parting them with his hands like a swimmer cleaving the waves, desperate for shore.

'I'm starving,' he said in the kitchen an hour later. 'Anything to eat round here, to go with this fab wine?'

'Pepper stew. I can make hot. You drunk much already.'

'Had to raise a glass with those Chinks.'

'I hate you are always late.'

'Darling.' He kissed her again, sucking her mouth inside his. 'You're a very understanding woman.'

She watched him open the fridge door stuck with magnets holding notices from Helen's school. So silly that sometimes she didn't believe him. When they were together, everything was wonderful. Everything.

'What Balkan crap've you got in here? *Caviar*. Shall I make Melba toast?' She loved it when he cooked in her kitchen. 'Tess could eat Melba toast for ever!'

They'd be living together if it wasn't for Tess. He couldn't leave a little girl of four with big blue eyes like pansies. Anka adored the love in his voice when he talked of Tess. She'd begged to see photos; he always forgot to bring them.

'Tess – how is?'

'Don't get me started. Walking round with a parasol of happiness over her gorgeous head.'

'And brother?' She'd have loved Helen to have a brother. She'd heard the boy's voice once, five years ago, at the beginning when she didn't know not to call the house. The little boy had answered the phone. She felt that gave them a connection. She pictured him teaching Tess to catch a ball. Then she added Helen, taking Tess's hand, smiling at those blue eyes.

'Crazed mess at the moment.' He was standing by the toaster, big like Pavarotti, back hunched. 'Never had a dad,' he muttered as the bread went down. 'Never know how to play it. I say some loony thing . . .'

'Please?'

'Where are the plates, girl? Quick!' He sat beside her. 'Here, sweetie. You never eat all I give you.' He raised the toast to her lips. She ruffled his hair and he slipped his hand over her breast, over the nightdress he bought her last Christmas, from Harrods. 'Mmm.'

He kissed her throat, nibbling down to her collarbone. Suddenly he was smearing caviar over her nipple, she worried about the fabric but he was sucking, licking, gobbling his lips round one breast after the other till the lumpfish roe was gone.

42

Friday 11 March, Primrose Hill, London, 4.00 a.m.

Standing on a wheelie bin in Rosamund's front garden is a dog fox in his prime. Two years old and these gardens, front and back, belong to him. Tyler would be outraged that any other male should feel possessive about them but from a fox point of view Primrose Hill is a patchwork of one-kilometre territories, re-fought for each December.

He is trying to push the lid up. He took his mate the slice of toast Russel had flung away earlier, but cannot get at the chicken bones he knows are in the bin. He leaps to the ground, hears a footstep and flattens. A figure staggers up the steps, fumbles at the door, opens it and totters through. The door closes, the fox jumps up to the bin again, but freezes when he hears a car. It is not easy being an urban fox. Most don't live more than two years. This one's sister was run over as a cub; the sound and sight have stayed together in his synapses.

He jumps off and melts under a bush. The car stops with one wheel on the kerb. A larger figure emerges, also unsteady, slams the door, points at the car, which flashes its lights, and lurches through the front door. The door swings to but does not close. A crack of light remains. Then the light goes out but a warm whiff of house stays on the air.

The fox is used to doors that stay shut. He noses the door. It moves. He studies the smells. Dog and human everywhere but food, too. He is halfway in when he hears another car coming fast towards the square.

43

2

Rosamund is on an island. There's a child she's got to find, a little girl. A tsunami is crashing on the shore – or is it the ticking laugh of a magpie? She lies still, heart beating. Was the child on the beach when the wave hit?

Gradually she realises where she is. When she moved into this room there was a proper dawn chorus. Now it's just magpies. In orange light shining through her eyelids she pictures baby birds cowering in a nest, a sharp beak stabbing. This changes to a black speck in a wheel of orange fire.

She opens her eyes, gets out of bed and looks at her garden. Gold crocuses stare perkily back. The mauve ones lie crumpled on the grass. She flosses her teeth, remembering how Father at breakfast would wait to pounce on whatever was wrong. 'Don't pour milk so fast, Rosamund. Use two hands or it will spill.' She looks critically at the greenish hollows under her eyes. Nothing kills your looks like a husband addicted to other women.

Passing Tyler's door, she tightens the cord on her dressing gown. Russel's trainers lie at the bottom of the stairs. How can a boy of fourteen have such giant feet? The stairs feel draughty and the front door's open. Is Tyler outside? And where's Bono?

She runs out. On the far kerb is a heap of pale rubbish. No . . . no . . . Oh God! She races across. Bono is half over the kerb, back legs horribly mashed. How long has he been there; has no one seen? She strokes his head. White fur lifts in gulpy shallows over his flank. She hears a whimpery moan.

'Bono,' she whispers. Now he's deaf, the only way to reassure is by touch. '*Good* dog,' she whispers anyway. 'I'll be back.'

The emergency vet is down in Victoria. It'd take longer to drive there than to wait until the local one opens at nine. She runs into the house. She can't face Tyler, he's so bad-tempered when woken, but she can't do this alone. She runs up to the third floor. Russel is sleeping face down on his bed. The freezing room smells of boy, socks, sweetness, sweat. The window is open, the computer humming. In here somewhere is the child she lived for, the body she cared for inside and out. Now she's almost afraid of it.

'Russel. Wake up, darling. We must get Bono to the vet.'

Russel opens his eyes. They are gummy, slightly pink. Does he have conjunctivitis?

'Can you help me carry him to the car? He's been run over.'

Russel heaves himself out of bed and runs so fast he almost falls downstairs. Rosamund scutters to the kitchen, grabs the dog basket and catches him up. They ease Bono into the basket and up to the hatchback. As Rosamund takes the awful hind legs, she hears a faint snarley squeal. Russel fetches Bono's water bowl, crawls into the car beside Bono and holds the bowl to his muzzle. After a moment a tongue emerges. They watch Bono lap.

'I can manage now, darling. You have to get to school.'

'Fuckin' stayin', Mum.'

'Shall I bring you something? Tea?'

'Nah.'

Rosamund forces herself to drink coffee. Who came in last? Russel will have to blame himself or blame his dad. After a silent drive, she parks on double yellow lines outside the vet's. They lift the basket out with Bono's head lolling on the edge. The waiting room is crowded with women holding crates on their knees, a young man with spiky hair jerking at a yapping terrier and a man with a squirmy black puppy.

Heather, the nurse, has known Bono all his life.

'Bring him straight in. Sorry, everyone. Emergency.'

A sudden hush, except the terrier. Every pet-owner's nightmare is carried silently through the waiting room. In the consulting room, Rosamund and Russel kneel on the floor like pilgrims while Barry the vet runs his hands gently over Bono. Barry has taken grass seeds out of Bono's ears, glass out of his paw. When he touches Bono's tummy there is a yelpy snarl that turns to a shriek. Russel tips forward convulsively. Rosamund puts a hand on his arm and he shakes it off. Russel's face is green, his eyelids vermilion. She shouldn't have brought him. But Bono is his dog.

'I'm very sorry, Russel,' Barry says. 'His back's broken and several vital organs smashed inside. Both back legs too. All I can do is relieve him of pain.'

A pause.

'How?' says Russel.

'Put him to sleep. Shock's numbing the pain now but he'd never be without it. And he'd never recover.' Silence. 'All I do is inject anaesthetic. Numbness spreads, he won't notice. And the pain will end.' Rosamund watches Bono's ribs jerk in spasms.

'You can do this for him,' says Barry finally. 'He needs you, Russel. He needs the people he loves.'

Tyler should be here. Rosamund looks guiltily at the ads for roundworm pills. At legs of the table where Bono had his first injections before he got so big he had to be doctored on the floor.

'You can do this for him,' Barry says again. Russel puts his cheek against Bono's muzzle. Rosamund rubs Bono's ears. His eyelids twitch. A bubbly noise comes in his throat. He knows them all by touch. Tyler roughs him up and Bono loves it. When he was younger he used to put his front paws onto Tyler's shoulders, big male chest to big male chest, opening his jaws in a big dog laugh.

'OK,' Russel mutters. A year ago, Rosamund would have put an arm round him. Now she doesn't dare.

She sees a glint. Barry is sliding a needle into the paw dangling over the basket. Russel, cheek against Bono's moustache, has his eyes closed. Holding the shaggy head that has been with them everywhere, holidays, birthdays, children's parties, football and French cricket, she feels it grow heavier.

Bred for boar hunting indeed. Bono never caught anything larger than a fly, and only once. Some mad fly, perhaps dying anyway, caught in the pile of a carpet. Rosamund remembers Bono studying its struggles, taking it softly in his mouth then releasing it.

'That's it,' says Barry. 'He's not in pain any more.'

Bono's eyes are still open. It is upsettingly not like going to sleep. Russel rocks the big head against his chest. Rosamund puts her arms round them both and hears Barry leaving the room.

After a moment, Heather is here.

'We'll take care of him now. Sorry, but – do you want the basket?'

Rosamund shakes her head. She keeps her arm round Russel as they stand. Bono lies in his basket. At the door, Russel looks back with a little pull of protest, as though a rope had snapped.

In reception, everyone avoids their eyes except the large man, who is picking up his puppy to remove it from the terrier. It wriggles, trying to get back to the floor. Rosamund meets the man's eyes and feels warm for the first time that day. He is shorter than Tyler but just as broad and younger. Fortyish, with floppy brown hair, pleasantly squashed face and black tweed jacket.

Bono can be cremated, apparently. They will get his ashes in the post. Russel stands frozen-faced, his back to the room.

'Lost him?' says the man. Sympathetic, but not too sympathetic. Russel nods and to Rosamund's surprise repeats the last thing he heard with Bono alive.

'You c'n do this for him.'

'Right,' says the man. 'We're responsible for their death as well as their life.'

Russel pats the puppy, which sets its teeth in his sleeve and tugs.

'In for his injections,' the man says. 'Doesn't know what vets are for yet. I'll be able to take him out now, let him play with other dogs. Where can you walk dogs round here?'

'Depends where you live, innit,' says Russel.

'Round the back of Kentish Town police station.'

Rosamund knows Russel's opinion of the police. 'They pick on teenagers.' 'They're all bent.' Signing a treatment form, a putting-to-sleep form, she hears Russel say, 'Round the Lido. Back of Gospel. C'n let him off the lead there, innit. By the tracks.'

'Thanks. Only just moved here, you see.'

She hears Russel ask the question he had answered so often himself.

'What sorta dog?'

'Flat-coat retriever. Could you hold him a minute, while I sign the vaccination form?' Is he gay, chatting to Russel like this? No, not the way he looked at her. Maybe he does Youth Care. She presses her PIN in the handset. 'Heavy for a little 'un, isn't he? Won't get as big as yours, though.'

The receptionist gives her Bono's empty collar. Rosamund sees Russel stroking the puppy. The man puts his hand out.

'Scott Redington.'

His hand is strong and warm. She realises she's shivering.

'Rosamund Fairfax. And – Russel.'

'Sorry about your dog. Terrible.'

Russel gives the puppy back. At last Rosamund sees tears sliding down his cheeks. She hugs him and he buries his face in her shoulder.

Outside, there's not even a parking ticket. Any other time, Rosamund would have exulted. She opens the passenger door, keeping one hand on Russel as if he were ill, or old, or might fly up in the air like a lost balloon.

'You can't go to school. I'll write a letter.' If only he were seven again. 'How about the zoo, darling? Lunch there?'

'Biology project,' he mumbles.

Back home he sloughs off his trainers and mutters, 'Might sleep after homework. Don't want lunch, Mum. I'm good.'

Can she mention last night? No. She is at a loss. So is Russel, but he wants to be at his loss by himself and disappears upstairs. She goes into the kitchen and sees an empty plate, empty pan with a spoon in it, and the gold skin of scrambled egg hardening over the lot. Tyler has gone.

Friday 11 March, Parliament Square, London, 2.00 p.m.

Anka heard her number and stood up. She saw the plump man with black glasses whom she'd noticed the day before shut his laptop, zip it crossly in a case and stand up too. With ten other people, they shuffled down a corridor to a panelled room, took the oath and sat, Anka in the back pew, the plump man in front. Facing them from behind a balustrade was a child, a brown face framed in a halo of frizzy black hair, shoulders thin as wire coat hangers.

The young lawyer, whose red face was surrounded by a creamy wig like a pink marshmallow wrapped in a white one, said the prisoner was twenty, and came from Eritrea.

Anka had left her home at seventeen. She had climbed on the tractor of her cousin Pero, who later disappeared in the war. Twisting round, she had seen her mother sobbing, holding up a crucifix which Anka watched glitter behind her as Pero bumped between maize fields edged with yellow courgette flowers – to Koprivnica, where she caught the Zagreb bus. In Zagreb, she took the bus to London where the strange names for musical notes, crotchets, minims, seemed to remind her what a stranger *she* was, how strange everything was. As it must have been when this boy came. Eritrea? She pictured the Great Pannonian Plain and sprinkled it with sand and elephants. Then she removed the elephants and substituted machine guns. People came to England to be safe.

She heard the lawyer say this boy had locked a Russian woman in a room and tried to rape her. He looked too little to rape a Russian woman.

'We resume on Monday morning,' said the judge.

From this angle, she could see three gentle tiers of fat beneath his chin. She tried to imagine him in his own kitchen, cooking peppers. His eyes were very blue and she didn't know how she felt about any of this.

The plump man in black glasses sighed as if everyone else were enormously silly.

Friday 11 March, Mangalore, Karnataka, 8.30 p.m.; 3.00 p.m., UK

The night was brushed with stars as if someone had upended a salt cellar over black satin, tall trees were teasing the moon like a silver ball they wouldn't let through their net and stalls either side of the village street were lit like Halloween lanterns whose wicks were the vendors, sitting between strings of rubber flip-flops.

Girish led Richard to a cave guarded by plaster leopards ten feet high. He took off his sandals and ducked inside. Richard followed, watching where he trod. Priests often left saucers of milk for Shiva's cobras. Inside, stone cobras loomed above his head like giant umbrellas, guarding Shiva's lingam. Girish bowed and kissed the stone. Richard stayed at the door.

'Like entering your own subconscious,' Girish said as they came out and joined an excited crowd around a bonfire. Children ran everywhere: little girls in flounced dresses and gold bangles, small boys in shorts and women calling to them like birds, wearing green and orange from which the sepia firelight coaxed gleams of gold. By the fire, a screen of sewn-together sacks erupted in hemp bubbles whenever invisible actors brushed against it from behind. Drummers sitting on the ground were surrounded by shiny-eyed little boys. A figure with twigs on its ankles danced into the light.

'A hunter,' whispered Girish. 'The twigs symbolise forest.'

The actor touched the earth and Richard smiled. When he'd seen that action first and learned what it meant, he had written Irena the only love letter he'd ever managed. 'Now I know what we have in common, darling, actors and biologists – earth! It supports actors, they salute it and ask for its help. That's what you and I both know – that we depend on the Earth.' But now, suddenly, he felt exhausted. He hated packing. Whenever he was tired, he saw faces. And the two splits in that screen, with a crooked seam below, looked like a scowling mask. He felt he couldn't stand a moment longer.

Three girls in saffron silk danced into the firelight, the bangles on their naked arms shimmering like cloud trails brightened by lightning. Girish laughed.

'They're not Yakshagana, they're flames. At night, when lamps go out, people say the extinguished flames gossip about the houses they lit in the day.'

The lead flame, colour of the shadows in Rosamund's hair, began to sing.

'She's singing about a girl with long black hair like a king cobra,' whispered Girish. 'Her husband ignored her and went to prostitutes. Someone gave her a love potion but she was afraid to use it and poured it into an anthill. The king cobra who lived inside the anthill fell in love with her.'

Richard blinked. Arms, hips, molten gold, mysterious and flagrant – Rosamund was everywhere. So was the king cobra's golden throat.

'One night it transformed itself into the girl's husband and slid into her bedroom.' The crowd laughed. 'The girl began to think her husband was loving in the dark but cold to her by day. Then she fell pregnant and he accused her of adultery. She would be stoned to death. But the cobra told her to take the truth test.' The crowd's murmur was like wind in the hills. 'She had to swear she was innocent while touching the cobra. If she lied, he'd bite her. Cobras bite people who lie.'

The crowd pressed forward. Girish steadied Richard in the crush.

'She sank her arm into the anthill, brought out the king cobra and swore she'd touched only two beings, her husband and this cobra. The snake rested its head on her shoulder. Its long black body mingled with her hair.' The singer ran her hands down her body to her hips. Richard heard behind him the hissed breath of five hundred men. 'Then it disappeared. The villagers kissed the girl's feet, calling her Protectress. Her husband accepted the cobra's son as his own.'

A figure with a blue-painted face and wild snaky hair bounded in, tore off a lock of hair and struck the earth with it. The crowd stepped back.

'Shiva's angry,' Girish whispered. 'Striking the earth means disaster.'

Richard swayed.

'Girish, I'm sorry, I've had a long day.'

'Let's get you home.'

Two days later Richard entered Mysore with Ranjit, son of his Mangalore landlord, an engineering student with a whirl of wiry hair. Richard had watched him grow up and now paid him to look after his Gypsy, drive him to Chennai, and take the jeep back to Mangalore where it lived when Richard was away. Ranjit had spotted a paragraph in *Mangalore Today* about an auto-rickshaw driver whom they had arranged to interview as they drove across Karnataka: Mukund, who rescued the snakes that appeared in the city in the rains when rat holes were flooded and the rats, which it was the snakes' job to hunt, moved into houses.

Sunday noon. Children played in a cul de sac overlooking huge acres of rice paddy, which stretched into the horizon like a sea of sunlit jade. Ranjit drove over black seams with splashy edges tarring over gaps between blocks of concrete. Each small house had a concrete car space and concrete steps to the upper floor. Children's clothes lay drying on a hundred concrete banisters. With a few details changed, it could have been Dulwich.

Outside the last house was a motorbike and an auto-rickshaw painted with slogans: SAVE ENVIRONMENT! CARE FOR WILD! A barrel-chested man in a red cowboy-fringed shirt and handlebar moustache waited for them beside a woman with a baby.

'Welcome,' said Mukund, in English. Twenty children swirled round them as they shook hands.

'Nice to meet you,' Richard said in careful Kannada. Mukund replied very fast, grinning. Richard looked helplessly at Ranjit.

'He says he knows little English but only little. He gets ten calls every day. People find snakes behind water tanks and in bathroom.'

'How does he catch them?'

Mukund unclipped a stringless tennis racket from the motorbike.

'He attaches pillowcase to racket with clothes pegs. The snake goes in.'

The top of Mukund's thumb was glassy and on his wrist was a livid scar.

'Two bites,' said Richard. Mukund smiled broadly.

'Bite on wrist,' Ranjit translated. 'He waved handkerchief, to show cobra spreading hood. A child asked question, he turned his head, snake struck. Only one fang came in. The other stopped at his watch.'

52

'Saved by time,' said Mukund in English and reverted to Kannada.

'He was in hospital one night, one day,' translated Ranjit. Eight phials anti-venom. He felt like having drunk one bottle whisky. His arm hurt long time.'

'And the thumb?'

'He bites his nails! He was holding cobra that had already struck, poison entered crack in skin beside the nail. He did not notice. When he went to hospital, flesh was already rotting.'

The woman laughed.

'His wife says, she doesn't let him handle food.'

'Yesterday, I caught this,' Mukund said in English. 'You will be interested, Doctor.'

He led them to a row of plywood boxes and swung up a lid. The children pressed closer.

'He made these boxes to keep snakes safe.'

What about keeping children safe? They were surging to see. Three scampered up the steps to peer from above.

With a snake stick, that long shepherd-like crook which Richard knew so well, Mukund lifted a dark snake from a box. It curled back and down, trying to hide its head under its coils. Cream bands widened on the sides and broke into scattery spots towards the tail.

'Krait,' said Ranjit. Richard was already trying to back the children away. It seemed small for an adult, but a juvenile was just as deadly.

'No no,' said Mukund. '*Looks* like.'

Now the snake had given up trying to hide, Richard could see its head, waving in the air.

'Bridal snake,' he said with relief. A harmless snake, which copied the krait to frighten off predators but got a few details wrong. On the back of its neck he saw the identifying yellow mark like a wedding veil.

Mukund looked pleased.

'Was in children's nursery,' translated Ranjit. 'Hunting geckos. He says, very gentle.'

'Snakes not poisonous as people,' said Mukund in English.

Richard took it loosely in his hands. He never tired of admiring the delicate biology snakes had evolved to cope with life. They could curl round any shape, slide up any surface on the tips of flexible, easily smashable ribs. Their inner anatomy was brilliantly modified to fit a narrow space. Since there was no diaphragm the heart could move, when prey passed through the oesophagus, to protect it from damage.

The children whispered, thrilled by this presence among them. The snake flowed and stared into air. Snakes didn't have big brains. If you held them lightly they went on flowing, apparently unaware they were imprisoned. Perhaps it believed, whatever believing was for a bridal snake, it was getting somewhere.

Mukund replaced it tenderly and brought out a thin green snake with a beak-like snout, bronze eyes with horizontal pupils and a bright pink mouth open in protest.

'Vine snake,' said Richard, since Mukund seemed to want him to flash his snake credentials. 'Was that in a tree?'

'A woman saw, behind her wood stack.'

Now two cobras. One found in a water tank, the other in a drain-pipe. Mukund held one in the air, hooking it in the middle and gripping its tail. It spread its hood, confused. It was sensitive, Richard knew, to vibration, and trucks were thundering along the main road behind. It turned its head, uncertain where the worst danger lay. The spectacled hood, a reaction to threat, was like a face. To Richard, it simply looked upset. To everyone else, it looked wonderfully dangerous, like electricity – or a god. No old people in the villages killed cobras. That spread hood had sheltered the Buddha and shaded Vishnu from the sun. A little girl leaned from the banister and flapped her hand. The snake lunged, the children laughed, Richard licked his lips and Mukund jerked it back, then locked it away, opened a notebook and showed Richard columns titled in beautiful copperplate. Species, Place, Date.

'Thirteen thousand seven hundred and sixty-six snakes,' Ranjit said. 'In five years.'

Richard turned over the pages. Cobra, cobra, cat snake, python, rat snake, cobra, Russell's viper, cat snake, krait.

'Thirty-six species,' said Mukund. So many, in one small city. This year the rains had gone on and on. Bangalore film studios had a cobra problem. There had been snakes all over Mysore's factories, offices, schools.

'He never asks money because people will find cheaper to kill snake. Ten out of a hundred people give five or ten rupees for petrol.' Mukund riffled his record book, showing these sums. 'He needs four litres petrol each day. Morning, afternoons, he takes children to and from schools. All day, he works auto-rickshaw. At weekend, he goes to Bandipur, releasing snakes in forest.'

Mukund picked up a little boy.

'His son Abhijit is also catching snakes. Mukund doesn't want him to. Snake-catching makes too busy! He doesn't go to films or family parties. Always a snake, someone's house. He doesn't want Abhijit to be like that.'

The family waved them goodbye.

'Always, good things done by one person only,' said Ranjit. 'But after Mukund, what?'

Sunday 13 March, Primrose Hill, London, 8.00 a.m.; 1.30 p.m., India

Rosamund sits alone in the kitchen, as every Sunday morning, studying *Style* magazine. What about that facelift? She shudders at a picture of scissors on bare skin and turns to Horoscopes. For years she's tried to second-guess from Shelley von Strunckel what Tyler is up to.

Outside, under the Heidi Home, the vixen holds her top hind leg in the air so as not to squash three blind sausages beside her. Her front paw lies over the front cub like the finger of a velvet glove. She feels as safe as a mother fox can ever feel.

'Time to sort out things on the domestic front,' say Rosamund's stars. 'A rocky time ahead,' say Russel's. 'Your ruler, Venus, is smiling on all your ventures,' say Tyler's. Rosamund sips her coffee. Autumn, Daisy, Liza, Sara, Marta and a thousand more. They come, they go. Nails in the coffin of her marriage.

The space where Bono's basket lay emanates a chill like air from the Arctic. Yesterday she found Tyler staring at it, eyes shiny with tears. 'Why the *fuck* didn't you wake me?' he said. 'I should've *been* there!' She'd considered putting her arms round him but history stood between them, a wall of slime.

Will this lump in her throat ever go away? When she gave Bono's empty collar to Russel she tried to hug him but he shook her off. He's eaten practically nothing. Yesterday he hardly appeared. She'd hoped they might all three watch a video on Saturday night but Tyler said they had a dinner with important friends. Russel had vanished. All evening she worried how he was. She knew Russel would know she'd be doing that, and resent it. Oh, let him find solace with his friends. Whoever they are.

On Sundays they pretend to be a family. Soon she'll start making lunch. But she's always cooked with Bono beside her. He used to get in her way, nosing every dropped crumb. Recently he has just watched from his basket, moving his head. Umpiring, Tyler used to say. Bono had hated their rows almost as much as Russel did.

She puts *Style* down and starts snipping garlic into tiny ivory flakes.

Sunday 13 March, Karnataka, India, 3.30 p.m.; 10.00 a.m., UK

The main road, crammed with lorries, ran like a strip of black cotton through green fields stuccoed with white egrets. Away, thought Richard. Away from the poaching, from crimes against the forest. Away from Mangalore, where Brahminy kites wheeled above the city in damp white sky. Back to Irena, to Devon. He could finish that paper now, on king cobra prey.

Hemmed in by a hundred trucks, through air black with exhaust, they inched past an arch. Through it he saw a green garden with fountains and recognised the Summer Palace of Sultan Tipu, Tiger of Mysore. He'd gone in once with Girish, seen a portrait of Tipu in gold embroidery, sparkly murals celebrating Tipu's victories over the British, and an English painting of British soldiers sacking this very palace, where Tipu died. Also a temple with a gigantic stone Vishnu, the god created to right the balance between good and evil. Vishnu was asleep, smiling, on coils of the cosmic serpent.

How important India is to me, thought Richard. He saw again the dancers in the village, golden in the dark.

Rosamund was coming for Easter.

A MURKY PART OF THE WOOD

3

Friday 18 March, Kilburn, London, 7.45 a.m.

'I can't go to Katya's tonight, it's your *birthday*!'

Helen had put a cup of tea by Anka's bed, climbed in, given her a shell painted with blue nail polish and a card with coloured butterflies round every letter. Helen was brilliant at Art.

'Beautiful, *dragi*. Won-der-ful. Thank you.' Anka had hugged her, holding the shiny head close to her shoulder. 'I keep, always.'

But now Helen was standing crossly in the cold and Anka sat against her pillows feeling guilty. Usually she had birthday dinner with Helen but late last night she'd had a phone call.

'Sweetie, get out your glad rags. I've booked the coolest restaurant in town. *Impossible* to get into, but I pulled strings. Chap must cosset his beloved on her birthday.' After five years, they were closer than ever. And Helen loved going to Katya.

'We are doing different this year, remember?' she coaxed. 'Today, when you are coming from school, we have cake. Supper, we have tomorrow, with Budimir, Lasta, Katya.'

'But it's your birthday *now*,' said Helen.

At lunchtime, having made it up with Helen, Anka went into the church beside Westminster Abbey, crossed herself, prayed, then sat up and contemplated the stained-glass window. This afternoon, when the court closed, she would rush to the hairdresser, rush home for birthday tea with Helen, take Helen to Lasta's, go home again, change, and take a minicab back to town.

All week, they'd been called in and out of court, which had enraged the stout man in the beautiful suit and black spectacles. Today the Russian woman had given evidence. Anka didn't believe her. Rape stories from her own village, after the war, made you want

61

to weep and rage for ever. This was different. The woman so large, and the boy from Eritrea so thin, so small. The woman said she'd been shopping after work in Carnaby Street and it was hard because someone in her office had given her a microwave to carry too. The boy was beside her in the crowd. He smiled and said he could carry her bags to Oxford Circus. At the entrance to the Underground there were so many people, he said come and rest in his room. The Russian woman said yes she would if he had anything to drink, she needed a drink.

Oh yeah, Anka could hear her boyfriend say. We know what's going on there, then.

Then, said the woman, he locked the door and tried to rape her.

Cabbage-shit, thought Anka. Anyone, especially a large red-haired woman twice as broad in the shoulders as the boy, can open a door. The boy said she had finished the whisky a friend left in his room, then showed him her new vibrator. This was a word Anka had not encountered before. The boy said the Russian woman had bought a vibrator in Soho and was angry there were no batteries. He took batteries out of his alarm clock and put them in for her. The she rubbed the vibrator up and down his cock, so he touched her breast. But she hit him and made him put his cock back in his trousers.

'She didn't like it,' said the boy, as if everything would have been OK if his cock had looked different. Twenty years old. Poor boy must talk about his cock, and a woman who didn't want it, to lawyers who didn't look as if they even had a cock.

Anka considered the judge in this connection and dismissed him too.

The Russian woman said there was no vibrator, all she bought was a dress in Carnaby Street. The other jurors believed her, except a blonde woman with a purple birthmark on her chin. None of the jurors were black like the boy. A girl with a shiny face and no make-up said all men were rapists.

Anka's phone rang.

'Happy birthday, sweet thing. How the hell are you?'

'So old,' Anka whispered.

'You're twelve years younger than me, with the body of a sixteen-year-old and a face that wouldn't just launch a thousand ships but burn them too. How's your case?'

'Is attempted rape.'

'How cool, how sexy.'

'Must not use mobile, in church—'

'What are you doing in a church, what's the *matter* with you? See you at eight-thirty. Can't wait.'

Friday 18 March, Chennai, Tamil Nadu, 8.30 p.m.; 3.00 p.m., London

Richard sat on a bed in his Madras hotel. He had a hundred people to see: conservationists, colleagues, forest department officials. His room stank of disinfectant. He'd have to leave later than he planned to get it all done. He must tell Irena he'd be a week late. At least he'd be there for Easter.

And he must phone Kellar. The very thought made him tense. Irena had asked once, 'What's so special about Kellar?' That was in his fourth year when Rosamund had dropped out of college, out of his life, and Irena had called to see if he wanted to go to some play in a pub. At first, talking about Kellar was a way of talking about Ros. Then he got interested in the question itself. He'd never asked himself what made Kellar great.

'His way of trying to know,' he replied, surprised into making the kind of woolly answer he despised. 'Kellar goes after truth, it's the only thing he cares about, but never says he's got there. Reptiles suit him because they're mysterious, so much not known. He doesn't *pretend* to know.'

'I see,' said Irena and he felt she did. He was beginning to realise that she listened to people not only to understand, but also to enlarge her own work. It made her both fun and peaceful to be with. He could talk to her as he never did to Ros, except in fantasy. For the first time in his life he felt met, in his mind, by someone who was interested in what he thought. About his work, about the world. And who thought about her own work in, he found to his amazement, rather the same way.

They'd gone to Rosamund's wedding together, they didn't know anyone but talked to each other, and Irena helped him garner the courage to talk to Kellar. To his amazement, the scientist he most revered in the world invited him to come and see his research in India. Walking away, Richard felt he had lost one dream but might be fulfilling another which mattered more.

Before he finally started work in India, though, he had been summoned to a late-night drink in King's Cross by Kellar's former colleague Vic Browne. 'Must give you the lowdown on Keller, young Ricardo,' he'd said on the phone. 'Meet me at Andy's Bar before I take the night train to Glasgow.'

Vic Browne had been their external examiner at King's, but Richard hadn't met him then. As a postgraduate, he'd admired Vic's papers on mambas and heard the gossip: how Vic was married once and now was famous for the dangers he ran, not with snakes but with women. There were not many women in herpetology but there were some pretty bitter husbands. When Vic had a drink he was impervious to everything and everyone. Richard had ignored the gossip. He admired Vic's work as he admired Kellar's and preferred his heroes unsullied.

He had found Vic sitting, a shabby corduroy cherub, in the corner of Andy's Bar. 'Cheers,' he'd said as Richard put a whisky in front of him. 'So you're off to India. Pity it's not the dark continent. Still, old Kells is the best. Data, interpretation, ideas, contacts, he'll see you right. But watch it, Ricardo, he's tense as a krait. Any criticism and it's war.'

Richard had sipped bitter lemon and contemplated gingery hairs on the back of Vic's hand. Everything about Vic seemed both touchable and tainted.

'Jesus, the *fuss* there used to be in the lab about washing test tubes. Anyone who did things any other way than his was wrong.' Vic laughed. 'We were scared as hell.'

This from an expert on genus Dendroaspis, whose toxin shuts down the lungs and heart.

'What were you scared of?'

Vic pushed forward his empty glass.

'Well now. Wasn't his temper, though he shouted all right if

64

anyone put a toe out of line. Lab was a fucking Chekhov play, really. How about another?'

Richard ordered a double at the bar while Vic contemplated spilt water on the table.

'He panicked, as if something might break inside him,' he said when Richard returned. 'That was it. Over tiny fucking details. Drop of water on a slide and you'd murdered a baby. *We* were scared 'cause *he* was scared – of losing it. Wanted to seem invulnerable, silly bugger. We knew he'd break if we confronted him.'

Richard had felt nervous. He was starting work in a new place, Kellar had suggested it, and Kellar would be his closest colleague for a thousand miles.

'He's a weak man, Ricardo, but wields a tyrant's power. You can't point out how silly the bastard is.' Vic had drained his whisky. 'Work's wonderful, of course. In the field. On the page.'

Richard sighed. Poor old Vic. Quick, coarse, brilliant and damned. And now dead.

His mobile rang.

'Richard? Girish. Bad news. A forest fire in the sector where you were working. People say it was started deliberately.'

'Why?'

'I've heard the director wants to cover evidence of poaching. He *says* they're bringing the fire under control. I'll email. Nothing you can do.'

Those precious eggs. The dry leaves heaped up so carefully, towering into flame, scorching birds off trees above. Did the mother get away? The leopard? The elephant?

He thought of Mukund's slogans. Of Shiva, the Destroyer. And Vishnu the so-called Preserver, snoring on his cosmic snake.

Friday 18 March, Primrose Hill, London, 8.00 p.m.

Rosamund pounces on Russel's rucksack by the front door and carries it to the kitchen. She feels like a wolf taking a fawn to its lair but she must enforce some rules. Russel pads in, searching for it.

'Not tonight, love. If you go out now you'll spend all day asleep,

65

and there's the dentist at eleven-thirty, remember?' Russel turns on the TV. Bono's corner beams emptiness at them both. 'Like to watch a film?'

She puts down two plates, gleaming sausages and pale farfalloni. Russel looks blankly at his and turns back to the TV. She pours herself a glass of wine. Blank is how he protects himself, just as she always did.

She sees herself at the end of her third year in college, holding a plastic cup of wine at the end-of-term zoology party.

'After next year,' said little Dr Lussers, 'might you stay on for research?'

She must have looked blank as hell. She did know Father was not the only reason Dr Lussers encouraged her. Father was zoology royalty but Rosamund herself, despite missing a few lectures, was doing pretty well.

Then, wondering when she could decently leave to meet Tyler, she had been accosted by the visiting examiner, Professor Browne, whom Dr Lussers had said it was an honour to welcome to King's. He had a wrecked pudgy face, stained corduroy trousers low on the hip which somehow made her want to hitch them up, gingery sideboards and strangely short earlobes. She would never, ever, forget.

'Hello, lovely! Bet I know who *you* are. Old Loose told me you'd fetched up here. Y' look just like your ma.'

'You knew my *mother*?'

'Intimately.' He scrutinised the shadow inside his paper cup and then Rosamund's cleavage. 'Daphne, the recorder player. Played duets with your dad but really dug the swinging sixties. Lovely dancer. Bet you are, too.'

He leaned closer, drowning her in breathy waves of Chardonnay.

'Always had an eye for the girls, old Kells. Didn't realise. Highminded.' He stared into his empty cup as if he saw a puzzle in it. 'Even while he had it off with that student. The lovely Vanona.'

'*What?*'

'The sixties, darlin'. Everyone was at it. Vanona lived in the house.' Rosamund felt every muscle in her freeze. Stay blank. Don't let them see how you feel. 'Why Daphne chucked herself under that train,' Professor Browne added, and the room went dark. 'You were a baby, darlin'.' She focused on saliva under his bottom lip. 'Filthy stuff, this. Fancy peeling off to a decent bar?'

She turned and walked out. Out of King's, out to the street. She stumbled through Aldwych, eyes streaming with tears, and was nearly knocked down by a van in Covent Garden.

She'd known it was a train. But . . . But she'd always believed Father was moral. Not kind or warm, she hadn't known those were things fathers could be. But he was always right. Now he was the liar. The betrayer. Crossing Charing Cross Road, Rosamund forced herself to say it. 'My mother killed herself.'

She'd have nothing to do with Father ever again. Nor with zoology.

In the John Snow pub, Soho, she'd hurled herself sobbing into Tyler's arms.

'What is it?' he whispered. 'I'm here, sweetie. You're safe.'

She poured it all out. The train, the lovely Vanona . . .

'I'll look after you,' he said. 'I'll be your rock.' Burrowing into his chest, she thought of all the knowledge Father had stuffed her with, while keeping quiet about the only thing that mattered.

She left betrayal behind, she thinks now, watching one lone far-fallone vanish into Russel's mouth. And I walked slap into new betraying.

Your dad doesn't know how to love, Tyler said once, as if he himself were the truest lover of all time.

'Eat up, darling.'

'Not hungry.'

'Must eat something.'

Russel stirs the farfalloni with his fork like a builder demonstrating what inferior cement he has been given.

'Pancakes for pudding.' He always used to love pancakes.

'I'm good,' says Russel. Which means, she knows, that he's not.

Friday 18 March, Covent Garden, London, 8.30 p.m.

The receptionist showed Anka into an underground bar whose wooden walls shone black-red like wine. Every sense alert, as if the air were fizzing over her skin, she checked the edge of her cleavage. Very low. And the silk dress rather tight. But he'd love it. She ordered gin and tonic. It had been a terrible rush, her last cash had gone on the minicab and all bank machines were down, but he'd pay. He'd be late, like always.

She smiled. Her untameable *crni lav*! The first time she'd called him that he had looked very suspicious. 'What in hell's that?' 'Is black lion,' she laughed, running her fingers through his mane. 'Sounds like a particularly vicious toilet-cleaner,' he'd muttered. But he had also been, she thought, rather proud.

Anka sipped her drink. Her blow-dry looked lovely. And Helen was happy with Katya. Now for her birthday dinner.

Friday 18 March, Primrose Hill, London, 11.15 p.m.

Rosamund switches channels. Ads, quiz shows, politics. A Honda flying through the air, four men answering dopey questions, and the courtyard of a London mosque full of banners saying 'British and Americans must be killed'. She switches off and looks round. When they did up this living room, they had installed a gas fire of false logs.

'That fire's *lying*,' said Russel when he was seven.

'When you get into Oxford, old chap,' Tyler said in answer, ruffling his hair, 'we'll have the champagne right here!'

'But Daddy can we have Coke?' Russel said anxiously. 'Don't like champagne.'

Rosamund looks at the uncurtained back window and sees little bubble-specks of air like jet jewels caught in the glass. Four years ago, this house was full around her like a flower. Children's parties, music lessons, Hallowe'en lanterns, football boots, ice creams. The petals have fallen so fast.

How's Russel doing, upstairs? She goes out, up to the first landing, and listens. Then into the bathroom. She pulls the door nearly closed, sits on the mahogany seat and stares at a lamp like a burning torch which Tyler found in World's End, Chelsea. It is too big for the bathroom. It probably contravenes Health and Safety, too.

The phone rings downstairs and the answerphone cuts in.

Rosamund hears raspy sobbing and a woman's voice, floods of words in a foreign accent. Something something 'broken', something 'three hours', something 'always like this!' A lot of hoarse crying. She is yelling down the phone. Something 'turn off mobile', something 'love of your life'. More crying. Something 'all these years'.

The tape runs out. Slowly, as if after an operation, Rosamund pulls up her knickers. Her skin feels inflamed, her tights stick to her jeans like the inner skin of an egg to its shell.

All these years? Love of your life? Tyler's escapades are short. That's their point. They are humiliating, but mean nothing.

And what's her evidence for that? Only him. She walks downstairs as if steps are a dangerous new invention. The phone tape is whirring like a rattlesnake. She presses 1471.

'You were phoned, today, at twenty-three forty-eight hours. The caller withheld their number.'

Tyler is occupied territory and she never knew. Her skin prickles as if the air were electric. She feels sucked out, like the seabed before a tsunami. *All these years.* How many of her years are those?

69

4

'Pity about your territoriality study.'

Tobias Kellar sat behind his desk at Chooramaya Reptile Research Centre, contemplating Richard through rimless glasses.

'North-east Bengal is good king cobra country still. Would you like me to mention you?' Kellar always clipped the front consonants of each word but swallowed the end as if there was something he was afraid of letting escape.

'Yes, please,' said Richard.

'Should you care to visit our holding pens, for rescued king cobras?' Kellar rose. 'We have had only males this year, but a new snake has come from a beauty spot. People were throwing stones at it. It is small. If female, it's a chance to breed. There's something on its eye. I intend to investigate.'

They walked past roses on impossibly long stems, as if extra wood were needed in this heat to make a single flower, and a young man unlocked a door. Richard stepped into a corridor flanked by mesh cages. Behind each he saw a pyramid of coiled snake.

'This one,' Kellar said by the fifth, 'is twenty years old. The largest king cobra in captivity.'

A head, rearing out of coils. A hood, spreading. A creamy throat, framed by the black symmetrical brush strokes which Irena said looked like a pharaoh's hairdo. The underhood's gold flanges were sprinkled with black spots. That face – which looked so calm even while charging.

'Fourteen six?'

'Fourteen eight.'

The last cell held a basket with a lid.

70

'Should you care to help, Richard?' You have to trust the people you wrangle snakes with. Kellar was paying him an enormous compliment. The young man offered Richard a snake hook as if it were a billiard cue. 'You won't need that,' said Kellar, taking one himself, like a bishop handling his crozier.

Richard followed the two of them into the cell. The young man closed the door behind them. Why, wondered Richard, did he keep putting himself at risk? No one used gloves. They made you clumsy and anyway were no protection. Did the centre hold antivenin for kings? You make antivenin by injecting a non-lethal dose of venom into a horse's neck. When the horse develops antibodies, you siphon off the blood, mix it with anticoagulant and separate the antibodies. But people become allergic to these components and Kellar, Richard knew, had been bitten so often that any antivenin was lethal to him now.

The young man lifted the lid with a stick and a dark head shot over the rim. Round eyes, spread hood – Kellar had the neck hefted in his hook and the young man already held the tail. The snake glared that king cobra glare which looks so reproving – because, Irena once told Richard, the eyes were so close to the nostrils. One eye was covered in what looked like horn. When a snake sheds its skin, everything comes off, even tongue tip and eye scales. This scale had failed to detach.

'Very thin,' said Kellar. 'Eaten little recently, the poison glands will be full from disuse. That eye cap is opaque. It probably can't see to hunt, do you think? We shall discover the sex. We immobilise the head – thank you, Dhirendra – and probe the tail.'

Dhirendra already had the head. When a snake feels held it will double back and try to bite. If you pick it up with only a hook it will slip away, so you hold the tail with one hand and fend the head off with the hook. But if you want to do something to it, you have to hold the head.

Kellar hoicked up the tail and slid a plastic probe horizontally into the genital opening. If it was male, the probe would go in three inches over the hemi-penis, into its sheath.

'Won't go any further, I'll try a little more – no . . . only an inch.

71

Female.' He pocketed the probe, not relaxing his iron hold on the tail. 'Now her eye. If you would take the tail – don't relax your grip at *all*, please, Richard. Mind the opening, it'll be sensitive.'

Richard gripped the tail. He had handled captive kings in Thailand but never a wild one. They were terribly strong. And intelligent. You never knew what a king might do. He held tight as Kellar took the head. The mouth was open in fury or panic. Her body heaved. Dhirendra manoeuvred it so he could hold it down with one arm.

'Anti-bacterial spray,' said Kellar, pressing a nozzle, sending liquid over the snake's eye. She thrashed and Richard felt her tail muscles tighten. 'This won't be pleasant,' Kellar told the snake, closing tweezers on the edge of the eye cap. 'It's not coming . . . I don't want to damage – yes, a little – ah!'

More convulsions. Kellar, tugging at the eye, had his own eyes very close to the snake's.

'I've got most of it. She's shed three skins while it stuck, three years of near-blindness . . . It's coming, one layer still attached – this must be hurting . . . Yes – off it comes!' He brandished a triplet of yellowy lenses, held together at one edge like strung-together plastic spoons. 'Stopping her seeing, poor girl. Preventing her getting food.' Holding the poor girl's head between finger and thumb, he dropped the tweezers in his pocket. 'Now she must recover. Please hold the tail more *up*, Richard. *Much* more up.' His voice rose as the snake struggled. 'Dhirendra, if you could lift the body out . . .'

Another dangerous transition. Dhirendra lifted her free of the basket, nudged the basket aside with his foot and laid the furious loops on the floor like giant black knitting.

'I may not be able to hold her much longer,' Kellar said quietly. 'Richard, everything depends on you. Dhirendra will keep the head away with the hook. Hold the tail higher. High as you can.'

Richard's hands slipped and he felt the muscles beneath take instant advantage. She lashed and he tightened his grip.

'Dhirendra, I'm going to let go and move to the left while you move the hook under her throat to the right. Let us hope Richard holds the tail high enough that she can't get us. *Now*.'

Dhirendra's movements were quick as the snake's. The hook was under her throat and moving her to the right even before Kellar released her head and stepped back. The snake swung round at Kellar but Richard held the tail high so Kellar was out of her range. Kellar picked up the basket, opened the door and walked through.

'Well done, Richard.' His voice was calm. 'Back slowly towards the door . . . good. Keep holding the tail up. Don't panic her.'

Richard's arms were aching. She was heavy; he was holding the tail above his scalp. Dhirendra, supporting her throat with the hook, walked backwards behind Richard. With her throat almost as high in the air as her tail, threshing her huge cogs of body between, the snake was reversed to the door of her stall.

'Once you're near the door, Richard, let go and come through. Keep out of Dhirendra's way. No sudden moves.'

Richard let go and stepped through the door. The lashing tail shot the snake forward; Dhirendra fended her off with the hook under her throat, lowered the hook to release the head, and slipped through the crack as the snake flashed round and came at him, her face with its newly seeing eye four feet off the ground. She stopped and swayed, watching.

'I was afraid she'd strike the door and hurt herself. Thank you, Richard. We must feed her up. For the moment we'll give her the live prey she's used to. A rat snake, please, Dhirendra? If someone can find one.'

Dhirendra stacked the basket and leaned the hook against the wall. Richard found his legs trembling. Even at nearly seventy, Kellar could handle a snake. So awkward with people, but with snakes he was calm itself.

'Would you care for lunch?' Kellar said, as if they had just finished a set of accounts. 'When is your plane?'

Richard had never seen Kellar's house.

'Not till late, sir. I'd love to, thanks.'

Kellar followed a path above a chequerboard of green paddy field where, Richard knew, the Centre caught snakes to make antivenin, and up a drive to a peeling bungalow.

This was the house where Rosamund grew up, where Kellar

brought his baby daughter thirty-five years ago after his wife died. Why had Kellar thrown up his Cambridge chair and come out here to do fieldwork instead? Richard suddenly had a mental picture of the paper bag from the Outpatients pharmacy of Barnstaple Hospital which Irena had laughingly framed for him. It showed the ancient sign of healing, a squat snake twining up a staff. Whatever Kellar went through all those years ago, maybe turning to snakes was his way of healing himself.

A young man opened the door.

'We'll eat directly, Govind,' said Kellar. In a small dining room with a mysteriously thick white padded tablecloth and a ceiling fan clanking like an antique propellor, Govind served rice, *dal* and vegetables.

'Take more,' said Kellar stiffly. 'Govind makes excellent cauliflower.'

Richard took another spoonful and glanced for inspiration behind Kellar's head at a small bronze dancing Shiva, Girish's favourite god. 'What's wrong with Vishnu?' Richard would ask. 'We're doing conservation or hadn't you noticed? Shiva's the Destroyer.' 'He recreates while he destroys,' Gish would say. 'He's extinction *and* evolution.'

Once, waiting in a tree at night for a leopard to return to its kill, Richard had pointed to a snake hunting on the forest floor. 'OK, there's Shiva's cobra. Doesn't it symbolise Shiva's association with death?' 'Yes,' whispered Girish, 'but also his power *over* death, his life force. And his spiritual power. That one cobra sums up all Shiva's attributes.' 'I'm a scientist,' Richard whispered crossly, 'I like things to mean one thing at a time.' 'Too bad. You don't *get* one thing at a time. Not in India and I bet not England either. Everything means lots of things all at once.'

A twig had snapped then and as if conjured by Shiva the leopard stood in a flare of black and primrose at the edge of the clearing. Girish began filming.

'Very fine Shiva there, sir,' said Richard politely.

'Do you care for Chola work?'

'I don't know much about it, really.' Richard looked at his steel water beaker. Kellar had a genius for making people feel uncomfortable. His awkwardness transferred itself to you like a burr.

'That was delicious, thank you, sir. I must go and finish packing.'

'How long will you stay in England?'

'Eight weeks. If I'm relocating, I'll have to negotiate a new budget.' Filling out grant applications, weeks of arguing with officials: that was what he faced now. When he ought to be in forest.

'Come to my study. I have papers you may care to see.'

Kellar's study was a legend in the trade. Richard saw a brown room with a piano – that was unexpected – two scuffed leather armchairs and a desk piled with papers. Thousands of books lined the walls and the floor was an ocean of scientific offprints. There was a gecko on the ceiling, the only living reptile in this shrine to the reptilian. *Hemidactylus frenatus*, thought Richard. Tropical house gecko.

Kellar handed over some offprints and picked up a large envelope.

'I believe you are – your wife is – in touch with a member of my family. I wonder if you could do me a favour. This is a book for my my grandson. An anthology of Alfred Russel Wallace, after whom the boy is called. At my request.'

'I . . . yes,' said Richard, appalled.

'Could you bestow it on . . . on your wife, perhaps, to pass to him? I thought, now he is fourteen, Wallace would be appropriate reading matter. Don't you think?'

Driving back to Chennai in a taxi – his Gypsy had gone back to Mangalore – Richard looked at the luminous ocean and the trail of debris it had swept up the coast three months before, washing away beggars, picnickers, candy-floss sellers, villages, thousands of holidaymakers. He closed his eyes. This had always been a cruel coast but last Boxing Day had been worse than any history book recalled.

Waiting at the lights, he saw a boy wiping the neck of a white ox pulling a cart. One horn was painted yellow, one green. Boy and beast were swathed in clouds of exhaust. On Richard's other side, inky fumes billowed round a stout woman in an auto-rickshaw, eating something out of a paper bag. Blue and silver cloth swirled beneath her like a throne. A little girl in a frilly dress, circled by her father's arm on his motorbike, put her hand into the smog and laughed. Her young father laughed too, into her hair.

Saturday 19 March, Primrose Hill, London, 10.00 a.m.; 3.30 p.m., India

Tyler is *never* down first, but before Rosamund reaches the kitchen she smells the frying and hears Radio 2. Last night, afraid she'd never sleep, she took two sleeping pills. Now she feels swimmy. It is all too much, the egg-yellow walls, bright rugs, Indian hanging, the music – and Tyler the robber king, spatula in air, his ancient olive-green jersey dropping over the shelf of his stomach like an altar fringe.

'Now,' shouts the radio, 'the number you've all been waiting for!'

> *'Touch me, tell me who I am.*
> *Will I have to go, like flowers that die?*
> *Will nothing remain of me above?*
> *You are my earth and sky,*
> *You're everything I've ever loved.'*

The hoarse voice, the fingers sliding up guitar strings, are in the room with them. Tyler strides over and snaps the radio off.

'Oy,' says Rosamund. 'I like that song.' Her face is paper, stretched over emptiness filled with things she doesn't know the names of. *All the promises we break,* she thought. 'It's exactly like "All I Want Is You".'

'What a ditz. Believe me, sweetheart, it's crap. You should *hear* the girl we've just signed. Fifteen! Deeply fab, *drop*-dead gorgeous, great voice, just *oozing* warmth. Platinum hair down to her bum. The camera adores her.' He flips a fried egg. 'We're calling her Amba Fox – good name, don't you think? She's going to top the charts and this stuff'll be nowhere. Fancy some bacon?'

'No.' Tyler overrides people so crassly it is almost magnificent. 'Thank you.'

'One little sizzler? One gorgeous gorgeous Porkinson's Banger?'

He rolls a sausage on its side. He loves his cooking skills.

'There's a message for you on the answerphone.' He has his back to her but she feels him freeze like a jackal that knows it's been seen. Despite the wooziness, something in her is cocking its head, wondering. How will Tyler get out of this? 'A woman. You'd stood her up. She said you'd been with her for *years*.'

'Muddle over her contract, silly cow. I said I'd sort it, then couldn't get away. She's tried to monster me a couple of times, flashing her sweaty knickers. Become a bit of a stalker I'm afraid.' He flips the bacon. 'You know how these women misunderstand.'

'It was nearly midnight. Shall I tell you what she said?'

'Load of bollocks, darling. Heard it when I came in. Not worth a moment's worry from your beautiful head.'

He hasn't got that quite right. Rosamund stares at the table. She knows he's thinking, Balls in a wringer! He'll try to persuade himself it's OK by persuading her of it. Part of her wants him to succeed.

He carries his plate to the table, shakes salt over the bright pile of food and spikes a sausage. There will be a lie in everything he says. He knows she knows that. He also knows she doesn't know where exactly the lie will be.

He learned, long ago, to attach himself so ardently to a lie that he convinces himself it's true. He feels so entitled. If his lie isn't true, then it ought to be. Already, as she knows he intends, the trauma of the night is evaporating. Watching him shovel down breakfast, she feels the first shock frill away like mist. Why had she been upset? She misunderstood. Tyler's in charge. This is their life. Bacon and Radio 2 in their lovely glowing kitchen, and Russel asleep upstairs. Tyler lives in such a hyper world women are at him all the time, yet here he is, with her.

Even the way he's reading the paper is comforting. One hand – the hand with the scar on his finger where he cut it making *boeuf bourguignon* to impress that blonde girl from his office – smoothes a page while another spears fried bread.

No. She shakes her aching forehead. She always adjusts how she feels to how Tyler says things are. That's how she comes to think that what she knows to be wrong, is right.

'Seen this about downloading music?' Tyler doesn't bother with international news or politics. 'They'll be doing us all out of business. Everyone's shitting themselves.'

Rosamund pours coffee grounds into the cafetière. He doesn't know which way she's going to jump. She doesn't either. Cool is her one advantage. If she loses it, he'll make her feel worse for over-reacting.

'Oh!' He puts his hands to his forehead.

'What?'

'My eye. There are worms floating across my left eye.'

He shakes his head like a bull in a hailstorm.

'Let me see.' He looks up. She takes his cheeks between her hands. 'Seems OK to me.'

The grey-denim iris rolls like a ball on water.

'I've got little specks, Rosie. Like something under a microscope. When I look sideways there are flashes.' He flings his arms round her waist and presses his head against her stomach.

'Does it hurt?' She wraps her arms round his shoulders and rocks him. She knows she is the only person on whom he can rest. But if the opportunity arose, he'd betray her the very next second.

A lot is happening, in fact, to the back of Tyler's eye. His retina, like everyone else's, is studded with receptors. It has evolved to convert light into electric signals entering his brain. In some people over forty, the vitreous starts to separate from the back of the eye and they see floaters and flashes. If the retina tears, they'll need immediate attention to stop it detaching like wallpaper peeling off a wall. Anyone who suddenly gets floaters and flashes should run to a retinal specialist.

But Tyler's retina, as he presses his head against his wife's belly, is not tearing at all. The vitreous is simply peeling away in a gentlemanly fashion as a chap's vitreous should. Just as well, since Tyler never confronts anything if he can help it.

Rosamund slides to her knees. Her fingers seek, as they always used to, the deep furrows either side of his spine. The rest of him is compromised and greedy, his back is innocent. She massages his shoulderblades and spinal knobs. She used to marvel at his spine, the secret source of all that strength. She remembers him looking at a memorial bench in Cornwall overlooking the sea, lettered with a man's name and years of life.

'Seventy years,' Tyler had said. 'Not long, is it? Should be longer.'

She feels again, unwillingly, this bond she has never felt with anyone else, as if the years had stored it in their bodies like electricity. The mutual knowing which always seemed to heal a lifelong sadness in each other.

But what sadness was worse than this? She looks up at the window. Father not loving you, answers the window glass, and she has a sudden image of herself running through London, running to Tyler's arms in Soho after that awful professor told her about Father's affair. 'I wish he'd loved *me*,' she'd found herself repeating, over and over.

That was why she had come to Tyler. Tyler made a fuss of her. She learned to be a woman with him. You can't stuff that genie back in its bottle.

Grow up, says the garden beyond the glass. Get real, says the pile of half-eaten food, the smears of bacon fat, the yellow walls which have seen so many tears. He betrays you again and again. He's abused his gifts and his warmth. He's treacherous to other people and himself. His body, that you still stupidly feel you cherish, is smeared with years and years of L-I-E-S.

She rests her chin on Tyler's head. He's not meant to be like this, she tells the walls, the garden. He's not in control of who he is, because he's in a murky part of the wood.

She strokes his hair, lets her longing surface and sees a crack in the earth's crust opening in front of her, and a scaly hand reaching out to drag her down. The only way to deal with Tyler is refuse him. Otherwise she's in a chasm she'll never climb out of. Yes, he *is* in a murky part of the wood, and he likes it. He won't give up the murk, say the chorus of crocuses outside. She hears again that hoarse hurt voice on the answerphone. Can she find out what's going on from his phone bills?

79

She lifts her head from his hair.

'Shall I drive you to Casualty? I'm taking Russel to the dentist.'

'Hell no. I've got a computer desperado from the wilds of Pinner coming to fix that bloody laptop.'

Tyler is not technological. He's supposed to be writing an article about what voices he is looking for. Two weeks ago he bought a PowerBook but so far has only managed to tangle the wires. He asked Russel for help but Russel said he didn't know nothing about Macs.

So that's why Tyler's up early. Nothing to do with that message. Somehow, this makes her feel even more the message doesn't really matter. Maybe she'll give the phone bills a miss.

There is a ring at the door. Tyler strides off to answer it.

At one o'clock she brings Russel back and finds Tyler talking to a young man in the hall.

'Hi, Russ, how the hell *are* you? Any fillings? Dil has just set up my charming computer.'

'lo.' Russel escapes upstairs and Tyler leads the way to the kitchen. 'Take a pew, old man. Little snifter before lunch?'

'No, thank you.'

Dil sits down. He has expressionless eyes, a brown jacket with a little stand-up collar, and black hair in short gelled spikes.

'Thanks a million, Dil. Just *don't* have the time, alas, to sort the thing out myself.'

Rosamund takes out butter, bread and cheese. Tyler could never boot a laptop by himself. Dil knows that as well as she does.

'Let me find my chequebook,' she hears Tyler say.

'I only take cash.'

'Oh. Oh well, let's see if my charming wife has any cash in that beautiful bag I bought her . . . no?'

'Sorry,' says Rosamund. 'I used it all up yesterday.'

Dil writes a receipt. Tyler watches him, rubbing his eye.

'You a fan of pop music? Bollywood maybe? We've got some great singers. If you want any CDs . . .'

'I don't have time to listen to music. I'm studying engineering.'

80

'You from India? My wife grew up there.'

Dil's eyes turn incuriously to Rosamund, then back to his papers. He folds them, gives one to Tyler, puts the other in his case and snaps it shut.

'I'm British. My parents came from Bangladesh in the sixties.'

She has often cringed at the contempt she sees in other people's eyes for Tyler's affectations or crassness. She never knows which is worse, that or women reacting to the charm. But Dil's indifference is worse than either.

'Shall I drive you up the road to the hole in the wall, then drop you at the Tube?' says Tyler.

'You OK to drive?' she asks.

'Of course.'

Tyler claps Dil on the shoulder. Dil's face freezes further. As the front door bangs, Rosamund runs into the living room and presses playback. The message has been erased.

'OK?' she says, when Tyler returns.

'Fine. God he's hard work, that boyo.' Tyler sits down. 'I know I said we might see a film tonight, sweetie, but I have to get to bloody Brixton for a gig.' He doesn't usually go out without her on a Saturday. Is it the woman on the phone? Unlikely. He avoids confrontations if he can, and that woman was spoiling for a showdown.

Well, it's nothing to do with her.

'I'm really sorry, darling, you know I hate working on a Saturday. All those dark cellars and poisonous beers. But there's no one else to check this band out and the London tom-tom says they're really hot.'

She lays three places. She can't bear to imagine what Russel is feeling about Bono.

'You can come if you like.' Tyler cuts himself a large slice of Brie.

'I'll pass, thanks.' He'd have a fit if she said yes.

'Like to watch a film?' she asks Russel later. Tyler has left; they are eating macaroni cheese. The kitchen light looks mournful and dusky as if she's seeing it through tissue paper.

'Goin' out.' Russel rises. He has left half his food. Feeling as if she were a piece of mildly unpleasing wallpaper, she watches him walk away. The rucksack, she knows, is waiting in the hall.

'Have a good time, love.'

The front door closes. She washes up, pours a glass of rosé, takes it into the living room and puts on the *Purple Rose of Cairo*.

At night, this room gleams with gold, black, burnt sienna, ivory. The fake gas fire burbles, reflected as tiny bright points in glassed-over photos on the piano. It still hurts that Russel stopped playing the piano. So musical, said his teacher. He stopped when he went to big school and hasn't looked at it since. Now the piano is a photo repository.

Rosamund abandons Woody Allen to peer at Tyler in sideburns with Russel on his shoulder. Then Tyler in black tie with Russel aged five clinging to the leg of his dinner suit and Rosamund beside him, her hair like corkscrews of light. Tyler in California, arm around some singer. Herself, dancing with Tyler. She looks critically at the shape her right leg is making.

When she was growing up, the only room she was happy in was the kitchen, where the cook taught her to dance on the concrete floor. Parvati was fat, but when she danced she was beautiful. 'Move hands like this. Up above, sway. Back and forward, like flower in wind. Below, root into earth.' She would put flowers in Rosamund's orange hair, clip her own gold necklace round her, and set Rosamund going round the kitchen table like a clockwork toy. 'Now, how beautiful you are!'

In England, Rosamund tried to show the girls at school how to Indian dance. And it was while dancing – to Meat Loaf, nothing to do with India, just with her boyfriend Sean at the end of her second year – that she caught Tyler's eye.

Sean was short. She could hardly see him among the leaping bodies silhouetted against cuculoris patterns thrown by the strobes, diamonds swirling into hearts through shafts of lavender, orange and emerald light. Instead she saw a rock god capering like a satyr, point-ing his fingers up and down as he danced. When he opened his eyes and saw her, he snaked his pelvis wildly and started mouthing the lyrics. *Dragon ladies talk that talk!* He jabbed his finger at her. *Who loves who and who loves best.* Six foot or more. Broad shoulders, broad chest. *Silver bullets in the jukebox, spin another round.* Tangly black locks, Medusa snakes over a pink fluorescent shirt. *Everybody at the back of the line! It's midnight at the lost and found!* Rosamund threw forward her mane of hair in time with the beat but Sean whirled her to another patch of floor. Later she saw him again, looking at her, laughing, mouthing the words exaggeratedly so she could see he was singing, *Midnight at the lost and found, lost souls in the hunting ground.* He blew her a kiss. *A remedy for all your ills, here at the lost and found!*

After the dance Sean left her to push his way to the bar.

'You need a drink, young lady,' said a voice in her ear. 'Why are minions not at your side, catering to your every whim?'

'Someone's getting me one,' she said, sweat pouring between her breasts. Her first words to Tyler. Why weren't they her last?

'Take this, darling.' He handed her a glass beaded with ice-cold drops. They were both panting, she saw the breath in his sweat-streaked shirt jump as if dancing without him. This is my habitat, said his panting. Coloured lights, wild heat, smoke, swirl and heat. Her breasts were heaving. She wiped sweat off her forehead with her arm, saw a love-bite on his throat like a tattoo and found herself wanting to sink her own mark on him, deeper.

'I'm in the music business, darling. A and R, that's me. That's *Are* you coming out with me *Right* now? Or tomorrow? Anyone who can dance like you should explore a career in music.' He kneaded her shoulder. 'You have eyes to drown in,' he whispered.

By the time Sean came back with lager Rosamund was lost. Only then, of course, she thought it was found.

Next day, while 'All I Want Is You' was playing on the radio, Tyler came to her room. She opened the door, he lifted her off her feet, hands all over her body, lips all over her throat, undid with one finger the difficult Playtex bra whose lace trim covered the hooks, and made love to her on the floor so wildly the carpet burned her spine. He lifted his head from between her thighs, chin and mouth glistening. 'Ring of gold,' he whispered. 'Harbour in the tempest.' And buried his face in her again. The next day he turned up with champagne, spread caviar over her nipples and sucked it off. '*All I want is you,'* he murmured. The rest of that year was a whirl of parties, lovemaking and Tyler singing meltingly to his guitar. After she chucked college, she moved in with him and took a job doing PR for his firm. Then she was pregnant. When Tyler felt the baby kick tears poured down his face. 'Let's get married. Chap must marry his beloved when she's having his child.'

Moment of madness, she remembers him saying long after, in a row.

'We're having a baby,' she wrote to Father. 'And buying a house.' There'd been no communication with him since she left King's. Kellar wrote stiffly back, sending good wishes. If it was a boy, might they consider calling him Russel, after Alfred Russel Wallace? It seemed an interesting name and they wanted to please him, so they did. And Rosamund stopped work.

'You don't need it, sweetie,' said Tyler. 'I'm loaded, I'll look after you. Just get the house straight.'

When the house was straight, they got married. It was Russel's first birthday – and here's the photo from the wedding day with Russel clutching Father's thumb.

As Rosamund contemplates Father's eyes behind the unframed glasses, there is a ring at the door. She runs to the window and sees a man with his arm round a boy. The boy is slumped as if he's been drowned.

'He's not as bad as he looks,' says the man. He has a dog, its lead looped round his wrist. He half drags, half carries Russel over the threshold. Russel's feet trail like wool.

'Where did you find him? What's happened?'

'Railway tracks, where he told me to walk my dog.' In the hall light, she sees it's the guy they met at the vet. 'Where can we lay him?'

He rests Russel on the living-room sofa and positions the shaved head gently on a cushion. Russel is covered in dark splashes and smells chemical.

Someone has removed her gut with a scalpel.

'I'm trained in first aid. Didn't say when we met, but I'm a copper.' He gives her an ID and ties the dog to a leg of the piano where it sits riffling the carpet with its tail. Metropolitan Police, she reads. Scott Redington.

'We need a sponge. I'll check for internal damage but I bet that stuff's mostly paint.'

She starts sponging and he ruches back Russel's sleeves. She sees grazes but yes, most of the colour is paint. Red, brown, and a lot of black.

'I heard a scuffle,' Scott runs his hand lightly over Russel's ribs and stomach, 'and running feet, saw him laying inside the fence like a heap of laundry. Recognised him.' Russel flinches. 'Worked you over, didn't they, son? Nothing broken though. Few days, you'll be right as rain.'

'Who were they?'

'The other kids, his mates. You were graffing, weren't you, lad?'

Russel opens his eyes, sees her, closes them.

'C'mon, son, got to explain to your mum.'

'Graffing?'

'Writing on walls.'

''m OK,' Russel mumbles. Scott takes the basin to the kitchen and comes back with a mug. He seems to know his way round by instinct.

'Tea and sugar. Doctor's orders.'

She watches Russel sip, staring at the floor. The only sounds are the dog panting and the hissing of flames. Russel's eyes move along the carpet and up to Scott's face. An attractively ugly face, with kind brown eyes. His cheeks squash in close to his nose and on down to meet deep folds below the nostrils.

Rosamund thinks of little Russel, so eager and in love with the world.

'Oh, darling.'

He tries to get up and nearly tumbles on to the carpet.

'Get you to bed, eh?' says Scott.

They trail upstairs. Russel droops, clutching the banister he slid down so expertly aged seven. Scott supports him, an arm round the shivery shoulders. Rosamund opens Russel's door. The window is open: the stone-cold room smells sweet and stale. They remove his trainers, spread the duvet over him. Rosamund kisses his forehead, wet with sweat.

'Will he be OK?' she whispers as they go downstairs.

'Sure. Bit bruised, but he's OK. Mainly stoned.'

'*What?*'

'You must know he smokes dope? Don't you smell it? Keeping that window open doesn't get rid of it.' Rosamund feels bits of her life flying off in all directions. 'In the car, he told me he blazed all this afternoon, then slept. To blot out the dog, I guess.'

Rosamund sways. She feels Scott's hand under her arm.

'Told me he went out to get more draw.'

'Draw?'

'Dope.'

'How – where does he . . .?' She tries to pull herself together. 'Would you like a drink? Or are you on duty? Is this a – a drugs bust?'

'A drink'd be fine, thanks. I'm not that kind of copper. I'm in Wildlife.'

She gestures at the front room. In the kitchen she takes two Tiffany glasses and the Laphroaig. What's luxury for if not emergencies?

Scott is petting his dog in the firelight. He takes the drink and Rosamund drops on to the sofa.

'What else did he say?' What sort of a mother is she? What's she been doing, all these years?

'He said they'd done a big piece and were well stoned.'

'Piece?'

'Wall painting. The family in the flat above me have a lad who tells me the jargon. He says doing a big piece takes hours. First the black outline, then blocks of colour, then highlights. They smoke a *lot* of skunk.' Scott sips whisky. 'All the time.' Rosamund stares at the fire. 'Their eyes get inflamed. Pink eyes, you noticed? There were five tonight in his crew.'

'Could you – kind of – tell me in English?'

'The crew's the gang.'

'Russel's in a gang?'

'Just a group. Might be up to fifty, but never together the same

86

time. Some are rappers, some drug dealers. "He's safe," they say. "He's my crew." They get together for music, skunk and graffing.'

Russel saying 'Safe, man'. Closing the door on a phone call.

'They put their crew's tag everywhere, like a signature. Black scribbles, to you and me. They're marking territory, high as they can.' Scott smiles. 'Like male cheetahs spraying a tree.' Rosamund tries to smile too. 'Russel wrote "Bono" on a wall tonight. The crew didn't appreciate that one bit. They were tracking. Graffing on the railway, the most dangerous place.'

Scott balances his glass gingerly on his chair arm.

'When they'd finished, Russel said they were well fucked. Meaning lean. Stoned. They chatted about cops. Russel, silly kid, said he'd met a cool cop.'

'What?'

'Told him at the vet I ran the Wildlife Unit at Scotland Yard. He was trying to impress. They knocked him about – lucky there were no knives – and took his bike.'

'He hasn't got a bike.' Tyler had offered Russel a racing bike for his fourteenth birthday but Russel had shaken his head in contempt. Tyler was hurt. Tyler misses little Russel even more than she does. Tyler hurts her all the time but when *he's* hurt, she feels guilty. It's her job to prevent any of that.

'He had one tonight. They stole several in Stoke Newington.'

'He has a *stolen bike*?'

'Not any more. They all steal bikes, use 'em for quick getaways and getting weed. Everything revolves round weed. Rucksacks are for weed as well as paint.'

He looks at her softly, seriously.

'Your kid's very young, love. The others are older. He says they diss him. They give me disrespect, he said.' She gulps whisky. 'He's eaten up with shame because he's not cool like them. He said, "They say I'm toy."'

'What?'

'Toy. A baby. Shit at graffing.'

Rosamund puts her head in her hands. Nothing, in looking after a child, prepares you for this.

'They want people to be scared of them. If they're dangerous, they're safe. But no one could be scared of him.'

Rosamund starts crying. Scott sits beside her and puts an arm round her.

'When I found him, he tried to wriggle away, then recognised Bramble and said "Bono." I helped him to my car. He gave me your address. When we got here, he tried a dive under that tree in your front garden.'

'The House Tree. The summer he was ten, I wasn't here, Tyler said he practically lived under that tree.'

'He fell, trying to get in. Said I thought he'd be better off in the house.'

A howl is coming out of Rosamund. Her arm jogs her glass, which falls and smashes on the marble. She buries her head in Scott's chest, burrowing in the way kittens press into their owners.

'Bin a shock,' he says, rocking her. 'But it's not that bad, as these things go.'

She screams silently into his black tweed jacket. When was the last time a man put his arms round her? She feels like a bud in a calyx. *All these years.*

'It's come on top of everything else. A few days ago I – I heard a message on the answerphone. Just – terrible!'

The world has broken. All she knows is, she can rest on him.

'Nuisance call?' She feels his cheek on her hair. 'Horrible, those are. Very upsetting.'

'No. A woman, for my husband. He – has affairs . . .' Scott knows not to say anything. One sympathetic word would do her in. 'But this was different. She's been with him for *years*.' Scott's jacket is wet, her throat convulsing like a jellyfish. 'And she sounded so like me. *She* didn't know where he was, he'd let her down. But unlike me, she was – dissing him. Giving him,' she tries to laugh and it turns into a sob, 'a *lot* of disrespect.'

He rocks her gently, the fire murmurs, the dog breathes little sleep-sighs. Gradually her sobs come at longer intervals, like an engine cooling.

'Life,' Scott says softly. 'My girlfriend left me last autumn. We'd been together years. She was seeing someone else. I had no idea. She stole my chequebook and forged enormous cheques. Enormous by my standards, anyway. And my new camera.'

'How awful.'

'Must have been planning it for ages. I lost all my savings. Had to move and start over.' Her tears have stopped. Her face feels raw. 'Round Christmas, things got so lonely, I tried meeting women on the net.'

'How was that?' Rosamund has wondered about this.

'Nightmare. No one tells the truth. Lot of desperate women out there. One of them I met, I told her I didn't think we could meet again, she started stalking me. Had to change my mobile. That's what Bramble's for – not just company – protection.'

She looks up. His smile starts on one side of his mouth and spreads like sun moving across a valley. She tries a laugh. It turns into a hiccough and he taps her on the back.

'OK?' He's sexy in a quiet way, not in your face like Tyler.

'Fine.'

He smiles again and stands up. She feels cold when he's gone.

'Fine's not quite the word, I'd say, ma'am. You need sleep, like your boy. And I must take this chap out before he makes a mess of your carpet.'

'At least I won't need sleeping pills after this whisky.'

'Take 'em often?'

'I'm trying to get off them. Not doing very well, though.'

He unties the dog from the piano.

'Been having a rough time, haven't you? You and your son, both.' He glances at the kelims, paintings, plasma screen, brass coffee table. 'What's your work, love?'

'I'm – well, I haven't worked since Russel was born.' She hadn't realised she felt ashamed of that. 'Tyler's a music promoter, so . . .' She gestures at their living room, suddenly seeing it not as mysterious and full of history, just expensive. 'I've done a course in garden design.' Now he's not holding her, there's an ice wind blowing. 'But I've only had one commission so far. You must come and see the garden.'

The puppy jumps up. She presses her face to its ears, smells the sweet puppy breath.

'I can't thank you enough.' Now she feels awkward. And she must look awful.

'Russel's a good kid. Talked sense in the car. Bit lost at the moment. We all go through it. Feels like the end of the world, but it'll sort. Asked him if he'd help me train Bramble. Might help him get over his dog.'

'You somehow know what to say to him.'

'I remember what it's like, being a kid.'

'He and Bono were like that.' She holds up her fingers, crossed. 'But he took to your puppy.'

'He says you're brilliant at dog training.'

'Not so brilliant at teenagers.' Her nose must be red. But she is suddenly aware of her breasts, rising and falling with her breath.

'Bring Russel to Scotland Yard. Get him interested in what we do in Wildlife Crime, when we're not rescuing teenagers.'

He holds out a card. She takes it, their fingers brush and she flings her arms round him.

'You were sent from heaven,' she whispers.

'You be OK now. Ring me whenever.'

She lets him out into the night. Something has happened between them. What he said about his girlfriend was a cry from soul to soul.

She shuts the door and looks at the lock. Bono went through here and got run over. Who left it open? *All these years* . . . Tyler makes *everyone* unhappy. She should slide the chain across and lock him out. But the house is in his name.

In the kitchen she finds a gas bill. R BEATEN UP, she writes on the envelope. BEEN DOING DOPE AND GRAFFITI. Rain rustles on glass above her head. STOLE BIKE, she adds. She puts it on the table with a knife on it, so Tyler will see. It looks mad and dangerous like that and she takes the knife away.

The rain is a firing squad now. Tyler will be soaking when he comes in. If he comes in. R ASLEEP, she writes. DON'T DISTURB. She props it against a pile of loose CDs.

Sunday 20 March, Primrose Hill, London, 2.00 a.m.; 7.30 a.m., India

'Could anyone else give you so good a resting place?'

The python has made himself into a hammock of oozy coils. Russel gathers them in like a cable till the heavy head lies on his shoulder. Tears slide down his ear to the python's painted skin.

Kaa is a Rock Python. Actually an Indian Rock Python, Python Molurus Molurus, Russel knows that now. But Kaa appeared long ago and the name stuck. His colours change. Just now he has blood-red splodges, like the rugs on the kitchen walls.

Coiled over the desk is Bono's collar. Its silvery nametag glimmers in whitey-blue rays from the computer screen.

toys will be toys, said the top message on that screen, signed FENRISWOLF

yeah they get on my tits like a guy who turns up at his mates house and starts shooting his family what a fuckin joke KAA

shut it your less than a toy uve never touched a wall that isnt hidden away like bin ladens hidey EVILDOER

fukin head spins do you no who i am? KAA

naw so fuck off ya blackneck bastard bet ur family is a real benefit to the gene pool SLASHA 4 EVA

if i catch any of u fuckers i will behead u KAA

shit things happen to people coz its there own shit fault FENRISWOLF

where's the blame then man inside or out in tha world? KAA

haha look up just world hypothsis youngn FENRISWOLF

After the last message pulses a green cursor, tip of the longest lobe on a marijuana leaf.

Rain rattles outside. Russel closes his eyes. He left the door open. Bono died because of him. *I am an evil mancub.*

We be one blood, thou and I, hisses the python.

They hear footsteps and Kaa hisses like a sword drawn from its scabbard. The door opens. Russel half opens one swollen eye. Dad never comes up here! Once, he was here all the time. Russel lies rigid.

'Hey, Russ.'

Russel feels the python's muscles tense. The fighting strength of a python is in the driving blow of his head, backed by all the strength and weight of his body. Like a hammer weighing half a ton with a cool quiet mind in the handle.

A bulky silhouette sways in the doorway. After a long moment the door shuts. The python's head sways above him.

Thy trail is my trail, Kaa murmurs. Thy kill is my kill.

Sunday 20 March, Kilburn, London, 4.00 p.m.

Anka sat heavily on her bed. Katya and Helen were watching *Bridget Jones* in the living room and she had managed to get through the whole weekend without breaking down. If Helen had asked what was wrong, she'd have fallen apart. On Saturday everyone had sung Croatian songs and the girls did a play for her.

What was he thinking, what was happening? Did he hate her? How was Tess if there'd been a row? Terrible, this being shut out. Like out of her village, her country, in the war.

Sunday 20 March, Primrose Hill, London, 4.10 p.m.

All day, Rosamund has hovered round the kitchen and hall. She's been up to check, but Russel is still asleep. Light from the windows seems milky as if a wall of mist had enveloped this house which she has tried, like the blackbirds building a nest in the overgrown jasmine, to make safe. There have been few sounds except the noises houses make when they breathe.

At twelve Tyler came down, took one look at her face and wrapped his arms round her. They stood at the bottom of the stairs like babes in the wood.

'Spuds and bacon?'

Comfort food, like a siege.

'The drug stuff had to come, didn't it?' he said as he sliced potatoes. 'Specially after he refused the school I lined up and went to that
dump up the road.'

'Drugs are in posh schools too, Tyler. More, because those kids
can afford more. They're everywhere.'

'You're an expert all of a sudden?' He poured oil in a pan. 'Just
hope he never asks *me* to score for him.'

The way he spoke made her feel it wasn't really so bad.
Teenagers take drugs. So?

Tyler has disappeared to his study to write his article and now,
at last, Russel is limping into the kitchen like a ghost.

'Tea, love? Scrambled eggs?'

'C'n we have telly?'

Voices flare behind Rosamund as she breaks the eggs.

Russel stares at black and orange zigzags where Bono used to sloop
by the fire. It's a dark drizzly afternoon. They are in the front room,
all three. Four, with Kaa. Waterfalls roar past him like angry glass
trees. He keeps his eyes on Kaa, scarlet and purple today, ready to
strike.

'Is that clear, Russ?'

'I'm sure things'll be better now.'

Silly cow. How dare she feel hurt because of him when he's the
hurt one? It's her fault anyway. Separate rooms – doesn't she *know*?

'No more drugs, old boy. No more – er – graffing. Or bike-steal-
ing. If you want a bike, we'll get you the best in town. If you want
art, I'll get you art lessons. But let's concentrate on schoolwork, shall
we?'

'I'm sure it'll be OK, now.'

She's not fucking sure of anything. Especially not his skanky dad
who never tells the truth. Behind Dad's head is the phone which first
told him Dad was evil. The moment Kaa became Avenger.

All this is his own fault, though. He got lean, and left the door
open, and Bono died. When you do bad, you get bad.

93

'Good man, Russ. Why don't we go fishing next holiday, like we used?'

Answer, whispers Kaa. It'll be over quicker.

'Maybe.'

'Well, now, how much of that stuff is stashed away upstairs? It's illegal and, dammit, I'm responsible.' In the jungle, there you feel free. 'C'mon, Russ – show me and let's get rid of it. Then we can forget about it, OK?'

His dad stands up. After a moment Russel stands too and follows him out of the room. Kaa flows beside him. He feels his mum sitting behind them worrying as if she were wired to electrodes in his brain. He hates her for not crying because it would upset him.

In his room, Dad treads through Kaa's beautiful mottled coils. Kaa gives an angry hiss and dissolves. His dad looks awkward and afraid, like he's too big for the room. Really, it's Kaa he's scared of.

'Where's the stuff, old boy?'

'There's nothing here. Honest. Used it all, las' night.'

He looks at the tumbled duvet, computer, shelves of dinosaurs, Lego, Harry Potter books. The fishing net they got in Cornwall. Model aeroplanes they made at the table that the computer now occupies.

His dad didn't look too big in here then.

Kaa could constrict him with one, maybe two of his coils.

'I need a drink.' Tyler opens the cupboard. 'Oh!'

Two Tiffany glasses gone now. Rosamund watches him take one, slice a lemon, ease out the ice tray, drop in three cubes and pour himself a large gin and tonic.

'Didn't even touch the sides. How about you, sweetie? For fuck's sake let's get a Chinese and watch a vid with him.'

'He likes pizza and horror.' Rosamund is wiping the hob. The limp cloth is something to cling to. Telling Russel off like that, formally, watching Russel glaze over as if she and Tyler were aliens, has pierced her in a place she never expected to revisit: sitting across from Father at Sunday lunch, frantic for his approval, flinching at the anger that came out of nowhere like monsoon lightning.

She didn't think, then, it was unfair. You don't question things as a child, she tells the little splashes of hardened sauce. She remembers keeping her eyes fixed on a little metal statue over Father's shoulder, a rebellious black angel doing all the kicking she'd have liked to do and never did. 'Rosamund, we must have a *talk*.' The way Father said that! It felt, though she didn't know the word at the time, obscene. That's why she can never scold Russel.

Tyler hands her a gin and tonic. In a clear glass, which is a reproach, but he's being tender too. That's why she can't leave. Irena doesn't understand. Maybe she never tells Irena the good bits of Tyler.

She watches the lemon rind nose her white-seamed cubes of ice. Tyler takes such care over his pleasures – and, yes, over hers. Today they are treating each other with broken gentleness as if something has died.

There must have been something badly wrong with Father to make him feel everything was wrong with her; and to make her feel it, too. Tyler isn't like that with Russel. Tyler is the great apprecia tor. He was brilliant just now. But terribly anxious, his fingernails are more bitten than usual. The tips end in overflowings of skin like ice cream over-running its cone, and today they are pinker than usual.

He said the right things, though. She couldn't have.

Tyler empties another gin.

'I'll take him to the rental.'

'Can you get him down?'

Tyler marches to the bottom of the stairs. Through the passage she sees him put one foot on the bottom step, like a hunter who has shot a deer.

'Russ,' he bellows up the dark stairwell as he used to, never doubting then that he would be met with enthusiasm. He is drawing on the past like a long-forgotten bank account. 'Let's go to the vid shop. Get a film to spook your mother.'

Rosamund stands very still. All she remembers of her own mother are a few stills from a crackly old film. She hears dragging steps in the hall.

'Pizza or Chinese?' says Tyler. The front door bangs. Despair starts furling up in her, like a flower at night. They'll have an evening with a film, like the old days. Maybe both her boys will laugh at her, as they used to do, when she goes out of the room to wash dishes and avoid the violence.

6

Monday 21 March, Primrose Hill, London, 11.30 a.m.

'Hello? This is Rosamund.'

She hears an indrawn breath.

'Rosamund Fairfax. Russel's mother.'

'Hi. How are things?'

'Fine.'

Scott laughs.

'But you say "fine" at unlikely moments.'

She remembers his face, soft and serious. That sun-on-the-hillside smile. Her laugh mingles with his, like a duet.

'Well – *better*.'

'Glad to hear that.'

'Russel wants to see Scotland Yard.'

'When?'

'Tomorrow afternoon? His term ends at lunchtime.'

'How about four?'

Monday 21 March, Parliament Square, London, 6.30 p.m.

'What in hell's name did you think you were *doing*?'

'So, so sorry,' Anka said for the third time. They were sitting in a pub by Westminster Bridge. She had begged him to meet her after the court closed.

'She nearly hit the roof. Luckily we've had goings-on with my charming son, some crazed drugs binge, and that took her mind off it. But those weirdo things you said. Began to think I had a stalker.'

'So, so sorry, *dragi*. I was mad. I did not mean.'

Mutinousness came and went in her, in little flurries. Her new dress, the expensive blowdry. Sending Helen away, precious time with her lost – and he hadn't come! What did he expect if he switched off his mobile? *She* gave up what she most loved for him, why should what *he* loved be protected, hers not? Of course she'd called, to reach him the only way she could. But she felt so guilty.

She started to cry again.

'You know I'd have rung if I could. My mobile ran out of battery—'

'Where you were?'

'The wife made me take her to a bloody film. She said I was always out, she didn't even have the dog for company now.'

'Dog, where is?'

'Run over. I've had one hell of a week, sweetie. And, the damnedest thing, she said about that song – oh, never mind. Come here. I tried to phone you outside the cinema, told her I needed a pee. But the phone box was vandalised. Poor darling, what a birthday.' He put his arm round her. 'You look so beautiful when you cry. How do I love thee, let me count the ways . . .'

She stroked his jacket collar like a pet. This, at least, was her friend.

'Allow me to make it up to you. How about the Ivy, my girl?'

'Where, I do not mind. Only to know I *see* you. Tonight?' She might arrange a babysitter by phone.

'Can't tonight.' He took out his BlackBerry. 'I'll blow Roger out tomorrow. And bring your birthday present.'

'I will make supper.' She was a rose, back on its trellis. 'I have much food, you greedy thing. Special, Croatian.'

'Can't wait.'

Tuesday 22 March, Central London, 3.00 p.m.

London is full of graffiti. How do boys reach so high? Rosamund looks down from the top of the bus. When Russel was little she took him all over the city on buses. The Tower, the Toy Museum. That time has floated away from her for ever, like the envelope on a mobile sending a text.

'Look, the Horse Guards. Remember?'

They get off into cold wind, under sky the colour of dishcloth, the washable white thick ones Irena uses, not throwawayable blue ones. Her nose – she squints at it – is a lavender icicle. They walk past Westminster Abbey to the famous sign.

'NEW SCOTLAND YARD! We've seen it so often on telly.'

Inside is like any office, except for the uniforms. A policeman takes them in a lift to the top floor.

'Welcome,' says Scott in the same dark tweedy jacket, 'to the Wildlife Crime Unit.'

Why did she think he was ugly? She feels like a migrant bird reaching its home.

Scott puts a hand on Russel's shoulder and leads them to an airless office overlooking grey roofs. Desks, cabinets, cupboards, a large stuffed bear and a very pretty girl at a desk; who smiles.

Rosamund's heart sinks as she smiles back. But what's it to her who Scott works with? Russel pushes back his hood. Feeling, Rosamund knows, even shyer than she does.

'Will I explain what we do?'

'Yes, what is wildlife crime? We're dying to know.' Russel is hating her gush. She feels nervous and hot.

'Illegal traffic in endangered animals, live and dead. Biggest type of crime in the world after drugs, arms and people trafficking. London's market in endangered animals funds criminal networks across the globe.'

Rosamund wriggles out of her cardigan.

'But there ain't no endangered animals, in London.' She hasn't heard Russel's engaged voice, his interested voice, for years.

'What there is here, son, is money. Animals go extinct in other countries because people buy things here.'

'Like what?'

'African bushmeat. Luxuries. Asian medicine.' He hands Russel a bottle. 'That's a baby king cobra in wine from Bangkok.'

Russel stares at the tiny forked tongue and eyes like stale opals.

'People, like, drink this?'

'Men do. Think it makes them potent.'

'A friend of ours studies king cobras,' Rosamund says.

'So does Grandpa! He's a herpetologist, in India.'

'Is he now,' says Scott comfortably. Rosamund knows he has clocked her surprise. 'In South-East Asia they slit 'em open, catch the blood while the snake's alive, and drink it. Did you know a snake can moan, in agony? Read that in a book. Never heard it, thank God.'

He takes up another bottle.

'Bear bile wine. Illegal to import, but legal to manufacture, in China. They put the bear in an iron wringer, squeeze out bile, wait till it has more, and do it again.'

'Why?'

'Said to be good for the liver. The bears live with tubes in their gut, the wounds get infected, infection gets into the bile. But it's big business. They even put it in shampoo.'

'That can't help their livers much,' says Rosamund. The fingers of her right hand seem to want to run through Scott's furry brown hair.

'But the rich pay more if it comes from wild bears. Wild's always supposed to be *better*. So despite thousands of bears in cages, wild bears are dying out.'

Scott hands Russel a box. Rosamund makes herself stay where she is, not go up close.

'Sticking-plasters, made from ground-up tiger bone. Supposed to kill pain. We raided Chinatown last week, impounded five thousand items with tiger parts in 'em. Tiger penis soup, tiger bone wine . . .'

'Where are the tigers, like, from?'

'Poached, from reserves in India and Russia. Or farmed. The Chinese farm tigers and pretend they don't.'

'Farm *tigers*?'

'Breed 'em in terrible conditions – you don't want to know.' Rosamund wants Scott's attention all for herself. But Russel is basking in it. 'Internationally, it's illegal to use tiger parts, but Chinese factories make this stuff and it gets sold secretly everywhere: LA, Amsterdam, Sydney. It's my job to stop that in London.'

Russel strokes an elephant tusk.

100

'Looks like plastic.'

'Look at the tip in strong light.' Russel takes it to the window.

'He looks good,' Scott says quietly to Rosamund. She feels approved and laces the fingers of both hands together to stop them touching him. His rough hair looks like beaver fur.

'I feel I'm tugging in the opposite direction from him.'

'All animal mothers feel that. You want to keep him safe, he wants to explore.'

So Scott too thinks in terms of animals. She feels nervous suddenly, as if he knows that she does.

'Have you got kids? You'd be a great dad.'

'Probably fuck it up with my own. Haven't met the right woman yet, anyway.'

'How's your dating site?'

'Haven't looked, not since we talked.' She sees his chest rise and fall. 'People there aren't the kind I feel OK with, somehow.'

'Needs time.'

'I know excellence when I experience it.' Their eyes meet. Her nipples tingle.

'There's marks on the point,' Russel says. The light from the window shimmers like oilskin. 'Kind of a dark line, under the surface.'

'You've got a good eye, lad.' Scott joins him and Rosamund feels bereft.

'That's *hard* ivory, West African.' He gives Russel a box and Rosamund comes up to look. 'See the difference? These are East African, easier to work. Softer.'

She sees a set of shaving brushes with handles like frozen cream. Tyler would adore them. He wouldn't know they were illegal but if he did he'd be even prouder of them.

'Ivory's been banned since 1990. But five thousand wild elephants are killed every year. A Mayfair barber was selling that lot for a thousand quid. We got him fined ten thousand.'

Watching Russel handle a long dark spike, she looks aside and meets Scott's eyes. He's looking at her, not at Russel. She looks away embarrassed, then realises looking away is even more intimate. So long since she was so aware of anybody. She's forgotten how it goes.

'Nice to see you when you're not in trouble,' he says softly. 'How's the gardening?'

'Nothing.'

'Might have something for you, in a few weeks.'

''s this a horn?' asks Russel.

'Black rhino. In Asia, people say it cures AIDS.'

'*What?*'

'Taiwan, South Korea, a kilogram was sixty thousand dollars ten years ago. Now it's double that. And dead rhinos everywhere, Nepal to Africa.'

'So animals are dyin' just for magic, innit?'

'And vanity. Eight fur coats yesterday, two tiger, six leopard, and one made from *three* snow leopards. Plus these.' Scott throws a shawl over Rosamund's shoulders. Swirls of red, brown and gold float round her.

'So light. Gossamer. Why's this illegal?'

'That's shatoosh. Fifteen hundred little antelopes were killed to make this lot.' He points to others under the table. 'They have very soft throat hair. Eight died to make each shawl. Poachers drive to the calving grounds and gun 'em down.'

'It's like wearing warm air. Softer than silk.'

'You're wearing six thousand quid there. Other beautiful women fancy it too. Diplomats' wives in New York. Heiresses in Rome. That antelope is going extinct fast.'

'D'you, like . . .' Russel wants, she can see, to get the words right, 'do undercover?'

'Sure. Here's my camera. You tape it under your jacket.' Scott ties a black bud under Russel's arm. His hoodie swings and hides it.

'Cool.'

'Last used on a housing estate in Epping. Pretended I wanted to buy a reptile. Belle, my colleague, pretended she was my girlfriend.'

The girl looks up and smiles. Maybe she really is his girlfriend. Maybe that stuff about dating sites is a blind. But why should Scott lie? He's not Tyler.

'Belle chatted the guy up while I filmed him showing us his hoard. Said I wanted something with a bit of oomph. That's rare and poisonous to you and me. Poisonous is what turns collectors on. Gave him three hundred quid for a poisonous lizard.' Scott hands Russel a photograph.

'Can I see? I did biology once.' She sees a bubble-wrapped dinosaur, blistered in yellow and black. Despite the heat, she doesn't want to take off the shawl he put round her. She wants to snuggle in it, into his side.

'Lucky you. Then you'll know that's a Mexican Beaded Lizard. Smuggled from Oaxaca. This guy wasn't a registered holder of dangerous animals – and he had no locks so there was a health angle, too. Can't have Egyptian Spitting Cobras loose in Epping.'

'What happened to him?'

'Fined fifty pounds per snake. The punishments aren't enough to deter. As species go down in numbers, their value goes up so the trade's worth *more* billions every year. I haven't the men to stop illegal trade in London.'

'Terrible.' She's being too gushy.

'But we try and prevent crime, too. There are endangered animals in London, son. We're watching peregrines nesting on the Tate, to check no one steals their eggs.'

'How's Bramble?' Russel looks round.

'Fine.' Scott smiles at Rosamund. 'Fine' is their word. 'Could you help me train him? We're no good even at the basics yet like – *Come!*'

He barks it. Russel laughs.

'Tomorrow?'

'I could manage the afternoon.' Scott turns to her. 'I daren't ask *you* to help ma'am, but may I borrow your assistant?'

'Russel's brilliant with dogs. You'll be in safe hands.'

On the landing, Russel goes ahead to press the lift button.

'Lunch, some time?' says Scott quietly. For a moment she is speechless, as if she'd had a blow to the stomach with a flat object. Her heart beats faster.

'Love to. After Easter.'

'Fine.'

The doorbell. Was Helen's choir practice cancelled? Had she lost her key again? Anka skittered out of the flat and down to the front door. There was her lion, her all-forgiving lover, early for the first time ever, waggling a bottle of champagne. An enormous box stood beside him on the pavement.

'Happy birthday, sweetheart!'

She was in his arms, his tongue down her throat.

'Helen will be here, one minute.'

'Let's open the champagne.'

In the kitchen she peeled off wrapping and opened the lid.

'Oh.'

A huge musical instrument, the pale colour of bare skin. Six strings and a sound hole like gold lace.

'So galling, that one's girlfriend can play so many instruments. But something you have *not* got, my little Slav cookie, is a lute.' She stroked one string. 'From the best lute-maker in England, sweetie. I checked him out.'

Five years ago, Anka had been busking, teaching guitar, writing songs. In *Cosmopolitan* she'd read about a music manager looking for unusual talent. She had taken him a demo tape and been invited to lunch.

'Very original idea,' he'd said, 'to write folk-pop in English to, um, Croat songs.'

'*Croatian.* Using songs was not my idea, was Josef Haydn's. Haydn was Croatian composer.'

'He was . . . er . . . German, surely.'

'No no, Haydn is Croatian name. Hajdin, Hajdna, Hajdinovic . . . from *hajda.*'

'What in fuck's that? You have such bewitching eyes, Anka, I can't think about anything else.'

'Thank you. *Hajda* is buckwheat. Many people in Croatia are called Haydn.' She felt herself flowering. 'Josef Haydn spoke Croatian! He was child in Croatian community, Austro-Hungary border. Then, lived in Austria. *Austria,*' she'd teased, 'not Germany, O big music manager.'

He'd laughed and refilled her glass.

'Haydn uses many Croatian songs. In Drum Roll Symphony, is famous song Croatian people sing. *Divojcica potok gazi.*'

'What in hell's that? Fuck me, Anka, your voice is as gorgeous as you are.'

'"Little girl treads on stream." We have big music tradition in Croatia. Byzantine music, Glagolitic . . .'

'Glago*whatic*?'

She was laughing, his arm was round her as she'd explained what was most precious in the world, except Helen.

'Church music. And we have also old carols. Twelfth-century. More than five hundred carols Croatians sing.'

'Fantastic.' He kissed her. 'Where, er, exactly,' he put his head on one side with a twinkle in his blue eyes, '*is* Croatia? What are your – um – customs?'

'Older women in my village, my mother, all have tattoo on hand. A cross – here.' She'd held out her bare arm, palm downward, to show him the back of her hand. He'd taken it, turned it over, kissed her palm.

'And when someone dies, one we love, we light candle on place they are buried. At night, so moon will see. To show we love, always.'

'Oh, Anka,' he'd said. 'Light a candle for *me*. I'll be your rock – always!'

She was poor, immigrant and a single parent. He'd be her saviour.

'Can't manage you m'self,' he'd said later. 'Not my type of thing. But it's as if – you don't mind me saying this? You don't *speak* very good English, but the words you put to these tunes are strangely – they really hit the spot. I'll get you the right person.' And he did.

'The damnedest thing,' he'd said after introducing her to Max who became her manager. By then they were lovers. 'Max said it too. "Because she speaks crap English," – forgive me, sweet thing, you know it drives me wild . . .'

'Tsss . . .'

'". . . her lyrics are wickedly effective."'

Two years ago came a song that changed everything. They'd been making love; he was running his hands over her naked skin as if casting a spell.

'I worship your body,' he whispered. 'You're my earth and sky. Touching you reminds me who I am. You're everything I've ever loved.'

'When we can be together?'

His hands were a night breeze on her skin.

'When the kids are older, I swear.' Street light from outside lay in tiger stripes on the pillow. 'Didn't you say, in your village you light candles for the person you love?'

'Yes, when . . .'

'Oh, sweetheart, keep a candle burning for me. Rescue me, Anka. I'm so lost.' He'd buried his head in her breasts.

When he left at three that morning, she'd sat down in this kitchen, floppy with love and also with pride, that *she* could help *him*, and wrote him a song.

'You like, *dragi*?' she said next time. 'Fleeting moment? Everything I ever loved?'

'*The* fleeting moment, young lady. The, the, the! This is English, dammit. How do you – never mind. Where on earth did you find *fleeting moment*?'

'Helen's homework.'

'Mmm. But how dare you steal my words! Come here,' he said, pulling her across his knee, 'and take your punishment.'

'It's rough,' he said an hour later, 'but the tune's amazing. Another of your Croat specials?'

'Old carol,' she said anxiously. 'I think, it goes.'

'Damn right it does. Take it to Max, sex it up and you've got a pop bestseller.'

Her black lion. She owed him Helen's school, everything. Now this. She stroked the shimmering lute and plucked a string. It reverberated through the kitchen, prelude to all the love songs ever sung.

'Happy birthday, beloved.'

'You forgive?' She twisted on her knees to look into his face.

'This is Forgiveness Hall. Oh, Anka . . .' He was hard, he was kissing her throat. 'You make me feel such a hero.'

They heard Helen's key in the door. When she walked in they were sitting on separate chairs and Anka was holding the lute on her knee.

'Look! You remember, my friend?' Helen had not seen him for nearly a year. Anka usually made sure she was at Lasta's before he came.

'Good evening, young lady.'

''lo,' said Helen, hot in her school blouse.

'So,' he said, looking at her, 'how does it feel to be in possession of a bust?'

Anka nearly dropped the lute. Helen looked at her and looked away. Anka felt she really had opened her door to a lion. Or maybe a wolf.

Wednesday 23 March, Parliament Hill, London, 4.30 p.m.

'Musn' punish him when he comes back even though he ran off. He thinks you're punishin' him for comin' back. Makes him not *wanna* come back.'

'Why didn't I think of that? Good *boy*, Bramble.'

Russel looks at the puppy, flanks heaving, pink tongue lolling like it would never get back in his mouth.

'But how do you stop him running off? Can't chase round for an hour every time he sees a flying duck. He could've run on the road and got killed.'

'Need a long lead. Practice comin' back on that. Then like, start letting him off.'

Bramble rolls upside down wetly over Russel's feet.

'Mustn' let him *be able* to disobey. 'f he disobeys, he's dissin' you. Gotta get his *respect*.' Russel rubs the dog's damp belly. Mud has arrowed the feather-ends of his tummy hair to little points. Is he being disloyal to Bono? Bono was always kind to other dogs. He'd like Bramble, he'd understand. Or would he? 'Gotta reward him. Bono used to run off, chasin' squirrels and shit. We kept crusts in our pockets 'n gave him one when he came. Gotta make him *want* to come to you.'

'I'll get a long lead.' Scott looks down at luminous lumps below them in the distance.

'London, eh? There's my office, where you came. And the Eye, bin on that? And the Post Office Tower. Like a giant shish kebab, I always say. Make a good photo, this view.'

But Russel is looking at the kites like red and yellow eyebrows, like angelfish roaring through blue air. Most of the guys with them are well old. Dads. Maybe grandpas.

'Make a racket, don't they?' says Scott. 'You'll want your tea. Shall we go?' They start downhill, Bramble straining on the lead. 'Sorry, son. Shouldn't've said that about being killed.'

''s all right.' They walk in friendly silence. Except Bramble, panting.

'Shouldn' let him pull like that. Oughta walk to heel.'

'How d'you do that?'

'Mum's got dog books. She could lend 'em.'

Dad opens the door.

'*There* you are, Russ. Who's this?'

'Hi there.' Scott puts out his hand. 'Scott Redington. Russel's been teaching me to train my dog.'

His mum appears behind Dad.

'How did it go? Come in.'

Dad's arm is across the door like a rope.

'Don't want to hold you up, Mrs Fairfax,' Scott says after a moment. 'Russel was great. But I've a lot to learn. He says you have dog-training books.'

'I'll look them out for you, Scott, after Easter.'

'Thanks. Well . . .'

Russel walks forward.

'Cheers,' he says, mostly to Bramble. Dad's arm goes down to let him in.

'We'll keep practising, son,' Scott says behind him. 'Happy Easter.'

Inside the house, Russel turns round. Scott is walking down the road with Bramble trotting in front of him, not at heel, holding his plumy tail high.

*

'Who's Mister Happy Easter?' says Tyler in the kitchen. He is cooking and Rosamund is washing up after him. Tyler always leaves a trail of sticky pans. She is taking Russel to Devon tomorrow. Tyler is working over Easter weekend with a Japanese company, but he'll join them for Sunday lunch and stay Sunday night. They'll have to share Irena's spare room.

'He found Russel when he was beaten up. I took Russel to see him at Scotland Yard, I told you. We should have asked him in.'

'What in hell's name's my son training a cop's mutt for? First he talks like a barrow boy, now he's hobnobbing with rozzers. And I didn't like the way he looked at you, young lady.'

'Come on, Tyler, he was just being nice.' That's what Tyler says, after chatting up a girl. 'And he's brilliant with teenage boys.'

'Then he's obviously gay. Out of the way, darling, I've a hot pan.' Tyler strains sauce into a jug. 'Glad he helped Russ, but does he always have BO? Three yards *and* some! Can't he find anything else to do but cavort with teenage boys?' He tips duck breasts into a copper pan. 'Pour me another glass of Gran Reserve, sweetie. Over there, look.'

LORD OF THE DANCE

7

Maundy Thursday 24 March, Parliament Square, London, 12.05 p.m.

Anka sat with eleven other people in a room with a buzzer to push when they reached their unanimous verdict. The blonde lady with the purple mark on her chin was sure the boy was innocent.

'She was leading him on.'

'Yes,' said Anka. *'Željela bi probati tvoj nekatar!'*

'What on earth's that?' The plump man with glasses was leaning against a wall. He doesn't like me, Anka thought.

'I love to try your – what is bees drink, in flower?'

'Nectar,' said the girl in a pink blouse who worked in Aquascutum.

'She could easily have walked out,' said the blonde lady.

'How could she? She was confused and terrified,' said the girl with no make-up. 'He was a sexual predator. He had probably done it before and got away with it.'

'She'd bought a dildo, for Heaven's sake, and got him to put the batteries in. Honestly, I don't know why the police have brought this case.'

'Why would you believe that?' said the elderly Irishman. 'He's perverted. He made it all up. Disgusting.'

'They've treated *us* disgustingly,' said the plump man. The glass in his spectacles was very smeared and their black frames made him look angry all the time. He is angry all the time, inside, thought Anka. 'They've kept adjourning, wasting our time. Let's vote him guilty and go to lunch.' He smiled at the girl from Aquascutum. She smiled back.

An official came.

'Have you reached a verdict?'

'We didn't ring,' said the foreman, a car salesman in a blue suit. Anka was the only person not from England, except the Irishman. She wasn't sure Ireland counted.

'I heard the buzzer.'

'Where's that?'

'There on the wall – Oh, sir, you must have leaned against it.'

The plump man in black glasses grinned unpleasantly. He did not apologise. The official left.

'We're going to be here all day if we don't reach a verdict. It's ridiculous. All they want to know is, is there reasonable likelihood that he tried to rape her? Of course there is.'

'I can't vote him guilty when I don't believe he is,' said the blonde woman.

'I, too, not,' said Anka.

'Let's take one more vote,' said the foreman.

Still ten against two. The stout man sighed ostentatiously. Anka, an expert on breathing, watched the pinstriped waistcoat strain as it expanded.

'We'll have to say we can't agree,' said the foreman. 'Anyone against? Excuse me.' He edged past the plump man, who did not draw in his legs, and pushed the bell.

When the judge asked if they had reached a unanimous verdict and the foreman said no, the judge seemed surprised. Also sad, Anka thought. The boy looked straight ahead under his black halo.

'He'll have to be re-tried with another jury,' said the judge. The boy disappeared.

Anka wrote her expenses on a form and walked unhappily away. The buildings round this square were for keeping safe. A court. A parliament with gold flags like little flames. An abbey with a door of holy saints. That boy, was he safe?

She was free now. To work, to feel her thighs move under her skirt, to buy new underwear, eat Easter lunch with Lasta and Budimir. Always, they cooked Croatian dishes and prepared a basket to be blessed in church. And on Saturday she would have a whole night with her lion! The first ever. He was not going to take a holiday abroad this year with his family.

But the boy who had faced them alone, where was he now? He was in a cell one year already, waiting for this trial. He'd helped a woman with her shopping and his life had changed. Who did he talk to, in prison? He was a child when he came to this country. What did he think of it now?

Maundy Thursday 24 March, Devon, 7.00 p.m.; Good Friday 25 March, 12.30 a.m., India

They are in a place where three lanes meet. His mum is nearly crying, silly bitch. Above a giant bank is a half moon like a slice of tangerine.

'No signposts. *All* the lanes have high sides, you can't see.' Her voice is squeaky. 'I knew all this once, when I stayed with Irena. Now it's a maze of muddy nothing.'

'Phone.'

'No signal. What about yours?'

Both networks are dead.

'GPS.' His dad gave her an electronic routefinder but she never uses it. 'What's Irena's postcode?'

'No idea.'

'Gotta have the postcode.'

A stripy face is looking at them from the dark.

'Look, Mum.' A shadow trundles away up a lane.

'Let's follow,' says his mum. 'Irena sees badgers, maybe it'll lead us to her.' Now there's grass in the middle of the lane. 'This is going to end in a farmyard.' They are in a tunnel of trees underlit by the headlights. 'Oh. I think – there should be an opening here – yes! There's Irena's gate.' He sees a yellow light through trees. And Irena waving.

'You found the way. Brilliant.' Irena hugs him. 'I've made soup.' She leads them to a stone passage so low Russel has to bend. Then a front room with a fire crackling and primroses – he knows they are primroses – on a table.

'Lovely!' says his mum. 'Isn't it *lovely*, Russel?' She always over-does it.

Irena pours soup into thick green mugs. Russel sits on a stool by

115

the fire. Kaa coils round his ankles, on a floor like pavement. Kaa doesn't mind the stone. He likes it. He likes the real fire, too.

'Haven't been here for *ages*,' says his mum.

'Not much has changed.' Irena laughs. 'Not much *to* change.'

Rosamund watches Russel give Irena his old sweet Russell smile. He keeps his head in its hood like a tortoise and his hands wrapped round the mug as if sheltering a candle. He is not drinking much, but does keep sipping.

'The big news,' says Irena, 'is that otters have come back to the stream. Richard will be thrilled.'

'Where is he? I thought he was back already.'

'He had to wait in India a bit longer.'

Irena kneels to put more logs on the fire, darting her hands among the flames as she did that rainy summer after her parents died, and Rosamund closes her eyes. She'd loved biology then. Funny Scott said that about her being lucky to do biology. She's never thought of it like that. She didn't say she hadn't finished the course.

She's been here twice since then. Once, she drove down alone with a bay tree for Irena's wedding, embarrassed because Richard used to be so weird about her, but he seemed fine. Happier than she'd ever seen him.

Then she and Tyler brought Russel for a weekend. They had a picnic in the woods and Irena stuck candles in a tree. On the train, Russel played with his magic set, poking the wand over the edges of a label on the train window to feel the bump. 'Daddy look, a white *car*,' he said as you might say white peacock, white tiger. She and Tyler looked at each other and laughed. The sunny fields, the beautiful boy, the magician's wand. Whatever Tyler had been up to the night before, that moment at least was happiness. Richard picked them up from the station and from then on it was probably downhill for Tyler. But he did his best. Tyler can be so sweet.

The voices of Irena and Russel sound like wind in the trees. She's never asked Irena if she wanted children. How would she look after them with Richard away? And her acting? And no money?

*

116

'Your mum's asleep,' Irena whispers. She's shorter than he is now and it's like they're alone. Russel hasn't been alone with Irena since she used to take him to puppet theatres. 'Will you come in the summer and see me at the Globe? I'll need all the friendly faces I can get. I'm playing Emilia in *Othello*.'

'What's that?'

'Shakespeare. I'm the heroine's friend.'

'What d'you do?'

'I'm married to someone very nasty. He's turning my friend's husband crazy by telling him she's keen on someone else. But I don't let myself know how nasty he is.'

'What happens?'

'I do an awful thing by accident – I give my husband my friend's handkerchief. He uses it to make *her* husband think she really is cheating on him, and so he kills her. It's a horrid story but it makes you wonder. Why do bad things happen? We never discover why my husband's bad.'

'Why do you stay with him?'

'You can have a good love for a bad person.' Kaa raises his head. 'And sometimes a good person, or someone who started out good, does bad things.'

'There's reasons bad things happen. The Just-World Hypothesis.'

'What's that?'

'Bad things happen because you're bad.'

'But my friend's good. So's her husband. Bad happens to them because my husband *makes* it happen.'

'Must be a reason.'

'Maybe there *aren't* reasons. Not always. Sometimes bad happens to good people, or people who are good-ish with bad bits, like most of us. Sometimes it's just bad luck.'

Maybe Irena sees Kaa but isn't saying.

'I'm so sorry about Bono, Russel.'

'Yeah, well . . .'

'He had a lovely life though, didn't he? I remember him racing around the woods with you. It's bad luck dogs age faster than us. But you made him gloriously happy, when he was alive.'

Yes. Bono was old. Dogs have to die. Better to go fast.

With Irena looking at him, quietly, from the rug, Russel feels held. A log falls in the fire and his mum opens one eye.

'I forgot the way,' she says sleepily. 'We were lost, weren't we, Russel? A badger led us to you.' She closes her eyes again.

'The badgers must know us,' whispers Irena with a smile. 'There's a sett in the woods.'

'C'n we see?' Russel is whispering too.

'It's too early in the year to see cubs. The mother keeps them underground when they're small. Must have been a male that led you here. But the Badger Rescue Centre has fifty orphaned cubs, we can go and see those.'

'What happened to their parents?'

'Killed on the road or – in other ways. They'll go back to the wild when they're old enough.'

His mum sits up.

'You look exhausted, Ros,' says Irena. 'Why don't you take a break? Go to India. Why not? Reconnect with your roots. You could stay with my friend in Darjeeling, there's lots to do there, and drop in on Richard – he's going back in May.'

'Cool, Mum.' Russel thinks of Grandpa in the photo. 'Why don't you?'

'I can't go anywhere, darling. What about you? Dad's out all day. I need to be at home.'

'You always, like, make yourself a victim.'

An owl calls outside.

'Could you stay with me, Russel?' says Irena. 'No, you've got school.'

'I c'n stay with Scott. An' Bramble.'

Wu wooo. Wu – woooo!

'That tawny owl roosts really close by.' Irena stood up. 'You're sleeping downstairs, Russel, in Richard's study. The end of the other passage, through that far door, see? I put a camp bed there. Fancy a hot-water bottle?'

'Thanks.'

*

118

Rosamund watches Russel go out of a door which hangs in its frame like a piece of jigsaw in the wrong hole. Irena hugs her.

'Lovely to have you here.'

'Do I make myself a victim?'

'Well . . .'

Rosamund stops herself crying.

'Tea?' says Irena. Her kitchen is simply the end of the front corridor. Rosamund watches her light the Calor gas. Twigs scrape a small black window. Irena doesn't draw curtains either. She too likes feeling part of the night.

'Who's the Scott he might stay with, if you go?'

'I can't go, Irena.' India, of all places. A door into terrible dark.

'Richard won't be in the south any more. You needn't go near Madras.' Irena knows she doesn't want to even think about Father. 'He'll be in Bengal.'

'It isn't that.' But it is, of course. 'I can't leave Russel.'

'Might be good for Tyler and Russel to be on their own.'

'They hardly talk.'

'They might, without you.'

'Russel's so inturned. I can't get through to him. Not since he was ten, really.'

'He's growing up his own way. Loads of people live their lives without finding themselves, but he will. Stop worrying, Ros.'

'Scott works in the Metropolitan Police. He protects wildlife.'

'And?'

'Russel's helping train his dog. To stop him thinking about Bono.'

'Fanciable?' Rosamund remembers her hand trying to touch Scott. Irena, watching her, smiles mischievously. 'Russel's got your animal thing, Ros. Must be from your dad.'

She's never told Irena she sees human beings as animals. And yet Bono was the only real animal she's known.

'I think he's lonely. Scott, I mean. Maybe he'd *like* Russel to stay.'

'Sounds as if you'd like to stay with him yourself.'

'I hardly know him.'

'So?'

They look at each other and giggle. Why did she feel like crying a moment ago?

'How's things with Tyler? You're going to have to share the room on Sunday. Or else make him sleep on the sofa.'

'He was brilliant about the drugs. But . . .'

Rosamund watches Irena lift the hot-water bottle to the kettle's spout. The stitches in its woolly cover stretch as water goes in. Irena's mother must have knitted that. Irena can't knit, and yet most things in Irena's house are home-made, part of Irena and Richard's past. Tyler likes everything designery. Toss the old away.

'I heard an *awful* answerphone message for Tyler. A woman. It sounded as if it was a serious, really long relationship.'

'Tyler's *connected* to you, Ros. Without child and house, she's on a losing wicket, if winning's what you want.'

'I don't know what I want.' She pictures Scott's smile. 'That woman was really angry. Tyler's probably seeing someone else too.'

'Fuck him, Ros. At college, you were this fantastic life-enhancer. Tyler's taken that away, you've got to get it back. Being *you*'s more important. Let Tyler dig his own grave.'

Again Rosamund feels like crying. Irena burps air out of the rubber, screws the stopper and hugs her. 'I'll take this to Russel. Then I'll make one for you.'

Good Friday 25 March India, 3.00 a.m.; Thursday 24 March, 9.30 p.m., UK

People had contaminated the earth, how did they feel about poisoning the sky too, this heaven they used to think so holy?

Richard was drunk. Well, slightly. It helped you sleep. Drops of condensation like crystal beetles raced over the scratched plane window.

Should he give Russel Kellar's present or ask Ros first? He remembered Tyler swinging the baby to the ceiling at the wedding. And later the boy in Devon, his hair a pale gleam in summer green. The old tree which Irena's father put candles in, when *she* was a child – Irena had studded with nightlights like stars, while that ridiculous dog scared wildlife for miles around.

Richard poured tonic from a tiny can, out of an egg-timer-shaped hole with a thin metal strip curling back from it.

He'd never wanted children. Irena had accepted that. He'd explained about his father, a terrifying man with spiky blond hair, nearly white, and very pale blue eyes who'd been away a lot. Driving cars, his mum said, to sell to other people. They'd lived in Manchester, a small house in a big city, and his mum was terrified of his dad. They all were, except Wanda.

Richard stirred a plastic chalice with a knobbed transparent wand. Tiny bubbles danced a sabbath up the side.

Until he was twelve, he'd shared a room with Wanda, his sister. He'd adored her. She'd been five years older; she teased him and complained about sharing the room but was sometimes very kind. They were allies. When his dad was there, she'd had terrible fights with him. Then one day Wanda wasn't there. His mum said she'd be back. His dad said over his dead body. Then he'd see him mum drinking. Once he found her passed out on the kitchen floor. When he was doing A levels, Mum said Wanda was dead. Later she told him Wanda had stolen money from them. But she never told him what happened to her at the end.

Richard looked out at black screws on the wing joining grey fabric stained with dribble where the metal had rusted. One island of metal was surrounded by extra studs like the Meccano he used to play with as a boy. They were going at four-fifths the speed of sound on a patched wing.

He remembered his mother telling him his dad had left too. Good riddance, she'd said.

The cloud below was white lace over duckweed. Underneath were miles of paddy field which had all been forest, once. Every year, he thought miserably, we use up four centuries' worth of animals and plants. Four centuries, of life that had left its passage on this heavenly body we call earth. The biology he spent his life studying seemed a frail lone candle in a relentlessly expanding universe.

He should ask for more gin.

'My dad wasn't a kind man,' he remembered telling Irena, 'but he was trapped. We all were.' His father had disappeared and died, unreconciled. Irena had never met his dad but she knew just how bitter his mum was. She'd been wonderful with her.

Those cloud-fronds were hospital gauze, staunching an unhealable wound. He had a vision of himself stationary in this metal tube, while the earth streamed below like a cassette ribbon unspooling.

From this moment, no more Ros fantasies, ever. They never came in England, only in tropical forest when he was strung to the intensity of leaf and spore. He didn't let himself think about them except when they happened, but up here, out of the world, he knew how deep they went.

Nine hours later, shifting stiff legs, feeling like some old scroll locked in a chest that would never unroll again, he opened his eyes.

'There's a blanket of cloud over London,' said the pilot. 'But we'll be down on time.'

Richard slid up the window blind. Black was fading to grey. In the roaring grey yeast of cloud, his exhaustion faces began: misty demons scowling, bearded men, madonnas with pewtery pythons of hair. His mouth fizzed with a taste like rotten eggs.

Ros would already be in Devon. She'd be sleeping the other side of the wall, two inches of lathe and plaster away from his and Irena's bed. He should have come home earlier, when he'd originally planned.

Good Friday 25 March, Devon, 12.45 p.m.

'That's the sett,' whispers Irena. 'That hole in the bank. See the pile of earth they've dug outside?' The badger sett is a letter D on its side. 'We shouldn't go near, we'd alarm the mother. Let's look for their tracks.'

Russel bends over gingery earth. They've left his mum up the slope looking at some plant. Dead leaves shine under his feet. Trees touch over their heads, reminding him of Grandpa's bricks. He used to make arches like that by putting the curved ones together.

When they were here before, Bono was too.

'Look at this stone.' Irena's voice is like breathing. 'See the claw marks?' The reddish stone is gouged and scored as if with chisels. 'Some badger prised it out of the ground.'

Russel sees a paw print, big as Bono's.

''s this badger?'

'Well spotted.' They listen. Nothing. 'Let's leave them in peace. She'll be worried.' They walk towards the end of the wood. 'I've known these woods all my life, Russel, I made a map of them when I was ten. But I'm no naturalist. You must come here with Richard.'

His mum is standing by an old black tree. An oak, oaks have those ripply leaves.

'Gonna stay a bit on my own.'

'Will you be OK?' says his mum just as Irena says, 'Stay as long as you want.' He sees them look at each other. Parents think they know you, because they saw you in days you don't remember. But those days belong to them, not you. They put their own shit into that. They remember a life they say is yours, but it's not.

He misses the net. Last night he slept under Richard's computer but it was bagged up, he didn't dare undo it.

'Coming back, turn right at that tree with a branch like a hook.' Irena points. 'Follow the path to the Candle Tree and you'll see our gate.'

'Don't get lost,' says his mum.

Kaa slides up the tree to watch them disappear round a bend, their wellingtons making tracks in the mud like a long-pawed animal.

He misses weed. The first time he smoked alone was after his dad cut his hand. Dad was chopping meat, his mum was crying and pretending not to. Dad shouted, Kaa hissed, the knife slipped and Dad screamed. There was blood everywhere. Mum took his dad to hospital while he went upstairs and got fucked.

Being lean doesn't just make things not hurt, it draws things together. At the blue hour, twilight, you can feel everything's connected. Like there's nothing that doesn't add up. But maybe finding it hard to connect things is more real than being able to see things joined up. It's OK to think that. It means the world means something.

Out of his pocket he takes a strip of twisted leather. Kaa is hanging from the tree, pointing at where two roots make a little chair in the earth. Russel squats, balances the dog collar on one root and scoops wet earth and leaves from between the two. Behind him, three jackdaws watch from a branch. He curls the collar in the hole like an ammonite. The magpies drop to the ground for a better view. Like all corvids, they are opportunists and take a professional interest in holes.

Wind sighs in the branches. Light rain begins, tapping the last few leaves on the tree. Russel covers the collar with earth, and sits down facing the forest, hand on the new-packed soil, his back against the tree. He looks at raindrops on his knuckles.

A frayed oak leaf floats down. It has clung on all winter. Now it has landed on his leg. His last link with Bono. It has a long central vein, little yellow spots, and small sideways brown veins, like string, over holes insects have eaten.

He tucks it in his pocket, puts his hand up into the space it floated through and feels cold air between his fingers.

*

'When's Richard coming?' Rosamund is restless. 'Can I do anything?'

'Nope, all done. He'll be here by two. He's getting a lift from Barnstaple.'

'I'll tidy his study.'

'Don't bother, it's only a couple of nights.'

'I'm sure Russel's left it a terrible mess.'

She follows the passage to the study. The small window looks onto the rough grass at the front of the house. As in Father's study, books run up the walls to the ceiling. Richard's computer is covered in plastic. Unlike Tyler, he can probably handle computers himself. If she'd said yes, when Richard had asked her to marry him, something like this study would have been her life.

It's dark, even at midday. She switches the light on. The camp bed is squeezed between filing cabinet and desk. She leans the bed up against the wall so Richard can reach the computer. On the floor where the bed had been is a book. *The Jungle Book*, say gold letters on the cover. Where is this from? She used to read Kipling in paperback to Russel – but this?

The pages are soft as a worn Bible. Inside is an inscription with Father's Greek 'e's. 'For Russel from his grandfather, on his first birthday, November 15th 1991.' Underneath, Russel has drawn a snake with a round head like a bun. She spent years praising drawings like this. Father must have brought this to the wedding. Did he give it to Tyler? No, Tyler would have said. To Russel? He was a baby, he'd have forgotten the next minute. Maybe it got lost among their books and Russel found it later. She remembers Tyler buying the *Jungle Book* video, Russel whispering he didn't like it but don't tell Daddy. The books must already have been a big deal. She doesn't like thinking Russel kept things secret from her even then.

Russel has written as well as drawn in it. 'When KAA came to the Jungle,' he has written, copying Father's 'e's. Rosamund riffs the pages. The first illustration is a baby playing with wolf cubs and Mother Wolf defending him against the tiger.

'It is I, Shere Khan, who speak!'

The tiger's roar filled the cave with thunder. Mother Wolf

shook herself clear of the cubs and sprang forward, her eyes like two green moons in the darkness, facing the blazing eyes of Shere Khan.

'And it is I, Raksha [the Demon] who answer. The man's cub is mine, Lungri – mine to me! He shall not be killed!'

Something rips open in Rosamund as she reads. Through tears, she sees herself reading these words lying on her bed in India but trying to remember some other scene – tickly grass, real English grass, with daisies. Woodpigeons, burbling. And a woman's face.

Shere Khan might have faced Father Wolf, but he could not stand up against Mother Wolf, for he knew that where he was she had all the advantage of the ground, and would fight to the death. So he backed out of the cave-mouth growling . . .

This is all she has. Her mother is a memory of a memory. She's been crying these tears all her life.

She hears an engine. Through the window she sees a van, and Richard taking a suitcase and rucksack out of it, and Irena walking over the grass, carrying daffodils. Richard drops his bags and opens his arms, Irena runs into them, Richard lays his cheek against her hair and closes his eyes.

Rosamund turns away, puts the book on the floor, replaces the bed over it and wipes her sleeve over her face.

At the front door the sun is out, the sky blue, and Irena is waving to the driver. Richard, in an anorak with dangling strings, rucksack on one shoulder, is filling the doorway.

'Welcome back.' As Rosamund kisses him the rucksack slips off his shoulder and crashes onto her arm.

'Oh gosh, sorry, Ros . . .'

'Not to worry.'

'You OK?' says Irena, behind Richard.

Richard watched Rosamund go upstairs and followed Irena to the kitchen where a pan was bubbling on the gas.

126

'I've missed you terribly.' He put his arms round her, cupping her small breasts. 'Wish we could go to bed.' He rested his chin on her shoulder.

'I know, love. But they're only here a couple of days. Take these plates, will you?'

'Ros looks older. She's been crying.'

'She's in a bad way. The boy's sweet but very teenagerish. He's fourteen. She's got to give up control.'

'I've got something for him.'

'Really?' Irena looked round teasingly.

'Not from me.' Richard wasn't good at presents. This time he had an old Keralan actor's mask for her, which Girish helped him find. 'From Kellar.'

'What is it?'

'A book, what else? Have we enough gas cylinders for the weekend?'

'We'll need a couple more. What's the book?'

'The naturalist Alfred Russel Wallace. Shall I tell Ros first, or just give it?'

'Don't make it a big deal. Tell her, give it and that's that.'

Richard had never wanted children. He had disliked being a child too much to wish it on anyone else. Irena had gone along with that. We both have our work, she said. Now we have each other, too.

'Shall I take the potatoes in?' He picked up a bowl.

Irena smiled.

'Take anything in you like. I'm just so glad you're here, you're safe.'

She rested her forehead against his chest. She was wearing a pale pink shirt open at the neck. He held her with one arm, the dish in his other hand, and heard Rosamund coming down the stairs. You could hear everything in this house.

At table, Irena raised her glass and he watched her breasts move under her shirt like small animals.

'This is Dave's cider, Ros. Dave's the farmer next door – remember him at our wedding? He was a god when I was little. He farms where we were this morning. He gives us a batch every Christmas.'

'Long time since I saw a baked potato.' Richard looked at leathery skin split in a buttery smile. 'Rice and *dal*, rice and *dal*, breakfast lunch and dinner for six months.'

'Here's to your research, Richard!' Rosamund raised her glass. The cider was the same colour as the under-layer of her hair.

'I've brought something for Russel,' he said.

'That's kind. What?'

'I called at Chennai, where your – er – father works. He gave me a book for Russel.'

'What book?'

Rosamund's face was suddenly sharp. Her nose was shiny, and the lines below it ridged in round her lips.

'Alfred Russel Wallace. I suppose . . . well, he *is* called Russel.'

'He won't read it.'

He had never heard her voice so high.

'He can do what he likes with it, can't he?' said Irena comfortably. 'Light the fire with it, jump on it . . . How about cheese? Cornish Brie? Cambozola?'

'How are the otters?' Richard asked.

'Haven't seen. Maybe Russel's having more luck.'

'Not in the middle of the day.'

'He won't remember the way,' said Rosamund anxiously. 'We should look for him.'

'He can't come to harm. No tigers and cobras here! Richard'll find him after lunch. You're dying to get out there, aren't you, love?'

Irena smiled into his eyes. Hers shone like leaves silvered by light from the sea.

'Yes, it'll be – um, nice, to see spring in Devon. Spring in tropical forest's not the same. I'll find Russel, Ros.'

'Can you take him a sandwich? All he ate for breakfast was cereal. I'll make one.'

Rosamund slipped off into the kitchen. Irena put her hand on his.

'I know, it'd be lovely to go to bed. But she's having a tough time. Their dog got run over, Russel was beaten up, they've discovered he's smoking dope, and Tyler's having some big affair. I know it's small beer compared to what's happening to the planet. But it's a big deal for her.'

Richard kissed Irena's palm, folded her fingers over to keep his kiss in, and leaned to kiss her lips.

'Russel picks up Ros's worries,' murmured Irena into his neck. 'They're not very good for each other just now.'

Ros came in and they both stood up.

'Can you give him this cheese sandwich?'

'Here's your bag,' said Irena as they went into the passage. He always carried a bag in the field. He put Russel's sandwich in, feeling for other things he kept there, knife, camera, collecting envelope, and touched something else. Irena had winkled Kellar's present out of his rucksack and slipped that in, too.

'We left him by the big oak above Long Bottom, but I showed him the badgers' sett, and where I'd seen otters. He might have gone back there.'

'You'll never find him,' said Rosamund. 'He might be anywhere.' Maybe these woods looked like chaos to her. Richard thought of Kellar. Kellar was magic in the field. Soundless, tireless, tough as stone. He saw everything, down to the pit-viper on the branch you were just about to grab for a handhold.

'He's a sensible boy,' said Irena, putting her arm round Rosamund. 'Richard knows these woods like the back of his hand.'

'I'll find him,' Richard said.

And yes it was nice to be in forest, after Delhi. The canopy was a fretwork of black veins, touched by the pale green of buds-in-waiting. Everything holding its breath for spring. A pair of blue tits flew away, a green woodpecker dipped down the slope. Here was the twisted ash, painted on its windward side by a vertical swathe of green, the trunk spiralled as if some hand had wrung its neck a hundred years ago. Lichen had followed that twist down; rain ran through the lichen's bloom like tears. All this unshowy weblace, bare twigs instead of the panoply of tropical leaf, was home. No, this was home too. He could never give up the magic of Indian forest. He loved both.

129

Beechmast underfoot and grass shoots blushing up through. Here was the silver birch that looped down and up like a ladle as if something had trodden on it when it was a sapling: a stag, rubbing velvet off its antlers, or Irena when she was little. Irena said it had been like that always. The new trunk had been bent and nearly snapped, but sap forced its way up and now it was a strong sweep upward, gloved in that black scatter which patchworks every silver birch.

Richard turned right along Hog's Back ridge. In a month this would all be bluebells, the purply blue he'd never seen in India. He loved that he, who grew up in Manchester, had become part of this woodland and its history; of people whose families had lived here for ever. From these ancient hollies, gloss green among hazy pre-spring greys, Irena's parents used to cut branches at Christmas. Now he cut them too. *The first tree in the greenwood* . . .

Something bright was moving down the pale slope. A red deer fawn. There was the doe. *Running of the deer* – he'd stepped into a Christmas carol. And into the greatest privilege of all, seeing wild animals who think themselves alone.

The fawn butted the doe's side. She was heading upwards, towards – Richard saw now – a stag, who stood motionless at the edge of the wood. The doe stopped, the fawn began to nurse and, suddenly Richard saw a boy, gazing at the stag, sitting against a tree, hands on the roots either side as if enthroned. He was dressed in dirty white; his head was nearly bald. Had he been ill? Richard thought of Ranjit's thick black locks.

Suddenly the doe's head shot up. She and the stag turned their faces downhill and were away, the startled fawn galloping too. What frightened them? Not the boy, he was admirably still.

Richard looked in the direction the deer had looked. Four men, two black terriers at their heels, were walking in single file towards the stream. The last carried a sack and spades. The man in front was eighteen stone at least. A bloated Dick Whittington, with gun. Richard hoped the boy, now gazing at the men, would not move.

The men disappeared. Richard wasn't up to Kellar's standard but he could move in forest pretty silently. When he got close he saw the boy was whispering. Did he have a mobile? No, there was no signal. Just a kid talking to himself.

'Russel?' he breathed.

The boy looked at him, terrified. He'd thought he was alone. That's the Medusa, Irena had told Richard. You think you're alone, then hear a footstep behind. While you were watching other people, something else was watching *you*. That's what turns you to stone.

'I'm Richard,' he whispered. 'Remember me? Those men mustn't know we've seen them.' He squatted beside the boy.

'Who are they?'

'Badger diggers. *Very* dangerous.'

'What are they doin'?'

'Looking for a sett.'

'What'll they like, do?'

'You saw those terriers?'

'Yeah.' The boy moved his hand over the hollow beside him, like someone protecting a bruise.

'The men make them fight badgers.'

'Why?'

'Badgers never give up. Diggers like that. They make bets: which dog gets bitten first, which dog will kill. We should call the police.'

'Report 'em to Scotland Yard.'

'There are people closer. Local police, RSPCA or Badger Watch at Barnstaple. Or the farmer who owns this land.' But no. He hadn't seen all the faces. Some farmers encourage diggers. Dave gave them cider at Christmas but what else did he get up to? Diggers travel hundreds of miles for a fight but work through local contacts. And they had known where to come.

'We gotta *follow*.'

The boy stood up. Skinny, but tall. When Richard stood, Russel's eyes were well above his. Russel was right, they needed evidence, and he had a camera in his bag. Diggers were expert at avoiding prosecution. 'No, your worship, we didn't expect badgers, we were looking for rabbits.' 'The dogs got in a fight.' 'It was an accident.' Some kept dead foxes in the freezer and brought them along to prove that's what they'd been after.

'We must *absolutely* not be seen. Will you do whatever I say at once?'

'Course.'

'And totally quiet. All we want is evidence, their faces, what they do. I'll take pics, then away to the police, OK?'

He moved down the slope. At the bottom he looked back. Russel was treading, soft as a leopard, in his footprints.

She is in a crawl space like the hole under Tyler and Rosamund's shed, but arched like a cathedral. Badgers are master diggers. This den is linked to hundreds of metres of tunnel made by badgers over two hundred years. Her long seamed pad ends in five oval toes and the claws at their end, now lying over the cubs, are as long again. Identical claws have created the labyrinth to which this den belongs. Human wars have made little difference to the badgers, though some were eaten when food was short. They have made their own history: foraging, raising young, extending their realm, creating hollows in the tunnel like this, where mother and pups lie in secret dark.

Head flat on the ground, she lies with her body curved round two tweed bundles. Her fur might seem grey but if you looked close you'd see each hair is white, delicately tipped with black.

The ground above shakes. She hears a dog's excited whimper and something bright comes down through the roof.

'Over here, Jeff.'

When the rod slipped through, suddenly easy, it meant there was space below. One man fitted a radio transmitter to a terrier's collar. The other terrier whimpered excitedly as he dragged the first dog, barking now like a small machine gun, and poured it into the hole as if stuffing a cushion into a bottle. The trousery hind legs scrabbled a second and then the barks were heard underground, moving along under the men's feet.

Jeff squatted by a black box, the receiver and depth gauge that would pinpoint where to dig. The beeps grew fainter, then stayed in one place. The terrier had found. The large man grabbed a spade. The badger would be getting away, badgers only fight if there is no other option. Dig your way out of every dead end is the badger motto. But not with cubs to defend.

He began digging furiously. To have the fight above ground they'd have to be quick, otherwise the badger would find another tunnel or the terrier might lose patience and attack. If it did, there was only one end. The dog was in the badger's home. There'd be fighting all right, but very unequal and they would not see. The remaining dog, tied up, was barking without gap.

'Dig, fucking dig,' they said to each other as the wood leaned over them, birds flew away into white-brindled sky and the gun stood against the tree, the one still thing.

The big man shovelled as if life depended on it. They'd made good depth and the chemistry of their bodies was changing satisfactorily too. From the upper end of eight kidneys, tiny molecules of epinephrine rushed out of four adrenal medullas in the inner part of the adrenal gland, rampaging through their blood like wildfire, speeding up violently the beating of four hollow muscular organs which had begun pumping about thirty years ago. One heart from Devon, two from Yorkshire and one Lancashire heart, very fatty. As faces flushed and sweat ran inside shirts, molecules were at work in their veins constricting small blood vessels, raising blood pressure, freeing sugar stored in four livers. They were textbook cases, men high on their own excitement.

Jeff flung himself on his stomach and put his ear to the ground.

'Fuckin' get on wi' it,' bellowed the fat man.

Underground, she parries again, then again, standing over the one living cub, head low. The terrier has killed one cub and is now tearing the skin of her neck, tugging sharp teeth through black-tipped hairs into her flesh. Suddenly, swinging up her head in the classic badger drive – no one has told the terrier about this – she slices her upper teeth through its temple bone, driving splinters into one eye while her lower teeth come up to meet them through the terrier's jawbone.

If you took that jaw between finger and thumb it would feel like porcelain. This terrier has been bred to be brave, that's all. Its barking

133

is screaming now. Swinging her head, the badger masticates bone, nerves, eye jelly. The terrier's body, pivoting on its pierced eye and tearing cheek, hits the tunnel walls again and again.

Light breaks in. Men pull them both up, the badger's teeth fixed in the terrier's head.

'Fuck'n' useless dog! Terminator terrier, oh yeah, Pete? Automated killing machine, *you* said.'

Someone loosed the other terrier while the big man swung his spade and smashed it into the badger's jaw. One terrier fell away and the fresh one danced around her, barking like a saw on steel, wagging its tail as dogs will wag at the most violent moments. 'I'm doing what God made me to do. What you have made me to do.'

Steadily, lower jaw broken, mouth full of blood, her own and the terrier's, the badger faced her second attacker.

'Ger on, Bessie!'

This dog was in the open, not a tunnel. It did not have to head straight into her jaws but could duck, weave, dance in from any direction. She bowed her wounded head as it darted in and out, ripping her sides and neck.

Ten minutes passed. Growls, grunts, smell of blood and shit, the sobbing panting of a mortally wounded dog on its side, blood soaking the ground. Sweat dripped down the men's faces, welled beneath their arms.

Attacked in the open, a badger keeps its head down between its forelegs, then snaps up, sweeping its head to lock on to its attacker. This badger's head was down, her hanging jaw nearly on the ground, her rubbery skin and hard hair her only armour, her hindquarters streaming red ribbons. The terrier pirouetted in and out of range.

'Ger on! Fuck'n' ger on!'

The terrier tried closer in and the badger struck upward, fastening her upper teeth in its unguarded throat. There was another small-dog scream.

'Need another fucker, Jeff! *Told* you to bring the lurcher.'

'Where's that useless bitch? See how hard *she* is? Best in East Riding, *you* said.'

The terrier tried to free its throat, but every tug made the badger's

134

teeth sink deeper. The dog was ripping itself apart. The men could see its windpipe, white and blue-madder like fairground rock.

The big man's eyes bulged, veins on his forehead stood out in the hard yellow shine of his skin, he swung his boot and kicked the badger's belly where the black fur was sparse. They heard ribs break and a *pfut* of skin rupturing over musculocutaneous tissue. She released the terrier and turned, sides heaving, to face him. He kicked the dog out of the way, raised his army boot and stamped down on the stripey head that had lain an hour ago beside her cubs. Head under boot she squirmed, swung her fore-claw at him, grey pad grimed with her own excreta, she was lying in that too as well as blood, but now he had a sheath knife, men knew it from seven counties, the US Marine K-bar sharpened like a scalpel, and he did at last what the men wanted, slid it between her ribs.

There was a small squeal as it grated on bone, then silence. Except the panting of four men, blood bubbling from a terrier's opened throat and the soughing of wind in bare branches.

Pete – for it was he, Pete Verrall of Ribblesdale, infamous from Leeds to the Sussex Downs – wiped his blade on the badger's coat. Below him, in the shadow of the opened sett, ants trickled towards two inches of newly dead tissue.

The living cub pillowed its head on its brother and shifted closer, questing for warmth.

9

Good Friday 25 March, Devon, 4.20 p.m.

Behind a boulder patchworked in silvery rosettes like fish scales with whitey-green frills, Russel crouches beside Richard as he takes photos, trying to shut out the smells, thuds, growls, thwacks, dog screams and the men's yells, more animal than any other sound. His stomach jumps bile into his mouth, his teeth are chattering like Bono's when he got old.

He looks hard at twisty roots of a thorn tree growing out of the boulder. There's sick on his feet. He's going to keel over, he's shivering, tears streaming down his fucking face.

Richard's arm comes round him.

'They're going.' The words are breath in Russel's ear. 'We'll give them time to get away.'

Richard kept his arm round Russel as the sobs, retching and shivers subsided. He was trembling too. Russel hadn't seen the details he saw through the zoom, but whatever he did see was appalling enough.

'Can you stand?'

He held the boy firmly, remembering Kellar with the snake. They rose above the boulder and saw the sloping woodland, gentle moss over rocks, glistening roots, and a bloodstained flat patch by a pile of new-dug earth. The diggers must have taken the bodies with them.

'OK?' The boy nodded.

'Russel.' The boy's eyes met his, blue and aghast. What should he say? 'We've got *really* good evidence. What she went through means hundreds of other badgers won't.' The boy nodded, face white as his clothes. 'Come.' He took a path through the densest parts of the wood. When it broadened out, he held the boy's shoulders.

'You're good in the field.' Russel said nothing. '*Never* go near men like that on your own. All over Britain they kill three hundred badgers a week. That's fifteen thousand a year. Police can't get evidence to convict them.'

'Scotland Yard'd help.'

'They've got their hands full with London. But thanks to your bravery and woodcraft – they had no idea we were there – these ones will go to prison.'

'Will the dogs like, die?'

'Probably. Diggers never go near vets. They'd get reported.'

Near the cottage they heard squeaking. Then Richard saw against the halogen of fading sky a mass of birds, tits, starlings, chaffinches, a mistle thrush and jay, buzzing open-beaked at a tree.

'That's the owl's tree,' he said. 'They're mobbing it.'

'What are they doin'?'

'Trying to get rid of the owl. He's roosting, trying to stay invisible.'

Close to the trunk, head twisted nearly 180 degrees, the owl watched its tormentors with big black eyes.

'Why don't it beat the shit outta them? It can fuckin' eat 'em!'

'He can't get them when they know where he is. They'll go to bed soon, then it's his turn.'

'Cos he can see in the dark.'

'He's not magic, he can't see when there's no light.' Enchant him, thought Richard, with science. Take his mind off the horrors. 'His cornea – know what that is?'

'Course.'

'It's fat, like an extra lens, to let in more light.'

The owl shifted; the starlings shrieked. Richard longed, as if the savagery they'd witnessed had burnt acid into his and Russel's psyches, binding them together, to give the boy the one thing he himself had always found consoling. Clear, beautiful, objective *explanation*.

'Millions of years ago, that owl's ancestors decided to hunt at night. Gradually, to see colours in dim light, their retinas evolved more rods than cones. *We* never did that, so we have more cones than rods. We only see colour in bright light.'

*

'There they are!' Rosamund peers into the gloaming. 'They've stopped!'

'They're looking at the owl,' says Irena.

'What that owl really depends on,' said Richard, looking up into the tree, 'is his hearing. He's got more nerve endings in the auditory part of his brain – that's the hearing bit—'

'I know.'

'— than any other bird. His right ear's higher than his left. His facial disc acts like a dish, and throws sounds into his asymmetric ears so he can target his prey.'

'Like two GPS signals.'

'Exactly. Thanks to fifty-four million years of evolution.'

'Fifty-four million? Heavy.'

Perhaps, thought Richard with a slight shock, he was better at teaching than he'd thought.

'*Homo erectus* migrated out of Africa two million years ago, but he became extinct. Our real ancestors only got going five hundred thousand years ago.'

'So these woods belong to the owl, not us.'

Richard fumbled in his bag.

'I've brought you something from India, from your grandfather.'

He felt the boy tense.

'We're in the same line of work.' Richard felt a tiny thrill as he said that, like handing on a baton. 'We're herpetologists. That means—'

'I know.'

'He thought you'd like something by your namesake. Alfred Russel Wallace.'

Russel whipped the package under his jacket without looking, as if the air might corrode it.

'You're named after someone very brave and profound.'

After a moment Russel said, 'What did he, like, do?'

'Tropical biology. He was an explorer, an animal collector. Brilliant. He invented evolutionary biogeography.'

Russel's blankness, Richard was sure, did not mean indifference.

'*Russel! Richard!*'

At Ros's voice there came a whirr above their heads. The owl had broken free.

Rosamund watches Russel walk into the front room followed by Richard, who has a strange gentleness on him like someone who's just seen a terrible car crash.

'We took a long way round. To avoid – er – poachers,' he says.

'Russel, do you drink cider?' says Irena, coming forward in a quick smooth movement as if some signal has passed between herself and Richard. Rosamund blinks. Is she being paranoid? What has she missed?

'Cheers,' says Russel.

'I found the map I made of the woods.' Irena shows Russel to the table. Richard and Irena bend over him like animals protecting their young. 'Here's where we left you. That black splodge is the oak. I spent hours in it when I was ten.'

Richard clinks his glass on Russel's. Rosamund has never seen Richard being fatherly. There's danger somewhere, or has she imagined it? Is she making herself a victim again, does she really do that? At least you know where you are if you're a victim. You can't be cast down, you're down already.

'Hey, Ros,' says Irena, putting an arm out. She's sorry for me, Rosamund thinks with a shock. 'Where's your cider? Can you help me peel the carrots?'

Alone at last.

Russel closes his door. Supper was well good, he likes food Irena cooks. But all the shit, the screams, grunts, barks, voices and faces, thwack of the spade, the blood, will never leave him, ever. Like Bono's legs, dark and mashed up with bone poking through.

He sits at the desk. *Infinite Tropics: An Alfred Russel Wallace Anthology*. He had a quick look before supper. He turns again to the writing, in exactly the same place as in *The Jungle Book*. 'For Russel, with love from his grandfather. Chennai, March 2005.'

He'd give anything for weed. The guy he buys from is probably wondering where he is.

The door creaks. He hunches his shoulders. Mum gets everywhere.

'You all right?' says Irena's voice softly.

He takes a jagged breath.

'There *are* bad people.' His words fall into the computer's plastic cowl like coins in muddy water. 'People are *shit*. They do shit things.'

'Yes, they do. What you saw has happened in England for over a thousand years. Badger baiting's been illegal for two centuries but it still goes on. I'm very sad you saw it.'

Tears spurt from his eyes.

'Shit . . .' He's shivering again. He feels Irena's arms round him. She's small, but she's strong. She lays her chin on his head. After a moment he rests his head against her and lets the tears fall.

'What sort of person would you be if you *weren't* upset? It's crucified Richard too. You saw a horrible part of the world, like war. A truth that's terrible to know.'

''s not true, the just world.' This shaking is like dying.

'No. But there are good things in the world too.'

Yes. He might see his grandpa one day. And proper jungle. Infinite tropics. He wipes his face on his sleeve.

'Not many people see anything like that. You're carrying a burden now. Richard blames himself for leading you into it.'

'Had to get evidence.'

'It's great you did. The police will act on it. But if you ever want to talk about it, or anything else,' she fishes paper out of the waste basket and scribbles on it, 'that's my mobile.'

'I couldn't tell Ros how awful it was,' Richard whispered in the dark. With Irena's head on his shoulder and Ros the other side of the wall he felt divided, like a pie chart. Even making love hadn't expunged Ros entirely. 'Should we?'

'Would that help Russel? I told her the basics, that you'd photographed poachers taking a badger.'

'It's everywhere, Irena. Wild animals killed, totally illegal – and nothing happens! At least in India they poach for food, not kicks.'

He kissed her neck.

'Your Badger Watch friend recognised that big bugger just from my description. He's from Yorkshire. Police in six counties have been trying to nail him.'

'Will you take Russel with you to the police? He'd feel part of – retribution. You were great with him, love, he really trusts you.'

'Of course. I like Russel. What did Ros say about Kellar's present?'

'Nothing.'

'I think Kellar's longing to see her. It was painful, he's so awkward. But he'd die rather than say.'

'I think she wants to see him too, but she'd never admit it even to herself. She's – there's something that stops her, Richard, doing what she needs. As if her soul was trodden on when it was young. She's the only one of us now with a living parent.'

Richard's mother had died two years ago from cancer. Irena had sat beside her in a Manchester hospice for weeks.

'I said, why didn't she go to India? Not to see Kellar, not at first anyway. Just for a break. She could stay with Alisha in June, maybe drop in on you in Bengal too – that'd be OK, wouldn't it?'

Richard felt the bed lurch beneath them both.

'In June? Crazy time to go.'

'She can't go till Russel finishes his exams. Would the weather matter? She's so ground down by Tyler, she needs to think about something completely different. Some other world.'

'Tyler's wrecked her life.' He tried to imagine Rosamund coming to him in India and felt terrified.

'Tyler made her happier than she'd ever been, at first.'

'He's totally fake. He's not worthy even of her *shadow*!'

'He's like a – a dictator. With some black hole he's terrified of falling into, underneath.'

'He's utterly crass. How are we going to get through Sunday?'

'We've got to be nice, love. We don't want Russel thinking we can't bear his dad. He's surrounded by absent heroes.'

'Heaven help anyone who takes Tyler for a hero.'

'But that's what he wants to be. I saw him at it last week.'

'Tyler? Where?'

'London. He didn't see me, I was with people from the Globe. He was walking toward us by the river, completely oblivious, arm round a girl not much older than Russel. Long pale hair. His eyes were glued to her face.'

Whooo! Then another *whooooo*, with tremolo. It sounded like all the disappointment in the world but the owl was just asserting his territory, or contacting his mate.

'Tyler was waving his hand and talking, edging his other up the girl's side. An old roué, whose strike rate's going down.'*Keweeek!* That was a contact call, a Where Are You? 'A vision of hell, stamped on the dark. The sinner beside the black river, condemned to repeat the same sin over and over.' Irena sighed. 'Tyler's forty-nine. That girl looked sixteen.'

Richard stroked Irena's shoulder. It's rare to be loved, he thought, because it's rare to be known.

'It was the Tyler Ros has never seen. At it all the time. Powerful men, expense accounts, girls on the make.'

'But he was so proud of Ros! Those ghastly meals when he sang at her. Tears in his eyes. Terribly embarrassing.'

Coo-wik. The owl was seeing off an intruder, maybe a barn owl. It'd be lovely to have barn owls. But the tawnies wouldn't stand it.

'He really did love Ros. Maybe still does. He's sentimental as well as calculating. Cold self-interest with a top layer of emotion, like marshmallow.' Her voice was dreamy. 'You could play Iago like that.'

'He *is* Iago.'

'No, he's not malicious, just lethally selfish. Like your poisonous snakes, he can destroy people, but it's sort of – incidental.' Her breathing slowed. 'He'll just never give up that greed . . .'

Her voice tailed off into sleep. Richard pressed his lips against her hair.

Saturday. The rain is like sheet glass but Rosamund has woken happier than she's felt for ages. She can do anything! Go back to biology. Or botany, why not? That'd be great for garden design. She watches Richard and Russel set off for Barnstaple.

'I'm making an Easter cake,' says Irena. 'We can't have an egg hunt if it rains like this. I've loads of little eggs, we'll have to hide them indoors.'

'Russel's way past Easter-egg hunts. What are you going to do to that chicken?' Rosamund starts washing the breakfast things. Domesticity is not Irena's strong point. She herself loves cooking, when she doesn't have to. When Tyler isn't showing off about it. 'Like me to make Moroccan *poulet*?'

'What would it need?' said Irena, as if it might involve a trek to the Atlas mountains.

'Nothing you haven't got. Onions, tomatoes. Spices.'

The rain drums outside. Baking smells fill the kitchen.

'What's my dad trying to do, Irena? Take over Russel?'

'Make contact, idiot. You're his only child and Russel's his grandson.'

Rosamund feels a sudden pang. She sees Father showing her when she was little a tailor bird's nest, hanging like a cow's udder from a tree, murmurous with chicks. Russel would have loved it.

Irena opens the oven.

'Moment of truth.' She sets a yellow balloon on the sideboard.

'Rioon! Amazing. Even the magpies wouldn't eat the last one I made.' In two seconds, the cake starts deflating into a primrose-coloured bucket. They look at each other and the old crazy giggle starts. They hug each other, weak with laughing.

'I've used all the flour. I could phone Richard . . .'

'Turn it into an Easter nest! Slather it with chocolate, put the eggs in . . .'

'Brilliant.'

They laugh again. Lovely, thinks Rosamund. Warm kitchen, Russel interested in something again, rain battering outside . . .

'Where's the icing sugar? And chocolate, for a shiny brown nest?'

'Somewhere.' Bottom up, head down like a terrier, Irena starts opening cupboard doors.

Easter Saturday 26 March, Kilburn, London, 7.00 p.m.

Anka smoothed the sheet, shook out the duvet and watched it settle like foam on the sea. He liked to shower in the morning, she knew that, so she'd bought some expensive Badedas. She'd also hidden an

Easter present in her cupboard. She felt bad. Helen did not know she was cleaning the flat not for Easter but for him, and Tess would not be waking up her daddy on Easter Sunday morning. 'But she'll have me all day,' he'd said on the phone, 'and I, sweetie, will have *you*! Exactly where I want you. Bliss.'

'Helen,' she called now. 'Your bag, *dragi*. Ready?'

'A *bag*?' said Helen, as if it were an instrument of torture.

'We go Mass, tonight. Then, you have sleepover. Night dressing, you need.'

'Night*dress*.'

'Tomorrow, Easter Sunday. So – nice *dress*.'

'Katya'll be wearing her tracksuit.'

'Not, at Easter.' Lasta would be going through exactly the same with Katya. 'Take dress *and* tracksuit *and* skirt. Maybe, the green?'

'It makes me look fat.'

If Anka said it didn't, there'd be a row.

'You choose, *dragi*. Skirt *and* dress. Then tomorrow, you have choice.'

'*A* choice. I can choose now, so I won't have to carry a stupid dress I won't wear.'

None of this would matter tomorrow. They'd have lamb, stuffed turkey. *Paprenjaci* were ready in the fridge, glazed with egg, honey, nutmeg, *lots* of white pepper. 'We can't have Easter,' Katya had said, 'without Auntie Anka's pepper cakes.'

'Blue, is more better?'

So *stupid*, to have phoned his house. His wife was even more demanding now. 'Their mother can't manage them without me. Tess can't eat without me, she's afraid of the wiggly spaghetti.' He needed cherishing. So many people around him making demands. 'Oh Anka,' he'd said the other night. 'You're a very understanding woman.'

He'd had girlfriends before, sometimes two at once. They never lasted long but sometimes, they got pregnant. Expensive, he said. Also sad, she'd thought but did not say. 'Not pleasant,' he'd said, 'telling them they had to have an abortion. But it had to be done.' The way he'd said it had somehow made her sorry for him, not them. But

144

what could he do, if his wife wouldn't sleep with him? He was a lion. The girls should have been careful, like she was. He'd *said* he didn't want another child.

She'd been a cow, a proper pig's ear cow, to make such a fuss.

Easter Saturday 26 March, Devon, 9.00 p.m.

'Wonderful, Ros,' said Irena. In firelight, Ros looked more like how Richard remembered. Could he see her nipples through her blouse? He was trying not to look. 'Have you had her Moroccan chicken before, Russel?'

'Dunno.'

Russel had been great with the police. Two witnesses plus photos made a cast-iron case.

'Let's dance,' said Rosamund. 'Got any Abba? Or something heavy and crazy – "Bat Out of Hell"? I haven't danced in so long.'

Irena got up. Guitars and girl voices filled the room.

'"Walk Like an Egyptian".' Ros laughed. 'The Bangles! Haven't heard that for years.'

Russel pushed back his chair.

'Going to bed?' said Richard 'Thanks for your help, Russel. You were brilliant. Sleep well.'

'Dance, Ros,' said Irena, clearing plates. 'I will too. But you start.'

Rosamund got up. Her hair sparkled on her shoulders. Richard stood self-consciously to face her. A ripple began at her hips and spread to her shoulders till her torso swayed like a vine. Hearing Girish say, 'Dancing is praying,' moved his pelvis nervously, side to side.

Easter Saturday 26 March, London, 11.45 p.m.

Chanting filled the dark church. The priest lit a candle.

Jesus who brings light, prayed Anka, *protect Helen. And my mother. And Tess. And my black lion.* She paused. *And all, all his family. And that boy from Eritrea.*

People at the front pressed forward to light their candles. Flames like yellow stitches filled the church. When Helen and Katya sheltered theirs with their hands, the blood glowed red through their fingers. They both held their candles well away from their hair. Helen spent all her pocket money, at the moment, on conditioner.

'*Krist je uskrsnuo!*' said Lasta and hugged her. Christ has risen! Anka kissed her back, '*Doista je uskrsnuo!*' Christ has truly risen. That beautiful word, truly.

'Goodnight, Katya,' said Anka as they left. '*Krist je uskrsnuo!*'

'Goodnight, Auntie Anka.'

'See you tomorrow.'

Anka hugged Helen, so warm and wonderful, and watched them drive off. Helen had life apart from her, she had life apart from Helen. That wasn't wrong, was it?

Coming home, she wondered if he was there already. She'd given him keys, specially cut for him. She opened the street door with that little twist to the left it needed. Had he found that difficult? But he wasn't there. She'd been so looking forward to coming home to him, as if they were living together. They *would* live together, when Tess was older.

She put on a jazz CD. At least she had time to get ready. She rubbed oil into arms, breasts and thighs and walked about the flat naked to let it sink in. Nice, if he came now! Naked, she set out clean glasses. He liked them sparkling, she'd washed them twice that afternoon.

One o'clock. He'd be here any moment. She put on a black silk corset. A basque. That's what the girl in La Senza had called it. 'Basque,' she said to the empty room. In the mirror, she looked like a porn star. She shook her hair round her shoulders, black like the silk, put on her new Spanish skirt, sat on the sofa and listened critically.

The CD finished. One-thirty. He was seeing someone else. She could never, ever trust him. Every coming was filled with his departure.

The phone rang.

'I'm on my way, just *couldn't* get away. They're talking big money, these Japs. Just passing Russell Square. Can't wait!'

146

Another CD. At last the front doorbell. She pushed the buzzer, heard him running up the stairs. His arms were round her.

'Your keys. You did not use.'

'Couldn't wait.'

Hands all over her, tongue down her throat, mouth gobbling her breasts. He lifted her off the floor, biting bare flesh between black silk and Spanish skirt.

She rested her forehead on his, wrapping his waist with her legs.

Easter Sunday 27 March, Devon, 2.00 a.m.

The remote island, and wild forest stretching on every side, determined the emotions with which I gazed upon this Bird of Paradise.

Lying on his front, Russel scrutinises a drawing of a long-tailed bird. Awesome, to have a bird named after you because you're the first to see it.

Six feet away, the other side of the wall, a young mole is moving through long grass. The faint swishing of his passage stops when he reaches a footprint left by Russel that afternoon.

Russel looks back at the inscription. He does not feel like the person he was before he came to Devon. Chennai! He sees the banks of the Waingunga. An elephant shifting its weight from one front leg to the other.

A note flops out of the book.

Dear Russel,

The man after whom you were named worked out in parallel to Darwin the understanding of evolution on which all biology rests. This volume contains his travels in South-East Asia. He did not journey with other people, like Darwin, but alone. He is my own great hero.

My best wishes for your fifteenth year.
Tobias Kellar

Outside, having reached the toe of Russel's footprint, the mole re-enters longer grass. Two wings open above him unseen like fanning hands. Flight feathers deaden the sound of air friction. Before he leaves the dint of Russel's toe the mole is dead in the stretching talons.

Easter Sunday 27 March, Kilburn, London, 3.00 a.m.

'Now young lady, this lovely lovely Sauternes. You've no *idea* how special it is.' Anka, wearing his shirt and nothing else, sat at the kitchen table heavy with love. He looked wonderful in his dark blue dressing gown. He must wear it every morning. She was more part of his life than ever.

'Oh Anka! You are the most heart-stopping creature.' He gave her a glass. 'To the most beautiful woman I've ever been in love with.' He gazed into her eyes and began to sing.

> *'Believe me, if all those endearing young charms,*
> *Which I gaze on so fondly today –*

'You're not the only singer round here, young lady –

> *'Were to change by tomorrow and fleet in my arms*
> *Like fairy gifts fading away,*
> *Thou wouldst still be adored as this moment thou art*
> *Let thy loveliness fade as it will.'*

She took a mouthful of wine like sipping sunlight and kissed him. As his lips opened, her tongue pushed it from her mouth to his. He kneaded her thigh and opened her labia with one finger.

Later, when he was asleep, she pulled the duvet high over his shoulders and listened to his breathing. That woman in his house had shut him out for years. She, Anka, was the icon he lived by. And he was paradise, the only one she'd known.

10

Easter Sunday 27 March, Devon, 1.00 p.m.

'Richard? Where in hell's name *are* you? I'm standing in some god-forsaken phonebox in the middle of medieval England, there's no mobile signal and it's pelting like rabid dogs.'

'Where's the phonebox, Tyler?'

'I'm dripping over the bloody – Dexham! Dexham Village Green. Looks like a superannuated car park.'

'Stay in your car. I'll find you. Ten minutes.'

'*Would* you? Good man!'

Richard looked up. Tyler overwhelmed him, even on the end of a phone.

'He's got as far as Dexham.'

'He always panics in a car,' said Rosamund. 'Specially if he doesn't know the way.'

'I hate map reading on my own,' said Irena. Richard knew she was afraid the lamb would overcook.

'We'll be half an hour,' he said.

'It's OK. I've turned the oven off. The lamb can breathe.'

'Like the wine. I opened two bottles, is that enough? Tyler likes his wine. I got three in Tesco's.'

'We can open the third if needed.'

'Irena's made a beautiful Easter cake,' said Rosamund.

'Irena *made a cake*?'

'Oy,' said Irena.

'A zoology special,' said Rosamund. She looked teasing and alive this morning, her hair scrunched up with little twisty curls at the side, like cowrie shells.

'Is Russel still asleep?' he asked.

149

"fraid so.'

Richard went out into the rain. If he had a son, he'd make sure he got up at the proper time.

Russel is a silky sausage of blue sleeping bag.

'Happy Easter, darling.' Rosamund sees no book, old or new. 'I've brought you some orange juice.' She puts a glass on the floor beside him, and a Smarties Easter egg. 'Dad'll be here soon. You can show him the woods after lunch if it clears.'

'Sleep a bi' more,' mumbles the blue cocoon. She thinks of little Russel, waking her at dawn to show her what the Easter Bunny brought. Even in that memory she is alone. Russel probably can't remember her and Tyler in one bed. She kisses the only visible segment of stubbled scalp.

'Here they are,' Irena calls.

'Time to get up,' she tells the sleeping bag. Through the window, she sees Tyler getting out into teeming rain and staring incredulously at the long sodden grass he is going to have to walk through.

Tyler enters the front room like a sandstorm, making the low ceiling, the primroses and bubbling fire which have held them safe for three days, feel suddenly dingy.

'Irena. How the hell *are* you? You're looking fab – those bewitching dark eyes.'

'Lovely to see you, Tyler.' Irena's face is pinkly oily from cooking. 'What a beautiful jacket. How dashing you look.'

'Do you like it? Paul Smith. Look at the stitching.'

Rosamund watches him kiss Irena's hand, put a box on the floor, glance in the one little mirror and smooth his dripping hair. All his acts of self-love, so flamboyant and exact. She knows them so well.

'Happy Easter, sweetheart.'

He kisses her. He smells of pine. Did he buy a new shower gel? Last week he complained Body Shop mango made him smell like a greengrocer. He takes a champagne magnum out of his box and delivers it into Richard's arms like a baby.

'In the cooler all the way down. I could use a drink after that drive!'

150

'We'll try to oblige.'

'The Mouton Rothschild should be opened now. I've brought three bottles.'

'What a Pandora's Box,' says Irena. 'You shouldn't have, Tyler.'

'What was Pandora's Box, exactly?' Rosamund feels as if she's on the ceiling, looking down.

'It held all the evils human beings suffer from,' says Irena.

'Unleashed on a poor male world by you women.' Tyler glances flirtatiously at Irena. 'But that's the *perfect* name for our new group! All our foxy babes. Pandora! Thanks, Irena.'

'What evils?' says Rosamund.

'Heartache, disease, overwork,' says Tyler. 'Everything we have to put up with, to provide you lot with the comforts you deserve.'

'There was Hope in there too,' says Irena, kneeling to look in Tyler's box. Even though Irena doesn't like him, thinks Rosamund, she too looks sleeker in Tyler's presence.

'Was Hope an evil?' she asks.

'Some people say it's the most dangerous one of all.'

'The pudding wine,' says Tyler, 'should go in the fridge.'

'Château d'Yquem,' reads Irena.

'Those in the loop say Château Yquem.'

'Is that Sauternes?'

'Madame!'

'My favourite.' Rosamund sees Richard look at Irena, surprised. 'I've only had it once,' she says, 'after a first night. Amazing.'

'Your fave too, isn't it, babe?' Tyler puts his arm round Rosamund. 'Got a whole case in, just for you.'

He takes a box out of straw and presents it to Irena.

'Fortnum's. Tyler, what luxury.' Irena thrusts her hands into tissue and lifts out a cake. A gold rabbit appears. Then chocolate butterflies, their filigree wings standing up like combs.

'Never seen a cake like that,' says Richard, struggling with the champagne cork.

Tyler takes up a white-chocolate egg, cameo'd in darker chocolate with a gun and hunting horn.

'For my charming son. Where is he?'

151

'On his way.'

'But this, my love, is for you.' He gives Rosamund a package and pushes her hair aside to kiss her ear. She lifts out a porcelain egg, midnight blue, painted with gilt silhouettes: crinolines, parasols and a man in a tricorn hat playing a lute.

'Like it, Rosie?' He gazes in her eyes. The pine smell is stronger. 'Got it in Burlington Arcade.'

'Exquisite, darling. *Thank* you.'

'Chap must get his beloved something as gorgeous as she is on a festal day.'

Russel is standing at the passage door.

'Hi, Russ, fancy some champers? How you doing with that cork, Richard, want a hand – Oh!' The cork hit the ceiling. 'Good man.'

Rosamund watches Richard pour champagne into the glasses she re-washed this morning while Irena placed eggs on her sunken cake. Tyler claps Russel on the shoulder, hands him a glass and waves at the white egg.

'Get yourself outside that, young man.'

There is a short silence.

'Cheers,' says Russel, looking at the floor.

'*Slancha*,' says Tyler, sweeping his glass in the air. 'Happy Easter, everyone. What have you all been up to?'

'Yesterday was too rainy to do much,' says Irena. 'On Friday we went to the woods.'

'See anything Russ?' says Tyler. 'Get in touch with your inner badger?'

Russel raises his head and stares at him, blue eyes into blue. Rosamund feels ice fingers on her spine. No one should look at anyone like that.

'I'll help you bring the food in,' she says and follows Irena to the kitchen. Tyler's idea of a party is people admiring him. She shouldn't have let him come. She hands melon slices out of the fridge. Blue plates with gold rims.

'You've used your lovely plates. The ones at your wedding.'

'Our only good china,' says Irena. 'What my mum called good, anyway. They were a present for *her* wedding.'

'Where have you whisked our own cake to? Sorry about that.'

'In the cupboard with our wine. Richard will enjoy them next week.'

Picturing them happy, alone with each other at last, Rosamund puts the melon on the table. Tyler is finishing a story, Richard is listening politely, Russel is looking out of the window.

She remembers Scott's face as she pirouetted in that shawl. Last night, dancing with Richard, she had imagined it was Scott. I'm enjoying being my body again, she thinks. And it has absolutely nothing to do with Tyler.

Dad empties his glass with a noisy sigh. Russel squirms, the sound is scratching his soul. He knows how the owl feels with those birds mobbing it.

'Hits the spot, doesn't it, Russ? Could you give me a refill, Rick? So, Irena, any TV work lately?'

'I'm in the education department at the Globe.' Irena unties her apron and sits down. Richard fills her water glass.

Richard was proper quiet, moving through the woods. The policemen thought he was cool, too. What if Richard were his dad? Or Scott? Irena's eyes are browny-green like bare woods with green buds. Forests don't lie. Nor do animals. Lying is all his dad knows how to do.

'What about you, Rick? How are the snakes? Bet you have some hair-raising stories.'

'I'm starting research in Bengal soon,' says Richard. 'I've got to learn a whole new India.'

'Oh come on, are they that different?' His dad does a singsong voice like the guy in the corner shop who sells Rizlas. 'We have very nice snakes here, sir, very nice.'

No one smiles.

'Bengal's *very* different,' says Richard. 'They worship a snake goddess called Manasa.'

'Lots of snake goddesses in the music business,' says his dad. 'Just signed a new one, matter of fact.'

Russel sees his mum glance at Irena.

153

'What's yours like, Rick?'

'Naked and wreathed in cobras.'

'How d'you fancy that, Russ!'

He hates it when his dad talks like that.

'They call her the Poison Remover,' says Richard. 'They say that if you don't die when a cobra bites you, Manasa saved you.'

'She must be the patron saint of every snakologist.'

'But I, being a scientist,' Richard catches Russel's eye, 'think the reason you didn't die was that the snake had no venom in its glands.'

He likes that Richard says things only he and Richard know about.

'If you die, they say Manasa's against you.'

'The bitch.' His dad is kind of laughing at Richard.

'Her left eye is the poison eye. The right is her nectar eye.'

'Nectar eye?' asks Mum. She is wearing a red dress. The top of her tits show. There's red ribbon in her hair.

'One look brings you back to life.' Richard is gazing at Mum like he did at the deer in the woods. 'Manasa is Shiva's daughter.' Richard pauses. 'Well, in a way.'

'How do you mean, Rick?'

'Shiva was sitting by a pond – er – thinking about his wife, Parvati, and ejaculated into the water.' Russel looks down. His dad laughs. 'His sperm dripped into the water on to the snake king. The snake king's wife created Manasa out of it.'

'I'll bring the lamb in,' says Irena.

'Allow me!' His dad doesn't like talk that's nothing to do with him. 'Can't let you sweat over a hot kitchen alone, darling.' Dad calls all women darling.

'Got a good biology teacher at school, Russel?' asks Richard.

'OK.'

'Biology and maths are his strong subjects. Aren't they, Russel?'

'Chill, Mum.'

'Where are the glasses for the red?' he hears his dad say in the kitchen.

'We only have these ones,' he hears Irena reply. His dad comes in and picks up everyone's glass.

'Russ? Finish your champers, let me wash your glass.'

'Don't want wine. Cheers.'

His dad returns with clean glasses, then again with a lump of meat.

'A triumph.'

'Bit overcooked I'm afraid,' says Irena.

'Shall I?' His dad takes a carving knife. 'Now, Rosie, little bit of outside for you? Don't like it too pink, do you, sweetie? I know what *you* like.' His dad looks at his mum like he's trying to make her share a secret but her face is shut.

'Perfect, Irena. Not dry at all. Well – not very.'

'Afraid you won't find much pink.'

'What about you, Tyler?' says Richard. 'How's your work?'

'Fab.' His dad hacks meat. 'Just done a deal with a Chink importer. Got a new singer going huge in America. You'll be hearing Amba Fox everywhere, soon.'

'Tell us more about Shiva and snakes, Richard.' His mum's face is red now.

'There are Tamil hymns . . .' Richard's voice trails off.

'Can you sing them?'

'I can *say* one or two, in English.'

'Like?'

'"Tell me friend, what strange man is this with a snake in his hand?"' Richard chants suddenly like a priest. '"He is god of all who live and move, beautiful god of the matted locks."'

'How cool is that?' says Dad, tossing his own locks.

'Which *is* Shiva, exactly?' says his mum. 'I get those Indian gods muddled up.'

'Better sort them out before you go back,' says Irena.

'Darling!' says Dad in that raised-eyebrow way, pretending to be polite but really sarcastic.

'Sorry, Ros,' Irena says to his mum softly.

'Just an idea. Irena thought I should get back to my roots.'

'When, may I ask?' says Dad.

'Not term time, obviously. Maybe after Russel's exams.'

Russel wants to say again he can stay with Scott but remembers

Dad holding the door and looking at Scott like daring him to come in. Richard hands him a plate.

'OK for you, Russel?'

'Cheers.'

'It'd be terribly hot, late June,' Richard says. 'Though you might hit the monsoon. You're welcome to look in on my work.'

'Wouldn't I be in your way?'

'Not at all.'

'C'n you go to Chennai?' Russel says. 'Or South-East Asia?'

'*South*-East Asia,' said his dad. 'Not Souf! That's nothing to do with India, don't they teach you anything at that school? It's the other side of the – er – Arabian Sea. Richard, correct me if I'm wrong.'

'Indian Ocean,' said Richard.

'Mind if I take my jacket off?' Dad is pissed now. The folds by his nose glisten with sweat. His fat cheeks are flushed. 'Chennai – that's Madras, isn't it? Get some good strong curries there, my girl.'

Dad gets up and his chair squawks on the stone. He goes round the table pouring more wine.

'Russ?'

'I'm good.' If only he were lean. Skunk helps him put up with Dad's voice.

'Are you going to leave me and Russ all on our tod, sweetie? Whaddya think, Russ? Shall we let her go, rough it by ourselves?'

He can't eat all the meat. He feels Mum looking. Irena will think he doesn't like it. He does, it's proper tasty, just too much.

'It was only an idea,' says Irena. 'Shall we clear?'

'What will this singer of yours sing, Tyler?' says Richard. He's not interested in Dad's work any more than Dad gives a shit for his. He's trying to be polite.

'I'll let you know when it's recorded. Get you an advance copy.'

They all know he won't. And Richard wouldn't want it if he did.

Irena carries in a cake. His mum said they'd made one like a bird's nest but this one's flat.

'A work of art, Tyler,' says Irena. Russel pushes back his chair.

'Goin' for a walk.'

'Had enough?' says Irena lightly.

156

'I'm good.'

Kaa slides beside him to the door. Maybe Richard and Irena can hear his scales whisper over the stone floor.

'There are boots in the passage,' says Richard. 'Take my anorak if you want. Might start raining again.'

'Don't worry, Tyler,' says Irena as the front door closes. 'He'll change.'

Tyler always has this effect, thinks Rosamund. All women, even Irena, try to soothe him.

'He just wants to be alone,' she says. 'He's fourteen.'

'He's brilliant at being blank,' says Irena.

'Too right,' says Tyler. 'Got it down to a fine art.'

'It's self-protection, isn't it?' says Irena gently.

'He's a bright boy, Tyler,' says Richard. 'Can I have some more cake, please?'

'Fantastic cake, Tyler.'

'I can't have a second helping,' says Rosamund.

'Come on, angel, one teensy weensy bit?'

Tyler cuts himself and her a slice. She knows he finds Irena and Richard hard work. But this is OK, isn't it? Her perfectly normal sullen teenager. Her husband being nice to her friends.

'Are you really coming to India?' asks Richard. 'You're welcome, but it's not that interesting in the rains. Good for snakes, but not much else.'

'She can visit Darjeeling,' says Irena. 'Tea gardens. Hill stations. Stay with my theatre friend there.'

There is a short pause.

'Well, bottoms up.' Tyler brandishes a glass of gorse-yellow Sauternes.

'Nectar,' says Rosamund. The wine is sweet fire. She too feels the need to soothe Tyler. How does he make you want to pamper him? 'I just *know* the gods drank Sauternes.'

'Specially Château Yquem,' said Tyler. 'Nothing but the best for the gods. And you, beloved.' He gazes at her, head on one side. 'Here's to your snake goddess, Rick, and her nectar eye. Aaagh . . .

better than ever! Have to say, I did have a slug myself last night, to make sure.'

'Could be dangerous to toast Manasa,' says Richard. 'There's Shiva energy all round her.'

'What Shiva energy?' Rosamund pulls off her ribbon, shakes her hair down and feels both Tyler and Richard looking.

'It's so warm,' she says apologetically. Tyler's eyes are bloodshot. Hasn't he slept? What will happen tonight? She hasn't shared a room with Tyler, not a whole night, for ten years.

'Destruction, isn't it?' asks Irena.

'*And* creation,' says Richard. 'Shiva's dancing all the time. Now, this minute, he's dancing the universe into extinction, and recreating it. He's Lord of the Dance.'

Tyler smiles winningly.

'I danced in the morning when the world was begun,' he sings. 'I danced in the moon and the stars and the sun.'

'That's it,' says Richard. 'That's Shiva.'

Rosamund remembers Tyler singing this years ago, in her student room.

> '*I danced on a Friday when the sky turned black;*
> *It's hard to dance with the devil on your back.*'

'I thought Lord of the Dance was Christ.' Irena lays her head on Richard's shoulder. 'It's today's song, isn't it? Easter. The sky turned black on Friday when they crucified Him.'

> '*Dance, then, wherever you may be,*
> *I am the Lord of the Dance, said He.*'

'Maybe it's both,' says Rosamund. 'Shiva *and* Christ.'

Tyler refills his glass and hers. He starts a new song, gazing ardently at her.

> '*Believe me, if all those endearing young charms,*
> *Which I gaze on so fondly today . . .*'

She remembers Tyler singing that on Waterloo Bridge, the Thames plaiting and sparkling below. Tyler kissing her, still humming, his throat vibrating with the tune, and necklaces of lights twinkling along the Embankment.

'Thou will still be adored as this moment thou art . . .'

He means it, completely. When he sings.

'How do you remember all the words?' says Richard. Richard is hating this, she knows. As Tyler often says, Richard is a stiff old stick. She could never have married him.

> *'You say you want*
> *Diamonds on a ring of gold . . .'*

'Tyler!' Rosamund feels a kick in her gut and hears her voice screech. 'Not "All I Want Is You"!'

'Indulge me.'

> *'Water in a time of dryness,*
> *A harbour in the tempest . . .'*

How dare he sing that? Even if they had sex tonight, which they won't, he wouldn't stop whatever else he's doing. He just wants to know he still has power to pull.

> *'All the promises we make*
> *From the cradle to the grave*
> *When all I want is you.'*

Rosamund slams down her glass. This wine is poison now. She's had enough lunch party. All Tyler needs is an audience. The only thing he loves is himself.

'Shall we try a walk?' says Irena, stacking plates.

'It's nearly dark,' says Richard.

'I'll wash,' says Rosamund to Irena. 'You put away. I don't know where your posh plates go.'

*

Outside, tucked behind the ivy where other birds cannot see, the tawny owl feels a tickle and opens his eyes. One lone parasite, a dipteran evolved from an insect which now exists only as a fossil in limestone deposits, has discovered it cannot puncture his skin. It is the larva of a fly which breeds in nests and sucks blood only from the silk-soft skin of nestlings. Last night this owl perched on the nest and it strayed on to his feathers. Now it is searching for softness, for food.

Tickles are part of the owl's life. He supports two species of louse, several blood parasites and more intestinal ones.

He closes his eyes. The air is not dark enough yet.

Whu whoooo . . .

'Fucking owl!' Tyler's impatience fills the little bedroom. It is eleven o'clock. Rosamund is lying under the duvet trying to finish *Othello*. She must give it back to Irena before she goes tomorrow. 'How does anyone get any sleep round here?'

'You'd rather have screeching brakes and police sirens?'

'What I grew up with, darling. How human beings ought to live, having a fab time with their own kind around them.' He kneels on the floor to open his bag. 'There's no space for even a chair.' He pulls out his dressing gown. He never wears pyjamas. Is he going to undress in here? 'Irena looks rather draggle-tailed.'

'You said she looked bewitching.'

'I was being *galant*. As for Richard, opening that bottle – what a wuss. And his nails. Does he never wash?'

'Keep your voice down.'

She knows his body so well. The broad chest, the rivulets of curly hair on muscly legs. She knows exactly how it feels. That body made her enjoy, for the first time, being a woman. For a second she feels a deep shock of desire, as if from an electric fence. It is replaced by a blast of pain. His body is smeared with years of treachery which turns desire to toxic waste. For three nights this room has been asylum. Now it is danger.

She hears her heart, like hoof-taps. Some harmless animals pretend they are dangerous. Moths disguise themselves as hornets, wolf

160

snakes copy the colours and smells of the krait. But what about the dangerous species? Some, like rattlesnake and cobra, have warning signals: leave me alone or you'll be sorry. Animals who live near them are born with the instinct to recognise the signals and keep clear. Like the women – she's seen them – who take one look at Tyler and move away.

But other dangerous species copy the colours of their surroundings. And some women walk right into the ambush where the predator is lying in wait. The path through the wood is never safe.

'They have no idea how much that Sauternes cost.' Tyler is willing her to look at him. 'Or the claret.'

'Does that matter?' She keeps her eyes on Shakespeare. 'They loved them.'

'And no TV. How can anyone not have television?'

'It's only one night, Tyler.'

'I could have taken you to lovely lovely Marrakesh for Easter! Russ could have gone scuba diving and met some charming houris.'

'Not much scuba diving in the desert.'

'Well . . .'

'And you said you had to work.' She is married to a monster. There is a tiny sweet vulnerable part of him that's genuine, but most of him is monster.

'Well, sure . . . but if I'd said I'd *booked* a holiday, I'd have swung it.'

Swiftly, but not swiftly enough, he disappears an indigo spongebag piped with emerald under the dressing gown.

'That's new.'

'Cool, isn't it? Got it when I popped into Fortnums. Little treat to myself.' He stands up. 'Only mirrors in the house are in the bathroom and that poky smoky room downstairs.' He goes out. She hears him lock the bathroom door.

Whu – whooooo.

She remembers what it was like, feeling stunned with happiness that she'd found a home in Tyler's love. Someone she could lay her self against and be safe. I gave my heart to him, she thinks. Can't get it back.

Should she go to India, just for a couple of weeks? Break out of the mould of hopelessness that encases her? Father needn't know. And it might get Russel closer to Tyler. But what about Tyler himself? Give him carte blanche and then what?

He's back, in his dressing gown. He stands looking at her, head on one side, a cautious twinkle in his eyes. He sits on the bed, which sinks like a beast of burden. Hot from his shower, he drops an arm round her, lifts his legs to the bed and leans back on the pillow. Her heart beating like a trapped bird, she contemplates Tyler's naked toes.

'Tragically undersized bed, isn't it? What cheap crap are you reading?' He bends back the cover. 'Fuck me, darling, what's that for?' He pauses. 'You looked fab today. Your hair's got more volume in it these days. Suits you.'

'How *could* you sing that song?'

'Just trying to make the party go.' He does injured brilliantly. *Harbour in the tempest. All I want is you.* 'But, sweetie, they were bags of fun, weren't they, those days?'

'Do you ever think what the words of that song actually mean?' *You say you want your love to work out right* . . . 'Get out,' she hisses. 'Just get the fuck out.'

Russel has been trying to see the owl. But now he is lying on his bed. On the pillow is a dead oak leaf. The waste-paper basket holds a white-chocolate egg in an unopened box.

'The Aru Islanders,' he reads, 'begged me to tell them the real name of my country. They said I was deceiving them. Whoever heard of such a name? they said. Ang–Lang?'

That's England, whispers Kaa.

'I know, man,' Russel whispers back.

'Angerlung? Un Lung? That can't be the name of your country! Whoever heard of such a name?'

Through the window is one white star. Betrayal is everywhere. The men, the badger, the dogs. And him, he's evil as those men. Bono died because of him. Never, in all his life, would Bono's pain stop being his fault.

162

He hears steps in the front room, and a clatter as if something has fallen. He squirms out of the sleeping bag and stands, shivering.

Kewick? Kewick?

He goes to the window, sees nothing, pads down the passage and hears Kaa following. At the end is a vertical splinter of light. Through the crack he sees his dad, mouth folded like he is furious, carrying a blanket. Dad picks up a fallen chair, lies on the sofa and presses buttons on his mobile. Russel knows that mobile. Well good at getting a signal. He'd like a phone like that.

'Darling,' his dad whispers into the stub of black and silver. 'Just wanted to wish you goodnight. Happy Easter again. And all my love – to the end of the world!'

Kaa circles Russel in a spiral, a tubular eggcup of iron.

'Sorry I couldn't ring before, couldn't get a second alone.'

The python is a vine stem holding him up.

'Everyone's asleep. *Such* a dreary day, thought of you *all* the time. How was Easter, how was Helen?'

Kaa's head is on his shoulder.

'You're breaking up – signal's hopeless here in the sticks – go to sleep, sweetheart. Just wanted to say I adore you! Sleep tight in that beautiful bed. Wish I was still in it.'

The corridor is freezing.

'Oh, sweetheart, me too. More than anything I've ever loved. Take my heart with you, into your dreams.'

The wood in the grate has red edges like windows of burning cities.

'Go to sleep with my breath in your ear.'

His dad snaps shut the mobile. Then, with the flick which Russel used to practise copying, he opens it again.

'Hello, sweet thing,' he whispers, in a different voice. 'How the hell *are* you? Couldn't let the day end without wishing my best girl a happy Easter.'

Russel stands without breathing.

'*Really*, Amba. Big girl like you? What did you get up to on Saturday night, after I *tore* myself away?'

We be one blood, thou and I, breathes the python in Russel's ear.

'What's the most luscious arse in London wearing tonight, young lady?'

Russel retreats towards his room. The door clicks. He stands motionless till he hears Dad's murmur again. Pressing his face to the window he sees the star. And round it other stars, like white full stops. The cold of interstellar space.

Un Lung, where no one can breathe. *Anger Lung,* where he has to live.

His dad is full of shite.

MOUSE LEAP

MOUSE LEAF

11

Monday 11 April, Primrose Hill, London, 11.00 a.m.

'It's a mad idea, Irena, India in monsoon.'

  'Go somewhere else then.'

  'I'd be in Richard's way.'

'He says you won't. And you'd love my friend Alisha. She's a theatre director in Darjeeling and runs a B-and-B there. You can stay with her.'

  'But my dad . . .'

'He's the other end of India, for fuck's sake. You're halfway through your life, Ros. *Do* something!'

Rosamund looks at the garden. Two camellias are out now, one red, one white. Richard's like my dad, she thinks. Might this be a first step back?

  'How's Russel?'

  'Up and down. He loves helping that guy train his dog.'

  'Scott.'

  'Yep.'

  'Going to shag him?'

  'Hey.'

  'Come *on*, Ros. What's with this paralysis?'

The doorbell rings.

  'I must go.'

'Russel Fairfax?' says a man in a crash helmet, holding out a package. Has Russel ordered some weird thing online? She takes it to the kitchen and puts it on a shelf. Irena's right, she's paralysed. As if she'd been bitten long ago by one of Father's damn snakes and the toxin never left her veins. Maybe she should try hypnosis or cognitive therapy rather than India.

*

167

Outside, the fox cubs want to use their new-opened eyes. The vixen chivvies them down to the den but they flow back up, drawn to the light. Eventually all three sit under the brambles, watched anxiously by both parents. A new, more dangerous phase of child-rearing has begun.

At teatime, Rosamund hears Russel in the hall.

'Hi, love,' she calls. 'Parcel for you. Want some tea? Toast?'

'I'm good.'

She pours milk into her own tea and looks up. Russel is standing by the shelf, trousers silting off his hips, staring as if his whole being has been wiped. In the opened shell of paper is a black canister.

'Looks like a bomb. What is it?'

'Bono's ashes.'

'Oh, darling.'

Silence.

'What do you want to do with them?'

'Like I know?'

Wednesday 13 April, Covent Garden, London, 1.30 p.m.

'My dad was in the army.'

Rosamund sits opposite Scott. Between them are red and green stripes of a tablecloth in a Cypriot restaurant. Tufts of brown fur spill from his open collar. She wants to stroke them.

'How's your salad?'

'Lovely. How are your meatballs?'

'Very tasty.'

Rosamund sips red wine. Scott is calming, like a friendly animal.

'My gran came from the Hebrides. Why I'm called Scott. Saw seals with her once, on the rocks.' He smiles his up-and-down smile. She feels as if she can see her life spread out beside her but doesn't know what's in it. 'My most treasured memory,' he says. 'You must have a lot of those yourself.'

'Some,' she says cautiously. He waits, but she says nothing.

'Dad wanted me to do the army. I picked police to be different.

Hated a lot of it but I did wildlife courses and worked my way to this. I'd have liked to have done photography, really,' he adds wistfully. 'I take wildlife photos, my spare time. I'm getting a new camera next week.' He looks at her anxiously, the way Bono used to look back in the park to check she was with him. 'That wine OK? I don't know wines like your good man.'

'Oh, Scott. Don't call Tyler my good man.'

'What should I call him?' He takes her hand. His fingers are strong and warm. She feels as if she's on fire.

'Whatever Tyler is, he's not good.' She hasn't fancied anyone for so long. How did Irena know? Once, Scott would have seemed boring. Not now. She feels she's struggling up through waters she thought had closed for ever over her head. 'Well – a lot of Tyler isn't. But he *is* Russel's dad. When Russel was little, Tyler made me realise what I'd missed as a child.'

'How come?'

'I never knew fathers played with children. Cuddled them. But when Russel stopped thinking the sun shone out of Tyler's arse, Tyler couldn't cope. It's cold war between them now. And Tyler and I – we're such a mess. I'm no *good*.'

'You *are* good. Trust a policeman.' He rubs his thumb over hers. She curls her fingers inside his palm. She's not used to talking, except to Irena. Suddenly, being married to Tyler feels like a tapestry with thousands of little stitches all starting to fray at once. Scott's gaze, though, is butterflies, feathering her face with their wings.

'We're very different individuals,' says Scott, and the butterflies are gone. How tricky it is, fancying someone. It comes and goes, minute to minute. Why did it fade at *individuals*? Because he's so earnest.

But what's wrong with earnest? It's precisely what Tyler is not.

Tyler's fun, though. I'm locked, she thinks, in an underground war with Tyler. If I let him spoil me for other people, he's won.

'Should I go to India for a break?'

'Great idea.' He looks at her with the blue-brown eyes of a shaggy mammal. *Beautiful*, they say. Tyler's compliments mean nothing and are often a smokescreen for guilt. This accolade is silent, therefore true. Or is it? She realises she doesn't know how it feels, to trust. 'Your dad lives there?'

'In the south. This'd be north. Bengal. My friend Irena's husband will be there so there's someone to touch base with.'

'Where's your mum?'

'She died when I was two.'

'Sorry.' He pauses. 'Illness?'

'Train accident.'

His hand tightens round hers.

'Crash?'

'At the time, I was told she fell on the line. Later I met someone who said it was suicide.'

'What does your dad say?'

'I've never asked. He was having an affair when it happened. That's when I left college, when I knew it was Father's fault. So I never finished my biology, you see.'

'Maybe it wasn't suicide. Or his fault. Why not ask?'

'We haven't spoken for thirteen years.' Suddenly she feels like crying. Father was a monster, but he was what she'd had. She'd realised suddenly, long ago when Russel was little, that she had been close to Father, once. She'd been telling Russel about the garden she grew up in. In her stories, she was always in it alone. 'What about your daddy?' he said. He knew her mum had died. My daddy was always away in the jungle. 'What about school?' Grandpa taught me. 'In the jungle?' No. At home. 'Then you weren't alone,' Russel had said with satisfaction.

Now she feels her upsetness washing over Scott like waves round a rock. His hands cup hers. A crying human baby can trigger a care reaction in a grizzly bear and something about her seems to trigger one in him.

'So you became a mum,' he says, 'without knowing what it was to have one.'

'I suppose – yes.' Fancying him is back again. She feels her vision clarify, as if she'd lived in half light before.

'Those books of yours are working a treat. More to dog training than I thought. And Russel's great.'

'He loved seeing you on Saturday. But then Bono's ashes came in the post. He's so unsee-throughable.' She sighs. 'Tyler calls it sullen.'

'It's the age.'

'How old are you, Scott?'

'Thirty-six. You?'

'Thirty-seven.'

'Another bottle,' says the waiter.

'Must get back to work. Coffee?'

'Fine.'

'Maybe you mean fine, this time.'

They smile shyly at each other. Her heart bumps as if she'd dreamed of falling off a ledge. Is she lost, or found? How do you tell?

'An RSPCA guy called Dennis, old wildlife spy of ours, has retired and moved house. He and Sarah want a new garden. Don't know if they can afford you . . .'

'I'm not expensive! Oh, Scott, I'd love to.' Is she overdoing it? Surely her signals are as unmistakable as the mating ritual of a demoiselle crane.

He hands her a neatly written name and address.

'Dennis and Sarah. Give them a bell.'

Wednesday 13 April, Kilburn, London, 9.30 p.m.

'Where's the corkscrew, sweetie? God, I need a drink.' He was a sad, angry lion today and his mouth was a thin zip.

'What is, *dragi*?'

'I don't do boring.' He spat the word bitterly, pulling the cork with a vicious pop. 'That's what my charming son calls me. No point staying around for someone you bore, is there?'

Anka put her arms round him.

'Never boring,' she whispered, and gave his throat a little bite.

'Those glasses are filthy. Can you give them a wash?'

She stood at the sink, soaping beneath Papa Haydn. Suddenly he had lifted her skirt and was in her from behind.

171

'Oh, Anka . . .' He squashed her against the sink and thrust deeper. 'Oh, sweetheart. We fit so perfectly together.'

'That's what sex should be, you hot bitch,' he said afterwards, over the wine. 'Unexpected. Raw.'

'Always?' Papa Haydn looked suddenly contemptuous. But which of them did he despise?

Saturday 16 April, Primrose Hill, London, 12.30 p.m.

What is a naked Barbie doll doing on the lawn? Rosamund has found odd things in the garden lately. An empty Flora oil bottle, a plastic stegosaurus. Who's chucking them in? She looks severely at the fence but the family this side is away. On the other is a retired civil servant. Does he have grandchildren? She looks back at the house and sees Tyler and Russel facing each other in the kitchen, their eyes nearly level.

By the time she goes in, Russel has gone.

'What was that about?'

Tyler shrugs, holding a bottle of Tio Pepe.

'Snifter before lunch?'

Maybe things would be better if she wasn't here.

Saturday 16 April, Parliament Hill, London, 4.00 p.m.

'Good *dog*. Look at that. Came back straight away. You've done wonders, mate.'

Bramble looks up, adoring. Russel plays with the tasselly ears.

'D'you think the world's like, just, Scott? Fair?'

'People can be fair.' Scott doesn't bullshit like Dad. 'They're often not. But they know what fair *is*.'

'No but, like, the world. Bigger than people. There's so much shite.'

'I know, son. Can't be a copper and not.'

Wind rustles the trees. Scott's new camera swings from his neck. Scott has let him use it to take photos of Bramble.

172

'Fucking game's over for the planet, innit? That's people. But somethin' bigger must've, like, let it happen.' All the time now, he feels Bono watching him. Maybe he shouldn't take photos of Bramble. Why should one be dead and not the other? Not himself?

'Must just be as fair as we can,' says Scott.

Next day, at the computer, Russel hears Bono breathing behind him with a raspy snuffle, but when he turns there's nothing there. What he does hear is Dad, climbing heavily up the stairs, now opening the door. There are white threads on the rubbed edge of his collar. His belly is going out and in fast. The furrows between his cheeks and mouth look as if his skin has been hung up wet then dried wrinkled.

'Can't get this bloody machine to work, Russ. Can't get online. Could you give me a hand, old man? You're so fab at it.'

'Dunno about Macs.'

They stand, looking at each other. Dad turns away.

'Your mother says it's lunch in five.'

He hates it when Dad tries to talk teenage.

Rosamund feels all wrong, sitting at Sunday lunch pretending to be a family. Her head feels tied with a band of fog.

'Are you going to India?' says Tyler. 'We need to know, don't we, Russ?'

Tyler doesn't want her to go. His life is a delicately constructed pile of falsehoods, he must be worrying what would happen if the central piece, the wife at home, disappeared.

'Will you go into jungle with Richard?'

This is the first thing Russel has said all weekend. Why does he want her to go? Because Tyler doesn't?

'Maybe.' She removes their plates. 'What about those ashes, guys? We could scatter them on Primrose Hill. I'd love to think of Bono up there, his ears blowing in the wind.'

Russel gazes at Tyler's chest as at a wall of sewage, stands up and pads out of the kitchen. Rosamund thinks of little Russel, refusing to sit at this same table unless it was by his daddy. She puts a hand on Tyler's shoulder.

'You think India's a bad idea?'

'What'd you do Rosie, for fuck's sake? If I have to fork out for an expensive holiday for you, make it somewhere fab like LA.'

'I want to do something of mine for once. Like you do all the time!'

'Think I *want* to be here at weekends?' he says, suddenly vicious. That doesn't happen often but when it does his mouth goes tight and his voice reverts, more Eton than Brixton. 'I could be in a million places.'

'Bet you could.' She starts loading the machine. 'Dammit, Tyler, I *will* go. After Russel's exams. He'll still be at school, you don't have to worry about daytime. But you'll have to look after your son evenings, mornings and weekends. And I'll pay for my trip myself.'

'How, may I ask?'

'I'm seeing someone about a garden tomorrow.'

'Blow me down. You dark horse. Well, good for you.'

In the front garden, a fox cub chasing a leaf emerges from the rhododendrons and is seen by three boys in the road. One throws a stone. It hits his spine and he lies there, twitching. Two magpies fly down. The vixen runs at them. One flies up over her head while the other pecks the cub's eye. The other cubs see snapping teeth and flapping wings. As the vixen drives one magpie into the air the other plunges its beak into tissue behind her, slicing shreds of live muscle from a tiny belly. The life span of an urban fox is two years, average. Most never get that far.

As dusk falls the vixen rejoins the other two cubs with a whimper like a tuning fork struck underground.

Monday 25 April, Potters Bar, 10.30 a.m.

Before knocking at the yellow door, Rosamund turns her mobile off. No one will phone her anyway but this is work with a capital W.

'Come in, pet.' Sarah has eager brown eyes and fluffy hair.

'Pleased to meet you.' Dennis, wide-shouldered with rosy cheeks

174

and grey moustache, walks her into a sitting room looking out on bare clods rimmed with a raw new fence.

'That's a good space,' says Rosamund, as Sarah brings coffee. 'Lots of light and mature trees. South wall. It could be really lovely.'

'We only had a yard before,' says Dennis. 'Sarah wants a water feature.'

Rosamund opens her portfolio.

'I haven't done many of those. Haven't done much of anything yet. Here's a water feature. But very stylised.' Tyler's friends had demanded a silver ball with water frilling over it.

Sarah says nothing.

'Here's my own garden.'

'That's *beautiful*. I'd like one like that.'

'This is how it started, thirteen years ago. Trees at the back, like you. No rose arch. Boring straight side beds.'

'How long did it take to change?'

'This, here, is after two years. What's fun, is watching it find its own shape.'

'How would you proceed here?' says Dennis.

'You've got depth but not width. Make the most of that south wall – summer flowers, autumn colour, interesting winter shapes. Plant the other side with shade-loving bushes. Put a terrace here.'

'A patio.'

'Yes. Like this.' She draws on her new Ryman's pad.

'What about Sarah's water feature?'

'You could have a small pond *here*. Would you want a fountain?'

'Sure.' Dennis says it like Scott. 'Make a splash, why not?'

'We'd have to dig an electricity channel.'

'What would that cost?'

'I'll find out. That'd be the biggest single expense. I'd charge three hundred for my time, hire people, buy plants and give you receipts. How about patio lights?'

'How much would they be?'

'I'll find that out too.'

She walks out, measures, sketches. Rooks wheel overhead. Dennis and Sarah watch from the window.

'I'll post you my estimate,' she says, coming in, 'and a copy of these drawings. It'll cost over a thousand. You may not want to spend all that. You might prefer to do it yourselves.'

'No, pet.' Sarah puts a hand on her arm. 'We like you.'

'Don't undersell yourself,' says Dennis. 'We want to do it properly.'

They shake hands.

'You used to work with Scott?' She feels shy saying his name.

'Liaised with him all the time. Great man.'

Rosamund parks in a high street and sits in the car, watching people carry shopping bags. This is the Beginning. Her garden, rewarding her for the hours she's given it. She feels as if she's woken up in Sleeping Beauty's castle. She's lived so far away from who she was. Dropping out of college. PR in Tyler's office then dropping out of that too. The only thing she's done is the garden. She thought she was doing it for Russel and Tyler but it turned out to be for her.

She gets out. In a shop window she sees, behind her own reflection, a little girl with curly hair like herself aged seven. She remembers a birthday, she's sure it was seven, that magic number, when the housekeeper, a little shrivelled woman with enormous eyes – Alagu, that was her name – gave her a pink trowel and asked the gardener for a corner of earth, for Rosamund to plant things in. That thrill, of seeing the tiny specks she put in red earth come out green and big! Going to bed imagining how the flowers would look. Alagu helping her imagine, tucking her under the mosquito net.

There *were* things she loved, back then. It wasn't only Parvati and the dancing. It was Alagu and gardening, too.

Rosamund enters Sainsbury's. Frozen Foods blows cold on her arms. In Coffee and Tea she spots an indigo packet. Tea-Garden Tea, Darjeeling, with an orange tiger gazing over a darkling plain. She switches her mobile on.

'OK, Irena. Where d'you get cheap tickets to India?'

'I'll ask Richard.'

Rosamund pictures Irena's phone lying in the room where Tyler slept that Easter night. Next morning he'd gestured at the blanket on the sofa. 'She said I was snoring. I ask you Rick. Snoring. Isn't that our *privilege*?'

'Here's the number,' says Irena. 'You fly to Calcutta, then catch a train to New Jalpaiguri.'

'Sounds impossibly remote.'

'It is. But it'll be wonderful. I'm so glad you're going.'

Monday 25 April, Soho, London, 9.15 p.m.

In the Thai restaurant, Anka caught him gazing at a poster on the wall of a girl with long silvery hair. He glanced at her and propelled her quickly forward.

'What is, *dragi*?'

'Just one of my stable. Blimey, a table at last.'

The room was a sea of glitter. Even the tablecloths glistened. Gold dragons curvetted on the walls. Two girls pulled out bamboo chairs and lit a candle in a frosted-glass chalice where it pulsed like a star in mist.

He ran a hand through his black mane.

'How the hell *are* you? Friend of mine back from South America told me about the system there called – what was it – *Hacienda*. Should have it here.'

'What is?'

'On the estate, one has one's wife and family. In town, the mistress. Everyone does it.'

'Every man, you mean, Mr Music Master. What women are doing, when he is not there?'

'That's not the point.' He looked deep in her eyes, her soul. 'How gorgeous you are. I don't deserve you.'

'Weekend, was good?'

'Wife's so arctic! No one has the right to be so private.' Frowning, he tasted the wine. 'She used to tell such fab jokes. God she was funny. Not many women tell a decent joke, but she did. We used to laugh all the time.' He sighed. 'Dunno what happened, really.' Anka had never heard him speak like this before. 'I just can't measure up.' He finished the wine in one gulp and refilled his glass. 'I impress tor

177

ten minutes, then what? Person who gets me best is her fucking little friend.'

Anka's heart felt cold and dense as if packed in foil.

'Is five years am loving you, *dragi*. Not, ten minutes.'

'Sweetie.' He kissed her fingers, nibbling the tips.

'New laptop, is OK?'

'Doing my head in. Son won't lift a finger to help. Think I'm going off my own child.' He looked so lost.

'But Tess! Is playing in garden? Now, is warm?' Sometimes, late at night, he phoned her from that garden when his wife was asleep. She imagined a sandpit in it, like the one she had always wished Helen to have.

'Garden looks so fab. You should have one, sweetie. Wife's brilliant at it.'

This was upsettingly different from other dinners.

'But – Tess?'

'Fanfuckingtastic. Have another glass.'

'I think, I do not need.'

'Indulge me.'

'Your keys I made, *lav*,' she said as they stood outside her door, his hand sliding down her hip. 'Where they are?'

'Here on my ring, look.' He put a key in the door with one hand, sliding the other down her haunch. 'Fucking thing won't turn . . .'

'Wiggle, *dragi*.' She'd learned this word from Helen. 'Same time to push forward *and* to push left.'

'I'll give you wiggle and push, young lady.' He followed her up the stairs, tossed her on the bed and knelt between her thighs as at an altar. Anka saw her breasts pointing up, like eyes squinting away from each other, to the walls. 'You look like Liz Hurley. Black hair all over the pillow.'

'Not, like me?'

'Oh yes, sweetie, yes, you, yes . . .' His head went down between her thighs.

Half an hour later he looked down, still inside her, arms either side of her shoulders, chest above.

178

'You make me feel such a hero.' He collapsed gently on to her. She felt his heart thudding. "m I squashing you?'

'No, no.' She stroked his hair.

'Gentleman always keeps his weight on his arms.'

'You say such silly things.'

'The wife may go away for a few weeks. Might be able to swing another night together.'

'Oh. We can have *three* nights a week. Saturday, too.'

'Well . . .'

'You can come Croatia Day.'

'What in hell's name is Croatia Day?'

'For Independence. South Bank. I did not tell before because, is Saturday. I sing *your song*! Also Croatian songs.'

'Can't wait.'

'You will meet Lasta and Budimir. But good behaviour. Girls will be there.'

'Girls?'

'Helen. And friend, Katya.'

'Is her little friend as fab as she is? What fun.'

'Silly. Katya is very intelligent. I will get compliment ticket.'

'When is it?'

'June twenty-fifth. *Independence* Saturday.'

'I'll do my damnedest.'

Her tummy felt squashed. But she wouldn't move him for the world.

'I trust you, *crni lav*,' she whispered.

'Must be mad,' he muttered into her jugular.

12

'Mind the bones.' Gopal ran an electricity company in Alipur Duar, and also a circle of amateur naturalists in north-east Bengal. He heaped fish on to Richard's plate and sat back smiling. Richard had been staying with him for a week.

'That is *tapaswi*,' said Sheshadri, an architect with black glasses and a charming smile. His cheeks glistened. Everyone here existed in a sheath of sweat. 'A Bengali delicacy. The fish is marinated in onion and ginger paste.'

'*Tapaswi* means one who meditates. This fish has whiskers like a holy man.' Gopal laughed.

'The British called it Mango Fish,' said Nain, the elderly bookseller. 'Both appear in the same season. Fruit is the only thing that helps us bear this final summer month. We have a fortnight more at thirty-eight to forty-five degrees. We really earn our monsoon.'

Richard looked at his hands. How did other people get their nails so clean? He had spent the day at Alipur Duar's Forest headquarters, meeting officials, waiting to meet others, filling in forms to rent a Forest Department Rest House in Buxa. He would report each week to their local Outpost and was driving there tomorrow in a rented jeep. Tonight he was meeting the *un*official protectors of Bengal's forests.

'Buxa's *called* a tiger reserve,' said Sheshadri. He was the only one Richard could imagine in the field: thin and fit, with quick eyes. 'The foresters say they have twenty-six tigers. They haven't any! That forest's on its last legs. Buxa's a cow reserve, really.'

The signs across the road, Debnath Medical Agency, Krishna Fashions, Dentist, were fading in the suffocating twilight. If only he weren't so tired. The cross bar and vertical of the window looked like a mocking face. If Buxa Forest was dying, why was he here?

'Last Sunday,' said Nain, 'I went to a hill where for years I've watched tigresses raise cubs. No sign of tiger at all. Do tigers have a future in India today? No! Nor do the forests.'

'What does your Circle do?'

'We've all done training courses in field craft and conservation. Pretty tough, some of them.' Sheshadri refilled Richard's water. 'Jungle safety, botany, zoology, ecology . . .'

'We go into schools to talk about conservation.'

'And watch what the forests' so-called protectors are up to,' said Nain with a sad smile.

'Loggers and poachers run these forests. They pay forest officers to cover the damage they do.' Gopal added *raita* to Richard's plate. 'We do what we can. But the people who block us are the foresters.'

Richard remembered how uncomfortable he'd felt at the Forest Department headquarters. He'd wrung a research permit out of them because of pressure from high up. Somebody owed Kellar a favour.

'Recently,' Gopal said, 'our Environment Minister was jailed for a month. He'd allowed a secret timber yard, owned by his uncle's wife's brother, to operate beside a forest sanctuary and cut protected trees.'

'We were lucky to get the case to court,' said Sheshadri. 'He can't have offered the judge enough.'

Sitar music flowed round the restaurant like the rain they were all impatient for, tangling like carvings on the temples Richard had seen from the streets. He'd been learning this little town, gateway to Bhutan, ancient trade post on the Silk Route to Tibet. The green mountains he'd seen from every dusty corner made him impatient for the forest. Thank you, snakes, for taking him to places like this.

Gopal had eaten an enormous amount enormously fast. He now leaned back, smiling warmly.

'We are very glad you are here, Richard. Our new ally.'

Richard remembered, with fury, Tyler's parody of an Indian accent. Tyler didn't have a clue, did he? But suddenly he found himself feeling almost sorry for a man he'd always detested.

'Your king cobras,' said Nain, 'are nesting in the villages now.'

'They shouldn't be doing that,' said Richard. Everyone laughed. 'The king likes remote forest. He is hamadryad, Spirit of the Wood.'

'The king has to change, like the rest of us,' said Sheshadri. 'There are fewer snakes in the forest because they're killed for their skins, so he hunts in villages where there are more snakes around, for the rats. The villagers feel honoured by his presence but don't like him in the wash house.'

'Here's Shanta.' Richard saw a small girl with long black hair coming into the restaurant. 'Her father's an elephant biologist in Assam. She's a doctor, she could have gone anywhere but when she finished training in England she came here.'

With her wire glasses and smooth round face, Shanta looked about seventeen.

'She works at the hospital. But also in a village clinic, not far from where you'll be.'

'Sorry I'm late,' said Shanta breathlessly. 'We had an emergency. Welcome to the Dooars, Richard.' He liked the way she said Richard. 'I've read your paper on cobra–villager conflict in Karnataka. Very interesting.'

Gopal lifted dishes towards her, Sheshadri poured a beer.

'Probably much the same here,' said Richard.

'You should visit Shanta's clinic,' said Nain. 'The villagers will tell you all about king cobras. How's your Bengali?'

'I'm working on it,' Richard said slowly, in Bengali. They laughed. His accent was probably terrible.

'Where's your clinic, Shanta?'

'An hour from your Rest House. Driving towards the main road, you turn right at a big banyan tree for the Forest Outpost, but left for our village, then left again down a tiny track.' With her tiny fingers she rolled rice into a ball. 'We're beside a shrine to Manasa. A notice board that wouldn't disgrace Harley Street, on a mud path full of cows.'

'Manasa's worshipped everywhere,' said Nain.

'They do *puja* to her through the rains,' said Shanta. 'She's all that stands between them and death – except me, Tuesdays and Saturdays.'

She added fish to the rice and raised it to her mouth. Not a grain fell.

'Monsoon begins in the mystic month of Asharh,' said Nain. 'First comes Ambubachi, when the red earth flows with rain.'

'When there are so many snake bites you mean,' said Shanta. 'I've laid in dried antivenin and we have an old hand-turned ventilator. But last week a boy died from a Russell's viper. He got to us too late. "I fed him milk through Ambubachi," his mother said, "so why did he die?"'

Richard walked home with Gopal through the night.

'That was lovely, Gopal, thank you. It seems almost – er – cooler.'

'This is the night breeze, from the Bay of Bengal. How's the Gypsy?'

'Seems OK, thanks.'

Sunday 1 May, Primrose Hill, London, 11.30 a.m.; 4.00 p.m., India

Rosamund pulls *Style* magazine out of the Sunday papers. What does Shelley von Strunckel say about the stars for May?

The phone rings. As she gets up, she catches sight of something blue outside on the grass.

'Richard's emailed,' says Irena, 'to remind you to get your visa.'

'I'm doing it tomorrow. *And* collecting my tickets. You OK?'

'I'm hard at work, learning my part.'

'There's something weird on our lawn, Irena. Random things keep appearing. That looks like a pair of knickers.'

'Maybe you've got a poltergeist. They're attracted to houses with teenagers.'

'Why the garden, then? Russel's never in it.'

'No idea. Have you seen the *Sunday Times*?' Rosamund looks at *Style*. She can't imagine Irena ever opening it. 'It's published the Downing Street Memo.'

'What's that?'

'Minutes of a meeting, ages before the war, which *prove* Blair knew America was going to invade Iraq.' Rosamund has never heard her so angry. 'They *prove* Blair was lying, when he said there were weapons ready to attack us. And that he took us to war just simply because he'd promised America!' Guilt squeezes Rosamund's gut. She only gets upset at personal things, not about the outside world. 'Knowing you're being lied to and not being able to do anything about it – that's the worst.'

Irena should try living with Tyler.

'Thousands of people dying, a totally illegal war – and he's responsible. Now he's asking us to vote for him *again*.'

Rosamund sees a breeze outside, lifting the edge of those mystery knickers. When Irena rings off, she goes out and picks them up. They look clean but she throws them in the bin. She feels they must be something to do with Tyler, even if they're not.

Monday 2 May, Primrose Hill, London, 4.30 p.m.; 9.00 p.m., India

Light leaps through the green cage of willow leaves. Inside the tree, Russel scratches at earth with a kitchen spoon. His mum is out. It has not occurred to him there might be tools in the garden shed. It was dumb to put Bono's collar under that tree in Devon. It should be here, where he and Bono first met Kaa.

To begin with Kaa was only a friend, though he did once strike at Dad, when Dad hit Bono. But when Mum was away, and Russel answered the phone and heard a woman ask for Dad like he belonged to her, Kaa changed. When he said he wanted to go to the school Tom was going to, and Dad said he couldn't, Kaa hissed and puffed up and Dad was afraid. He didn't know why, but he was. 'Do as you please,' he'd said. That had made Russel feel, not good exactly, but like he'd won.

If Mum goes away again, there'll be Scott and Bramble.

But he suspects Bono *does* mind him training another dog. Bono's always around now. He scratches at the door and appears in the garden when Russel's in the attic, but when Russel gets downstairs, he's gone. If Kaa could change to Avenger maybe Bono can turn against *him*.

Russel scrapes. The top layer of earth crumbles but it's like iron beneath. He can't make a hole deep enough for this stupid urn. He tries twisting the lid. It sticks. He rocks it back and forth. Bono is in there and he can't reach him. It gives and he looks in. The ashes aren't white like he imagined, just grey gravel. Have they charged his mum a hundred quid for a load of random cinders? It's his fault Bono is here. Like the badger was man's fault. He closes his eyes, feels Bono's fur brushing his cheek and sees the badger swiping at the men, jaw hanging, blood pouring.

He opens his eyes and tips the ashes in the hole. The last ones don't want to come. He puts his hand in, feels grit on his fingertips and shakes them over the hole. He wipes his fingers on grass, tears it up, puts that in the hole too and scrapes the earth over.

He can't tell if Bono has forgiven him or not.

Monday 2 May, Leicester Square, London, 9.30 p.m.

'You are more than one hour late!'

'Sorry, angel – that traffic. From Brixton, of all godforsaken spots.'

The bar he'd suggested had mirror pillars up to the ceiling like a glass forest. All this time, she'd seen a thousand reflections of herself. And girls floating past her like jewelled dragonflies.

'Yes, sir. What would you like?'

The waitress hadn't come near Anka for half an hour.

'You've no *idea*, darling, what I've struggled through to reach your charming haven! Bottle of number thirty-six for me and my friend. And – do you do olives? Or bread and oil, like a good girl?'

'Both.' The waitress laughed and bridled, smoothing tight red silk split up one willowy thigh, the swell of her mons Veneris level with Anka's eyes. Anka felt dipped in the silence of someone who doesn't know the language others know. Has he been here before? She realised miserably she might not believe him, if he said he didn't know this girl. Where was the man who had claimed her as his saviour, the man she'd rescued from the mud of a million affairs that never lasted?

'What do you say, sweetie? Bread *and* olives?'

'Is OK.'

185

No, she was being unfair. She was his big love. He had so much on his plate. *On his plate.* She'd learned that from Max, her manager. She imagined her lover's plate brimming with bright red curry.

'You are coming from Albania?' she asked the waitress. 'My Albanian friend, musician, is talking like you.'

The girl looked down like a scalpel.

'I am from Kosovo.' She turned away. 'Olives *and* bread?'

'Thanks a million, babe.'

When she left he caught Anka's fingers and nibbled them.

'What a madam. Fuck difference does it make? Kosovo wosovo.' He dropped her hand. 'Decorative, though. Bet she's a goer.'

Anka felt as if a hand had come from the ceiling and smacked her. Did he know where Kosovo was? He had not known where Croatia was. She'd found that sweet and funny, once. Did he not know both countries fought the same people? Women raped, people tortured, homes burned, children lost . . . It was on television *here*!

Her lion did not live in a world where people died.

Friday 6 May, Primrose Hill, London, 8.30 p.m.

'What happened in your constituency, Ros?'

'Hi, Irena. Oh, the election. Labour, I think.'

'They've all voted for Blair *again*.'

'Maybe they think it's safer.'

'*Safer?* Knowing he lied us into a war that's still killing thousands of people – and making Muslims everywhere hate us?'

'Well . . .'

'Electing him again says they're right to hate us, now.'

Rosamund goes back to her plant catalogues. Russel is upstairs. Dennis and Sarah adore her designs and she's doing the costings. They want roses, a magnolia, colourful bushes. She's checking on Japanese maples. Maybe *Acer Palmatum* will rescue her from this Gorgon spell of doing nothing with her life.

Twilight falls outside. The dog fox leaps from the wall at the end of the garden, holding a toddler's sandal in his mouth. Six gardens up is a washing line, and two gardens beyond that a climbing frame. Both are perfect hunting grounds for fox-cub toys. Hamburger cartons, crackly crisp packets, plastic spoons, anything that can be rattled, stalked, chewed, thrown up and caught in the air.

Saturday 14 May, Buxa Forest, Bengal, 3.00 p.m.; 10.30 a.m., UK

At last the showers had begun. It was still swelteringly humid and hot, the forest felt parched, exhausted leaves hung shrivelled in hushed air, but the trails were muddy now, not steel-hard.

Richard squelched down a gluey path. He couldn't love this forest as he did those of Karnataka, but at least he'd had no Ros fantasies here. His drunken resolution had worked. Or maybe seeing Ros as she really was, at Easter, had done the trick. He was waking at four each day, working till noon, coming back to the forest at four and working till dark. At night he collated his meagre data.

His survey had depressed him deeply. Very few wild animals, even snakes, but hundreds of cows. Flouting India's basic forest law – no domestic animals in protected land – the villagers let cows into the forest to graze and the foresters let them. Richard had made one expedition farther in. There was better forest in the Sinchula Hills. He would try there when he'd finished this sector. There had been king cobras here once, he'd found old nests. Other snakes would appear now the rains were beginning. Maybe they would attract kings from further off.

He turned a corner and saw a snake across the path. Blackish-grey, two foot – could that be an Olive Oriental Slender? They were rare even in the western Himalayas and had never been recorded here in the north-east, nor at such a low elevation. Non-venomous, a genus all its own and hardly studied – what luck!

He took the GPS position, slid a stick under the belly, grasped the head. Take no chance till you're sure of identification. He carried it back to the Rest House and popped it in a basket. Quick, the books.

Smooth, slightly iridescent scales, head hardly wider than the neck, eye small with a round pupil. Yes. He turned it on its back.

Scales keeled in the anal region. Underbelly a beautiful bitter orange. *Trachischium Laeve*, definitely. Extraordinary.

But it belonged to the park. He could lose his research permit simply for picking it up. He made five pages of notes. At twilight, he let it go among the trees, looking after it so keenly he felt his gaze parting the darkening leaves. Then he saw a face swimming up at him out of the shadows. Golden twists of hair, falling to the tops of creamy breasts. He could, he really could, see the nipples. The force of her swept and shook him. He nearly reached out to touch. He *had* touched her, at Easter, when they danced.

So she was still around.

Wednesday 25 May, Chinatown, Soho, London, 9.15 p.m.

'Let's get home, sweet thing. I want to monster you in your own bed.' He was kissing her on the seventh floor of the Chinatown car park. Anka was holding his cock and his hand was deep up her skirt. 'No sense in necking like crazed ferrets here. Sorry I had to put off seeing you. But just you wait, young lady.' The car rolled down the ramp through yellow cement tunnels. Anka snapped her safety belt.

'You never use.' She did his up too. She loved mothering him. 'One month, is concert.'

'What's that?' He put a card in the exit machine.

'Queen Elizabeth Hall. South Bank. When you are meeting my friends Lasta and Budimir. And famous music critic Franjo Zubrinic, from New York.'

'Remind me when that is.' He turned up Charing Cross Road.

'Saturday, June twenty-fifth. Croatia Day.'

'Did I say I'd come?'

'I told you. I got compliment ticket.'

'May be tricky. That's the day she's going away.'

Sunday 29 May, Primrose Hill, London, 9.00 p.m.

'That's where I'm going.' With Russel, Rosamund kneels on the living-room floor over *The Times Atlas of the World*. 'Calcutta, here.

188

Amazing, isn't it? Then Darjeeling, I'm going to see some botanical gardens there, for my work. Then I'll visit Richard for a few days here. On some border. What's that country?'

'Bhutan, Mum.' Russel's laughing at her. He's much keener on this than the essay he's supposed to do on *Julius Caesar*.

Tyler is out. She doesn't believe in another band playing Brixton of a Sunday night, but who cares? She watches Russel swallow. His Adam's apple is huge. What's it like to cart that around in your throat? A son is a journey into the unknown. Such a mysterious process, creating a child out of two cells. Sometimes she sees Tyler in him, sometimes herself. But he seems, more and more, to be his own strong self, too.

'Where's Chennai?' he says.

'Down here. Bottom of India.'

He doesn't ask, Where's Grandpa, why aren't you going to see him? Maybe a daughter would have. Grief cuts through her, that old familiar lightning she thought her body had forgotten. Four years. How does a family gather shadows like this, full of things never said?

Outside, the dog fox shows the cubs how to strip flaking bark from trees to get the heaving sheets of woodlice. On the lawn he listens, head cocked, to worm-bristles rasping through grass, then grabs a worm by the tail. The head burrows frantically into earth and curls under, gripping the lip of the burrow. His black lips tug gently till the worm is taut, relax, then pull again. The worm emerges suddenly. He flips it to the dog cub, who gulps it down. The female cub watches. Her father shows her how to spoon craneflies off the grass, delicately, with her tongue.

Sunday 29 May, Kilburn, London, 11.00 p.m.

Write a great new love song, Max had said. Sitting at the keyboard, Anka picked out the song Haydn used in his symphony. *Divojcica potok gazi*. No. She changed it to triple time. *Little girl – treads on a – stream*!

No, it sounded dead. She tried the lute. No. Neither tune nor tone was the problem. The problem was words. And behind them, feelings.

She walked to the window. The street lamp shone orange on the tops of pitted bricks in the opposite wall. A plastic bag blew along the street, a sleepwalking jellyfish stretching its tentacles. Can you write love, for someone you're not sure is good? When you're no longer sure it's you he loves? Or if he's capable of love?

That's the song she should write. She doesn't want to bring it into words.

Wednesday 8 June, Baker Street, London, 10.00 p.m.

'I don't usually go for science fiction but that was *so* funny, Scott. Brilliant.' Rosamund squeezes his arm as they queue to leave *The Hitchhiker's Guide to the Galaxy*. Scott feels solid and welcoming, a tree she'd like to climb. But he's cautious somehow. Defended.

'You like Woody Allen, don't you?' he says. The foyer smells of popcorn. 'Saw a DVD in your living room that night. I've got the whole set if you'd ever like to see any more.'

Rosamund imagines a neat shelf of DVDs by his bed. And the bed, what was that like? They pass a poster of a smiley girl with flaxen hair like Rapunzel.

'June the twenty-fifth,' she says. 'The day I leave.'

'What's that?'

'London debut of Tyler's new singer. He went on about her at first. Now he's gone all quiet.'

'So?'

'So whoever left that message before Easter has been replaced.'

'How do you feel about that?'

'Couldn't care less.' Does he believe her? Does she believe herself? 'How's your camera? Russel says you got the new one.'

'Great. But don't get much chance at wildlife, just now. Most I see's not in a fit state to be photographed.' They walk down Baker Street. Arm in arm, keeping step. 'Saw Dennis yesterday. Sarah's excited about the garden.'

'So'm I, Scott. We'll start in September. I'm having a lovely time ordering plants.'

'How about India?'

'I'm terrified. But excited. I'm staying with a friend of Irena's in Darjeeling. She sounds fun. I'll see Richard for three days after that.'

'How's the boy?'

'School says things look good for starting his GCSEs. Pity he had to stop dog training to revise.'

'Did wonders for Bramble.' Scott stands still. She stops too. He puts his arms round her. 'And for me,' he says softly. 'One day, ma'am, I'd like to try and photograph *you*.'

She feels desire flare in her like a tropical storm and presses herself into his arms. But he just strokes her hair, kisses her cheek and carries on walking.

'Bite in the Indian?'

Scott is more of a mystery now, not less. She knows he likes to read the sports section of the paper and doesn't read thrillers because he wants to get away from police things. He's told her about the hares he saw one evening outside London, dancing on a hillside. He'd like to make a collection of hare photos. She knows all this but it doesn't make him feel closer. It's not like talking about his girlfriend who left him. They haven't talked about that again.

At home, she goes upstairs and finds Russel at his computer. She kisses him.

'You'd love that film! Why not go with Dad while I'm away?'

'Maybe.'

Thursday 16 June, Kilburn, London, 11.55 p.m.

'God that was good.'

He reached over, still inside Anka, and took a cigarette from the pack beside the bed. From underneath, Anka saw grey hairs under his arm, beaded with sweat, and felt him inhale. He tipped ash in the packet's lid, rolled off her and lay back. She must open the window afterwards or Helen would wonder tomorrow why her mum's bedroom smelt of smoke.

'Croatia Day, is OK?' He hated being reminded of promises he'd made, but this was important.

'Be harder to get away when the wife's not there. Tess is only three.'

'Must be, nearly five?'

'Yes, of course.'

'You don't want wife going! Are fearing I demand, like her.'

'Nonsense, sweetie. I'm just not sure how it'll work out.'

Friday 24 June, Primrose Hill, London, 6.30 p.m.; 11.00 p.m., India

'When are you off?'

'Oh, Irena. There's a cab coming at six.' Tyler hasn't offered to take her to the airport and she hasn't asked.

'Richard emailed to ask about Russel's exams.'

'Russel, Richard wants to know how your exams went.'

Russel is sprawled at the kitchen table, doing busy things to his mobile.

'OK.'

'He says OK.'

'Richard says don't forget malaria tablets. He'll meet you Monday morning. Get out quick. He says Indian trains don't hang around.'

'Jesus, Irena, can I really do this?'

Tyler looks up from cooking and laughs.

'Stay with us, kiddo.'

Next morning, with a money belt round her waist, bracing herself for a twelve-hour plane ride, Rosamund opens Russel's door. He lies on his back. The screensaver is flashing a sequence of jungles at him like a guardian angel. She stoops over the pillow.

'Bye, darling.'

A sweaty arm comes round her neck.

'Bye, Mum. Have g'd time.'

'You too, love. Look after Dad.'

She finds Tyler in his dressing gown, cigarette in hand, leaning against the open front door like Rhett Butler in *Gone with the Wind*.

'Are you going to smoke in the house the minute I walk out? I thought you didn't want to get up early.'

'Chap must get up to bid farewell to his beloved.'

He likes to see himself as playing by the rules. Whatever his rules are.

'Bye. Thanks for a lovely supper.'

Tyler takes her in his arms. He presses her head into his shoulder where it used to rest. She feels his heart, which she once thought she knew. He is naked under the dressing gown while she is armoured in money belt and safari jacket, in *going away*.

'Dangerous world out there, sweetiepie. Take care of yourself. I'll miss you.'

13

Saturday 25 June, South Bank, London, 6.00 p.m.

'Can't do tonight, I'm afraid, sweet thing. I'll make it up to you,' he added in the voice of someone ignoring an open wound on someone's face. 'I swear.'

Anka was in the green room. Helen and Katya were eating the performers' crisps from tables with a red-black ripply wood grain like shiny jam. Lasta was laughing with the other Croatian musicians. Anka took a breath. Every word her lover spoke felt cut in her bare arm.

'I'd love to be at your side in your hour of triumph but Tess has gone ballistic about her mother leaving.'

'Oh . . .'

'Her nursery put on a play this afternoon, there's a party for parents – the wife didn't tell me till I took her to the airport. Can't leave Tess the first night her mother's away.'

Anka turned off her mobile. All round was a comforting Croatian murmur. Jokes, laughs, instruments tuning. It was a big concert, she was only part of it. They were celebrating Independence while a raven was plunging its beak in her innards.

On stage she kept her eyes on Helen, trying to ignore the empty seat in the front row. Except for that one gap, the hall was completely full.

> *'Touch me, tell me who I am.*
> *You are my earth and sky,*
> *You're everything I've ever loved.'*

She hated this song now.

'Light me a candle when I die
To say I'm everything you loved.'

Everyone stood, clapping, stamping the floor.

'Mum?' said Helen in the artists' room after. 'You're white.'

'Just – is tiring, *andele moj.*'

'Auntie Anka, you're a queen.'

'Thank you, Katya.'

Lasta brought over a man in a dark suit and silvery tie. Franjo Zubrinic, from New York.

'Happy to meet you, *Gospodica.*'

He kissed her on both cheeks.

'You make the old carols truly new. Even more original, with the lute.'

'Thank you.'

'You trained in opera, I think? That song you are known for – it hides what you can really do.'

For the first time since leaving the Guildhall, Anka felt really met, by someone who saw and heard her not as she was, but as she could be.

'Here's my card.' His nails were beautiful. Like his suit. 'I could help, in New York. There's a bigger community, a wider market.'

'I know. London Croatian community is smallest in world.'

'Why call yourself Shadiyah when it's not your name?'

She was all wrong, and this man knew it. Voice wrong. Name wrong. Song wrong. The man she loved, wrongest of all. She felt held together only by the varnish of the hour. And by Helen. Helen knew she was anxious.

Anka suddenly felt protected by Helen, rather than the other way round. Her lovely, watchful daughter, so creative, so strong. She smiled across and Helen, watching her, smiled back. A golden smile that boldened her to explain to this man who knew the wrong turn she had taken.

'My manager, he said I needed mysterious image. My friend chose this name. It means singer, storyteller.'

'Why not your real name? And real music. *Prava muzika?*'

Anka was silent.

'Call me, when you have something I can use to help you.'

Sunday 26 June, Buxa Forest, Bengal, 1.30 p.m.; 9.00 a.m., UK

Richard waited in streaming rain at the Forest Department Outpost. The violent downpours had gone on for weeks. Nain said Bengali farmers, afraid of their raging rivers, prayed for rain but also for its moderation. The stream below the Rest House was swollen, forest paths awash. But at last there were snakes. A White-Barred Kukri snake, the first he'd ever seen. A Green Bronzeback Tree Snake, slithering through branches. But no kings.

Anand Singh opened the door. There was only one guard on Sundays and Richard was delighted to see Anand, who helped him practise Bengali. Anand was in his mid-fifties, a thin man with bloodshot, protuberant eyes. He looked bleary; Richard realised guiltily he'd probably been asleep. All the guards were the wrong side of fifty.

'How are you?' they said simultaneously in Bengali.

'How is your son?' added Richard, coming in out of the wet. Anand's son, whom Richard suspected of being alcoholic, had just been fired from a gas delivery job and was supposed to be getting a motorbike to start a messenger service.

'Good. Thank you.'

'My guest is coming next week. I'll bring her to sign in. Very kind of the Forest Department to let her stay.' Anand produced two little cups of *chai*. 'Have you ever seen one of these?' Richard opened his *Snakes of India* at Olive Oriental Slender Snake. Anand studied the picture. Richard had seen in the field that he was both observant and knowledgeable about snakes.

'Sometimes, farmers find.'

'I saw one in the forest. I'd love to examine another.'

The deputy director, who was usually in Alipur Duar at weekends, came in, stared at them and disappeared into his room. He clearly disliked Richard hobnobbing with Anand. He had given permission for Rosamund to stay at the Rest House only, Richard was sure, because she was Kellar's daughter. Ros would die if she knew that. There was a maze of unspoken suspicion round here that she would never understand. Nor, for that matter, did he.

Anand's face was less welcoming now.

Sunday 26 June, Piccadilly, London, 9.30 p.m.

'I've said I'm sorry about yesterday, but don't go on about it, there's a good girl.'

Anka looked into the night. She was holding his arm. They were walking away from Piccadilly tube, Eros was about to launch into the sky, and what she felt was alone. Distant, like outer space.

'And don't try and make me late tonight. You don't know what it's like, to have to get back in time for a small child.' How could he say that? He knew she brought up Helen alone. Did he never think what *her* life had been? 'Their mother's away, I've got a babysitter. Don't sabotage me.' His car was parked off Haymarket. When they got in he flung himself on her, 'It's been so long . . .' His tongue was in her mouth, his hand pulping her breast, dragging the bra-cup aside. 'God, I've missed you! I'm taking you to a fab little bar, you'll adore it . . . we've got an hour . . .'

'You said we are having more time. Now she is away.'

He started the engine. Anka snapped her seatbelt. It was tighter than usual and the seat was closer to the dashboard. Had Tess been with him? He never had a child seat. Maybe the son? But there was scent, too. Who else had been in the car?

Proud of knowing his way through the back streets, he turned into a dark road leading to Piccadilly.

'The damnedest thing. We got the dog's ashes through the post in an urn. I thought, now he and I are alone—'

'Except Tess.'

'Of course. Thought I'd invent a ceremony, open champagne, toast the damn dog. I opened the urn to see what was inside and it was empty.' He braked. Parked cars sleeved the road, another was blocking the way. 'Sorry, madam,' he yelled out of the window. 'You'll have to exercise your reversing skills, I'm afraid.'

The two cars faced each other in the dark. He turned off his engine and folded his arms. Anka said nothing. He drove with panache on a clear road but when things became tricky he panicked and snapped, even at her. The other driver slowly backed round a corner, into a space between parked cars. As he drove past, he raised both hands off his wheel. To sign thank you, Anka thought, but instead he clapped a slow clap, ironical, implying it had not been difficult at all.

'Oh dear, was that a trifle *ungallant?*'

He pressed the button to wind up the window and sped triumphantly on, then stopped at a red light, facing buses and cars streaming along Piccadilly. Anka undid her seatbelt, got out and slammed the door. The lights changed. He had to drive on. She saw him looking back, gesticulating, borne across Piccadilly as in a devil's chariot over a river of tar.

She walked up Piccadilly. Street lamps lit her tears to orange jewels.

Sunday 26 June, Primrose Hill, London, 11.30 p.m.

Russel stares into depthless blue. *Increase your pennis size three inches!* Everything around him is dark. The cursor throbs on screen like the only living thing.

Outside, the language of the garden is pure and still. Night flows, silver, soot and ultramarine, over black-latticed grass where Russel and Tyler once played French cricket. The vixen sits motionless in the moonshadow of euphorbia like a bacchic thyrsus. Yellow potentilla flowers, on a bush planted by Rosamund when Russel was two, shine up at the sky, each blossom a dim circle like the end of a doll's telescope.

One cub pounces at her mother's tail-tip, the other chases after. Their eyes are no longer cloudy indigo but citrus, their ears not baby-round now but triangles. The male sees another shadow and for the very first time goes up into the mouse leap, the birthright of every vulpine fox. Genes, nerves and muscles curve him into a circumflex at the top of his jump. His four paws dangle, his brush points down behind as if God, or a genetic code handed down through millennia, has picked him up under his elbows. He lands on his shadow and springs away again. He does not know that landing on his forepaws is designed to counteract the up-leap of a mouse.

The vixen sits. Once you stop being a cub, conserving energy is everything. Her son is using his to learn life skills as fast as possible. The female cub gallops up to see what her brother has found. New-grown vibrissae on their muzzles mingle like fingers in water. Nerve-threaded fur touches. Black lines over their mouths draw back as if they are smiling. Or so a human eye might suggest to a human brain.

Industrial logging in rainforests promoted by World Bank is out of control! Russel hears the front door bang. Kaa hisses.

Fight global capitalism now!

Downstairs, the phone rings then stops as if Dad has snatched it up.

Protest against global conglomorates destroying forests with agreement of World Bank! Action meeting, Thursday 7 July.

School doesn't matter. Rainforest does.

Picket World Bank on Pall Mall! Our office, High Holborn, 9.00 a.m.! Banners available.

He types High Holborn into StreetFinder. He can get there via King's Cross.

Next morning, he walks into the kitchen and sees his dad pouring milk into a bowl of Berry Burst Cheerios.

'Get outside that, young man.' His dad puts the Darwin mug beside him. 'And here's your tea, monsieur.'

Russel stares at the Cheerios as if they block his view of the universe.

''m good, thanks.'

Monday 27 June, Charing Cross Road, London, 4.00 p.m.

Drum kits! Where could she put all that? And what about the neighbours underneath?

Anka walked up Denmark Street. Helen was learning drums at school and she had promised at least to *look*. Plectrums and valves are laid out here in these windows like bullets.

199

'I am your rock,' he'd said. *Drkadžijo!* She could see that rock, black with jagged edges, spray boiling round it. The rock that ships are wrecked on. She stared into a red sparkling guitar, pointing up like a gun.

Better off without her. She could hear him saying it. Like a sudden hot message in her brain she realised he must be *pleased* she'd gone. He was *used* to disappointing people, to letting them down. He was not worrying about her as she was worrying about him. He was thinking only of himself.

At the end of the street were one, two, three Korean restaurants. So many Korean people, too, in London? What were *they* escaping?

She saw a church, walked up white steps into a lobby with tiles on the floor like brown-black snakes, sat in a pew and began to weep.

Monday 27 June, Primrose Hill, London, 8.15 p.m.

'There now. Duck breasts in honey.'

Russel looks at his plate. His dad puts down a glass.

'Corton, my boy. First-class Burgundy. Little treat for our first night. How was school?'

Russel slices half a centimetre off the meat.

'Don't want wine.' His dad says nothing. Russel pushes his plate away and stands up.

'Thanks.'

He goes out of the kitchen. Before he reaches the first-floor landing he hears his dad on the mobile.

'Sweetheart, you're on. Bind up your golden locks. Your chariot will be at the door in half an hour.' Russel stands at the top of the unlit stairs. 'Going out for a few hours, old chap.' That voice has been calling up this stairwell all his life. 'Got to see someone for work.'

The front door slams. Then the house phone rings. It rings several times through the night. He doesn't know if he's alone in the house or not. Fuck does he care? But when he comes down in the morning his dad is there, pouring the milk.

Father is drowning! Rosamund sees him choking and helpless in a forest pool. 'You can't save him,' says a voice. Now it's Tyler, eyes bulging, terrified. She's got to help. She can't.

On the top bunk of the Kanchenjunga Express to New Jalpaiguri, Rosamund opens her eyes. Above the air conditioner's roar, rain crepitating on the roof, clatter of wheels and five separate snorings, she hears a mosquito. The only sure way to avoid malaria, the chemist said, is not get bitten. She puts her head under the sheet, which is stiff as a cardboard coffin. Is this how she's always lived, head under the sheet? Her watch glimmers blue. What are Tyler and Russel doing? She has hardly been away from them since Russel was born. Nor away from Tyler since they met.

Breathing through the harsh cotton, she thinks back to Calcutta. Richard's friend met her off the plane, steered her through a million people into sauna-bath air, through a city of klaxons, lorries, beggars, buses, more lorries, cars and rickshaws to a hotel. Then, next day, to a menacingly crowded train station. India is where she grew up but she knows less than nothing about it. India is loss. India is her mother dying when she was two.

'Deal with it,' says a voice.

She closes her eyes and is standing in pinkish air in a winter beech wood. Bare trunks, like sliding columns of a cathedral nave, disclose a path to the forest's heart where there is, she knows, an altar. And under that a sarcophagus, a Pandora's Box holding something that will make her life make sense. Tyler is coming towards her, head on one side, as he looked when she used to run to him with that lift of heart that said, 'You're home!'

There is hissing in the faded damask air and Tyler turns into Father. 'Both incapable of love,' says the voice. She knows this is true. They reflect each other as a star is the after-image of another star, long gone. All her life she's carried an image of Father round her neck, an iron key that fitted Tyler too. Both are horribly fused in this one figure striding towards her like a cowboy through the door of a saloon.

She runs away, deeper into the wood. There's the altar, but lapping it are glistening black coils and a giant snake rears up behind it like a periscope. Fatal rays beam from the chitinous scutes of its golden throat. Even in dreams, she knows the language. But is this dream? It feels like her whole life encrypted in one moment. The snake's eyes flash bronze. If she meets them, she'll turn to stone.

Heart pounding, enveloped in sweat, Rosamund opens her eyes. There's something she's forgotten. Some vital thing she's supposed to bring with her and has lost.

An hour later, she is standing among prone bodies in the dim corridor. The train stops with a wrathful bump. She checks the station name, shifts somebody's leg, and steps down. The door slams, the train departs, she is alone on an empty platform swarming with raindrops like glass ants, under a night sky alive with constellations that haven't beamed at her for thirty years.

She's soaking. But she's warm. Monsoon rain, tender and violent. How could she forget waiting, through scorching days and sticky nights under chemical-drenched mosquito nets, for that first growl of thunder like a slammed door? Seeing dark clouds at the edge of the horizon and running out into the garden at the first drops, dancing in the rain among smells of exhausted red earth and plants coming back to life. And Parvati, beloved Parvati, cooking dishes to welcome the monsoon. Everyone smiling, laughing, moving differently in the relief of rain.

And the smell. Woodsmoke, dungsmoke, wet grit. Yes, *that* smell! Calcutta didn't count, she never knew an Indian city, but this smell here is part of her. She's coming back to something utterly forgotten, where there really had been things she loved. Black trees crowd into greying distances where the rails come nearly to a point like lead in a pencil. This is India, her dreaded deep past, and she is in it alone.

It comes to her why she was always afraid of forest. It wasn't Red Dog at all. It was *alone*. She was never physically alone as a child except that moment when Father went ahead up the track.

There were always people. Yet she lived inside a solitude she never labelled, sharpest when she faced Father over lunch on Sundays.

She watches silhouetted branches wave against a smudge of rainy orange, the first faint fingerprint of dawn.

Real forest, what Father called with that revering voice 'the field', was the closest she ever got to naming the loneliness. Forest was where Father belonged. And yet imaginary forest, the jungle in her head, *Jungle Book* jungle, was where she felt at home, companioned.

Mad. But you don't question what you're given as a child. Nor the rickety mask you make of yourself, to deal with it. Or she hadn't, till now.

Tongues of water are running down her face and neck. Suddenly she recognises what it is that she's feeling, coming back. Angry. Very angry. Russel was right, she sees herself as a victim. Was that her own making, her response to the reptilian unease that spread out from Father?

She pulls her bag to a dark building with one lit window and stands under the clock as directed, watching the second hand glide round the face like a long-handled spoon.

Five minutes. Ten. Twenty. A small beige man appears, sweeping the hall. Where's the car from Alisha's Guest House? Then out of the shadows floats her own name, held up by a dripping young man.

'Darjeeling, mam?'

'Thank you,' she says shyly and follows him to a dark car park full of pouring rain and lorries. They get in and he steers round a bunch of wet cows, and a sleeping calf curled like a cupcake. Ahead, black sky is lightening into banks of cloud splitting like cobweb. This rent begins glowing, a luminous yolk in a black fried egg, and a red ball pops up into it.

'*The sun plays hide and seek with us*, mam,' says the driver. 'Rabindranath Tagore. He wrote poem about Darjeeling.'

Now the world is misty grey lace. The road rises to black hills furry with forest and silvered by rain. Hours later, they are among steep valleys covered in blobs like sea anemones, like the bright green jelly with which *Ghostbuster* scientists splattered the Statue of Liberty in Russel's favourite film when he was six.

'What are those bushes?'

'Tea, mam. Welcome to Darjeeling, Queen of the Hills. Gateway for harmony with Nature.'

DOORS

14

Richard hurled his shoulder against the door to open it. In a month of rain the wood had swelled and everything stuck. He stumbled out into the pewtery drizzle that had replaced the monsoon's first violence. Before meeting Ros, he was due to meet Gopal at the market in Alipur Duar. One hour to the Forest Outpost, another to Alipur Duar. Another hour there, then two hours back. Half a day lost. He was doing this for Irena.

'Remember Ros at college?' she'd said. 'That free spirit? Maybe India will help her get it back.'

'Will Russel be OK?' Richard had asked. Now, walking to the jeep, he saw again Russel's thin white shoulders heaving as the badger diggers left. Irena was usually right but he didn't like thinking of that boy left alone with the crassness, the whole huge unawareness, of Tyler.

'Tyler wants to be a good father,' Irena had said. 'I'm sure he'll *try*.'

The Gypsy's engine spat feebly like a kitten and died. He was so dependent on this jeep. He listened to each beat of tappit and sparkplug like a lover. Today it seemed as reluctant to face the next three days as he was. He couldn't envisage Ros here at all. Reconciling the real with the fantastic, he thought irritably, holding the key down hard in the ignition, is not what scientists are for. Especially herpetologists, whose lives depend on recognising the real. He flirted the accelerator and the engine juddered into life.

Tuesday 5 July, Kilburn, London, 9.15 a.m.; 1.45 p.m., India

Anka picked up her shopping in the High Street. Everything in the bags was for Helen. She could not eat. She'd left messages, he hadn't replied. His mobile was always off. For five years, they'd rung each other all the time.

He must feel so lost. She put the bags down again and redialled.

'We're sorry, this number is unavailable at this time. Please call later.'

Tuesday 5 July, Bengal, India, 3.00 p.m.; 10.30 a.m., UK

'The one land all men desire to see, and having seen once, even a glimpse, would not give that glimpse for the rest of the world combined.'

That's what Mark Twain said about Darjeeling. Re-reading her guidebook in the train, Rosamund looks out at misty valleys, feeling grateful to that rainy little town. She's coping with India, alone. At Siliguri station she pushed through the crowds and found her seat all by herself. When did she last feel she could *do* things? Darjeeling has given her that. It would have been nice with no rain but Alisha, a sparky forty-year-old who'd met Irena at some theatre festival in Canada, made up for rain. Rosamund's world has completely changed, or she feels it has, after one week of Alisha's jokes, gossip about the Darjeeling theatre scene, who's sleeping with whom – and no one with Tyler. Of no sleeping pills (she left them at home and hasn't missed them) and lots of emailing from the Cyber Café at the Red Rose Hotel.

She loves Scott's emails. He's giving up photographing wild animals, Bramble frightens them away. But might she come with him, to photograph London?

Yes, she emailed back, not sure whether to put an exclamation mark or not. She remembers asking Irena, 'Is Hope an evil?' And Irena saying, 'Some people think it's the most dangerous thing of all.' Scott isn't hope, exactly, but he is a promise of spring. Even seeing his emails makes her feel warm. She feels little pieces of her soul flying out to meet him. Tyler and Russel, though, are not chatty. It feels strange, emailing their computers in different parts of her own home. Still, they seem OK.

Who cares what Tyler gets up to? She's *sorry* for whoever he's with. From here, she sees how hollow his act is. He polishes people with charm, so they shine his reflection back and enhance him. Why should he be the centre of her life? There are more important things. Like the Gorkhas from east Nepal, who want their own Gorkhaland. Or the tragic Tibetan refugees. Or Lepchas from Sikkim, with yellow faces and turquoise-studded necklaces, whom Alisha called Ravine People. She's told Scott about them all. Sometimes she thinks of Scott as a creature from another solar system, blown in by accident to help her life make sense. Sometimes it seems daft, telling him what she's seeing. But he's become a centre, like the doughy softness at the heart of a not quite cooked loaf.

The train crosses a foamy river, alongside a road full of lorries piled with logs, and she thinks over her research. She felt silly calling it that at first but Alisha said, 'Why not?' Succulents in the greenhouse of Darjeeling's Botanical Garden. Alpines, in the dripping rock garden. She could specialise in Himalayan plants. Put that on her brochure. Again, why not?

Now for three days roughing it with Richard. And there he is, spectacles running with water, blue shirt wet over his ribs. She gets out into silvery drizzle.

'Welcome to the Dooars. Were you all right? I should have met you at Siliguri.'

'I was fine.' She dances beside him, wanting to unload, tell what she's seen. 'I *love* getting round India by myself. I thought Darjeeling was noisy till I saw Siliguri. Then I realised how quiet it was.'

'Siliguri's the business hub of the region.'

His jeep smells of mud, damp and oil. On the seat are feathery ferns with wheel-tops like ammonites.

'What are these?'

'A favourite monsoon dish. The woman who sold them called them *boudaga shak. Bou* is bride, *daga* is tip.'

'Tip of the *bride*?'

'The blushing Bengal bride, my friend Gopal said. Looking down, in her sari.'

'How do you cook them?'

'I've got instructions.'

Clouds of exhaust, black dumplings of smoke. Honking trucks.

Auto-rickshaws like overgrown bees, yellow and black. UPER-MARKET, she reads. ALIPURDOOAR FINEST. She feels cocooned from this strangeness by Richard, who seems to belong to it. He moves more freely here than in England. More male, somehow.

He swerves round a dappled bull with an enormous hump and swinging wash-leather testicles. SADOSH! says a faded board in curly script.

'That track you were on is causing frightful problems at the moment.'

'Why?'

'Elephants. North Bengal is the highest man–animal conflict zone in India. There's terrible logging everywhere, legal and illegal, but still enough forest for three hundred and fifty elephants. At night, they cross the tracks for food and water. The drivers are supposed to slow and whistle, but don't. Ten elephants were run into last year. One took a day to die. There are rows about it in the press, but nothing's done.'

'Why not?'

'Oh, Ros. India's so complicated, every issue's politicised. So many wonderful people, so many vested interests. Eco warriors have a rough time of it here.'

'What direction are we going?'

'North. You came east through the Dooars. That's Bengali for door. This is the gateway to Bhutan. That's Bhutan, straight ahead.' She looks through lacy drizzle at dark mountains, their tops invisible.

'Tomorrow, if you like, we can walk in nearby forest. The day after, I thought we could take the Gypsy to the Sinchula Ridge, core of the reserve. On your last day, I've asked a Bhutanese student to drive you to the sights nearby. Such as you can get to, in the rains.'

'Does he speak English?'

'Oh yes. Very sophisticated. The Bhutanese used to own all this. The Brits grabbed it in the 1860s so now it belongs to India. Buxa Fort was built by a Bhutanese king to guard the Silk Route from Tibet. The British imprisoned Indian freedom-fighters in it. Now, alas, people are planning to build a road to it.'

'Why alas?'

210

'*Any* road is bad news for a forest. It disturbs animals, and poachers can get carcasses out more easily.'

They are on a red mud track with grass fringes sparkling like chartreuse. Suddenly the jeep curtseys wildly on the mud like a falling skater. Tyler would be hysterical, but Richard holds calmly through the skid.

'Mud from now on, I'm afraid. Back in Calcutta you'll know what India's really resting on.'

They slither along a glutinous track with walls of bushes either side, as through a tunnel of green jam. So this, thinks Rosamund, is The Field! Trees around them and above. No sky. God knows what would be coming in with the rain if it weren't for the plastic windows. But she's not a little girl any more, trailing after Father in the jungle. She'll be fine.

Richard stops outside a bungalow surrounded by dripping scarlet flowers.

'This is the Forest Department's Outpost. I report here every week. We're in Buxa Reserve now.' Does Richard want her here? It has never occurred to her he might not. She suddenly feels shy. She hasn't been alone with him since they were students. She doesn't really know him at all. 'They have total power over me. They gave permission for you to stay. We must be *very* polite.'

An elderly guard opens the door.

'Good afternoon, mam. How are you.' His grey moustaches are too big for his thin face.

'This is Anand Singh. He's helped my Bengali no end. He knows a *lot* about snakes.'

Anand Singh shows her into an office with a bare electric light, a computer, a poster of animals.

ENDANGERED FAUNA OF THE DOOARS. BENGAL
TIGER! ASIAN ELEPHANT! REGAL PYTHON! HISPID
HARE!

Richard scowls at the poster.

'That's a sick joke. There are none of those animals here now.

Well, this is the director's computer. Want to tell Tyler you've got here OK?'

Back in the jeep, bushes scrabble at the windows. The jungle is closing in. After an hour the trees open out, rain stops and Richard pulls up by a red-brown stream streaked with cream like marbled endpapers of an old book. Beyond, the ground drops. They are looking over the rounded tops of a million trees, with dollops of steely cloud tossed over them like a crumpled coat. Up the slope, behind them, is a bungalow.

'This really is roughing it, I'm afraid.'

'I love it,' she says, and follows him to the verandah. Richard holds open a mesh door.

'Keep this closed, it's the mosquito door.'

Rosamund remembers a mosquito door, always shut, and herself pretending to be a panther in a cage behind it. Sniffing the trellis marks it pressed into her skin.

Inside, the bungalow smells damp. Velvet cushions on the sofa are spotted with mould. A mahogany table holds papers and books: *Snakes of India*; *Jeep Maintenance: A Handbook for Fieldworkers*; *Herpetological Review*.

'No electricity or phone signal, just paraffin, Calor gas and cold water only, I'm afraid.' She looks at the bathroom's stained grey marble. A real flush lavatory, thank God. A tap low in the wall and a red plastic jug on the floor. What's that for, Russel might ask. She knows, she has remembered: to wash yourself with, after shitting. Russel would want to try at once. Tyler would die.

Her room is bare boards and patched netting over an iron bed.

'I'll bring a lamp. Leave your shoes upside down. Never leave clothes on the floor, there are scorpions. I'll make supper.'

'I'll help. Where are the blushing brides? I'm dying to learn Bengali cuisine. And I've brought you gingerbread and oatcakes. Irena says that's what you miss most. And two bottles of Bordeaux.'

'Er, well for tonight, I've prepared rice and *dal*. I thought you'd be tired. We can have the ferns, um, tomorrow.'

Someone's shy round here. Is it her or him?

*

In the night there's a thump on the roof. Rosamund wakes. The pores of her face feel clogged as they do when she's had no sleep. Her skin is so annoying, it reacts to the slightest thing. Or maybe it's this foul metallic smell. *Scuffle scuffle, flub flub, thump*. Those sounds are right above. A panther? No, what would a panther be doing up there? What about snakes? That picture of the regal python in the director's office . . . She grits her teeth and sets out to not be afraid. Darjeeling was a lovely break from her fears. Now, squarely in Father's territory, she's got to face the swords where she belongs.

At nine next morning, plastered in insect repellent, she enters the central room and finds Richard writing. He rises politely.

'Would you like rice and *dal*? I made some when I got back.'

'Got back?'

'I've been in the forest since five. Do you mind Nescafé?' He lights the gas ring on which he made supper last night. The table feels clammy, like skin that has sweated and cooled. Everything's damp, even her clothes. How can Richard bear this for months on end?

'What jumped on the roof in the night?'

'Monkeys, probably. Grey langurs.' He smiles. He's in a khaki shirt today. Not weedy at all.

'Did you bring strong shoes?'

'Are these OK?' She sticks her feet out. They both look at her trainers. After she's finished eating he kneels before her like the herald presenting the glass slipper to Cinderella.

'Can you put these on over your socks?'

'What are they?'

'Leech socks.'

Oh God. Slowly, as if pulling on evening gloves, she drags the white fabric up her calves. Richard ties each tight below the knee. Her feet look like Christmas puddings about to be boiled. She thrusts them back in the trainers and laces them like a warrior putting on armour before battle.

'The leeches will be at you instantly. They have so little time to get to work. But it doesn't matter if they get you. They don't hurt, don't carry disease.'

213

He raises his hand and touches her hair very lightly. 'Can you – er . . . bundle this away somehow?'

'Why?'

'It'd get smothered in leeches. Mustn't give them anything to grab.'

She ties a scarf over her hair, tucking every tendril in, and stands up. Richard watches as if he'd never seen her face before.

'OK?'

Outside, in a break from the rain, she sees a line of denim hills below iron-bellied monsoon clouds. In among the trees, the sky disappears completely. She's a gardener, her soul should revel in all this botany. But what is it hiding?

Richard points to a leaf covered with inch-long elephant-trunks swaying like rubber pins on a pincushion.

'They're searching for us,' she whispers. 'Like triffids.'

Two leeches tangle their top ends and wave free. Every leaf, now she looks, is bristling. Millions on millions.

'They feel our vibrations,' whispers Richard. 'And the pulse of our blood. You OK?'

'Yes.' Whispering seems natural, not only because they might disturb animals but because this feels like church.

On her Christmas-pudding feet she follows Richard along a path so overgrown she can hardly see the mud. Each bush seems to grow in the act of writhing over her shoes. Gradually she gets used to flicking off the black sperm that gallop up her sleeves and wriggle into eyelets of her trainers.

A black bird flies across the track, trailing two tail-feathers ending in splodges like black lollipops.

'What's *that*?'

'Racket-tailed drongo. Wonderful, isn't it? And look.' Richard points at the stream where a snake's head breaks the surface, drawing two ripples after it like silver whiskers. 'Rat snake. King cobra's favourite food.' He takes a stick and lifts leaves round the base of a tree. 'Let's see . . . snakes love tree roots . . . Yes!' He straightens with a small snake hissing like a soda siphon hanging from his stick. Grasping its head, he carries it over as if offering a sacrament. 'It's OK. I've got him quite safe.'

A white V flows back from the snake's nose over its head. The pale body, writhing between hand and stick, is painted with red peacock-eyes outlined in cream.

'Russell's viper. One of the Big Four. You should tell Russel. This snake is a teenager too. The adults are much bigger.' Gently, he pinches its jaws and a translucent blue-pink gullet opens, showing two sugar-white front teeth, each with a white skirt behind. 'That membrane protects the fangs. When the mouth's closed, the teeth fold. They have to be syringe-sharp, they're very delicate. Kraits and cobras hang on and chew till they've pushed in enough venom, but these guys strike and retreat in the same millisecond so as not to get hurt by their prey.'

She feels as if its venom is beaming in through her pores. Is this what has sat at the bottom of her soul? The wild nature which she seems to have been born knowing, but which she's never actually seen? The eyes have vertical pupils. What is it thinking?

'What's the Big Four?'

'The snakes that cause most deaths. Cobra, krait, saw-scaled viper and this fellow. You must have grown up with them all round you. Russell's viper bites aren't fatal if treated, but they cause more deaths than any. People can't get help.'

'So little, to be so dangerous.' And Richard so large, holding it. She hasn't ever thought of Richard as large. He puts it gently on the ground, releases it and steps back. It shoots into the wet grass with a liquid zigzag, like a crack spreading across a saucer. 'Most people,' she says, aghast, 'well, like me, live such unaware lives.'

Richard says nothing. What does her life look like to him? She has a vision of human beings, the ones she and Tyler know anyway, zooming down the motorway with mavericks like Tyler weaving in and out, making things dangerous for others. But alongside are these other creatures, living their lives secretly in the silent lane. That grass looks so innocent, beaded with rain. You could walk through here and find death. But it'd only be one small creature, defending its life.

She'd wanted to forget the past but here it is, popping at her out of the grass like Hope from Pandora's Box. Damn this forest. Things are coming alive in her she hadn't expected.

215

'Our blushing brides were gorgeous, weren't they?' Rosamund smiled at Richard after supper and raised her glass. She had carried out Gopal's instructions for cooking *dhenki shak* and seemed delighted with herself, with him, with Bengal. They were sitting in a booth of light shed by one paraffin lamp. All around was shadow and the rustle of rain on the roof.

'Wonderful.' Privately, Richard was scolding himself for picking up that viper against all his principles. Disturbing an animal in its home, picking it up in protected forest: he could get banned from Indian forests for that and quite right too. Examining an Olive Oriental Slender for scientific purposes was quite different. He almost felt irritated with Ros for tempting him into betraying his standards. It was showing off in just the way he disapproved of. Not that Ros meant to tempt. She simply was temptation in herself.

Before supper, he had opened his bottle of duty-free whisky. He never normally drank out here. Rosamund had refused to let him open the wine.

'They're for celebrating your king cobras when you find them.'

Smiling, elbows on the table, Rosamund was a different creature from the woman afraid of her son getting lost in a Devon wood. So many different colours in her hair: amber, honey, cinnamon. Zoologically, he'd be hard pushed to describe it. Close to her temples, the almost pubic curls seemed brighter than the flame itself.

'What's it *like*, handling poisonous snakes?' She tipped her head on one side so the longest ringlet disappeared between her breasts.

'I learned a lot from a snake-catching tribe in Tamil Nadu, doing my snake musk study.'

'Snake *musk*?'

'We've learned a lot about that just in the last ten years. Nasty musk to discourage predators, nice musk to – er – attract mates. Vipers produce a fine spray, kraits a thick paste. Krait musk really stinks. Cobra's quite pleasant.'

She laughed. Her lips glistened in the soft glow.

'You're like those men who catch poisonous snakes on TV?'

'Rosamund! I *can* wrangle snakes, but only when I have to. *Herpetological Review* did a profile of the average herper. Irena said I ticked hardly any of its boxes. Only, she said, "indifference to wealth" and "sloppy dress". Your dad ticks even fewer. He dresses so correctly.'

'What are most herpers like?'

'Oh, motorbikes, beards, hard-drinking, fast talking . . .'

'Hard-womanising too, I bet.'

Richard pictured Vic Browne at King's Cross. '"Exhibit vigorous heterosexual behaviour while avoiding romantic commitment" is what the survey said.'

'How about the women?'

'It was one of the last scientific fields to have any women. They tend to do frogs not snakes. But there are some very good snake women, now.'

'But what's it like, handling snakes? That viper could have killed you.'

'You have to imagine how *it* feels.'

Nice, he remembers one Irula man saying, standing by a ditch with a Checkered Keelback running through his hands. That keelback had been aggressive but the Irula gentled it, then gave it to him. He felt it flow as if he himself had become part of its quest for pattern, for escape. Intense green all around, he remembered. Steel-grey sky. Colours of monsoon. The moment he first realised how connected he felt to these creatures of the earth.

'But why snakes? What do you see in them?'

'Your dad had a lot to do with it. He's a fantastic scientist, Ros. I don't know why *he* chose snakes but it's what he does with them in his work, how he sees big questions from tiny things . . .'

'How do you mean?'

'Like Darwin, deducing general laws from tiny details. Like . . .' Richard hesitated. It felt wrong to tell Ros what he talked about with Irena. But why not?

'Irena says one small gesture on stage, one person moving a chair, can make the audience feel, this is how all people suffer.' He felt he was breaking a taboo. 'You learn so much from the person you love, don't you?'

'What does Irena say about snakes?'

There was an edge to her voice now.

'We, er, talk about how there's so much you don't know. You only see a tiny part. Science is a – a journey.' This was the most naked thing he could say. Did Rosamund realise? After marrying Irena, he'd felt awkward with Ros. For years before that, he'd behaved to her like human clingfilm. How had Ros seen him then? Tongue hanging out! No wonder she turned him down.

'Scientists must always be the first to say they *don't* know, and go forward to the truth. Your dad's brilliant at that. And, er – with snakes, there's the – the mysteriousness.'

Irena, he realised, always knew what he meant, sometimes even before he said it.

'What about danger?'

'Irena says there's risk in anything worthwhile. She says she's so terrified when she goes on stage the boards feel electric.'

'She's never told me that.'

They were silent. He listened to the thudding rain. His own heart thudding, too.

'I've always been terrified of forest,' said Rosamund suddenly. Her breasts rose and fell. 'Today was the first time I've gone into it for over twenty years.'

'Really? You always seemed to know so much. I thought your dad must have shown you jungle. I was so jealous.'

'He took me once, on my ninth birthday. I don't know which I was more scared of, the forest or him. When he was ahead, round a corner, I met a dhole. Really close, staring at me from some bushes. I was petrified. I thought if I ran, I'd trigger the pursuit mechanism, I knew about that. I was small and skinny, I don't know how much real danger I was in . . .'

'Very little, unless it was rabid.'

'But it felt like everything I was afraid of in – well, Father himself. The watcher in the undergrowth.'

'You should have said, Ros. We don't need to go tomorrow.'

'What Father did give me was a kind of empty knowledge. Genus, behaviour – it's how I still get through life. I translate what people do, even what *I* do and feel, into animals.'

She sipped her whisky.

'Isn't that mad? I've never told anyone else. It's how I got through college, as far as I did get. I was having fun. First time in my life, you know? I did fuck-all work. You helped me with experiments, remember? I knew so much *stuff* from Father but only in my mind. I was petrified of the real thing. Snakes, forest, everything.' She was twisting her fingers. Should he take her hand? 'In the forest today – you weren't cross, you weren't going to criticise me . . .'

'Of course not.'

'It made me see how stupidly scared I've been. Of everything.' He was out of his depth. Oh for Irena. But she hadn't told Irena this, she'd told *him*. 'I'm scared of tomorrow, but I survived the leeches, didn't I? It'll help me face other things – I'm really trying to change.'

'Actually, you do seem, er, different. Not so – held back.' He took a surprised breath. That seemed, somehow, the most personal comment he'd ever made to anyone. 'Coming to India seems to be good for you.'

'It was always easier,' she was gazing at the flame dreamily, 'to go on being how I was, and do nothing.' He felt the night around them like wings. 'Things are going to be different, now.' She raised her glass. 'To the forest!'

'I'll drink to that.' He couldn't believe he'd bared his soul about science. And she'd bared hers in return. He saw her shirt falling away, the nipples on her breasts, he was stiffening, this never happened in her actual presence. And never indoors, only in the field. As if a metal plate left in his brain from an operation had begun glowing, he felt a kind of reckless glory—

No! No getting turned on. The fantasies hadn't gone at all. And here she was, looking just like them. He closed his eyes, then opened them. She hadn't noticed. She was clearing the plates.

'Will we see animals tomorrow?'

'I hope so.' He stayed sitting.

'What if it's one of your king cobras?'

'We freeze.'

'Richard!'

'Honestly, we're *very* unlikely to.' He was OK now. He began washing up. 'India's not Africa,' he said over his shoulder. 'You have to work to see our animals. I'm looking for signs, not contact.'

He felt every move she made behind him as if it were tattooed on his skin. She was scared of forest? He was scared too, now. How would he feel with her there?

Wednesday 6 July, Devon, 10.00 p.m.; Thursday 7 July, 2.30 a.m., India

The beech leaves, black sequins against a night sky streaked with purple, keep rain off the stream where four otters tumble round the empty badger sett. They slip into the water. Four round heads write four long Us on the surface. Downstream, the owl watches a hole where the rats who live behind the drain, whom Irena does not know about though she has her suspicions, will soon emerge. Over the grass before him lies a parallelogram of light. In the middle, like the pupil of an oblong eye, is Irena's shadow.

The only movement outside is the falling rain, the only movement inside is the shaping of Irena's lips as she memorises *Othello*. And the hand of the clock moving on, like clocks all over England, to twelve.

Wednesday 6 July, London, 11.30 p.m.; Thursday 7 July, 4.00 a.m., India

In bed, Russel looks at his mobile. He hasn't seen Dad since supper. He's nearly out of credit and the battery's low.

Charge it, says Kaa.

Na, it'll be OK. Russel sets the alarm for seven-thirty. Outside, two fox cubs tug a pigeon wing in opposite directions. Downstairs the house phone rings. Russel switches off his bedside light. Five minutes later, he switches it on again and fumbles at the table. He finds the phone and changes two digits. Eight o'clock is OK. Downstairs, the ringing stops.

15

Thursday 7 July, Buxa Forest, Bengal, India, 5.15 a.m.; 12.45 a.m., UK

'That's a bad sign,' says Richard, opening the mesh door. Rosamund sloshes through pouring darkness to the Gypsy.

'What is?' she says as he swings up beside her.

'Hang on – you always have to pray – ah!' The engine chokes into life. They bump down the slope. 'Did you hear a gecko as we left the house?'

'No, why?'

'There's a Bengali tale about Manasa the snake goddess. A merchant refused to worship her and she killed six of his sons in revenge. The seventh married a girl called Behula. When they left Behula's house, a gecko made a noise like this.' Richard smacks his lips. 'It's inauspicious, apparently, for lizards to chirrup when you leave the house.'

'Why?'

'Just is. Manasa sent a cobra to bite the groom on the wedding night.'

The jeep lurches and sticks. In the headlights, the slush looks like the inside of a giant Mars Bar. Rosamund grips the dashboard. Wheels churn, the engine whines. With Tyler, she keeps quiet when things get tricky. He gets venomously angry if he loses control. But Richard's back wheels hold and he drives on.

'Suppose we really get bogged down?'

'I get us out.'

'Aren't you frightened, driving here alone?'

'I've always done it. We all do.'

She looks at his silhouette against plumes of bamboo, high as houses, lashing in the rain. A sight most people never see, she knows this now, because India's national parks are closed to visitors in monsoon. What she is seeing is the forest replenishing itself.

221

Richard looks relaxed, planing the jeep over mud lit by the headlights into magenta toffee. Very different from the man Tyler laughed at for the way he opened champagne. He's the only person she's ever told about the weird way she thinks, and maybe the only one who would understand. After all, they did zoology together. 'You learn from the person you love.' What has she learnt from Tyler? And why, when she was young, didn't she see how interesting Richard was?

Jealousy shoots through her. She douses it. How dare she feel anything but gratitude towards Irena?

'So he died on his wedding night?'

'Yes, but Behula refused to cremate him. She guarded his corpse and drifted it downriver on a raft to the gods' abode where she danced so beautifully that Shiva persuaded his daughter Manasa to resurrect Behula's groom.'

It's light now, the trees are melting green sugar running with water. The jeep bumps over knobbly rock and she hears the chassis grate. Branches snap in at her window and a giant spider with yellow hairy legs swings in with them. Richard leans across, sweeping it gently out, the jeep slews across slimy furrows and stops, almost vertical, top wheels churning in air. They hang a moment, bounce down and go on.

Eventually the track peters out. Richard turns the jeep and switches off the engine.

'Now we walk. I'm amazed we've got this far.'

Rosamund gets out. The drizzle is fine muslin on her face, the dripping canopy sounds like spinach being washed. Richard feels in his bag.

'Compass, water, knife, binoculars, snake bag, camera, first aid, torch, stick, notebook, GPS . . .'

'My car's got one of those. What do you use it for?'

'To record where I find things. Let's go.'

Thursday 7 July, Kilburn, London, 12.15 a.m.; 4.45 a.m., India

Broken tunes raged in Anka's head. Ten days he hadn't called. His mobile was always off, or his message box was full. She'd managed to leave one message. She'd begged him to call. He hadn't.

Her pillow was fire. She turned on her other side. He never thought about his effect on other people. He made you feel he knew you deeper than anyone, then he left you alone, feeling still connected. 'We're so close it's like having another skin.' How could he heap such terrible silence upon her? She heard Helen going to the bathroom. You could hear everything in this flat.

Helen was choking. She flung off the duvet and raced to the bathroom. Helen was on her knees by the lavatory, sobbing, shaking. Anka put her arms round her. The bowl was full of orange vomit. Helen was hot, trembling, whimpering.

'I didn't tell you, Mum, I had a *horrible* kebab after school. Katya only ate a little of hers, even though she'd paid for it.'

Anka held her, smoothed the hair from her face, stroked the forehead where sweat stood like froth. Helen was twelve. She looked eighteen sometimes, but she was a child.

'It cost £3.49! I didn't like it but I'd paid so I ate it. Katya threw hers away.' Helen howled, as appalled by the money as by being sick. Her sobs turned into retching. Anka filled the tooth-mug with water.

'Wash mouth, *andele moj*. Not to drink. Rinse, only.' They knelt side by side, as if the lavatory were an altar. Anka rocked her, feeling Helen's hot flesh through the puppy-printed T-shirt.

'I keep trying to be sick and nothing comes.'

'You have taken everything out. Ev-er-y-thing! Bad kebab and supper, too.'

'Haven't you got medicine to stop me *trying* to be sick?'

'No, *dragi*. But now, will be better.' She helped Helen up. 'Sleep, little cabbage. Best medicine.' She helped Helen to her room and put a saucepan by the bed. 'If again you are sick.'

'Yuk.' Helen snuggled into the duvet dotted with dinosaurs.

'Tomorrow, I make soup we drank in village, when I and my brothers had *stomachi*. No school.'

'But Katya and me are showing our artwork.' Helen howled like a six-year-old. 'It's *very important*. It's our project on front doors. We've been doing it for ages. I *must* go to school.'

'Baby, you cannot. I ring Lasta. Katya will show project and tell you.'

Helen buried her face in the pillow.

'We did all that *work*.'

Anka stroked her hair.

'Will watch DVD.'

Helen's sobs grew weaker. Anka turned off the light.

'*Divojcica potok gazi*,' she sang softly, stroking her daughter under a blue diplodocus. 'Little girl treads on stream . . .' She hummed till she thought Helen was asleep. This was what mattered. Never mind lovers. Helen breathing, Helen calm . . . She stopped humming.

A muffled voice said, 'Can we watch *Titanic*?'

Thursday 7 July, Buxa Forest, Bengal, India, 9.15 a.m.; 4.45 a.m., UK

'Stand still,' Richard hisses. 'Completely.'

A dark snake gliding across the path stops and looks round with black full eyes.

'They don't focus with muscles that change the shape of the lens, like us,' whispers Richard. 'They focus by moving the lens towards or away from the retina. They mainly see movement.'

'Hard not to think it sees us.' The snake looks as if it knows all her secrets. It slides forward again.

'How *can* we understand them, really?' Richard sounds proud and obsessed, like a father displaying his baby. 'We learn things bit by bit but nothing explains the whole thing as you see it like this, in the wild.'

The snake's tummy is startlingly white. It is aquaplaning on milk.

'Moving without limbs,' whispers Richard. 'Imagine starting out to design that.' Such love in his voice. On the snake's back are pairs of white lines, wobbly as if chalked by a child. Each line veers towards then away from its partner. Some pairs cross. 'Of course no one did,' he murmurs, as if to himself. 'The fossil record's patchy but as snakes evolved they may have grown limbs and lost them several times over. Some have more than four hundred vertebrae. So many different ways of supporting ligaments and tendons to let it flow like that.'

'What is it?'

'Oh – thought you'd recognise it, after what you said last night. A krait. *Bungarus caeruleus*, because of that iridescent blue sheen. You only notice it in daylight.'

She puts her hands on Richard's shoulderblades to feel him solid in front of her. She remembers a row in the kitchen when she was little. A dead snake dangling from a stick. And Father very angry, shouting.

The head is in grass on one side of the path, the tail still hidden on the other. Then it's all gone.

'This is the only krait we saw in the south. Here they have two others. The banded and the black krait – which I've never seen. Fantastically rare. But it's rare to see any krait in daylight, they're active at night. So glad you've seen it. So close.'

'Horribly close.'

'It wasn't feeling threatened, Ros. Just going about its business. Most snakes only bite in defence.'

'Didn't you say kraits chew till they've pumped in enough poison? Aren't they unbelievably toxic?'

'But their venom's all they have. It's energy-expensive to make; they don't want to waste it on things they can't eat, like us. They evolved quick-acting toxins to catch little quick things like frogs, which have equipment they don't, like legs. Just bad luck they harm us, too.'

They walk on. Something bounds over the track in front of them, a large deer with muddy flanks and terrified eyes, gone as quick as it came. Rosamund hears galloping feet. Then silence.

'Sambhur.' Richard points to scratches on a tree. 'That's leopard, I think. Almost high enough for tiger. There is life here, still.' He stops so suddenly she bumps into him. He points to his feet, then up to a bent-back bough. 'Bicycle wire, look, across the track. Then running up that tree beside us – see? – and lashed to a clutch cable. Hell.'

'What . . .?'

'A snare. If any animal touched that wire, the cable would snap down round its throat and lift it off the ground. It would dangle here, throat half-severed—'

'And?'

'And die. Strangled, starving. Or they'd come and kill it. With guns, clubs, sticks.'

'Who?'

'Poachers. A tiger can fetch ten thousand dollars. Clouded leopard, leopard or simply that deer. The park director ought to be sending out patrols to clear these snares.' He sighs. 'This is why India's forests are emptying. I must record this.'

The wire is a silver cobweb. Rain hangs off it, a row of fat tears. Rosamund imagines a leopard half garrotted by this wire. Wild desperate yellow eyes. She hears Scott. 'Did you know a snake can moan?'

'A friend of mine works in wildlife crime in London. Some of the beasts killed here end up there, I suppose.'

'All over Asia there's a great dying.' Richard is taking a GPS position. 'In India it's getting worse and worse. Especially in the rains, when it's harder to police the forest.' He's taking photographs. 'Last year, in monsoon, Sariska Reserve lost *all* its tigers. That director tried to deny it. Said the tigers migrated, which tigers don't do.' He cuts the wire. The branch swings back, showering them with drops. 'My Indian colleagues are up against this everywhere.'

He drops wire and cable in his bag.

'Aren't there laws?'

'Masses. India has brilliant laws. But they're not enforced. The politicians don't care about wild animals. They care about development, which makes money for the rich. Wild animals don't have votes.'

'But you'd think – now India's booming, so sophisticated . . .'

'India's always been *sophisticated*, Ros. We're children in comparison. But billions of rural poor are desperate. Development takes away their homes. Where there still are forests, they try and make money from the animals.' He looks at the path. 'One animal saved, for now. But thousands of these things are being set in India's forests, this very minute.' He puts a hand on her shoulder. 'Let's go.'

She follows like a squaw. He dismantles four more traps and stops at a stream, a torrent of russet foam.

'Lunch-time. I used your oatcakes for sandwiches.'

'They were for *you*.'

'Now they're for us.' She sits on a boulder. The forest drips and spatters like Morse code. 'Perfect habitat;' he whispers. 'Stay here a second.'

He vanishes. She looks up. Trees rocket towards a sky she cannot see. Raindrops roll down every leaf, plashing to ten thousand more leaves below, hiding God knew how many small lives. She is alone in the forest.

Thursday 7 July, Kilburn, London, 8.00 a.m.; 12.30 p.m., India

'Lasta? Helen cannot come to school. She is sick. Sick all night, you cannot imagine. Will you tell Katya?'

'Oh no! They're presenting their art project today. Katya has gone on about it for weeks.'

'Can Katya text, to say what teacher said?'

'Of course. Tell Helen to get better.'

Anka put the phone down. Helen was still asleep. His message box wouldn't be full so early in the morning. She could leave a message *now*, break it off properly. Jumping out of cars in Piccadilly did not count.

She remembered that terrible time she phoned his house, five years ago. He'd given her the number, she didn't know he had a child and a wife. He didn't behave as if he did. She was whispering love when the phone was picked up and then, to her horror, she heard a child's voice. 'Hello?' So proud, the little boy had sounded. Confident. 'Hello?' he'd said again. She'd hung up.

She looked now at her phone as if she'd never seen it before. The rounded edge of the bit she put to her ear, stained brown. Ten black holes below, a little net. Round buttons, faded numbers, and one black dot for speaking into, the mouth of a tiny snake.

She pressed buttons and got voicemail. And she left her message.

Thursday 7 July, London, 8.10 a.m.; 12.40 p.m., India

Russel is among the Man Pack. Shadows of people on the pavement are stretched-out wolves they none of them see, running in front of them. It will never be this moment again, when he's walking to the Underground to save the forests and hates his dad. Not just ordinary teenage hate but real and for ever. Is there someone in another country, exactly like him, who has these same thoughts? Chennai perhaps?

A bit of paper somersaults past, opening butterfly wings, jerking like it's in pain, whatever written on it lost. Maybe a promise, an offer that'll never be made again, a spell torn from a magic book that holds the world together.

He'll forget this minute. He's overtaken the paper, he's already forgotten it. There are so many minutes. How can you keep track of the person you are in them all? No, he'll remember this minute for ever. Because this is life. All you get of me-in-the-world.

Here's the Tube. He turns off his mobile. At the black and silver vendor he presses the Zone 2 button. A ticket falls in the trough and Kaa, grey-blotched to match the pavement, rears to look. Kaa is interested in how things work. Bono was, too. He can feel Bono looking now, over his shoulder.

Shitloads of people, squashed in the lift. 'Doors closing,' says the recorded voice. 'Mind the doors.' What's it like, standing in front of some machine saying doors are closing when they aren't?

He feels dizzy, pressed against all these bodies. He hasn't eaten or drunk anything, he had to get out quick to avoid Dad. He sees Dad at supper, doesn't have to see him mornings too. Who needs breakfast? Maybe Dad wasn't in the house last night. Maybe he was alone. Shit he cares.

Going down. He'll be with the marchers at nine-fifteen. They won't all have left. It'll take time to move off, a big crowd like that.

Doors open. People shuffle along the tunnel just not touching, like they have sensitive whiskers either side of them. Over the bridge he sees a train pulling in and lopes down the steps, through the crowded platform, to get to the front. It has to be the front carriage, that's where he goes.

Inside, jammed against the Man Pack, he holds a yellow pole, like a liana in the forest he's speeding through this blackness to save.

'Upon arrival, the last doors will not open. Please move down the carriage to leave the train.'

Euston's a boring station, pale grey tiles. At King's Cross, a moment of relief, of feeling untouched as he changes lines. He hurries to the Piccadilly Line, for Holborn. A train's in, he races to the front carriage again but there are too many people in the way, the doors are closing, the train's proper full, one guy holds the door for him, the last door of the first carriage, but he can't get in. No room.

The guy, rather fat with shiny cheeks, wearing a blue baseball cap, gives up and pulls back his hands. As the doors shut he smiles and mouths SORRY. The train pulls out.

If he'd left his alarm at seven-thirty he'd have got there on time, easy. He looks at the tunnel roof. People think of the bit the trains go through as tunnels because they're black, but the stations are tunnels too, only higher.

He's made a study of the black electric boards that hang from them. Northern Line boards have one fat cable, a black python twisting away at the end into the roof. Circle and District boards have a black concertina each end, to protect live wires from rain. On this one, orange letters made of little separate bulbs twinkle like fish scales and chase each other, left to right. They disappear when an oblong block comes and shoos them all before it.

There's another train due in two minutes.

Thursday 7 July, Kilburn, London, 8.45 a.m.; 1.15 p.m., India

The sun was shining, her coffee was still as hot, but love was gone.

Anka squeezed the white flange to pull the phone cable from its socket and sat down at the keyboard. The only thing to listen to now was how she felt. She pressed three keys. First came the reluctant electric buzz, then the welling chord: C, E flat, G, the minor triad. From there, goodbye would come.

Helen appeared, face seamed where the pillow had pressed it, blue-painted toenails shimmering, the eyelashes of cartoon puppies on her T-shirt wobbling over her breasts as if the animals were winking.

'What time is it?'

'Quarter to nine. Katya will text you, after art lesson.'

'Can I watch telly?'

'Sleep now, *dragi*. Or read, till sleep again. Sleep, is medicine.'

'I'm hungry.'

'Later I make soup. Now, drink water. Sleep.'

Helen disappeared. Anka heard the bed creak as she got in and she stared at the spark of fake gold round her biro.

Somewhere a wave was gathering, carrying with it everything she had not wanted to see. A wave of grief and pure wrongness raced towards her over a sea of feeling she'd thought unshakable. His face, looking at her from on the pillow. Her heart, rising to meet his gaze. Love had lit everything she was, Anka the mother, Anka the musician, the Anka she'd been all these years. Her black lion. What would become of her now? *Che faro senza Eurydice?*

Should she have stayed with opera? Franjo Zubrinic was right, she had not been true to her voice. Nor to what she knew. That lion of hers had betrayed so many women before. He'd told her the stories – sometimes three at the same time. And always the wife, not knowing, at home. Why had she not asked herself what sort of man he was? She'd believed he was good. Maybe not in all things, but in loving her.

But he must be feeling terrible, after her message. Angry. But also hurt. She turned her mobile back on and pressed the number she knew in her sleep.

'I'm sorry. The number you are calling is unavailable. Please call later.'

Thursday 7 July, London, 8.49 a.m.; 1.19 p.m., India

Russel closes his eyes, holding another pole. He's in the jungle behind a tree, there's a tiger in the clearing ahead. But then there's a crack, the train shudders and stops, he is flung against the man beside him, everyone's falling, there's a noise like rocks crashing, the window has a white snake on it like lightning. The lights go out. He's on the floor, everyone's on the floor, arms, legs, bodies, they've hit another train, the tunnel's fallen, he can't breathe, can't see, someone's screaming, someone's shouting, 'Help me, help me!'

He struggles to his knees. His shoulder hurts. Where's Kaa? Thrashing among these bodies, getting trodden on.

'We've got a problem,' says a voice on the loudspeaker. 'Stay calm and we'll get to you.'

Someone bangs the door. Everyone's up now, they are standing, squashed and dark, he can hear their breathing. He closes his eyes and feels Kaa twining round him. 'We be one blood, thou and I.'

They wait, like in the jungle when man passes. After a long sweaty time someone says, 'There's a torch.' He opens his eyes and sees a little white flicker, like a falling coin, in the carriage behind. The end door opens.

'This way, please. One at a time.'

They go back through the unlit train. One carriage, the next. Everyone quiet. Shuffling. Someone whimpering. Bono. This is his fault. Bono has finally become the Avenger.

Last coach. The end door is open. A man is helping people step down into the tunnel.

'What's happened?'

'Something wrong with the train in front. An electrical fault, nothing to worry about. Keep calm, we'll sort it out. Follow the track to the station. All right, madam? Want a hand?'

Russel's legs tremble. When his turn comes, he yelps in pain. Holding the man's hand sends pain burning through his shoulder.

'All right, mate?' On the track another man puts an arm round him. Shiny lines stretch ahead.

'Don't touch anything,' hisses a voice.

'It's OK,' says another. 'They've turned it off.'

They walk in single file, like in a dungeon on a computer game. Ages in the dark. The gritty thud of feet. People hold up mobiles, they don't work but shed little blue lights. Then real lights begin on the walls, slung from sagging cables like a music stave. Between people's backs he sees the tracks glistening like silver snakes. He keeps his eyes on a spark of gold under the ear of a woman in front. She has her arm round another woman, who's limping. When she turns her head, Russel sees this spark is a gold loop. She catches his eye.

231

'Chin up, kid. Nearly out.'

One foot in front of the other. They come out below a platform. This must be how train drivers see a station. What happened to the driver? What about the train in front? And the guy who tried to let him in?

A guard is helping people on to the platform.

'Here you go, son. Upsy-daisy.'

His shoulder on fire, Russel walks along the platform. The escalator isn't moving, people are talking about a crash, the barriers are stuck open, the ticket hall is a bad dream, rows of people on the ground under Sock Shop and Body Shop, people covered in blood, people with red blankets over their faces, other people's hair grey with dust. Some with burnt faces, bleeding, sobbing. Ambulance men carrying stretchers. Loads of policeman. Is Scott among them?

Russel's eyes go black, this is his fault, the train that crashed was meant for him, he was nearly on it, Bono got it wrong. He should be on those stretchers.

'Go to Marks and Spencer,' someone shouts. There are loudspeakers but he can't hear what they're saying. His white trainers are black, he's covered in soot. Outside, there are sirens, ambulances, police cars, lorries and buses jammed and hooting.

'Are you all right?' says a man but he keeps walking.

This way, says Kaa.

Thursday 7 July, Buxa Forest, Bengal, India, 3.50 p.m.; 11.20 a.m., UK

'Quick,' Richard whispers, looking as if he's seen God. He takes her hand.

Rosamund trembles.

'Richard, I'm really afraid.'

'They can't hurt. It's once in a lifetime – quick.' He leads her off the path among leaves and leeches. Her legs feel wobbly.

'What?' she whispers.

'*Babies,* just hatched. Forty, at least. There *is* a breeding population. Don't worry, the mum'll be a long way away by now. She leaves the eggs before they hatch.' He puts his arm round her, encouraging. 'We think the eggs start smelling different before they hatch, which makes her leave so she doesn't eat the babies.' He pushes her under dripping boughs to a clearing like a bower. 'They've just left the eggs, the nest's in those bushes. See the umbilicus?'

Rosamund sees a heaving knot of tiny snakes. Eager, white-striped faces, big jet eyes, red threads glistening on their bellies. They are gliding over the grass, tongues darting in and out, ribboning away from each other like tentacles of an octopus.

Richard bends over them with a tape measure. They slide over his hands, ignoring him, intent on discovering the world. She watches him take photos, write in a notebook, face and hands close to their noses.

'Most are twenty inches. They grew nearly two foot in the egg.'

'Where are they going?' She thinks of Russel manoeuvring his rucksack to the front door, closing the door, stepping into ferocious London. 'What's the – the plan?'

'They have to take what comes. Mongooses and birds will eat a lot. Nature always over-produces. But they're strong, they've absorbed the yolk – want to hold one? They won't use their venom in the first few hours.'

'No, thanks. When will their hoods grow?'

'They have them, just haven't used them yet.'

He swings his cap in front of one. It stops and stares, mouth pursed as if whistling, rears like a bendy stick of black candy and spreads a tiny hood. Richard takes away his cap. It stands swaying, hood subsiding into sides of the head. Then it flows on again.

'Your dad would be in heaven. How right he was to send me here.'

'He sent you?'

'He suggested it. *Fantastic* we came today. A one in a million chance.'

He turns and kisses her. His mouth is scaly and hot. '*Thank* you, Ros. You've made me believe in this forest.'

She stands circled by his arm, watching king cobra babies wriggling into undergrowth, starting their lives. How's Russel doing without her? All her life she's explained people in terms of wild animals. Now here she is in the real intimate wild, wilder than wild, and what does she think of? Russel. Always Russel.

'Watch where you put your feet, darling.'

Richard heads towards the path. When Tyler calls her darling it's ironic, the ghost of something she used to think wonderful. He says darling to everyone anyway.

But Richard said it naturally. She feels like dancing.

They reach the trail.

'Must start back. Don't want to be here when it gets dark.'

Soon she can't see the leeches on her shoes. The light is thickening. The trees here have pinkish-red bark. There's more space between them. She can see a patch of purpling sky. Richard waits for her.

'Can you go a bit faster?'

'I'll try.'

'The jeep's just round that bend.'

'I need a pee. I'll catch you up.'

Thursday 7 July, London, 11.30 a.m.; 4.00 p.m., India

Russel walks. Each step feels like a precipice. His tongue feels enormous and dry. His shoulder throbs. Where is he? Here's a road sign with familiar round black letters. He thought he'd never see anything homey again. He doesn't deserve to. This was how Bono felt when he wanted water and was too weak to move.

'Ossulstone Street. Where the fuck . . .?'

This way, whispers Kaa.

The march must have gone without him. 'A train crashed,' he imagines telling them. 'Because of me.'

Dizzily, he passes cars, jammed and hooting; a row of parked ambulances, ambulance men leaning on them like they've been in a boxing match. One is being sick, another wiping his eyes. Now a street he recognises. He sees two dwarfish scarlet figures. His eyes and head feel strange, the red jumps up and down like blood. When he's close, he sees they are kids in fancy dress. Red cloaks, plastic swords. Is this a just world? Little kids go to fancy dress parties while all *that* is happening?

But maybe back there wasn't real. Maybe it was only for him. A warning, a message. He left the door open and Bono died. There's a reason bad things happen. It's always someone's fault.

What happened to the man in the baseball cap?

The kids are waving their swords. Fuck's the point, pretending the world's OK? It's a sign, what happened to the train, or seemed to happen.

What's real is here, his home. Here's the door he left open that night. He puts his hand in his pocket and finds his key. It could have fallen out in the tunnel. He can't believe, now, he walked in that tunnel and saw those people in King's Cross.

Inside, the black and white floor makes his eyes jump. His shoulder hurts, he feels sick. He pulls himself upstairs by the banisters and stops at the bathroom.

Drink water. Wash these black paw hands that don't look like his at all.

Call Mum in India, hisses Kaa.

Won't get through.

Call Irena. She said, call any time.

But Russel's looking at white. White bath, toilet, wall. He doesn't belong here. Tears sting his eyes. He opens the cabinet, takes Mum's bottle of sleeping pills and slips it into his pocket. He feels Kaa disapproving. But where was Kaa when Bono got run over? He fills his Thomas the Tank Engine mug with water.

It takes a long time, clinging to the banister with Kaa holding him up like the woman in the tunnel held her friend, to walk downstairs without spilling. He closes the front door. The phone starts ringing on the other side, as if he'd set it off.

Stupid bitches. How many nights has Dad stood there talking shite to them?

He kneels on the earth he packed over Bono's ashes. The grass hasn't grown back properly. This tree used to be their jungle, his and Bono's. It's the nearest he'll get to Chennai, now. He pictures the Waingunga at night and Bagheera crouching, a black shadow on the bank. Kaa makes himself into a hammock under him. Russel balances his mug on the grass and takes out the bottle.

The pain will stop. He will have paid for Bono.

Thursday 7 July, Chennai, Tamil Nadu, 4.45 p.m.; 12.15 p.m., UK

The man comes into the room. The gecko on the ceiling does not stir. Each of his toe pads has half a million tiny hairs, tipped with a thousand fibres, whose molecules generate a tiny charge with the molecules of the ceiling. He can stick to any surface on the planet and allows no intruder on this ceiling. But he shares the room with this man, he's used to him. When the light comes, he expects it. Notches in each slit iris of his pupils are already closing, like little guillotines, to control the glare.

The man switches on the computer. It groans, then hums. The gecko is used to that, too. But then the man slews back his chair and stands up like an earthquake. If tropical house geckos could read, this one would see 'London Rocked by Terror Attacks. Scores Dead. Hundreds Wounded!' But what he has evolved to react to is sudden movement. He whisks into a crevice as the man, clumsily, as if from a great height, drops his hand on the phone.

Thursday 7 July, Kilburn, London, 12.30 p.m.; 5.00 p.m., India

Anka sat back. Her song was truthful but there was more to say. And other tunes. Carols. Hymns she sang in Zagreb Cathedral. Could she write a sequence of goodbyes? For many instruments, not just keyboard and lute? Many people, saying goodbye to different things, not only her and her stupid love?

Helen came in, rubbing her eyes. Dust motes swirled round her legs in a ray of sun.

'Katya hasn't texted me yet. Art must be over.'

'No more sleeping?'

'No and I'm *really* hungry. Can I watch telly? Please?'

'Not TV, *Titanic*. We watch, together.'

Alone with her work, alone with her daughter, she would shut out the world completely, this one day.

Helen settled on the sofa, Anka fetched the dinosaur duvet, wrapped her in it like a parcel and put her arm tight round it. Soon, Helen would not want to watch films with her any more. With

Helen's head on her shoulder, Anka remembered saying goodbye to her own mother before climbing on to Pero's tractor like these Irish boys walking up a ramp to the *Titanic*. What about the boy from Eritrea, alone in a British prison? The people who worked in those Korean restaurants? The waitress from Kosovo? All their goodbyes?

This was Helen and Katya's favourite film. Helen had watched it a thousand times. Anka knew it scene by scene, just as she'd known *The Wizard of Oz*. Helen watched films repeatedly, then abandoned them.

Anka's arm tightened. Helen grunted sleepily. *If* she could write this cycle and Mr Zubrinic liked it. *If* she could sing it in New York, with her own name. Then, then, she could face her mother. Look. Your lovely granddaughter!

Later, she might try this first song on her neighbour Maureen's piano down the road. She never left Helen alone but Helen was nearly thirteen. And it was only two doors away.

Thursday 7 July, Primrose Hill, London, 12.40 p.m.; 5.10 p.m., India

The world is just. An eye for an eye. On one side the front door, on the other side the road.

'*Good* dog, Bono,' Russel says to the willow leaves above him. Kaa is squirming underneath. There's yellow sick on his trousers. His mouth is sour, his stomach jumping. Kaa's nose hammers his chest.

Call Dad.

Kaa is Dad's enemy. Why's he saying ring him?

His hand is floppy, a limp-dick hand. He wobbles it into his pocket, which is sticky, and pulls out the mobile. His fingers are nearly too feeble to press On. As he waits till the SIM card is ready, the phone gets heavier, like it wants to drop to earth. He fumbles, scrolling to 'Dad', and presses 'Call'.

Engaged.

'See?' he mumbles. Even his lips are floppy.

He hears Irena. 'There are good things in the world.' In the green lace of the tree above, he sees Mum's face.

Call Scott, says Kaa.

'Hi there, sorry I can't take your call. Please leave a message.'

'Scott.' His tongue is dangling. 'My train crashed.'

Say where you are, hisses Kaa.

'I'm at home.' The phone beeps, the battery's going. 'I took Mum's pills.' The battery pips like a bird, and dies.

Thursday 7 July, Buxa Forest, Bengal, 6.15 p.m.; 1.45 p.m., UK

Peeing in the jungle! Rosamund stares, overwhelmed by the beauty above, the intricacy of citron sky through black-leaf silhouettes. But she's still not keen on leeches and pulls up her trousers fast. She can hardly see her feet. Richard is a shadow ahead, reaching the jeep. She walks on. Nearly there, just step over this fallen bough lying across the path.

But the bough rears and twists round her leg, it's not wood but supple cable, thick as her arm. The end, clubbed like a pollarded branch, thwacks her on the chest. Rosamund screams and catapults backwards to the ground.

Thursday 7 July, Chennai, Tamil Nadu, 5.20 p.m.; 12.50 p.m., UK

Tobias Kellar holds the phone as if weighing a baby, listening to the ringing of a number he has not dialled for thirteen years. A voice in the instrument squeaks like a departing ghost. 'The person you are calling cannot come to the phone at the moment.' From its crevice, the gecko watches him hold the receiver in the air a moment, then set it back in its cradle.

Thursday 7 July, Buxa Forest, Bengal, 6.30 p.m.; 2.00 p.m., UK

'Did it get you?' Richard knelt by the dim heap on the ground that was Rosamund, shining his torch over her hands, legs, feet, face. 'No pain? Burning pain, anywhere?' They should never have stayed so late. He shouldn't have left her for an instant.

'No. What was it? Christ, what *was* it?'

'Can you stand?' He helped her up.

'It *hit* me! On my chest. On purpose.' She sounded indignant, not afraid.

'Get in the jeep, quick. It might decide you're a threat after all and charge.' He dragged her in, closed her door, ran round to his own door, swung in, slammed it and took her in his arms. 'You've found what I've been searching for. A really large one. Fifteen feet. Must have slid on to the path after I passed. It head-butted you.'

'It *what*?'

'King cobras do that. When they want rid of a threat but don't want to waste venom. It was saying "Piss off." I saw it getting away, as surprised as you. Not many people have trodden on a king and lived to tell the tale.'

He didn't say this was one of the very few snakes that *did* come after you, if it felt you were a problem. He switched on the engine. The trees lit up like a stage set and Rosamund laughed a wobbly laugh.

'Fancy just getting *butted* by something that could do so much worse.'

'Attagirl.'

He put one hand on her knee, steering between trunks with the other. Animal eyes glowed. He saw a python. And another krait, a ribbon of stripy tape. He loved this forest now.

'How do you feel?'

'I'll never be afraid of anything else, ever. I've escaped a king cobra!' A mongoose flicked to the side. Tree trunks processed past in the dark.

'How was it in Madras,' she asked suddenly, 'with Father?'

'He gave me lunch in his house. Your house. I saw his bronze Shiva.'

'Where was that?'

'On a shelf in the dining room.'

'I only saw that room on Sundays. Otherwise I ate in the kitchen. There was a little black angel behind Father's head in a hoop, kicking. Like *I* wanted to kick, when he shouted. But I was too scared.'

'That was no angel. It was Shiva Nataraja, India's holiest symbol. Shiva dancing his eternal dance, playing a drum to create the

239

universe, bringing fire to destroy it. And a cobra on his arm. Shiva's all about snakes.' Liquid ruts shine in the headlights. 'Did he shout at you a lot?' He felt close to Ros now as he never had, except in fantasy.

'When I did anything wrong, like spill something on the table-cloth. He panicked when things were not as he wanted them. As if he was afraid he'd break.'

'That's what Vic Browne said.'

'Professor Browne?'

'Did you know him? He worked with your dad in Cambridge. But before you were born, I should think.'

'He was at the end-of-exams party, our third year.'

'So he was. I only knew him later, as a colleague.'

'He was drunk.'

'He did hit the bottle. That's what killed him.'

'He's dead?'

'Yes. Lived by the snake and died by the snake. He handled a mamba after drinking. When bitten, he did nothing about it for an hour.' Richard put the Gypsy into a bend. The wheels waggled and skidded.

'Have you been bitten, Richard?'

'No. I'm pretty careful. They say people go into denial when they're bitten. "It didn't get me – well maybe it did get me – all right it got me, but I'm going to be OK."' He paused. 'What was it like, Ros, growing up with Kellar?'

'Well – he taught me, lectured me, read to me. The other people, the servants – though I didn't think of them like that – were very kind. The gardener let me grow flowers. The cook taught me to dance. That kept me going.' Something tiny fled across the track. 'Was that a mouse?'

'Tree shrew. A very wet one.'

They both laughed. He might open one of her bottles of wine when they got back.

'There was someone I loved who put me to bed when I was little. I only recently remembered her name. Alagu, the housekeeper. I remember crying hysterically when she left. And Father being furious I cried. I was always breaking rules I never understood.' The going was easier now. 'Mostly it was Father educating me or ticking me off. The only ordinary thing we did was when I helped him pack the car for his expeditions. A white car, creamy and curvy.'

'An Ambassador.'

'How do you know?'

'That's what everyone had. Another national symbol, that car.'

'It was a privilege, helping him pack. I'd trot in and out of the house carrying things, proud if he put something where I suggested. Then he'd send me in, take everything out and rearrange it. I'd watch from the window, feeling so *unnecessary*. As if there was never any point to what I did.'

'Here we are.' The clouds had lifted, leaving layers of striated amethyst, black and purple sky over the inky forest. 'Drinks on the terrace? I've never needed to celebrate more. *That's* where I'll do my study. You found the spot, Ros. Thank you.'

'First,' she said, 'I'm going to the bathroom to check for leeches. All over!'

An hour later, they were sitting side by side, mosquito coils at their feet like incense burners, her head on his shoulder as he'd always dreamed.

'When you danced at Easter, they were Indian dance movements, weren't they?'

'Parvati taught me. I longed to be a dancer. "Walk in circle, spread hands" – whoops! Sorry, are you OK?' Her hand had banged his cheek. 'She'd hang her necklace on me. "Hand is snake. Gold snake, sway up and down."'

'Parvati was a Shiva devotee. The dancer's hands are Shiva's snakes. My friend Girish's a fan of traditional dance.' He heard a gunshot in the forest. Poachers. Rosamund hadn't noticed.

'The moon's a white plate,' she said, 'over those hills.'

'The Dooars.' He smoothed a curl on her temple, awed to be so close. This moment would stay with him, etched in glass. It was his, to keep. He leaned his forehead against hers. But what was he *doing*? He pictured Irena's eyes.

Suddenly he hated Ros. If it wasn't for her there would be no shadow between him and Irena. But Ros looked up as if asking to be kissed, his lips touched hers, her tongue slipped into his mouth, curled round his teeth and ran over the back of his top lip. He found his hand stroking her breast.

For twenty years he had dreamed this in shy, tortured detail as only a scientist can dream.

I've been in love with you ever since we met. I've taken you with me into the jungle for years. Today you were really there and I nearly got you killed.

His fingers worked into her bra and found her nipple. He felt he was touching her soul. How could it be so small when she'd had a child? But what did he know, he knew nothing about this woman he had yearned for. The nipple stiffened in his fingers.

A double gunshot cracked in the forest. Another animal dying.

He slipped to kneel before her, resting his brow on her knee like a medieval knight, then picked up the mosquito coils, took them indoors, lit a lamp and hung it by the gas ring.

'I'm going to make you the most beautiful rice and *dal*,' he said, 'in the world.'

Thursday 7 July, Kilburn, London, 4.30 p.m.; 9.00 p.m., India

'Can we see *Bridget Jones* now?'

'I think, sleep.'

'The soup made me unsleepy. *Please?*'

Anka slipped *Titanic* back in its sleeve. She brought out *Bridget Jones* and fed it into the machine.

'C'm on, Katya,' said Helen, frowning at her mobile. 'I don't know why she's not answering.'

'Maybe, battery.'

'She always charges it at night. She's much carefuller than me. She remembers.'

An hour went by. Helen's head dropped on her arm. This had been a healing day. Twenty-four hours with Helen, cut off from the world. She had written the song that freed her. She could feel others waiting to be written. She'd love to try this one on a proper piano.

The duvet had fallen off Helen's bare thigh. Anka hitched it up

242

but Helen kicked it off and stretched her toes over a cherry red stegosaurus.

'Hot.'

Anka laughed.

'OK, little apple, if I go later to Maureen's? To piano, one hour?'

'Course. I'll be fine.'

Helen turned and hugged her neck.

'Thanks for looking after me, Mum.'

Thursday 7 July, Buxa Forest, Bengal, 10.30 p.m.; 6.00 p.m., UK

What is she doing? This long forgotten moment of *about to*. About to make love. But – to *Richard*? They're on the sofa, his head between her breasts. She's never fancied him before. But he saved her from the snake, she's been so lonely and his lips are round her nipple. The one thing she wants from this life, she suddenly thinks, is to know herself loved.

Suddenly she sees Scott, looking puzzled and hurt. Then Irena, laughing when they iced that cake last Easter.

What *is* she doing? Has she been tainted by Tyler? Did something bad in her, that Father always said was in her, recognise something corrupt in him? She hears Father's voice. 'You're a devil, aren't you?' Maybe Father was right. Maybe it was the other way round, maybe Tyler was tainted by *her*.

Richard sits up. He picks his spectacles off the floor, tucks in his shirt and stands.

'I can't, Ros. Irena's my *life*.'

Rosamund presses her face into the rusty velvet. It smells of mould, of hopelessness.

'I'm sorry, I shouldn't have —'

They hear footsteps. A knocking at the door.

'Mam, mam! Telephone,' says a voice. 'Urgent.'

Rosamund buttons her shirt. Richard opens the door to Anand, the guard.

'Mam, is all right. But urgent, urgent.' Eyes fixed on Richard, he speaks in rapid Bengali.

'He's bicycled here in the dark,' says Richard. 'Must have taken hours. Something's happened in London. Russel's OK, but you should leave at once. Get your stuff, we'll try and change your ticket by phone, I'll ask the Bhutanese boy who was going to show you round to drive you to Calcutta. If he can't, I will.'

In ten minutes, with Anand's bike in the jeep and Anand sandwiched between them talking excitedly, they are slithering along the track, headlights flashing on bushes and lancing rain.

'It was a bomb,' says Richard. 'Some friend of yours phoned. Anand didn't understand. Only that Russel's OK.'

At the Outpost Anand shows them his notepad.

'Mister Tyler, one time. Mister Scott, two times.'

Under Endangered Fauna of the Dooars she tries the house phone. No answer. Then Tyler's mobile. 'The number you are calling is unavailable. Please call later.'

But Scott – Scott answers.

'Thank God! What's happened?'

'First thing, love, Russel's OK. He was caught in the bombings, but wasn't hurt. Just a shoulder sprain.'

'Bombings?'

'On the Tube. Russel's train was only stuck in a tunnel. He's shocked, but the hospital say he'll be fine.'

'But – but –' she can't think – 'why was he on the Tube at all?'

'He was going on a march to save the rainforest.' She stares at a mosquito floating round the desk light and starts to cry. 'He tried to get on the train that was hit but couldn't squeeze into the front carriage.'

'He always goes in front.'

'Five minutes earlier, he'd have been on that train. Those five minutes saved his life.' She gazes into dimples in the beige computer cover. 'He had no idea it was a bomb. He thought the train had crashed and it was his fault.'

'What?'

'Steady. Listen. This isn't as bad as it sounds. He went home and swallowed all your sleeping pills.' Her eyes go black. 'I got to him in time. Luckily he had the bottle so we knew what they

244

were. He's right as rain. They wouldn't have killed him anyway, apparently.'

'But – *why*?' Her voice is a wolf, a howl.

'He'd been brooding about the dog. He feels guilty. He thought the crash was punishment.' Papery moths waltz round a bulb in the ceiling. How could she not have known? How could she have *left* him? 'He knew it was silly, he phoned me before he lost consciousness. He was under that tree of yours in front. Mobile networks were down, it's chaos here, but his message got to me. Took him to Edgware General. Casualty everywhere else was full.'

'Where's Tyler?'

'Can't locate him. Left a message at yours. Tracked down his office, no one. The bombs hit in rush hour, see. Found his mobile, left a message. If he doesn't make contact tomorrow, I'll take Russel to mine. Hospital knows I'm a copper, they're happy to discharge him to my care.'

'How's he feeling?'

'"Fuckin' stupid!" That's what he said. He also said to say hi. I left him asleep.'

'I'll come soon as I can.'

'Take care now. This place is like a war zone. Everyone's lost someone or thinks they have, everybody knows someone who's hurt. Phone when you land, I'll tell you where to come.'

'I . . . Scott, thank you . . .'

'We'll be waiting for you.'

Thursday 7 July, Kilburn, London, 10.30 p.m.

Anka closed Maureen's piano and sat looking at her knees. A strange, life-changing day. Now she could rejoin the world. She had rediscovered an excitement she had somehow mislaid. She felt humble and weak. Grateful, like after Mass.

She walked out of Maureen's flat into her own house and up the stairs. She gave her lock that twist it needed. The hall light was on. Hadn't she left it off? Maybe Lasta had brought Katya round to tell Helen about the art lesson.

245

In the living room, the TV was on. No sound. *Bridget Jones* must have finished, there was a police film instead, full of ambulances. She recognised the backdrop. That flesh-pink brick was the hotel in Russell Square, near the recording studio. The dinosaur duvet was a heap on the sofa. Helen must be in her room with Katya.

Did Lasta bring Katya and leave? There were two wine glasses and a nearly empty bottle of white wine. Did Budimir and Lasta bring it? Why had Helen not told them where she was?

Then she heard Helen's voice, high and afraid. And a man's. She ran to Helen's bedroom and by the My Little Pony shelf, all those big dolls' eyes and sparkly ponies, Tyler was standing with his arms round Helen, his flushed cheeks pushed out like a cherub blowing a trumpet. Helen's puppy T-shirt was crooked, her face flushed too, her black hair over one bare shoulder.

'*Isuse Krise!*' Anka hit Tyler's face. '*Gade jedan, kako si mogao?*'

Tyler pushed her away, Helen burst out crying and ran out, stumbling over slippers on the floor. Anka heard the bathroom door slam and hysterical sobs behind it. Tyler held his cheek looking at her, tousled and stupid.

'*Tako si Odvartanice –*' she didn't know bad enough English – '*da te ne mogu vise gledati!*'

She snatched a naked Barbie doll off the chest of drawers and advanced on Tyler, pointing the sharp feet at his eyes.

'*Izdajnice!*'

'Hang on, sweetie, you don't—'

'*Šupak jedan,*' she hissed. 'What you are *doing*?'

He fled unsteadily out into the living room. She chased after, saw him slam the door, heard him slither down the stairs, bang the house door and off into the night. Shaking, she laid the doll on the keyboard lid where it looked like a cut of raw meat on pitch. She stood by the frosted bubble-glass of the bathroom.

'Helen?'

No answer. Anka turned off the TV, plugged the phone in, turned her mobile on and listened to messages.

'This is the secretary at St Mary's. The school will be closed for the rest of the week, due to the bomb at Edgware Road Station.'

Anka stared at the phone.

Then Budimir, like an old, old man.

'We're at the hospital. Katya's alive, but lost a lot of blood. Lasta's with her. We're working all night, the corridors are full of wounded.'

She tried Budo's mobile, heard the rising quavers that meant it wasn't working, rang their house and got voicemail.

'*Dragi Budo, kako si mi? Stvarno mi je žao!* I was working, I cut off phone, *Gospode Bože* what has happened, how is *Katya*?'

The bathroom door burst open and Helen shot like a hot plump bullet into her arms.

16

Saturday 9 July, Heathrow, 11.00 a.m.; 3.30 p.m., India

'Scott?' Rosamund, dizzy with no sleep, sways in the passport queue behind an elderly man in an African turban. He too must have had an achingly long flight, with hours of hanging around in midnight airports.

'I've landed. Where's Russel? How is he?'

The elderly man shuffles forward. She follows.

'Fine. Here with me and Bramble. Got a pen?'

She scuffles in her bag.

'17B Regis Road, Kentish Town. Mind how you go. Roads are closed round all the bombed stations and the bus.'

'Bus?'

She watches the man in front show his passport to a uniformed woman at a booth.

'One bomb was on a bus.' Behind passport control is an ad for Credit Bank. The uniformed woman shows the old man's passport to another official who examines it as if beetles were crawling through the pages. 'Russel's saying can you get a top-up card for his phone?'

'Of course. Send him my love.'

'He sends love too. Take care now.'

She gets through quickly at another booth. That man is still at the barrier. No Credit Banks for him. Feeling guilty, she rescues her luggage, buys a paper and finds a cab.

Sitting back, she realises she's coming home to a different city from the one she left. A city in mourning, terrified, with people on a train, which Russel tried to catch, dead in a tunnel thirty metres below the pavement. With men cutting their way in a hundred

248

degrees of heat to pull those people out. A city with a bus in it which she must have ridden on, blown apart in a street she travels down all the time. A city of hospitals where hundreds of people are fighting for lives that have changed in one second, for ever.

Scott opens the door. At the tenderness on his squashed face, so happy to see her, so anxious for her, she nearly howls. She's exhausted. She's been holding herself in for this. She rests her forehead on his chest like a babe that has struggled out of the wood and found its mother.

'Come upstairs. Russel's here, he's fine.'

His living room is, as she always imagined, very neat. There is a dog bowl in a corner, a bookcase with paperbacks and, on the wall, a grainy black-and-white photo of a hare with worried liquid eyes and ears like razorshells.

'Hi, Mum.'

Russel's arm is in a lime-green sling. Will she know how to talk to him? It's as if he, or she, is back from a lunar expedition. What he did, what he went through – hasn't it set them impossibly apart, like people at opposite ends of the Sahara?

The dog bounds across the room, plants his paws on her thigh and licks the air.

'Down, Bramble. Knee him, Mum. Don't let him jump up.' She can hear how anxious he is to show he's OK. The spell breaks. She kisses him lightly.

'Glad you're OK, love.'

'What animals did you see,' he asks, 'with Richard?' He sounds more vulnerable, less unapproachable, as if something has burst. Maybe he feels that she's changed, too.

'Baby king cobras. And a grown up one reared up and hit me.'

'Cool.'

'We were plotting,' says Scott after a moment. 'Hope Russel can help us this summer. We're still monitoring that peregrine nest on the Tate, make sure no one nicks their second clutch of eggs.'

'Brilliant.' She sits down. 'Must take my malaria pills. Got to take them for a month after.'

'Bet you didn't eat.' Scott gives her a mug of Nescafé. No spoon, no sugar; he knows she doesn't like it. Her heart opens and closes like a sea anemone.

'I couldn't.'

'How was the flight?'

'I changed at Delhi. It's taken eighteen hours.' They are trying to be ordinary, but nothing's ordinary. Russel's lime-green sling burns her retina.

'Still no word from your old man. When does he leave for work, mornings?'

'Never before half nine.'

'Then he's fine. Those things hit ten to nine.'

'He takes the car anyway.'

'Dunno he was there,' says Russel.

'He wasn't at home?'

'Didn't see him. Did you buy the top-up card?'

'Here.'

They watch Russel manipulate his mobile with one hand.

'Three voice messages.' He presses the loudspeaker. Tyler's voice makes her jump.

'Russ, old chap, just wanted to check you're OK at school. Don't want to disturb your charming lessons but funny things are happening on the Tube. I'll try again. Keeping m'phone off, there's a stalker after me.'

Russel presses again.

'Hi, Russ, just making sure you're OK. Can you text me?'

And again.

'Russ, it's Dad!' Heavy breathing, slurred, as if Tyler is running and also drunk. 'I'm in Euston Road, I'm coming. Hang on, old man! I'm coming . . .'

'Friday,' says Russel. 'Twelve-thirty. Like, after midnight.' The phone gives a lolloping burp.

'Text. Did you text me, Mum?'

'No, darling.'

She sees Russel's face go blank. She rises and grabs the phone.

Yr number found under SON on phone of patient mr t
Fairfax unconscious univ college hosp falconer ward pls
contact sister.

Scott looks too.

'Four, on Friday morning. Thirty-three hours ago.'

Rosamund puts her face in her hands.

'Mum . . .'

The room whirls. Scott is talking on his phone.

'Driver I know will be at the door in five, get you there soon as he can. Russel and I will wait here. Stay with her, son, while I make her a sandwich. She needs to keep her strength up.' Rosamund sits, holding Russel's arm. 'How's your own battery?' says Scott gently. 'Phone us. I'll bring Russel whenever you want.'

They inch forward in blue veils of exhaust, half hour after half hour. ROAD CLOSED. DIVERSION, ROAD CLOSED. Her head aches, her skin feels like sand, when did she last moisturise? Everyone imprisoned in metal, everyone wondering where the next bomb is, with pictures they can't wipe from their minds, of people they love caught in wreckage they've seen on the news, wondering what they went through in their final seconds.

And not this city only. Dizzy with fear, fatigue, no food, Rosamund suddenly feels part of other cities all over the planet, where people live like this all the time. And sometimes – she remembers Irena's fury – because of things decided here, in this city. Baghdad, Fallujah, Gaza, Beirut. ROAD CLOSED, ROAD CLOSED. Everywhere, this is the world.

The nurse on reception, a Jamaican woman with hollows under her eyes as if she hasn't slept for a week, looks at her screen.

'We tried his house. No answer.'

'I was out of the country.'

'The wards are full. We've had seven hundred serious injuries in this city in one day. Your husband's in the corridor of Falconer, third floor.'

'What happened to him?'

The nurse scrolls wearily back. She had already gone on to something else.

'Car accident, Thursday night. He ran into a lorry on Euston Road. Police will contact you.'

Everywhere in corridors and lifts are stretchers, nurses running, porters pushing trolleys with tubes arcing over them. Falconer corridor is packed with bodies lying on wheelie beds or the floor.

'You passed him in the passage,' says the tiny nurse at reception. Malaysian? Philippine? She looks like an exhausted doll. As if her throat might snap. This is a world where no one sleeps except the dying.

'He has been conscious now and then. You may be lucky.'

She leads Rosamund past bodies lining the passage like parked cars, to a patient lying under a lamppost of transparent swagging. Perspex tubes bubble liquid and air down under the sheet, into the back of his hand and into a mask over his nostrils. Other tubes pipe liquid the colour of watery cider out of some sorrowful part of his innards. The lips are scraped frost, a crackelure of quartzy dead skin shrivelling at the edges. The girl has made a silly mistake. This isn't Tyler.

Rosamund looks at the next trolley, a man whose skin is the pitted texture of foam on coffee, with a mothy line on his upper lip as if he'd been drinking black soup.

The nurse, a girl really, touches her shoulder.

'Can you sit on the bed? We've run out of chairs.'

Rosamund sits on the rim of the trolley beside the first man, still as a knight on a tomb.

'I'm sorry, Mrs Fairfax. The doctor said it's only a question of time. There are severe internal injuries.'

'Could you give me – details – later?'

She takes the patient's hand. The nails are bitten below the fingertips, the skin swells up and over them. The hand she treasured when she and Tyler became part of each other, she had thought for ever. She strokes the gold band she put there on Russel's first birthday. *Diamonds on a ring of gold.* The ring Tyler has worn through everything, till now.

What was that madness in India the other night? It's with Tyler that she learned about loving and being loved. She brings her other hand up, swaddles Tyler's between both. Her thumb stroking Tyler's thumb, she leans forward and puts her lips against the bottom lobe of his ear, the only bit she can reach. Everything else is covered in bandage. He smells like a chemist's counter.

'*Harbour in the tempest,*' she whispers. He'd laugh; he always told her she was a hopeless singer. Then he'd whisper, 'I need you, Rosie. I love you beyond all the world.' '*All the promises we make, from the cradle to the grave, when all I want is yours.*' They are alone like Tony and Maria at the dance in *West Side Story*. She feels her breath come back to her from his bandaged ear.

She sees a denim glint between his eyelids.

'Russel?' he whispers through those terrible cracked lips. She can feel what an effort it is, expelling the air.

'Russel's OK, darling. He's fine. But he thought the bomb was his fault. He's been in agonies of guilt at leaving the front door open so Bono was run over. He thought it was a punishment.'

Tyler's fingers twitch. She watches a breath force its way in. The denim glint has gone.

The nurse is beside her.

'Can I stay the night?'

'Of course. The doctor will be round soon. Ask him anything you want.'

Rosamund rests her head beside Tyler's. Is that a sigh, or the creak of displaced tubing? She imagines Tyler driving, drunk – and desperate to reach Russel. Panicking the way he always panics at the wheel. And her not there to help.

She wakes when a hand moves her shoulder.

'Mrs Fairfax?'

A dark man in white is bending over her.

'Sorry.' She sits up. There are noises and echoes everywhere, feet clacking, wheels clattering, strip lights humming. She has slept in pandemonium.

The doctor looks Indian, she feels a bond, she has come from his home. He looks tired to death.

'Is there anything you'd like to ask?'

'She said it was a – question of time. What's wrong with him?'

'*Many* internal ruptures. Spine broken in two places, ribs, pelvis – we've put in drips and patched things up. We're concerned about the heart. Did he smoke?'

'Like a chimney.'

'The lungs are full of fluid. He's not in pain; he's on several drugs including morphine. He had severe concussion and there's massive secondary infection we're trying to control. But his temperature's right up now. I'm sorry, Mrs Fairfax.'

'How – long? My son . . .'

The doctor looks at his notes. She watches him watch Tyler.

'I think he'll last tonight. But your son should come tomorrow.'

'Can I phone?' Rosamund asks the nurse later.

'Phone and toilets that way, dear. No mobiles.'

Rosamund leans against the black cowl of a payphone. The coin slot, its scuffed silvery metal, is the vertical oblong pupil of a goat.

'Hello?' Scott's voice. She closes her eyes in relief.

'I'm staying the night.'

'What's happening, love?'

'He'll last the night.'

'I see.'

'Can you bring Russel early tomorrow? And – prepare him? Tyler's unconscious. There are tubes. An oxygen mask.'

'Sure.'

'Is he OK?'

'You OK, mate?' she hears him say. She opens her eyes.

'Russel says he's fine. Did you eat that sandwich?'

'I forgot.'

'Look after yourself.'

'I'll try. Thank you.' She feels her throat tighten. 'Tell Russel, Dad was conscious a moment. He asked about him.'

She puts the phone down, remembering a toddler with pale hair like sherbet fizz waiting at the window for Daddy to come home. She hasn't managed to forgive her own father but she must help Russel forgive his.

*

254

They lie side by side, their faces up to the ceiling like pages of an open book, in that mysterious safety which two bodies make for each other. Tyler is the road she has travelled to. The pipes carrying liquid into him sway above like twigs on the tree of life. If they hold each other close enough, or if she holds him since he is not in the market for holding, darkness will be kept at bay.

She lives every struggling breath. She whispers, like their first night together, that she loves him. He did love her, once. As much as he could.

'You learn from the person you love.' What she learned from Tyler was how to love. She'd never managed to know whether love was what she felt for her dad, or not.

She feels hot pressure in the area of her heart. What does Tyler's own heart look like now? Staring at the strip light's pearly unlit cylinder, she whispers to him, 'I danced in the morning when the world was begun.' She sees him as a dancing cowboy, alone inside his whizzing lariat. In the desert, with a dark horizon across and beyond him. 'I danced in the moon and the stars and the sun,' See, sweetheart, I do remember the words.

Saturday 9 July, Kilburn, London, 10.30 p.m.

For two days, Anka and Helen had talked only of Katya. Katya was going to live. Her face would be all right, the hospital had taken the glass out, her eyes were OK. They'd all sat with her, Helen had been brilliant, holding her hand, chatting. Budimir and Lasta had worked in the hospital for two nights and two days. Lasta's face was grey. Then Anka gave Lasta the meatballs she'd brought and took Helen home.

Now Helen was sitting on the sofa sobbing. She had cried so much her face looked like a puffball. At last she was talking about Thursday night.

'When he came, I'd just seen about the bombs on TV. It happened that day, Mum, and we didn't know!'

'Yes.'

'I phoned Katya's, no answer, I couldn't text, it kept saying "message failed". I thought I'd come and find you, but I wasn't dressed.'

Anka held her tighter.

'He had a bottle of wine and was, like, excited. His face was red.'

'Drunk.'

'He knew where the opener was and everything. How'd he get in, Mum? Didn't you close the door?'

'I gave him key. Long time ago.'

'He said he was going to drink this with you or break it over your head. What did you say to him?'

'Never mind.'

'He said he got your message and felt so upset he turned his mobile off. I felt sorry for him.'

'He is good at, making women sorry for.'

'He said he didn't deserve it. He was nice at first, Mum. He called me a sweet thing.'

Little girl treads in a stream . . .

'He made me drink wine, he said the bombs were a shock, I needed it.'

'Drkadžijo!'

'He told me how *he* heard about the bombs. He was going to drive to work from his girlfriend's, but the radio said London traffic was all stopped so he thought he'd make a day of it with his girlfriend.' Anka breathed deep. She remembered him saying, 'Other people are salvation.' 'Then he realised it was, like, bombs. He tried to phone his son. I didn't know he had a son.'

'Is fourteen. Where his daughter was?'

'He didn't mention her. Like, he seemed not to be living with his son either. He said it was crazy; he loved his wife. "She freezes me out," he said. "Hence the girlfriend." He talks funny. He said his son and his wife were the only ones who mattered and his son was OK because he was at school – Oh, Mum!'

Helen sobbed again. They knew, now, a pupil from the school had died at Edgware Road and many had been hurt along with Katya.

'He said this was it, he was going to turn over a few new leaves, everything was gonna change. I didn't really listen, I was worrying why Katya hadn't phoned.'

'Should not have been going, to Maureen's.'

'He poured more wine. The next didn't taste so bad.'

'*Izdajico.*'

'He asked what boyfriends I had. I said I didn't have any. He said what was the matter with boys these days? I could be a model. He said I had a gorgeous mouth.'

'*Seronjo, zašto si to učnio.*'

'I was dizzy. He said I should lie down. He said he was in loco pantis and I must go to bed. I didn't want to, but he took me to my room.'

'*Drkadžijo!*'

'As soon as we got in, his mobile beeped.'

'Mobiles not working nowhere, Lasta said, that day.'

'It must've come back on. He suddenly got a voice message.' Helen's voice trembled.

'He started shaking, Mum. Crying. Like, a grown-up man, crying? He said his son was in hospital. He put his arms round me like he couldn't stand, his breath smelt really yuk. He kept saying, "Jesus". Then you came in.' Helen burst out in sobs.

'*Duso, popij! Malo caja od mente.*'

Mint tea, what else? Just as her mother used to make it. Anka stroked Helen's hot damp hair.

Sunday 10 July, University College Hospital, London, 8.30 a.m.

Rosamund watches Tyler's chest rise and fall. A chair has appeared. She looks at its plasticky sheen and stays where she is, her head on the pillow with his.

'Russel's coming soon, darling.'

Now Russel is sitting in the chair. She sits up. Tyler's eyelids have parted.

'Hey,' he whispers. Russel glances at his mauve lips, then back at the floor.

'Old—' whispers Tyler, and stops. There is a guttural silence. Tyler breathes like someone who has just been swimming in rough sea.

'Clap.' Rosamund takes Russel's hand. He tugs it away but she lifts it to Tyler's hand lying on the sheet like a lost glove. Russel's convulses in a little parody of a handshake.

'Remember how he drove through the night,' whispers Rosamund, 'to get you that train set?'

Russel's head goes down slowly till his forehead is touching the sheet, as if he's bowing. His shoulders shake. Tyler's eyes are closed, the skin grey like winter sky. But even with corrugated lips, trussed up like a mummy, Tyler can talk.

'Bono.' She feels his exhaustion, saying that one word. 'My – fault.' The glint of his eyes is turned to Russel's head. 'Front . . . door.' A whisper like brushing dust. More breaths, terribly uneven. 'Open.' The bruise-colour lips push out. 'Not –' a breath like gravel flung up on the chassis of a car. 'You.'

Russel's head comes up. Blue eyes meet blue.

'Dad.'

Silence.

'Dad, sorry I didn' help with your Mac.'

There is a sigh, as if Tyler has at last found something he can stay with. Russel tips forward on the bed, his cheek on Tyler's hand.

'I need to change his bottles, Mrs Fairfax,' says a nurse. 'Fancy a coffee for ten minutes?'

Scott guides her and Russel down. Tables in the canteen are the colour of stained teeth. In a mirror in the Ladies, the hollows under her eyes are lilac sacs, their edges sharp as bone. Everything in the canteen glitters, perspex over the muffins, black-crackle Mars Bar wrappings, chrome on the coffee machine.

Back with Tyler. Boxes of light moving over the floor.

Tyler's breathing is more jagged now. At longer intervals. Longer. Surely the next breath will come.

There are nurses. A doctor. Russel is holding her hand.

THE GANDHI IN
TAVISTOCK SQUARE

17

Richard wiped his face. The air vibrated with insect whines and amphibious burbles. After a week of driving to far-off forest twice a day – he couldn't camp here, his permit didn't allow it – Richard had terrific data but had never felt so tired.

He didn't want to think about what had happened with Ros. Anyway it was overshadowed by Russel and the bombs. He kept wondering how she was. He'd changed her flight, alerted Irena, Sanjay had taken her to Calcutta. All he'd had to do after that was get on with his work.

A breeze came, cooling his soaking shirt, and with it an odd sound, a faint rattly moan from a stand of *sal* saplings whose glossy leaves grew right down to the ground. He walked softly towards them, in among the trees, and was hit by a terrible smell. In a clearing covered in patches of what looked like peanut butter, overlaid with sequins of black quartz – flies, thick as anthracite – he walked into an overpowering stench. At the edge of the clearing lay a tiger, flat on its side, emaciated, crusted with shit. It had fallen in its own flux. The yellow splashes everywhere were vomit or diarrhoea.

He saw the white-striped tummy rise and fall. Little zebra stripes under its chin, where the white throat wrenched up to the light, twitched in a retching swallow. The face was clenched, eyes closed. It must be in agony. The ribs rose and fell in jerks, crinkles of yellow foam and bubbles of crimson crusted the black clown's mouth which was scrunched as though crying. Black streams welled over the one visible tooth. The huge legs and paws were stretched on the ground, and one paw twitched. No, that was

261

maggots, the foot was heaving with them. Yellow ichor oozed from it to the ground.

So easy to poison a starving tiger. You just tip fertiliser or pesticide into a goat carcass.

The tiger moaned again. Should he try to end its suffering? As he looked, there came a coughing sigh, blood rushed from the mouth, the belly gave one last convulsion and was still.

What do you do with a dead tiger? He couldn't get the jeep up here. Anyway, if he took it to their door, the deputy might try to pin something on *him*. Killing the national animal was a serious crime. Losing one from your forest was the worst thing in the book, foresters would go to any lengths to cover up a dead tiger. And Richard's permit forbade him to take anything out of the forest. The deputy could cancel his permit, stop his research, take him to court for killing a protected species. Anything to deflect blame. There was no money in protecting animals, but loads of it in allowing poachers a free hand.

Richard recorded the GPS position and walked round taking photos. That leg was festering, probably from porcupine punctures, the flesh must be soapy jelly inside. No wonder the beast was starving, it wouldn't have been able to hunt. He stood a moment in useless salute, feeling he should close the staring, fly-covered eyes, then turned away.

Tonight, he'd transfer to his laptop and USB, the photos of this and of the traps. Tomorrow, he'd go to Alipur Duar for supplies, email the deputy from there and give the evidence to Gopal too. There was no protection for animals here at all.

Friday 15 July, Kilburn, London, 6.45 p.m.; 11.15 pm, India

'Anka? Katya is home. Can Helen come tomorrow?'

'Of course, Budo. Brava!'

Anka's eyes throbbed like two hammers. After the weekend, Helen had gone into a shell. School had opened again but Helen cried every day on coming home.

'I am sorry your friend died,' said Budimir.

'My friend?'

262

'Who didn't come to your concert.'

'He died?'

'On Sunday.'

'But, he was not in bombs.'

'A car crash. It was in the paper. They said he was a great loss to the music industry.'

Saturday 16 July, Buxa Forest, Bengal, 2.00 p.m.; 9.30 a.m., UK

'That was absolutely delicious.' Richard leaned back in his chair. Gopal's wife, small, plump, outspoken and funny, had demanded to know exactly how they had cooked their *dhenki shak* and then produced a swathe of other mouthwatering Bengali dishes.

'Come,' said Gopal, and showed him the computer. Richard emailed the deputy, attaching dated photos, GPS positions, reports on the tiger and traps. The deputy would not be pleased. Richard turned with relief to Irena's email.

> Darling, Tyler has died, in a crash. Ros is devastated, we talk on the phone but I'm rehearsing like mad. It feels as if everything should stop in London, theatres have closed, but the Globe's going on. Wish I cd be with Ros. Her friend Scott is rallying round, her cleaner's living there. She says Russel's devastated too but they're getting on better. Maybe tell her dad?

Richard felt dizzy. He looked round at a photo of Gopal's daughter, getting her degree in America. At rain, weeping down the window. He saw Tyler sitting in his car in pouring rain by the phone box at Dexham. Tyler singing to Ros, putting a brave face on his night on the sofa. He'd never thought about Tyler in himself, only the wreck he'd made of Ros.

Suddenly he had a vision of the dead tiger, alone on its side.

When he set out for Buxa the rain had cleared. The sky was white as lard. He was so tired with all this driving, but he must thank Anand for coming to tell them about the phone calls. At the Outpost he knocked at the door. Anand opened it, sullen and unwelcoming. Had the deputy been angry with him for leaving his post last Thursday night?

'Thank you so much *again*,' Richard said in Bengali, 'for cycling all that way with that message.' He held out a thousand rupee note. Anand took it. 'I hope it didn't make difficulties for you.'

'Thank you,' said Anand in English. What was wrong? Maybe his son had got drunk again. Money, everything was money. The guards were in the front line. Richard suspected the director had not paid their salaries for months.

Had the deputy received his report? He might not have been in today, he spent most of his time in Siliguri. Taking bribes, Richard was sure, for signing away protected trees to timber companies. He'd seen timber lorries in the southern sector.

'Good night, Anand. Thanks again.' He turned to wave but the door was already closed.

Thursday 21 July, Kilburn, London, 1.00 p.m.; 5.30 p.m., India

Anka lit a taper, stuck it in the sand tray and prayed. For Helen, Katya, Lasta, Budo. For Tyler and his children. For London. 'Prayer is new life,' the priest in her village used to say. New life was badly needed, everyone was terrified. London was a different city. On the Underground, the bus, they were all afraid of the person beside them.

In the candle smoke flowing up into shadows of the church, she saw Katya's beautiful unscarred face at Easter. Tyler's blue eyes gazing at her on the pillow. Tyler laughing, head on one side, talking about his children. Such love, such pride. She imagined the boy she'd never seen, comforting his sister. And Tess's big blue eyes, running with tears.

She closed her own eyes. *When you pray, you are new.*

She sat in the back pew. In the gloomy light, everything looked faded and inevitable. In front of her, a Jamaican woman held a photo of a young man beside a very blue sea.

'I have seen violence and strife in the city and destruction in its midst,' the priest chanted. 'Deceit and guile do not depart from its streets.'

The woman crossed herself, kissing the photo. A tear like half a silver ball slid over her cheek.

Anka crossed herself too. She was writing Goodbye Songs all the time now, tunes and lyrics rippling out like rain, but she was afraid all the time. For Helen, for the city. Today, more men tried to kill people at three other stations, and on another bus. Their bombs hadn't exploded, but they had tried. And they were refugees, like her, they had come here as children. These were her goodbye-sayers, the people she was singing for. How could you do that to the country you came to, to be safe?

She thought of the boy from Eritrea, who held his head up like a saint on an icon when the judge said he must go back to prison. What was he thinking, what were people in his prison saying, about the bombs?

'You shall not be afraid of the terror by night, the arrow that flies by day, or destruction that lays waste at noonday.'

If Helen had not eaten that kebab. If Katya had been nearer the bomb. What angel marked the door of some people so they were safe, when they went out of their door in the morning, and others not? She did not deserve this angel. She had lied, she had stolen. Lied to her mother, not telling her about Helen. To Helen, telling her their family in the village was dead; and also not saying about Tyler. And for five years she had taken love away from a woman who had lost her husband, now, for ever.

Anka took a breath. She had kept all her jealousy and guilt about the person he called 'the wife' on a very short chain, like the huge dogs who guarded her parents' chicken yard on the Great Pannonian Plain. She'd tried not to think of the guilt. But she had been afraid of it, just as she'd been afraid of those dogs when her father unleashed them at night. They had not helped her father. Her mother said the soldiers had shot them before shooting him. And having kept guilt chained up for so long was no help now.

'Holy Spirit within us,' the priest intoned, 'our spark and our flame, *sanctify our souls, set our minds aright. Tread upon the lion and the cobra, the young lion, the serpent.'*

Anka stared at stubby scarlet glass round small flames on the chandelier. She must put right the wrongs she had done.

Tuesday 2 August, Buxa Forest, Bengal, 4.30 p.m.; Midday, UK

He'd seen a leopard here once, at just this time, the silver hour before twilight. Tonight nothing, just trees and gooey mud. Richard saw a leech on his forearm and pulled it off leaving a tiny drop of blood. Exhaustion flowed over him like boiling water. His hand was shaking with fatigue. At the Rest House, he saw a basket on the porch. Good. He'd put word out through Anand that he'd pay for any unusual species, but only snakes brought from the fields, not from protected forest. The basket was too small to hold a king but now, in the rains, there were so many snakes it could be anything.

He got out. This was the time of day he loved, when the rain lifted before twilight and you saw ivory sky under heavy cloud.

Should have remembered to fill up in town. There was an emergency canister in the back but he shouldn't let the tank get so low that sludge rose from the bottom. The Gypsy was temperamental as it was.

He must check on that basket. The snakes weren't always in good condition. In the shadow of the porch he lifted the lid and saw something slim and dark. Had Anand's friend found an Olive Oriental Slender at last? He craned over, holding the edge. No. A cream belly, not orange. The eye big and black, he couldn't see the pupil. The Oriental Slender had had a round pupil and grey iris. White skin between the scales—

Suddenly there was a burning pain in his middle finger. He snatched it back. The snake came too, swinging from his hand. Quick, get the teeth out, don't damage them by pulling or it won't be able to catch food. He squeezed behind the head, pushed gently forward and disengaged the fangs. Drops of liquid glittered in the dulling light.

He held the snake in both hands and watched the tongue flick. It was nervous, tasting the air, keen to get away. The face, now he saw it properly, could only be a krait.

But it was all black. He'd seen photos, one taken by Kellar. The black krait occurred only here, in the north-east. West Bengal, Sikkim, Bhutan, Nepal. Yep. *Bungarus niger*. A small one. Juvenile.

He dropped it in the basket, fastened the lid, walked out to the light in the open and kneaded the bitten area with a fingernail. He couldn't see a puncture. Probably too young to be dangerous. Despite, of course, those drops.

Oh, he'd be OK. He'd write a paper on it. Even better than an Oriental Slender. Black kraits had hardly been studied.

He'd look at it tomorrow. He walked to the Gypsy to get his bag. God, he was tired. He opened the jeep door to get his stuff and heard himself telling Ros about denial. 'It didn't get me – well maybe it did get me – all right it got me but I'm going to be OK.'

He paused, hand on the handle. The sky looked down at him, a man alone in a darkening world. If it had not been a dry bite, these two hours were critical. He should make a tourniquet, slow the toxin getting into his circulation. And move slowly, movement worked it round the system quicker.

He saw Irena's eyes light up when he came home, the corners of her eyes when she laughed. Running with daffodils into his arms.

The trees around him swayed. Tree-shadows splintered on glistening grass. He heard Shanta's voice. 'A clinic an hour from the Rest House.' If the worst had happened, paralysis would be gradual. Shanta had dried antivenin, but ordinary polyvalent serum would not work for black kraits. It was developed for the Big Four whose bites caused the most – say the word – most deaths.

Shanta's manual ventilator could be his only hope. If he lived, the neurotoxins would work their way out of his system in forty-eight hours. But if he wasn't helped to breathe for those hours there'd be internal damage, irreversible – kidneys, brain . . . this hour might be all he had to act.

Suppose he was perfectly OK as of course he must be, it didn't hurt now? People would say he knew nothing about snakes. Too bad. For Irena's sake, he must try.

267

He climbed wearily into the seat. How about the snake? He'd be back in a couple of hours. No one came here except forest guards.

He felt his finger tingle. Or did he imagine it?

Half an hour. Bump, slide and skid. The headlights shone on marbled ruts under the grass like opened flesh under absurdly green hair. The gauge said EMPTY. His hand was tingling. So was his wrist, where the pulse jumped, slicking toxin up his arm. Should have made that tourniquet. Couldn't stop now, might stick in the ruts. Would his muscles lift the emergency can? His whole arm was tingling. Here was the banyan tree and the right turn to the Outpost. Left or right? It would be an hour beyond the Outpost into town.

'Turn left,' said Shanta's voice. 'Then left again down a tiny track.'

His eyelids were flopping, it was hard keeping them even half open. And hard to stay sitting. No pain or wound at the bite itself: typical of krait. Unlike cobra where all hell broke loose in the flesh at once.

A second left turn. Very narrow – would the Gypsy get through? These ruts were deeper, wet undergrowth everywhere, and the needle two thirds down the red square of EMPTY. This was a jungle path, going nowhere.

He held one eyelid up and the other shut at once. His breathing was raspy. But the trees were sparser. The rivulet he was sloshing through was dotted with the darker pools of cow pats. And here were the cows themselves, lying like pale pyramids in the path, chewing their cud. He swerved round them, engine pinking because he had no hand to change gear, and saw a building on the right. A notice board. Though one eye he saw a tiny hut lashed to a tree and in it a large doll, with big black eyebrows, shiny black eyes like the krait's, a pink and gold sari, marigolds round her neck and cobra heads behind like a crown.

Manasa, Remover of Poison, help me, for Irena's sake.

His head fell back on the headrest. There was no light in any window. He was going to be sick. He was sweating like a squeezed sponge. All he could do was slump on the horn. The noise was a fart on the empty road. He let his eyelid fall.

268

'Who's that?'

He couldn't speak, his throat muscles had gone, his lips flaccid, his tongue a useless loll in the mouth.

'Richard? Is that you? What's wrong?'

His hand reached up to open his eye. Shanta was standing under an umbrella like a wet sparrow. Two sparrows: he was seeing double out of one eye. His lips were no longer his, but he made them move.

'Bitten,' he said. It came out 'witter'. He could hear, he was conscious, he just couldn't move.

'Krait . . .' It sounded like 'ray' but she got it.

'Krait, Richard? I've got serum . . .'

'No.' How could he say, with no lips and no tongue, that polyvalent serum wouldn't work and no one knew the black krait's toxins?

'Black . . . *black*.' It came out 'At, at.' Did she get it? Words were everything, and were useless.

'When, Richard? When?'

'Nearly . . . two . . . hours . . .'

He was vacuum-packed in his body, sweat rilling over testicles and thighs. Someone took off his shoes.

'Richard, can you hear? Can you move at all?'

Small firm fingers held his own, which were flopped flower stalks. He forced the top joint of his thumb forward like a shy lover.

'Good, Richard. You can communicate.' Above, a spot of brightness. Two spots. Was he seeing double behind closed eyes? 'We're going to keep your heart going manually while we set up the machine. Then we'll transfer you.' Hands bumped his chest, breath came up and out then in and down. Air rough as a cheese-grater was filing his throat. 'Can you squeeze my finger to say you understand?' Thud, bump on his chest. Breath in, breath out. He summoned all his strength and hooked the tip of a finger over hers.

'Good, Richard. We've got to keep your airways open. If they close we'll put a tube down. We'll only do it if we have to, OK?' Silence. 'Can you still move your finger?' It was like being set in toffee. He could hear and feel but not see, speak or twitch. 'Is there any part you *can* move?' He tried to clench all his muscles, scrunch himself, convulse. Breath in, breath out. He saw himself with toxin unfurling through his arteries like bindweed through clay.

'Watch his toes,' he heard her say in Bengali. 'They're farthest from the heart.'

He felt a hand on his right toe, and bent it.

'Yes.' A man's voice in Bengali. 'Look, mam.'

'Good, Richard. We know you're conscious, you're in there and hearing us.' *In, out. In, out.* He heard wheels. Creaking. 'Synchronise with his breaths, Bhargav. Like this.' Her mouth was over his. He choked, her mouth was soft but the breath she forced in was hard. She didn't stop but went on while hands kept thwacking his chest. *In, out. In, out.*

Twin silver dots looked at him through the marbled maroon of his shut lids. Rougher lips came now, tasting of betel. He choked again.

'Gently, Bhargav.' The rhythm steadied. *In, out. In, out.* More blows on his chest. 'Sit him up more, Sanjay, we'll attach him to the bag.' Arms under his arms, something hard on his mouth. Retching took him. Someone sponged his chest. 'Don't let vomit get in the trachea. Sit him up more.' Through scarlet and black he saw two glary eyes. Below them a mouth, pursed like the king cobra's, then opening to a smile. Shiva's smile.

'Richard, we're attaching you to the machine now.' *In, out.* Creak of a handle, breath in his mouth, too fast, too strong, he spluttered and retched. The rhythm steadied. *In-and-out. In-and-out.* Breath in his throat like a coarse file, backwards and forwards. Thuds bruising his chest. Her hand on his foot. 'You're hooked up, Richard. Can you still move your toe?' He tried to push. The muscle felt like bone. Hands tilted his head back, pulling his lower jaw forward.

'Barghav, keep the airflow, in and out of the lungs. This position, OK?'

In, out. In, out. A year, a hundred years. He heard a fan whir, a handle creak. He was choking, the breath was broken glass over his larynx, then stopped entirely.

'Turn it up, Sanjay. Harder! Keep the blood flow to the brain.'

There was a stab at his chest, a hoof forcing air into his lungs, blood out of his heart. Now the bright pouts of light, the Shiva eyes, had gone. Beyond his red lids there must be daylight. He was a caul of sweat.

'Keep it up, Durjaya, don't break the rhythm.' Creak of the handle. 'Mam, can someone else take over?' 'Don't break the rhythm, I'll call Satyavan.' *In, out. In, out.* 'Richard, can you move your toe?' He was fossil, he was iron. 'Check the pulse, Sanjay. Satyavan, keep the rhythm.'

He was the dark side of a mirror, Shiva's eyes glaring again, lighting the purpling and bleaching inside him, liver and kidneys, heart and crepuscular brain, crinkled and bulbous, paling and darkening. The skin of his throat was in ribbons, he could take it no longer. The thud-breath again, and again.

'Check the airways, Durjaya.' Shiva's legs flashed, the god of the matted locks whirling against his own red corpuscles and he was part of the dance, of the blood, of the universe, heart like a drum, cobra heads flicking from Shiva to the winds of the world. 'Keep going, Rajat.' A hand on his wrist. 'Can you hear me, Richard?' *In, out. In, out.* 'Keep going, Rajat, keep going.'

'Mam, my hands are sore.'

'I'll take over, get some rest.'

He was on the ceiling, there were lava and cinders, Shiva was striking the earth.

'He's not hearing, mam.'

'He's in there, I'm sure. Carry on, Bhargav.'

Vomit in the cave of his mouth, chainsaw breath slashing his chest. He was his own shroud of hardened cement. Let me die, he tried to say and knew he said nothing. He was red lilies broken, boiling dew, crashing and burning with Shiva, the god of nothing else.

'Mam, two days we have turned. No movement, twenty-four hours. Can we stop?' 'Please go on, Rajat. Go on till I say.' *In, out. In, out.* 'Richard, can you hear me?' He felt a hand on his toe, that half-inch of muscle which connected him, a million years ago, to the world. They had to let him die. Shiva was whirling him into dissolve, stripping every illusion away.

Every illusion but one. Now the face up there, the two eyes and mouth, was not Shiva but Irena. Irena's face. Irena's smile.

'Richard, can you hear me?' Shanta's words but Irena's voice. Her gentleness, reaching him. And her hand. He'd know her touch anywhere.

Not yet, said Irena. Like Behula, the bride in the story, refusing to let him go. *You're needed here.*

18

Richard opened his eyes. He saw a light bulb covered in dead flies, a room of bare cement and in the corner a dilapidated apparatus like a mangle with an elephant's trunk.

He sat up. His head swam. When it cleared, he inched his legs over to the floor. Shanta appeared in the doorway in a lavender sari brushed with blue.

'Sit, Richard. You mustn't get up quickly.'.

'I should fall down and kiss your feet. I heard you. You wouldn't let them stop.'

'Gopal phoned. The Forest Department wants you to leave the Rest House. You must eat, Richard, then I shall drive you in your Gypsy to Alipur Duar. We'll collect your things on the way. You will stay with Gopal. It is all arranged.'

By the time they got to the Rest House, Richard felt strangely shivery.

The porch was empty.

'You will never know who left that snake,' Shanta said, 'or what happened to it.'

'But it might die.'

'Richard.' She burst out laughing. 'Scientists are *not* like other people.'

'You're a scientist too. If you weren't, I'd be dead. And the black krait's *very rare.*' But he was laughing too. His first laugh, back from the dead. He opened the door of the Rest House. The room was chaos. Papers everywhere, sofa overturned, the shelf where he kept his laptop bare. He always emailed data to himself on Yahoo once a week so his research was safe in the ether. Plus he always backed up on his second USB. In the pulled-out drawers he found his passport and return plane ticket but no English cash and no spare USB. All the new data left was what he'd had with him in his forest bag. Notebook and camera, with pictures of the dead tiger.

'Oh.'

'What, Richard?'

'I – can't believe . . .' His head swam, his throat was sore. 'I think maybe the krait was left on – on purpose.'

Anand's face, after his report to the deputy. Snake expert killed by snakebite – nothing odd there, the causes of death were gliding in the jungle all the time. Guards had to do what the boss said. There were thousands of men in villages desperate to bribe their way, they had to bribe, into Anand's shamefully underpaid job.

'My USB had shots of a tiger I reported poisoned. I knew it made trouble for them, but—'

'If you suspect them, Richard, of taking your laptop and leaving the krait, you can do nothing. This is too complex for you to deal with. And you have no proof. Tell Gopal, then go home to your wife.' She put her hand on his forehead. 'Do you feel cold?'

'A – yes.'

'I think you have malaria. We shall get drugs in town. Where is your suitcase?'

He lay down while Shanta packed his papers, clothes and books, too weak to be embarrassed at a beautiful girl sorting his unwashed underpants.

To take his mind off his wrecked research, he pictured the malarial parasite responsible. When did it slip into his bloodstream? Within half an hour it would have been in his liver, multiplying. Then, unknown to him, his liver cells had burst, letting loose thousands of new ones that doubled back to infect more blood cells while he lay at Shiva's mercy. It would live in his blood and liver for ever now, invisible to surveillance from his immune system. Except in his spleen, his wonderful spleen, which would destroy infected cells. In its million-year war to win life from inside another organism's blood, the malaria parasite dealt one card after another to fox the body, adapting instantly whenever a new immune response blocked it. Always one step ahead. To avoid his spleen's policing, the malaria protozoan would plaster sticky proteins onto the surface of infected blood cells, and glue them to the walls of small blood vessels so it could circulate undetected. It would keep switching between different surface proteins ahead of the pursuing immune system, like a spy with multiple passports – or suicide bombers slipping past CCTV.

He still couldn't believe they were suicide bombers in London. English kids, attacking other English kids, like Russel?

By the time they got to Alipur Duar, Richard was burning and freezing.

'I *must* email. And talk to Irena, if I can.'

At Gopal's computer, shivering, Richard emailed the deputy. Had he received his report, did he find the poisoned tiger, was he on the track of the killers? The photo and report were on Gopal's machine; he attached them again, thanking the director for use of the Rest House. Even in fever, he could still do irony.

He took out his mobile. Early morning in England. Was Irena in London?

'Richard?'

'Thank God, oh thank God.' Through thousands of miles he heard his own voice echo. *God, God, God. . .*

'What's the matter, love?'

'Malaria . . .'

'Oh no. All these years you've managed to escape.'

'I wasn't taking my tablets. But they're not foolproof, I don't know if it was then . . .'

'Why weren't you?'

'I – got bitten.' In the silence he heard the fear she'd never said.

'OK now?'

'Completely.' He swayed on the chair.

'I'm on the train to London. Everyone's jittery. People started getting back on the Tube but then there were *more* bombs – the Oval, Shepherd's Bush, Warren Street.'

'Anyone hurt?'

'No. They didn't go off. People pretend not to be scared, stiff upper lip and remember the Blitz, but they're terrified. We have to get to work, we depend on trains and buses. Warren Street.' She laughed, but he heard how scared she was. 'I always thought Warren

Street so *innocent*. And the police killed someone in Stockwell Underground. They ran into the carriage and shot him in the head.'

'A bomber?'

'No, completely innocent. The police said he jumped the ticket barrier to get away but they were lying. The police – lying! This isn't England any more, we're a police state. And Al Qaida's promised more bombs.'

'I wish I were with you.'

'Richard – was it a king?'

'Krait. I was exhausted. I always promised myself not to handle a snake when I was tired. They're so quick.'

'Thank *God* you're OK. How's the fever?'

'I've got drugs, I'm at Gopal's. It should be just a few days, if there are no complications.'

'You sound – strange.'

'Irena, darling . . .'

'Yes?' Her voice, her breath close to his ear, was like warmth from a faraway planet.

'You saved me. They thought I wouldn't make it. I saw your face and heard your voice. You pulled me through.'

One more call.

'Hello, sir. Richard.'

'Ah, Richard. You were bitten.'

'A black krait.'

'You saw a *black* krait?' Excitement under the famous Kellar cool. 'I only saw one once. In Sikkim. What habitat?'

Kellar's priorities were oddly comforting.

'I don't know where it was found.'

'I see. Did they use serum?'

'Artificial respiration.'

'Lucky.'

'I wanted to tell you, sir – I don't know if you saw about the bombs in London.'

'I did see.'

'Your – er – family's fine.'

'Ah. Good.'

'I gave Russel your book.' Kellar was silent. 'He's a bright boy. I took him out in the woods, in Devon. Very observant.'

'Good.'

Richard swayed.

'I should tell you something else, sir.' He could hear Kellar's wariness. He remembered Kellar's face close to the king cobra as he peeled the lens off her eye. 'Your daughter's husband has died, in a car crash.'

Gopal caught him as he fell.

'Richard,' said Shanta. 'Go to bed.'

Tuesday 9 August, Primrose Hill, London, 11.30 a.m.; 4.00 p.m., India

Sitting on the edge of the bath, keeping her head down as Maria brushes in the dye, Rosamund stares at Maria's glitter-pink flip-flops.

'How are your children, Maria?'

'I have new photos. Carlotta, six birthday. And Juan.'

'How old is Juan?'

'Eight.'

'When did you last see them?'

'Five years.'

'There's a plastic hood on the shelf.' Rosamund feels liquid trickling and shuts her eyes tight. 'Now we cover my hair, so it'll cook.' 'Please?'

'So the colour soaks in. Can you see your children soon?'

'It is money. Better give to them, than use for go. Many people from Bolivia do this. Also, I cannot come back.' Maria is here illegally. When Rosamund first heard about Maria's children she'd told Tyler, who said it was the damnedest thing and then forgot. Now Rosamund aches for Maria. Mourning makes her feel Maria's pain more. Not to see her kids as they grow?

'Now,' said Maria, 'will be beautiful again.'

'What would I have done without you?'

Rosamund hugs Maria and begins to cry. Maria pins plastic round her head, wraps a towel round it, wipes her face with a flannel. For a month all she's done, Rosamund feels, is hug Maria. She looks in

277

the mirror. Eyelids like risen dough, puffed with crying. Cheeks sunk as if night had bitten them.

Maria has made her eat. So has Scott. What with Bolivian stews and Pizza Hut toppings, Russel has eaten more in four weeks than in four years of her own cooking. Sometimes she wishes Scott would take her in his arms again but maybe she'd flinch away. Anyway, he doesn't. He brings food, eats with her and Russel, chatting gently about his job, about London, and when he sees Russel is interested, he offers little memories of his own. Police work, his childhood, a seal he saw in the Western Isles.

She has learned things about Scott, small things she feels she is storing up for some future time when she will no longer feel like a fridge being defrosted. Scott takes Russel off to guard birds' nests, train Bramble, watch football. He brings Woody Allen DVDs and sometimes, at weekends, if he has taken Russel to a match, he stays over in Tyler's room. Which is being de-Tylered week by week. Rosamund is working on it. The cheval-glass has gone, drawers and cupboards are empty.

But mostly Scott lets her get on with her grief. She cries while she's turning out Tyler's things. Her cheeks feel sandpaper-raw. Maybe they'll never recover. She's lucky to be able to pay Maria to look after her. Money that comes, like everything, from Tyler.

Outside, theatres have reopened, and so has the Underground. The burst bus has been dragged away. Everything's back to normal, except for police with guns at Tube stations and letters from Tyler's insurance company enclosing the police report. Recorded on a speed camera driving at sixty-five, Tyler had sliced into a lorry while over-taking outside the Euston Road tunnel. No one else was hurt. He was three times over the alcohol limit.

But even drunk, Tyler wasn't usually reckless. No one knew where he had been that day. Maybe, Rosamund thinks as she inspects her reblonded roots, he suddenly went blind. No. His eyes were definitely seeing at the end.

'Got to show them we're not scared, eh?' says Scott, buying the tickets. Russel nods, but Kaa refuses to get in the lift. In the carriage,

Russel touches one of the upright poles. Everything people depend on is useless.

'All to ourselves,' says Scott, sitting down. Russel sits too. Mum sits on his other side.

'OK, darling?'

One ad shows an elephant with stubble on its head like a toothbrush, and a smile like a black banana. 'London drivers saved £190 on car insurance last year at elephant.co.uk.' He sees Mum smiling. She thinks she knows what he's thinking. But she hasn't seen ads saying stupid things like that while people scream on the floor.

Somehow Mum not having seen it makes it more like it won't happen again.

'OK?' says Scott and Mum says, at the same moment, 'Irena's playing Desdemona's servant, Emilia.'

'I know.'

'Her husband, Iago, makes Othello think Desdemona's having an affair . . .'

'Doh, Mum – Irena told us.'

'Did she? When?'

'In Devon.' Doesn't she remember anything?

'This is a Northern Line train, to Morden, via Charing Cross.' That woman seems to be there. Like she could really help. So much that seems real is not real at all.

There are four other people in the carriage. A guy with a rucksack on the floor. Another with a violet laptop on his knee. His mum says he can have Dad's white Mac soon. She's shown him the newspaper with Dad's photo, saying about stuff he did in his work. She wants him to feel proud of Dad.

There are two girls here too. One has a silver bullet through her eyebrow. Her chest is peeling at the top of her tits. She looks at him, then away.

You feel it on road, you see it in people's eyes: everyone looking and not looking. Fear everywhere. There are photos of rucksacks just like that in the paper. What the bombs were in.

They are sitting under a roof raftered like a Tudor farmhouse. Tourists have vanished from London and in these round walls the small audience feels brave, like pioneers. Afternoon air is turning from gold to silver and Scott's thigh feels warm against hers. There are no separate seats. Rosamund watches Russel take in the stage ceiling painted with clouds like crinolines, and the faux marble pillars, rose and violet, feathered with milky cracks.

How draining grief is. Oxygenless, like air on another planet.

Now she's out in the world again, she can take stock of her body, her mind, her guilt. Irena's behind that façade. She hasn't seen Irena since India, only spoken on the phone. In all her mourning, that awful scene on the sofa keeps coming back. Never mind being head-butted by the world's longest poisonous snake – nearly sleeping with your best friend's husband trumps that for nightmare.

Here's Othello, full of the romance of himself. Like Tyler, who always knew exactly what people wanted to hear. 'That's what's so seductive,' Irena once said. 'You're captivated, even while you laugh at how desperate he is to please.'

Now Desdemona in her nightdress, standing up for the man she's married. And her father turning bitterly away. This play is upsetting on so many fronts. Rosamund draws in her breath. When she was only reading it, she didn't realise. How did Father feel, when Tyler threw him out of their wedding?

Here's Emilia. Irena looks amazing. Rosamund feels she's never really *seen* her before. That yellow dress . . . She feels Russel stir in surprise.

Desdemona jokes with Emilia's husband, flirts with the other guy, but really she's worrying about her own husband at sea. Emilia knows that, she's full of jokes too but she's looking out for her friend, thinks Rosamund guiltily, all the time.

Here's Othello, striding off the ship, taking his wife in his arms, in that moment when nothing matters but the hug that closes down the rest of the world. Two bodies, and two hearts beating, each to each.

And then, so quickly, the jealousy.

By the world, I think my wife be honest and think she is not.

Rosamund feels bile burning her throat.

Think'st thou I would make a life of jealousy,
To follow still the changes of the moon
With fresh suspicions?

She hears a helicopter buzz in darkening sky. London is all surveillance now. What has a life of jealousy done to her? It's driving Othello mad. In her, it brought back the paralysis she'd opted for as a child. What if she'd never suspected Tyler, never let herself know he was lying – would she have been happier? But you can't make a life out of fooling yourself.

Emilia picks Desdemona's hanky off the ground, hoping to please her own husband with this tiny crime, not realising he's lying his head off. So easy, from the outside, to see he's a shit. Had Irena make the connection?

Of course. To play being married to Iago, she must have drawn on all the wilful blindness she'd seen in action, all these years. Rosamund clenches her hands. She has never really admitted Tyler was – well, bad. She sees herself going on to Irena about Tyler's betrayals; the humiliations, the really *wrong* things. Then feeling relieved she'd got rid of them by telling Irena, and carrying on as before. The familiar was comforting. Trying to change would spell chaos. Irena must have gritted her teeth a million times.

Othello points to Desdemona. *There, where I have garnered up my heart*, he says. *Where either I must live or bear no life.*

Garnered up his heart? That's what she'd done with Tyler. Now there is no more Tyler and no more heart, maybe, too. Finito.

The white moon above the theatre is looking down now at one woman alone, waiting for a man. Desdemona, bruised, bewildered, wanting to love. Rosamund thinks of all those nights she waited for Tyler, in bed or in the kitchen with Bono asleep in his basket. What stopped her doing something about it, *telling* him things had to change? Of course, Tyler would have promised to change and gone on as he was. But how did she get so hypnotised that she kept on playing his game?

Now, even smashed by grief, she at least feels alive.

How do you, my good lady?

Two women, gentle with each other. Emilia brushes Desdemona's hair. Rosamund closes her eyes before Othello strangles his wife and opens them as the penny drops: when Emilia has realised who made these horrors happen.

My husband? Irena's voice holds all the damage people do to each other and themselves. Scott leans forward and grips Rosamund's thigh. She puts her hand on his. *My husband?* Irena turns to Iago. *You told a lie, an odious damned lie, upon my soul.*

Iago runs at Emilia with a knife and Irena falls. Rosamund feels Russel jerk in protest. Irena didn't tell him about that.

Backstage, the theatre's modern. Like, normal. Russel sees flowers everywhere, and actors in clothes like *Blackadder*. Desdemona's old, twenty-five at least. He can see her tits through the nightdress. Standing back with Scott, he watches Mum with Irena. They're kissing, laughing, hugging, crying. Irena hugs him, too.

'Russel. It's been so awful not to be *with* you.'

She kisses Scott, though she doesn't know him.

'Interesting, eh?' murmurs Scott as he steps back. Russel knows Scott feels as strange as he does. But also, like him, Scott's pleased his mum's having a good time.

Monday 15 August, Alipur Duar, Bengal, 5.00 p.m.; 12.30 p.m., UK

'Your temperature's down. You're on the mend.' Shanta sat on Richard's bed in Gopal's spare room.

'Were you worried?' Richard's head ached. He felt feeble and stale.

'After all those toxins in your system, Richard, yes. Lucky the malaria wasn't cerebral.' The blue cloth over her breasts and shoulders was whorled with turquoise like a complicated promise. 'Why do you not have children, Richard?'

'Don't bully me, Shanta. I'm ill.'

'Richard, I'm your doctor.' Rain thrummed outside. 'Richard?'

'You don't give up, do you? They warned me about Bengali women! OK – I'm not good with children. And it's a terrible world to bring life into.'

'What does your wife feel?'

'She cares about her work, I care about mine and we share . . .'

'Share what?'

'The way we look at the world.'

'What about sharing the world, Richard? And a family?'

'I'm not equipped to be a parent. I hated being a child. My sister – she disappeared and then died – I'm just not *qualified* to have children.'

Shanta's specs flashed in lead-coloured light falling on her from the window.

'Richard, I think you would be good with children. Like animals. Even that snake – you even saw that snake's point of view.'

'You saved me from it, Shanta. And so did Irena.'

'I didn't know she was there too.'

'I was just about to give up. She got me through.'

'Richard, there's something you're not happy about.'

'Shanta, shut up, I'm ill . . .'

'Richard!'

'OK.' He sighed. 'Yes. Something I'm ashamed of and don't know – how to talk about.'

'Richard, I saved your life, you belong to me.'

'Do you always cure your patients by third degree? OK, there's – it's a woman. Irena's friend. Mine too, long ago.'

He fell silent.

'Richard . . .'

'You see, Shanta, maybe you'll understand, science was always my escape. From home, from – narrowness. I walked into a lab my first day at college and there she was. Like I'd walked into a long-lost dream. I – fantasised about her.'

'Richard, this is normal.'

'But it went on. She married a lout. He was always off with other women. When I was working in forest, I associated her with – all the mystery, the . . . the life, the diversity. I fantasised about her *there*.'

'Again, normal.'

'Not when I was married. It was terrible, a secret I've kept from Irena. Then she came to stay in the Rest House.'

'And?'

'Nothing happened. It nearly did but – I – stopped.'

'I think she is a manifestation of your wife. Every myth is a version of the truth.'

'Irena says things like that.'

'I think you love your wife very much. This woman is her avatar.'

'Rubbish. They're completely different.' But the face he suddenly saw was Wanda's. Wanda teasing him, her face framed in new-dyed green and white hair. Wanda holding the book he wanted out of reach. He felt again the shivers and nausea when Dad told him to forget he'd ever had a sister.

'Richard, do you know why we have many gods, not one?'

Was everything he'd felt about Rosamund a hangover from losing Wanda? Guiltily, when he was ten, he'd fantasised about her, too – and tried not to, in just the same way.

'You talk about diversity in the forest, Richard, what about diversity in *us*? We are so many things. I've never seen the point of only one god. One god, what good is that?' The air now was like soft smoke. He thought of Shiva's face as he'd seen it in his fever. 'There are gods in everything we do, Richard. All connected, like your forest. We cook, make phone calls, we eat, we love. All those are gods.' She took a sharp breath. 'I'm just saying what it's *like*.' She suddenly sounded anxious.

'OK, Shanta.'

'Every god has avatars. Same god, different name and face. They hurt and help us, each in their way. Manasa kills and saves through poison. Also love – desire, fantasy, sex, tenderness. Same god, different avatars.'

'Sounds like Tyler's creed.'

'Tyler?'

'Her husband. He went after women like a disease. What you said would justify him. A different god for each relationship? That's just plain wrong.'

'I don't mean you should act on it. Just honour each for what it is. You didn't act on your fantasies, did you?'

'No. But I was terrified it meant I loved her, not Irena.'

'In the forest, you don't always see things clearly, do you?'

'Not at first. You think you've seen a tiger and it turns out to be a patch of yellow fern.'

'We say, you mistake the rope for the snake. Those fantasies were some other god, not love. Every god's powerful. But who you love is your wife.' He closed his eyes, feeling suddenly peaceful. 'You should live with her all the time. That's my diagnosis. Now, Richard, you must sleep.'

19

Monday 15 August, Primrose Hill, London, 8.30 p.m.

'Peter Vere d'Abney-Fairfax? Who on earth's that?'

'That was Tyler's real name.'

Irena starts to giggle, almost their old crazy laugh.

'Why didn't you tell me?'

'He didn't want anyone to know.' Tyler and his names. 'He lived by keeping things dark.'

Irena bends her head over the papers again. Rosamund looks at them shakily. She has given Tyler's cheval-glass to Oxfam, taken the SIM card out of his phone, paid someone to wipe his hard drive, given phone and laptop to Russel and thrown away six blister packs of Viagra she found in various jackets. Little chips of blue sky, some missing from each. But worst of all are Tyler's accounts. Thank God for Irena. She feels they are reading Tyler's bones. What's really lain under her life, all these years?

It is a soft summer night under the conservatory glass. She looks at moonlight on Irena's mothy hair. Suddenly Irena throws down the biro.

'Sorry, Ros, you're going to have to sell the house. This mortgage is *insane*. All there is here are bills and an enormous overdraft. Two-hundred-pound dinners, sums like I've never seen just for drinks in a nightclub. A running account at a wine merchant, another at a jeweller's.'

'What?'

'Here, just at random, is a £2260 receipt! For – what on *earth* did Tyler want with that?'

Rosamund snatched it up.

Mr T. Fairfax. Replica Renaissance lute in A. 23 ribs of Rio rosewood. Striped neck and pegbox in snakewood and holly.

'Seen one of those lying around?'

'When was that? March.'

Irena plugs in the kettle.

'Never mind the past, Ros, it's the future that matters. How's Russel doing in Greece?'

'Loving it.' Richard has found Russel a volunteer job protecting sea turtles on the island of Zakynthos. 'The locals race motorbikes on beaches where the turtles lay eggs, but Russel and some girl saw a hatch. They saw the babies finding their way to the sea by moonlight. Russel was thrilled. Brilliant idea of Richard's. And everyone thinks he's a hero, because of the bombs.'

'Now you can take him to see your dad.'

'God's sake, Irena, stop sending me to India. I've only just come back. Anyway, you say I haven't any money.'

'When you buy a smaller place, you'll have tons. This must be worth a fortune.'

Rosamund looks at their reflections. Nothing belongs to you, really. The garden will go on growing, without her. What we think is ours floats away to thin air. Why had she let Tyler persuade her not to work? She knew what a self-deceiver he was. He told people what he wanted to be true, then believed it because they did. If only they'd trusted each other enough for him to tell her he was up to his ears in debt. *She'd* have been happier, working. Everything could have been different.

Irena puts tea in front of her.

'Russel needs to know his grandpa.'

Rosamund begins to laugh. Hysterical, to hear Kellar called anything as cosy as a grandpa! Laughing turns into crying. She puts her head on her arms. Will these tears at the slightest thing never stop? She feels Irena's hand on her shoulder.

Next morning, they hear the flop of post from the letterbox. Rosamund goes into the hall. One envelope is handwritten in thick black letters.

I am leaving England with daughter for holyday but before, I
invite you to coffee. I am very sorry, about your husband.

Is café in Southampton Row by Tesco Express. Near, I
work. If you meet there I would very much like.

Here is phone. Sincerely, Anka Vladic

Rosamund flips it onto the table.

'How many of these are there going to be? I could make a whole
website of girls' names from his address book.'

'You'll always be sorry if you don't go. Why not arrange to meet
Scott after?'

That afternoon, Rosamund rides down Eversholt Street in a minicab.
They had to get back on the Tube for Russel's sake but she can't face
a bus, not yet. She's always felt at home on top of a London bus and
the top is where the bomb went off. Meeting Tyler's cast-offs seems
small beer beside that.

London is a ghost city still, the sunlight saturated with danger.
Fear everywhere, like light on the surface of a pool. The cab has white
cotton tied over the seats and a sign saying THANK YOU FOR NOT
SMOKING. The driver's hair curls against his head like wool on a
black lamb. They cross Euston Road. The mayor has lifted the
Congestion Charge; he knows no one wants to come in. She always
feels strange sitting in a car and not talking but there's only one con-
versation in London these days, especially in Bloomsbury.

'Traffic's OK now,' she says. 'They've taken the bus away.'

'Fifty-two people died here.' He turns his head. Black glasses,
wispy under-chin hair. 'But thirty thousand died in Iraq, who is
minding about them?'

The pavements of Woburn Place, edged in grey-pearl granite cut
from some calm Cornish mountain and laid here a hundred years
ago, slip by them in silence.

'I'll get out here, thanks. I'm early.'

She gets out by a wall plaque saying Dickens once lived here, and
another saying British Medical Association. The Belisha beacon is
crooked and headless. At its base is fresh cement, in which she sees

the footprints of a pigeon like knots in barbed wire. The bird must have walked on it wet. Could it fly afterwards, with cement on its feet? Her eyes well with tears.

This is where the bus blew up. She crosses into Tavistock Square.

'Four o'clock,' the husky voice on the phone had said. She'd recognised it at once from the answerphone message. Now she stares at bronze words on a rock. 'Placed here on Conscientious Objectors' Day 1994.' A cherry tree with a plaque. 'For victims of Hiroshima.' This garden is a hotbed of peace, and in the centre is a bronze Mahatma Gandhi. 'To celebrate the 125th anniversary of his birth, 1996. Set up by the High Commissioner of India and the Mayor of Camden.'

Rosamund sits on a bench among geraniums. Gandhi's bronze has bled green streaks into the white plinth. His hand is strangely large, touching the ground between his knees. The world's great symbol of peace, come out of violent partition. Again, London was involved.

She thinks of the cab driver. *Who is minding about them?* She has never thought these things before.

'Strange it was here the bus blew up, dear, isn't it?'

A small birdlike woman with thick eyelids and surprisingly bright eyes is sitting beside her. Her hair is vivid black-brown, the memory of the colour it must have been fifty years ago.

'Were you here that day?'

'I live in the square, dear. I've watched it become a peace garden. Now this.'

'It seems impossible. Even after only six weeks. A *bomb* – here!'

Pigeons strut on the path. Rosamund watches a white seed drift over Gandhi's arm.

'When I was young, we called those fairies. We thought it was lucky to catch one.'

'Did you hear the bomb?'

'I was coming back from shopping. I had my cornflakes and eggs and sardines. I was walking down Upper Woburn Place. I stopped, surprised to see a number thirty.'

'Why?'

289

'We don't get the thirty here. The driver was lost. He was diverted from King's Cross because of *that* bomb. He'd stopped to ask a policeman where to go. I was by a traffic warden. It was so odd to see a lost bus. Then we heard a bang and saw smoke. I didn't fall, the warden held my arm, but I dropped my bag. I saw red metal fly through the air.'

'Metal?'

'The roof, dear. The top of the bus. There were bodies too. People, flying in air. When the roof came down, it seemed to be slow but it wasn't. The people came down too. But,' her voice trembled, 'mostly pieces of people. Torn apart.' Someone should be looking after her. 'After that, red wings stuck out of the bus. People screamed from the top. Some jumped and fell. The stairs weren't there. People said bombs were all over London.'

'Yes. My son . . .'

'Was he hurt, dear?' The woman lays a hand on her knee.

'He was on a train behind one that was hit.'

'The thirty was packed. Everyone got on buses you see, when they heard about the Tube.' One pigeon perches on Gandhi's head. Others watch from the path. 'There was blood running down the walls of the Medical Association like paint. The traffic warden said, "I've got human flesh on me." People were covered in blood. Other people were lying in the road.'

'What did you do?'

'I picked up my shopping. Doctors ran out of the Medical Association. Everyone was saying their mobile wouldn't work but I don't have a mobile. I had no one to call. My husband died in 1996.'

'I'm sorry.'

'My son's in Thailand. So I didn't worry about anyone of mine. I came here. It seemed safer with him.' She looks up at Gandhi, shivering. 'Five eggs were broken.'

'Would you like me to see you home? Is your son coming to be with you?'

'I'm all right, dear, thank you. I'll just sit here. With him.'

Her eyes, under their waxy lids, are gazing at Gandhi.

*

Anka held herself in from the diaphragm as if about to sing, and looked at dimpled froth on her cappuccino. She knew this café, she came here to be alone in breaks from recording. She stared at the green frog, high as her shoulder, which stood inside the door holding a wooden lily like a parasol.

Through the door came a slender woman with hair like pale fire, in a tank top and matching shrug, the colour of apples when the sun has left them. No bra, just a drawstring over loose breasts.

Anka smiled, tentatively. The woman gave a nervous smile, here and then gone like the flash of a windscreen on a distant hill.

'Anka Vladic?'

Anka stood up.

'Please.' She gestured to the table. They sat opposite each other.

'Cappuccino, please,' the woman told the waitress.

So this was the enemy. Demanding and cold. Making him take her shopping, take her to films. Crushing his lion's spirit.

Anka saw a delicate face, wide, generous mouth, no lipstick or make-up, and felt coarse. This woman was older than her, yes, but so fragile and so alive. How could he cheat on her? And be so frightened of, so *nasty* about, all these years?

This woman had been the enemy because Tyler said she was. Because he felt guilty, he made his wife the bad one. Not him.

Holding her pink-lustre cup in front of her like a shield, Anka said, 'Is difficult.' Rosamund said nothing. 'He said many things. But I, was fantasy. You, he loved.' She looked at the giant ice-cream cone by the door. The three lumps, pink, green and white, made you never want to eat ice cream again. 'Children – all right? He loved, so much!'

'My son's better now. Thank you.' Rosamund spoke slowly, as if she thought Anka wouldn't understand. 'He was on the train behind the bombed one at King's Cross. But he's OK.'

'Katya, friend my daughter, also. In Edgware Road. Is alive. But hurt.'

They looked at each other. Anka felt a lump in her throat, heat in her eyes. 'Little Katya . . .'

Rosamund's hand stretched jerkily, as if against her will, to Anka's.

Two women, face to face. One with her arm across the table.

'It's a terrible time,' said Rosamund. 'We all feel so helpless.'

Tears on both faces, now. They were the only people here, except the waitress leaning against the espresso machine, examining her split ends. This woman, whose husband she had stolen for five years, was comforting her! Anka gave in to crying. For Katya, for Tyler, for herself, for Rosamund. For human beings. Such mess they made.

'Little one – is OK?' She wiped her eyes with a paper napkin. At least Rosamund had Tess.

Rosamund looked startled.

'We haven't, I haven't – got another child. Only Russel. Our son.'

Anka's spine was a strip of ice. She felt a chill spreading round her ribs. She couldn't breathe.

'But, little Tess?' She remembered when Tess was born. His frantic lovemaking afterwards. They were new then. So good together. 'He talked about, all the time. Four years. Tess!' Why remind this woman of her own lovely child? 'Melba toast, she loves.' She saw pink drain from Rosamund's skin like bleaching marble. 'Is afraid, from wiggly spaghetti. Only her daddy can feed.'

'That,' said Rosamund, biting her hand as if she'd seen a ghost, 'was the name . . . that's what we were going to call . . .' She looked as if she was facing the jawbones of hell. 'We did have a baby four years ago, but she was born dead.'

Anka put her hands over her eyes.

'Being afraid of wiggly spaghetti was Russel. Melba toast was *his* favourite. He ate nothing else for a year.'

'Tess.' If Anka could have blocked out every sense, ears as well, she would have. 'Does not – exist?'

'She did exist. But she never saw the light of day.' Anka opened her eyes, Rosamund was lacing her fingers over her lips, as if trying to keep something safe inside. 'She was born dead. The hospital made me hold her. She had amazing hair. My colour. And was dead.' Rosamund's eyes were dark and smoky now. 'Tyler broke down. It was dreadful, everyone was upset. Tyler made a fuss, blaming everyone. I was in another hospital afterwards, on medication. Russel stayed with a school friend. It was the last minute he could choose big school . . . You know . . .'

Anka nodded.

'And somehow he turned against Tyler. He adored him before. He insisted on going to the school his friend was going to. Tyler seemed to wash his hands of him. When I came back, Russel didn't feel like the same child. As if I'd lost both of them.'

Anka shook her head, feeling like a battered animal. Tyler saying, 'Don't get me started.' Going on about his perfect little girl. She had thought she was the only one he did not lie to. But he'd covered it all up. Death, grief, everything.

Why? Because he'd wished, so much, the baby was alive? But Tess was why he couldn't leave Rosamund. He knew that she, Anka, would do anything for Helen.

'He said he'd always, always wanted a little girl,' Rosamund said.

Anka took a deep, calming, singer's breath.

'Before Tess, we'd been getting on very badly. He was unfaithful from the start. I don't know what he'd told you, but you weren't the first.' Anka said nothing. 'I'd stopped sharing his room, I couldn't bear him coming back from other people. But we really wanted that baby. We knew it was a girl. I'd always longed for a daughter. Tyler was thrilled. When she was born dead he just – fell apart.'

Anka put out her hand. Rosamund's fingers gripped hers.

'Tess,' said Anka. 'Where is?'

'What do you mean? Oh. I suppose the hospital cremated her. At least, that's what they said. They didn't tell us where they put the ashes.'

'What hospital?'

'Whittington.'

Anka closed her eyes.

'Maybe,' she said, 'you like to know, about night he died? All, I do not know.'

Rosamund nodded, like a child who's told a story and expects one in return.

'He was angry.'

293

'Why?' Rosamund's voice was suddenly sharp.

'He came, drunk. Was drinking with girlfriend, all day.'

I had just broken it off. No. *He was using you, to me, to cover up seeing someone else.* Not that either. And nothing, nothing, about Helen. She wanted this beautiful woman, much more wounded than she'd known, to feel as good as she could about her husband. She'd promised God to try and make up for what she'd stolen.

'I, too, angry. Because, girlfriend.' Rosamund nodded. 'He got text message and ran away quick. I think, to your son.' She looked straight at Rosamund. 'He did not want you going away, to India. It was you, he loved. Is true.'

'Very generous of you, to say that.' Rosamund was watching her mouth as if truth could fall out of it onto the table, like pearls. Their hands clung among the crumbs.

'My daughter, Helen. Never I tell my mother in Croatia because, was shame. Now, I will take Helen to village.' She squeezed Rosamund's hand. 'When bad things come, you needing family. Mother. Father.'

Rosamund stared at her.

'You're right. Thank you. I hope I can be as brave as you.'

The Romanian waitress, nothing to do on a Wednesday afternoon in a stricken city, watched them walk out to the street, press their faces against one another as if there was something in the other that soothed what each had lost, and walk away in opposite directions.

Rosamund is walking down Southampton Row through reeling London. High Holborn, its clocks and hanging eaves. Holborn Viaduct. Newgate Street. She is reeling herself. Pandora's Box is well and truly open now. Everything she has kept going by not thinking about is creeping from the crevices, streaming at her like rags of horror in a ghost train, from the London streets.

Herself, four years ago. Drugged and crying, with a tiny cold bundle in her arms. Tyler crying and shouting, casting blame.

She has felt empty inside for years. But really she'd been full, hadn't she? Full of loss. Of things she never told even Irena. She'd been almost angry with Irena, away in Canada, leaving her alone.

Afterwards she told her the facts, but not how she'd dreamed and longed for that little girl. How she'd bought a babygro with a white rose on the front. Tess, supposed to be her and Tyler's new start, had become the road to nightmare.

When Rosamund got back home, everything had changed. They never spoke of Tess. Life flowed on like bark of a tree growing over an iron spike, hardening till no one saw what lay beneath. Tyler must have dealt with his grief through women. But also, it seems, by denying it. By inventing a life.

Rosamund shivers. She'd shut grief in an iron vault. Now it has cracked wide open.

St Paul's is a stone breast in blue sky. There's the courtyard and Scott, bless him, is the only customer at the wine bar. There's a glass of lager on the table and his jacket is hanging on the chair. His shirt stretches in smiles across his shoulders and he is reading a letter. Rosamund walks past a Piccadilly Ices van doing no trade at all, and puts her hands over his eyes.

'Only you could get beer at a wine bar.' She sits down. 'London's scary, isn't it? Specially after the second bombers.'

'At least you can see it. This place is normally overrun with tourists. I've tried to photograph that so often.' He waves at a buttress of the cathedral. 'How was it?'

'OK. She was nice. Sad. Very sexy, but not trying to be. I've no idea what she does or where he met her but – he had good taste.'

Scott smiles. Now they're out of the house, she feels he's looking at her breasts even when he's looking at her face. These past weeks at home, he's emanated a held-back kindness. Here, somehow, he feels less constrained.

'Your usual? Nice soft red?' He looks for a waiter. He takes a cautious pleasure in finding wines she might like.

'What's your letter?'

'They're cutting half our department. Moving us to the outskirts.'

'But you only have five men! Are you going to have two and a half?'

'Two. Everything's antiterrorism, now.'

'Oh, Scott.'

'What difference will two men make, combing London for suicide bombers? To us, they were crucial, but animals don't have votes.'

'I'm sorry.'

'Glass of the Merlot, please,' he tells the waiter. Behind his head, up beyond the gold cross of St Paul's, silver clouds like chefs' hats are racing over blue sky. He looks at her, his soft serious look. 'Shock, was it?' he says gently.

She starts to cry. She seems to have spent the last six weeks in tears.

'I've never told you. We had – I had – a baby. My baby girl,' the words bring back the flooding despair. 'Born dead. But,' she gulps, and Scott takes her hands, 'Tyler told that woman she was *alive*!' Is there no end to the horrors Tyler can fling at her from the grave? She feels like a raw egg blopping out of its shell. 'I don't know which of us was more shocked, her or me. All the time he was with her, however long that was, he pretended we had *two* children.'

'Now why would he do that?'

'He lived off fantasy.' She looks at black metal posts marking the wine bar from the rest of the courtyard. The silky ropes between are pallid and fibrous, like toffee. 'She asked what happened to the ashes. I don't know. It doesn't bear thinking about. There'd been a scandal in 2001 – some hospital somewhere keeping parts of dead babies.'

Scott comes round the table, leans over and presses her into his chest.

'The hospital asked,' she says into his shirt, 'did we want them to cremate her? I think even with miscarriages, now, they cremate the – remains. But we were in no state – Tyler just said OK and they took her away.'

She feels Scott stroking her head gently and she remembers him stroking his puppy the night he brought Russel home.

'She has a daughter.'

'Not—'

'Not Tyler's, thank God, she'd have said. No, she's from Croatia. What on earth did they have in common, except sex? He was completely uninterested in foreign countries.' She hates the bitterness in her voice. How can she get free of that? 'She said she'd never told her mum in Croatia about her daughter but now she's going to take her to see her. She said, when bad things happen you need your family. Maybe I should take Russel to see Father. But how *can* I?'

'One thing at a time, love. Brave of you to see *her*.'

She hears his heart beating.

'Must drink my lovely wine,' she says shakily after a minute. He goes back to his chair. He doesn't flirt or pay empty compliments, he simply looks concerned. Why doesn't he make a move?

She has been so self-absorbed. All these weeks, she hasn't really seen Scott at all. Today is not about Scott. Or is it? Does he feel, as she does, a large piece of something, her Tyler-self, calving off her like a chunk of iceberg, melting into the sea?

She will always be mystified by what Tyler did. Maybe one day she'll manage to be sorry for him. But she'll never feel *wed* to him again. Her life with him, and the hidden life he lived, now seems like coloured tat in a tourist window in a town she'll never revisit.

She breathes deep. As, she noticed, Anka Vladic did, too. Inside, she feels some crucial space being cleared, brutally but completely, by what that woman said. Maybe feeling this space in herself is all she needs to do, now, about Tyler. She can move on.

She looks up. Scott smiles.

'Mmm?'

'Is there a movie we can see?'

297

20

Monday 22 August, Alipur Duar, Bengal, 11.00 a.m.

'Richard, you're in a chair!'

'I wobbled into it like an old man.'

Richard had been gazing at the tyre-recycling yard beneath the window. He looked at Shanta. She was wearing green and orange with ambery swirls, spring and autumn both, and he felt as if he'd been through some noxious tunnel and come out to clear day.

'Why did you come here, Shanta? You did a PhD at Oxford, you could have gone anywhere. Why here in the sticks?'

'Many medical students study abroad, England, America, and stay there. Better jobs and you don't have to bribe people. But I wanted to help here.'

'You're Joan of Arc.'

'There are so many problems here. AIDS, for instance. In many places, people don't admit it. Regions like this, so poor, so ignorant of medicine, especially women – this is where doctors really matter.'

'What does your mother say? Marriage prospects, all that?' Shanta was silent. 'I never used to ask personal questions. I've learnt that from you.'

'Black kraits have unknown toxins.' She laughed. 'New things in your blood.'

'Shanta – she's gone. I feel free. Of the fantasies, I mean.'

'You've let her go.'

'Anyone there?' said a voice. 'I've come to see Richard.'

'Girish!' Richard tried to get up and failed. 'All the way from Mangalore.'

Girish came in like sunlight, beautiful, casual and quick. His eyes, searching for Richard, stopped at Shanta in surprise.

'I had to see what trouble you'd got yourself into without me. I see you've been living it up.'

'This is Shanta, my doctor. She saved my life. But watch it, Girish, she's a terrible bully. Her father is Mukul Kumar.' Everyone knew everyone in conservation. 'Shanta, my friend Girish – photographer, philosopher, dance expert.'

Richard knew there were nuances he would never understand behind every meeting of two people in this country. Girish and Shanta would know more about each other in one second than he ever would. That was OK. He knew he was clumsy, but also that the people he liked forgave him. These were his friends and he loved them.

'Shall I get tea?' Shanta stood at the door in a moment of complete grace. Green cloth fell over her shoulder in liquid folds. 'You have a lot to talk about.' She went out.

'Gopal emailed me your pics of the baby royals.' Girish sat down. 'A lot to be desired in the composition, I thought.'

'*Photographers*. You're impossible.' They were laughing. 'Fantastic, weren't they?'

'Amazing. I wish I'd seen them.'

'What shall I do about this tiger?'

'You'll embarrass the forces for good here, like Gopal, if you stay. Gopal filled me in, by the way. The laptop, the krait.'

'Yes.'

'You've provided evidence of tiger poisoning, at least. Gopal's circle will use it as they can. The foresters will try to discredit it. You're better out of it now. Come back to Karnataka. Or go to England and publish from there.'

'That's giving up.'

'You've done what you could. Others will do what they can.'

'But we're fighting a war! For the wild – and – and for science, for truth. I've worked in this country fifteen years, Girish. I've seen habitats lost every day, mining and logging leases granted illegally, destroying protected forest, all done by corruption, for greed.' Richard found himself trembling.

'That beautiful doctor will blame me for exciting you.'

299

'Species disappearing every day.' His voice shook. 'Orissa gave permission last month for two elephant forests to be cut by a bauxite company. Two! Forests destroyed for ever, villagers losing their fields and turning to poaching in despair. Rich corrupt bastards getting even richer.'

'We are fighting a war, but you won't be giving up on it in England. This isn't your country. You can make a noise, so people try to silence you. That's probably what happened here. But you can still do great work for us from England. Research, conservation programmes, reports.'

'But the *losses*.' Richard felt like a child wailing in the dark. 'And that's leaving out global warming. The animals, ancient forests that will never come again, the incredible connectedness – science doesn't know the half of it yet and may never, before it's all lost.'

Girish walked to the window.

'None of us would choose to live in such a time. All we can do, you, me, Gopal, everyone, is what we can. And live our lives.'

Shanta came in with tea.

'I must get to the hospital. I've stayed with one patient, Mr Difficult Demanding Richard, long enough!'

'Can I go out today?'

'I think you can.' She smiled, as if giving him an amulet. 'But don't get ill again the minute you go outside.'

'Might he be well enough,' said Girish, 'for us all to have dinner tonight?'

On Gopal's computer sat a frosty email from the Forest Department attaching a receipt for his rent. No mention of tigers. Richard began an email to Irena, but then tried his mobile instead. He heard clicks and watery echoes.

'Hello?' Irena suddenly said in his ear. 'Oh – *Richard*!'

'Darling, I'm back Sunday week. The fourth.'

'Oh no, we're rehearsing that day, we've got two new cast members. I won't be able to meet you.'

'I'll come to the Globe.'

'Don't you want to go straight home?'

'I want to see *you*. Will you be at Annie's?' In London, Irena usually stayed with her dancer friend Annie. 'Can I stay there before going to Devon?'

'Of *course*. The rehearsal will break around six.'

'I'll be there.'

Tuesday 23 August, Potters Bar, 4.15 p.m.

'Milk no sugar,' says Sarah. 'Is that right, pet?'

'Perfect. Thank you.' Rosamund gets up off her knees. She's planted all day. The pond's looking good, the builders have dug the electricity channel, the water lilies are enjoying their freedom. Next month she'll plant the spring bulbs.

'We heard you lost your husband, I'm so sorry. Was it the bombs?'

'A car crash.'

'We're so sorry, dear.'

'Thank you,' Rosamund says again. Sarah looks like a squirrel that knows where it's put all its nuts. No room in her life for the ambiguous mess that was Tyler. She hardly knows Dennis and Sarah, but they are her first clients and she's made them a perfect garden. She loves them.

'What a worker,' Dennis says.

Rosamund smiles gratefully. So much has sorted itself in her mind while she soaked roots, teased them apart, pressed them into the soil. If only she'd started doing this years ago. But better late than never. Tomorrow she'll take the biggest plunge of all.

Tuesday 23 August, Kilburn, London, 5.15 p.m.

Anka put down the phone. Mr Franjo Zubrinic loved her sequence. He wanted to work with her on it. He would pay their fare to New York.

'Helen?'

Helen was always in her room now. With the door shut.

'We are going America, for holiday.'

Helen opened her door. There were spots around her nose. She wore black. No more dinosaurs and puppies. Her hair was short and spiky.

'New York,' said Anka proudly. 'Martha's Vineyard.'

'When?'

'Thursday.'

'Cool.'

Wednesday 24 August, Chennai, Tamil Nadu, 4.00 p.m.; 11.30 a.m., UK

A mosquito landed on the ceiling. The gecko gazed at it with eyes like mica buttons. His pink-grey spine, the chocolate streak down his cloisonné flanks and the almost translucent tail ending in eyelash-thin stripes were all completely still. He was a master of depth of focus. In bright light, notches in his irises closed down to four pupils, giving overlapping images. As the phone rang below him, he stared at four mosquitoes blending into one. The man stretched out his arm. Neither gecko nor mosquito moved. Both used whatever they could of what was around. The mosquito was interested in the man but not till twilight, the gecko was interested in the mosquito and the man was part of his habitat.

'Yes?'

Suddenly the man stood up and the gecko lost focus on his mosquito.

'Oh.' Recovering focus, the gecko regauged his range. 'Richard told me. I am sorry, Rosamund.'

'Sorry' was not a sound the gecko had heard before from Kellar's lips. Not that he knew. He was concentrating.

'I tried to telephone . . .' The mosquito shivered its wings. 'Please.' Silence, except a faint buzz inside the phone. The gecko's tongue shot out, captured the mosquito and returned to its mouth. A second later the tongue came out again to clean the protuberant eyes. 'Indeed.'

With the digestion process beginning in his tract, the gecko crept forward. Evening had begun. Hunting time.

'Naturally, Rosamund. Of *course* come.' The gecko was halfway round the ceiling. 'Both of you come – for Christmas.'

The gecko cared nothing for voice-tones. Nor about a hope, almost

302

a hilarity, that had not warmed this voice for fifteen years. 'I see. March, then, for his holidays? You are welcome, always.'

Kellar put the phone down and stood still as the gecko in the centre of his study, on boards into whose cracks the sloughed skin of human beings had sifted, like sand in an hourglass, for forty years. His own skin, his daughter's skin, little floaters of gecko shit and dust from the earth outside.

When the gecko reached the far corner, he heard a noise he had not heard in his whole four years of life, a sobbing like the pulse of rain on earth.

Sunday 4 September, Southwark, London, 6.30 p.m.

The Globe's back door was guarded by bins higher than himself. Between them, Richard waited wearily for the door to open.

'In the tiring-room,' said the doorman.

'Can I leave my bags here?'

The corridors met him with a soft Babel of sound. *Ay, ee, oh, ooh, ah.* There must be hidden microphones. The noises followed him into the Gents where he looked hopelessly at himself in the mirror, unshaven from a day and night on a plane.

Why should Irena be glad to see him? He'd been so selfish all these years. She must have known about the creepy infidelity at his heart. Fantasies about her own best friend! Why should she be glad he'd come back from the dead? She was an artist. He had failed her, he had nothing to give.

Back in the corridor, he stopped a girl rushing by.

'Where's the tiring-room?'

'That door. They're doing a costume check.'

He pushed it open. Walls, ceiling and floor like a box of nut-brown sandalwood. People in Tudor clothes, as if the inhabitants of the National Portrait Gallery had slipped their frames to rendezvous in here. And a glass, tilted to reflect a beautiful woman in a low-cut yellow dress.

He met her eyes in the mirror. The eyes that had saved him in the dark. Irena as he had never seen her. Voluptuous. Astonishing.

303

'Yes?' A man in doublet and hose blocked his view.

'For Irena?' Richard said hesitantly.

Suddenly Irena was hugging him. He hardly dared touch her.

'Thank God, thank God you're safe.' Forgive me, he wanted to whisper and didn't dare. 'We're just about to start. Want to lie down and rest?

'Can I watch?'

'Of course. My husband can watch, can't he, Bernard?'

The Elizabethan courtier turned with a dazzling smile.

'Was it you bitten by the snake? We were so *worried*, darling. What a hero.'

'We must be very quiet,' Irena whispered many hours later, outside Annie's. 'We mustn't wake her, she gets up at five.' They tiptoed into darkness. 'Take your shoes off. Mustn't mark the floor.'

Carrying their shoes, they crept past the dark mirror of a studio wall to a tiny bedroom where Richard put his arms round Irena.

'I didn't think I'd live to hold you again.'

'It's changed you, hasn't it?' she said as they lay in the single bed like children. Richard, propped on his elbow, couldn't look at her enough.

'I realised I'd taken the best thing in my life for granted.' He smoothed her hair off her temple. 'You. Love.'

'But it was granted. To both of us.'

'I felt I'd been sleepwalking through my own love story. Things never got said.'

'Not everything has to be said.'

'I've never been unfaithful, you know that. But why did you encourage Ros to come to India? Was it a – test?'

'I wouldn't do that! To either of you. I trusted you. I trusted us.'

'And Ros?'

Irena hesitated.

'She's been under such pressure. So all over the place. But it was OK, wasn't it? It helped her. She's a new person. Apart from the awfulness – Tyler dying, Russel, bombs, everything – she's somehow come back. You helped her, darling. Only I didn't know you were going to get bitten.'

'Such an idiot.'

'I've always been terrified of it. All your colleagues got bitten in the end. Somehow the terror in London brought that home.'

'What was all that whispering in the corridors?'

'Stage mikes. People warming up on stage. Wherever you are backstage, you've got to know what's happening out front.'

'It felt – I suppose everything feels like that to me at the moment . . .'

'Like what?'

'Like a message. It's silly, you'll laugh . . .'

'What?' Her hand traced his collarbone.

'That black krait – it's such a mystery snake, you've no idea. Even Kellar's only seen one once. I felt it was a messenger, a warning, to make me reconsider my life. Our life.'

He looked at the tiny gold hairs on her top lip.

'Irena, please, I – want a child with you. If you'd like that.'

When he'd said, long ago, that he didn't want children, Irena had said OK, all she wanted was to live with him and do the best work she could. She never said anything she didn't mean. He was asking her to go back on something that was part of them from the start.

'Bring a new person into a dying world?'

'I don't want to be away any more. I want to be with you. See it grow, show it any wilderness left. I can still do my bit. Teach conservation. Write. And spend my life properly, with you.' He pressed his head against hers. 'And our child.'

She was silent.

'OK,' she said at last. 'If we can.' She nestled into his arm. After a long pause she whispered, 'A child in the old barn again. My parents would be so, so happy.'

Saturday 10 September, Potters Bar, 4.00 p.m.

'I knew you were the right person, pet.'

Sarah looks happily at green turf, purple Michaelmas daisies, pink roses, a tiny pond and a fountain like a sapling of glass.

'It's turned out well.' Standing between two people looking at their future under September sun, Rosamund feels like a child who has pleased both its parents.

'Just as Sarah wanted, and some,' says Dennis.

'I gave your name to my sister,' says Sarah. 'And she told her neighbour what a lovely job you've done. *He* wants you now.'

'Just you take care of that lawn,' says Rosamund. 'Water it for three months, promise? Love your lawn. That's an order from your gardener.'

'Selling up?' asks Scott, as she opens the door that evening. He's been away, she hasn't seen him for a fortnight. Behind his head she sees the green willow and her sale board. The summer, which has been at her like a war, now feels tired. September light fills the street like aromatic oil: glittery, dusty, sticky as ambergris. The house she is about to leave sits solidly in its garden. Willow-shadows speckle the grass.

'Three lots of people are coming to view on Monday.' She kisses his cheek. 'I'm stinky, I'm cutting onions. You have love from Dennis and Sarah. How was Scotland and the conference?'

'It went. Can I do anything?'

'Get yourself a beer from the fridge. How was coming back to work?'

'Feels like all the world's vanishing animals end up dead in London. We got a haul of bush meat. A load of dead chimps.'

'You sound tired.'

He says nothing. She could always depend on Tyler's extravagant sentiment, even when she knew it was hollow. With Scott she draws a blank in funny places and sometimes feels disappointed, as if she is drowning and he's failing to pull her out. These weeks without him have been hard, full of estate agents, selling furniture and persuading Russel to feel excited about moving.

She watches Scott sit and pour lager into a glass.

'Sorry, love. Bit browned off. Five thousand animals've just been found dead and dying in a boat off south China. Three hundred crates, of lizards, turtles, pangolins. And *forty* bear paws.'

'Bear paws?'

'For soup. All that, and more, gets smuggled into China every day. Wouldn't have known if the boat hadn't broken down.' He gulps. His normally furry hair is flat like waterlogged silk and she wants to stroke it. 'What'll they *do* when the only animals left are disease-bearing insects with no birds and frogs to eat 'em, rats with no snakes to eat those, and scavengers like magpies, far more adaptive than us? Probably cleverer too,' he adds gloomily, watching her slice shallots. 'Where's the boy?'

'In Northampton. Staying the weekend with a girl he met in Greece.'

'Hey!'

She tips shallots into hot oil. What can she say? How she liked the hare photo he sent? They have lost connection suddenly. The kitchen feels very silent.

'Why are you selling?'

'Can't manage the mortgage. I'm looking at two-bed flats in Camden.' She laughs, but he is staring at his beer.

'Sorry to hear that.'

'Don't be. I'll miss the garden. But the house has always felt a bit – unreal.'

She hasn't realised that's how she's felt, as if the house was as fake as Tyler. Or her-and-Tyler. Watching the onions begin to glisten, she feels Scott's hands on her shoulders. He is kissing her nape.

'No one can say,' his breath tickles, his hands steady her arms, 'I'm after your money now, can they?'

'Scott!' She turns. 'Was *that* it?' Questions flop in her head, like a bat that has flown in through the window and can't get out. She remembers when he first came how he looked at everything, rugs, piano, paintings, chairs and that sofa. All bought by Tyler. Everything she's selling.

'Well . . . What's that we're having, for supper?'

'Coq au vin.'

'Very nice too.'

Feeling flooded, like an engine, she puts chicken pieces in the pan to sear them. In silence, with Scott's hands on her shoulders, they both watch the pearly fat-beads spit.

'You had all this,' he says into her neck.

'You make me feel more real,' she says at the sizzling pan, 'than this ever did. Sort of – confident.'

She tips the pieces into a casserole, steps back, and finds herself in his arms. One of her hands is creeping to his hair, some other hand, it has to be her right, or her left, is round his waist. Her eyes are closed. She opens them and sees his brown eyes, dreamy and rapturous. So much on his face that she feels she has never seen him before. Longing, elation, anxiety. And hope.

They kiss nervously, eyes closed, like teenagers. His lips taste of lager.

'Wanted to do this,' he says into her hair, 'ever since we met.'

'Why didn't you?' He says nothing. 'You've been hurt too, haven't you?'

Like Tyler, Scott keeps things light, but for the opposite reason. Feeling too much, not too little. Does she want to do this? All her life she's known where she is with *down*. You don't have to face actually getting what you long for. But yes, she's going ahead, her fingers are cradling the bottom edge of his shoulderblade. Other fingers, also hers, are deep in his hair. She feels light and alive, standing in his arms with the pot bubbling and sunlight pasting oblongs on the floor. Now he's kissing her throat. That hand of hers that was so wayward months ago, twitching to touch him when she told it not to, is rubbing his spine.

'How long,' he asks, 'does coq au vin take to cook?'

Saturday 10 September, Tottenham Court Road, London, 7.00 p.m.

'*This* shoe shop, Helen? Office? Is expensive.'

'So? You said I could have anything I liked, because of the money from America.'

'OK, little apple.' Anka sat on a bench among discarded sandals from the sale and looked out at Centre Point's fountains, at shoppers crowding into Oxford Street. Helen was examining clumsy sport shoes with ugly flashes. Why did her daughter want to disappear her feet in things like that?

'Why not this side? Pretty sandals, why not you want these?'

'No one wears that stuff. They're not cool.' Helen gave a clutch of trainers to the Japanese assistant, to find them in her size.

'Maybe,' Anka said, 'for school . . .'

'Oh, Mum.' Helen switched from contemptuous teen to wailing child. 'I hate school without Katya.' Lasta and Budimir had taken Katya to Croatia for a year.

'Maybe, school in New York?'

Helen's smooth brown face and spiky hair swung round.

'Like, for real?'

'They want me, for work. Maybe, we go for good?'

Trainers scooted across the floor as Helen hugged her.

'When?'

'January.'

Helen put her foot into a white trainer with green stripes.

'Also, duso, I must ask you forgive me.'

'What for?' Helen started tying laces.

'I said my family, all was killed, in war.'

'So?'

'Was not true. My mother, she lives.' Helen's fingers stopped.

'Like, she's in Croatia, now? You mean, I have a baka, like Katya? Why didn't you tell me?'

'Because I did not tell her, about you.'

'She doesn't know I'm – I'm here? I'm alive?'

'I was – shamed.'

'Of me?'

'No!' Anka hugged her.

'Mum! People are looking.' Helen picked up a black shoe with red slashes.

'Of you, am proud! Of me. Because I knew your father only short time. Because I was not marry. My mother, your baka, is Catholic. Is big shame.'

'You said my dad died. Was that untrue too? Because,' Helen stuck her foot into a rose-pink trainer, 'I was afraid that he – that man . . .'

'Tyler.'

309

'I was scared *he* was my dad.'

'*Isuse Krise*. No, baby, no. Was bad but not *so* bad. Is dead too, now.'

'Like, *dead*?'

'In car.' She watched Helen run a finger round the inside of her heel.

'But he *was* your boyfriend, Mum,' Helen said slowly. 'Wasn't he?'

'Yes.'

'Why didn't you say?'

'I – was shame.'

'So who was my dad?'

'*Good* musician. Very good! I knew only few months, first arriving London. He went home, Australia. Not knowing about you. Then, he died.'

'*Australia?*'

'If you like, we find his parents.'

Helen put on the other pink trainer, stood up and inspected her feet in a mirror.

'Nice,' said Anka, cautiously. 'More – female.'

'Doh . . .'

'I will tell my mother. We will go Christmas, to village.'

Helen did a little skip.

'I'm going to have a *baka*! But, if she's ashamed of me . . .'

'No, sweet. Of me, the shame. You, will adore. Over moon.'

'Over *the* moon. What's she like?'

'Not educate, not speaking English. She has tattoo.'

'A tattoo? Where?'

'A cross. On back of hand, here.' Anka spread out her left hand.

'Like a Goth?'

Helen looked at her pink toes, side by side like pigeons on a branch. Then she looked up at Anka and grinned, bouncing her heels on and off the ground.

'I've got a tattooed granny! A granny *of my own*.'

Later that night, when Helen was at a sleepover, Anka set out for Whittington Hospital. In Archway Tube she stared at the rising silver corduroy of the escalator, the speckled stone of crowded tunnels, and came out to a roaring circle of night traffic. In Whittington Hospital precinct she stepped softly round each dark building, looking at the names. Occupational Therapy. Jenner Building. Music ran through her head, something heard at college. *Pictures at an Exhibition*. The Ballet of the Unhatched Chick.

She glanced up at the orange-purple sky, trying to find the moon. Round the back of the Labour Ward refuse bins towered above her and a cat or fox flicked through shadowspaces between them like the cats did at night in the churchyard, at home. Out of her bag she took a white chrysanthemum and a night-light, like those she used to light when Helen was afraid of the dark.

When someone dies, she heard herself saying, *we light candle on place they are buried. At night, so moon will see.* She'd loved Tess, even if Tess had never lived. For Tess, she had sacrificed the love she'd had, or had thought she had.

She laid the flower on the tarmac and lit the candle beside it. The flame turned one ivory petal to a tiny crescent moon.

Sunday 11 September, Primrose Hill, London, 11.45 a.m.

'Nice room.' Scott leans back on the pillow. The air is perfectly still. Rosamund's bedroom looks different when her head is on Scott's shoulder. Sun pours in, on walls red as a toffee apple, touching her mother's photo on the chest of drawers.

'Didn't see as much of Scotland as I'd have liked,' he says dreamily, pulling her closer. 'Wanted to go back to my gran's place but was stuck in that conference. Maybe we could go there, some time? I could show you her beach. Take a few photos, maybe.'

'Love to.' Rosamund moves her hand through the thick hair that runs, she now knows, from his throat to his navel and further south.

'Isn't this hot, in summer?' she says.

'Don't know any different, do I?'

'Shall I make brunch? I'm meeting Irena this afternoon.'

'Why don't I take us out for pizza first? Or a pub?'

Pulling on tights, Rosamund looks up and sees him watching.

311

'Just enjoying it,' he says, smiling. 'Long time since I saw a woman do that.'

He goes to the window. This is an old house, there must have been moments before when a naked man has stood looking out of this window. But not in her time. She looks at the rivulets of hair feathering the backs of his thighs.

'You've got a fox,' he says suddenly and she joins him. They watch a young fox cross the lawn, his white front spotless as a dress shirt, his black-tipped brush bannering behind. His coat shines like conkers, fresh-split.

Rosamund is walking on air over Golders Green Crematorium's grass beside Irena. She's just paid for three hundred crocuses to be planted here for Tyler. In March, before they go to India, she'll bring Russel to see them. Some leaves on these trees are gold, some still green. The London sky is unbroken grey cloud but she feels like a ray of light, one of those shafts that finger down through cloud and make a distant meadow glow.

'You look brilliant, Ros. Selling houses suits you.'

'How about you? How's Richard?'

'He's got interviews at West Country universities. And Southampton, they're big in conservation science.'

'Russel's looking forward to us coming to you at Christmas.' They walk past lawns and shrubs. 'Every single plant here has a name. Kingsley Amis, Peter Sellers, Sigmund Freud, Ivor Novello, Marc Bolan – and Keith Moon from The Who! Tyler would love that.' She sees Tyler standing in their garden waving his hand, inviting people to indulge him – and finds herself shaking with loss. 'Here,' she says, almost choking. Irena puts a hand on her arm. 'Tyler's rosemary bush.'

The plastic label with his name is on a stalk as if it too is growing in the earth. *In Loving Memory of T. Fairfax, 1961–2005*. Forty-four years, for a man who thought nothing was enough, no woman, no glass of wine. And no child, either.

A blackbird streaks out of the tree above, squeaking like a rusty tap.

'At least now I know where he is.' Will this rollercoaster of fury and sorrow never stop?

'It's very hard, Ros, mourning someone who hurt you so much.'

'He was supposed to look after Russel. Instead, he used our dead baby to lie to that woman. As he always, always lied to me.'

'He must have been upset too, when the baby died.'

'Are you on his side?'

'You know I'm not. But he must have suffered too.'

'You said he was a narcissist.'

'That's still a human being.'

'He couldn't admit he'd fucked things up with Russel so he invented a fantasy he liked better, while his son . . . If it hadn't been for Scott . . .'

There is black fog round her now. Through it, she feels Irena hugging her.

'I don't know how Tyler lived with himself,' Irena says softly, 'but it must have taken its toll.'

'He got drunk, had a row with that woman, ran away and skidded to his stupid death.'

'He'd just heard Russel was in hospital. That's why he was speeding.'

'He *swam* in betrayal.' She's brimming with anger and despair. Their edges grate inside her.

'He wanted life to be exciting,' she hears Irena say, still holding her. 'I expect betraying was exciting. But I bet it was difficult sometimes, being Tyler.'

Rosamund turns away. This rage she gets hit by is bound up with Father, she knows that. And the terror, too. Russel is thrilled about India in March, but she's petrified. Father watermarked her life and Tyler somehow fitted Father's imprint. She'd thought the bitterness had faded. Can even Scott not help her be rid of it? She feels again the thud on her breastbone where the snake hit, and through the black fog sees her old solitary Rusty Spotted self lying like sloughed skin on the grass, waiting for her to step back in.

She steps round it and hears Irena's voice as if from another planet.

'It'll take time. You'll remember good and bad. It'll come and go.'

Sure. Like when he was alive. Was Tyler her one big love or the monster who blighted her life? If she never resolves that she'll never be able to forgive Father either. Can she forgive him, can he forgive her? How on earth will they face each other?

She turns to look back at the tree and the tiny bush below, and sees a bird fly into the branches above. She had a deep connection with Tyler; she can't wish that unfelt, unlived. Sunlight pours over the tree from a break in the cloud and she squeezes Irena's arm.

'Let's go and look in those dress shops with sales on the High Street.'

Behind them, the blackbird returns to his branch. He is establishing his winter feeding territory. He chirrups four rising quavers, followed by six descending. Each phrase lasts six seconds, then begins again.

VENOM EXTRACTION DAY

21

Saturday 25 March 2006, Camden, London, 7.00 a.m.

Rosamund opens her eyes. Scott is asleep on his back. She has woken curled up into him like fern. Being with Scott isn't all scramble and intensity, like with Tyler. It's comforting, with patches where she feels he'll never understand. But he often surprises her by under-standing more than she does.

What must she do now? Turn off the heating, check window locks, make sure Russel has his passport.

She's done so much in the last six months but facing Father will be worse. Selling the house was nothing in comparison, though saying goodbye to the garden in November was a wrench. The trees were bare. Next spring's leaves, now wintering in their furled-up buds, would greet new faces. She stood there picturing her old protector, Rusty Spotted, slinking into the brambles like the fox that showed itself the first morning Scott stayed.

The camellias she dug up that day are flourishing now. So is Russel. Scott is around at weekends; Russel likes that. Scott may not be the answer for ever, but it's great for now. Russel likes that Bramble sleeps in his room. His own girlfriend comes to stay, too. Lovely, though Rosamund suspects them of smoking dope.

This flat seems more hers than the house ever did. Her bedroom is no desperate asylum like the one she slept in for the last ten years. It is hers, and chosen. Photos on the wall show Russel at Christmas with Richard and Irena; Scott and Russel on Russel's birthday; a beach in the Hebrides where they took Russel for October half term.

The photo of Russel with Father is in Russel's room. She hopes Russel won't feel let down when he finally meets his grandfather.

The money she has earned from new clients is enough to go to

India with, so she's no longer living entirely off her capital. She thought that once she got here she'd be her same old pre-Tyler self, but it turns out she's some other old self. One she's not sure of, yet.

Scott grunts and gathers her closer.

'Nervous?'

'Petrified.' She ruffles the pelt on his chest.

'I'll miss you.'

'Me too.'

Later, as she makes for the bedroom door dressed for the journey, he grabs her by the arm, spins her round and kisses her hard, as if fire shut up in a stone had suddenly burst out. They stand together in March sunlight, wordless.

CHENNAI. There it is, white letters on a black airport board. Russel takes a photo of it on his mobile. He knows, now, that Chennai's a city. But there's jungle near, and Grandpa has promised he'll see it.

In the security queue, he watches women scrutinise the procession of squiggles on white screens: X-rays of toothbrushes, mobiles, brushes and spectacles, like bacteria in a microscope with sacs and bubbles round them. He looks down suddenly with a light shock. There is a large snake beside him, see-through like Sellotape. He'd forgotten about Kaa.

A man grabs his rucksack.

'Mind if I look in this?' He lifts out Russel's spongebag, iPod, condoms, bubbled foil of malaria pills. 'Going to India for long?'

'Five weeks.'

'Holiday?'

'Seein' my grandpa.'

'Have a good time.'

His mum is putting her shoes back on, after Security. Did she see the condoms? He took them from a drawer in his dad's old bedroom and keeps them because of Dad. With Zoe he uses new ones. He's shown Zoe the piece about Dad in the paper. Zoe thinks that's cool. Maybe he was a shit in some ways, she said, but you've got to live with that. Think of the turtles, finding their way to the sea.

*

318

It's nearly dark when they reach their seats. Outside the air is misty. Halos of light, like growing muscle, cling round the airfield lamps. Mum snaps her seat belt.

'Look at the films we can watch. How do you work this thing?'

'Doh, Mum, look . . .'

When they leave the ground, he is explaining the buttons so he does not see, or imagine, or whatever has been going on in their long companionship, a translucent python on the tarmac, rearing its diamond-shaped head for one last look at the plane.

Sunday 26 March, Devon, 1.30 a.m.

'You OK?'

Irena was a dim shadow, walking towards the door in the dark.

'Just having a pee.'

He heard the lavatory flush and remembered hearing Ros sobbing in there after she and Tyler had that row. His fantasies now seemed to have belonged to some other Richard. The black krait had saved him. It came, it vanished, he nearly died, and something was freed in him for ever.

In daily touch with Girish and Gopal, he was doing what he could. While from south and north India they did what they could, too, to hold back the destruction of the wild. The battle would never be won, but you had to do something.

Irena was back, an ice-maid in his arms.

'You're lovely and warm. Richard, was it only science that took you away? Or India too?'

'A bit of both. You never came with me.'

'I'd love to now.'

'We'll go together. *And* the baby. We'll go to Girish and Shanta's wedding.'

Sunday 26 March, Chennai, Tamil Nadu, 5.00 p.m.; 12.30 p.m., UK

'There he is. Oh God!'

'Chill, Mum.' She couldn't do this alone. Russel feels strong, as if the world were opening an eyelid. The clock says five o'clock but really it's midday. There are thousands of people.

A tall old guy is standing in front of them in western clothes. White hair, a thin brown face with scribbly criss-cross lines. Glasses with no edges. The eyes behind dark and greeny, with black rims round the pupils.

'Good afternoon, Rosamund. And – Russel.'

'Hello.'

His hand is wet with sweat. Grandpa's is dry and strong. His mum kisses her dad's cheek.

'We shall be home in one hour. We are just outside Chennai.'

'Madras, when I left,' says Mum.

'They changed the name ten years ago. Come.'

Outside is hotter than Russel ever thought he could bear. Sun stings his shoulders. Everything is dazzle and dust. A smiling man puts their bags in a jeep.

'This is Bansi.'

'Hello, Bansi,' says his mum.

'Welcome, mam.'

Russel has never been in a jeep. Inside, the air is even hotter and smells of plastic. Grandpa sits beside Bansi and a plastic elephant with a bulgy tummy hangs from the mirror between them. Bansi drives on the left like in England, through cows pulling carts, through lorries, through three-wheelers like yellow and black bumper-cars. There are skyscrapers beside the road. Then mud huts with skinny kids, dogs with curly tails and cows eating rubbish loose on the ginger earth. Below the road are bright green fields glinting with water like buried mirrors.

'Paddy fields,' says Mum. 'For rice.'

'I know.'

Now silver-blue sea and gold sand.

'Marina Beach! I remember paddling here. Making sandcastles.'

Bansi laughs.

'The Coromandel Coast.' His grandpa talks like a teacher in an old film. He waves at a line of rubbish. 'Those are the houses that collapsed in the tsunami.'

'*Here?*' said Mum. 'I thought – further south.'

'Several hundred people died here, Rosamund. It was Sunday morning after Christmas. A holiday. Fishermen's huts were flattened everywhere.'

'Father.' She hasn't said that word yet. It sounds uneasy, like a smell people pretend not to notice. 'What about you?'

'We were not affected.' Like, Grandpa was nearly in the tsunami and Mum hadn't known?

Bansi turns in through a hedge and parks by a house with no upstairs.

'Oh,' says his mum.

'You are in your old room, Rosamund. The spare room.'

'Where's Russel?'

'Govind put a camp bed in the kitchen alcove.'

His grandpa gets out of the jeep. He looks well strong for an old guy. Russel gets out too. This is the garden Mum used to tell him about like it was the best place she'd ever known, when he was a kid. The Dark Side, the Light Side. There are the paths like orange ribbons between bright broad grass like plastic. She used to run down there when *she* was a kid. He blinks. He feels dizzy.

'A mongoose visits the kitchen at night but I doubt it will disturb you, Russel.'

Inside, everything smells sharp. There is a metal net door in front of the ordinary door and propellers whirl on the ceiling.

'I remember this smell,' Mum whispers. 'Oh. My old room.'

Russel looks in. The wood bed has posts and a roof. In a passage, Bansi pushes back a checked curtain: Russel sees a camp bed under a window with mesh over the glass.

That night they eat curry off a table whose white cloth is thickly padded, as if there are other cloths beneath. A man Russel hasn't seen before holds metal dishes so they can spoon out their food.

'Thank you, Govind,' says Grandpa. They eat in silence. The food tastes different from Indian takeaways. Tastier.

'When your mother was four, she used to take her breakfast out to the garden.' Grandpa speaks to him more than to Mum, like he finds it easier.

'One day, the housekeeper heard her talking. She thought she had an imaginary playmate, as children do.'

Can Grandpa know about Kaa?

'One day, I heard her through the window saying, "No. Wait your turn." She was sitting on the ground in front of a cobra. I saw her tap it on the nose with one of these spoons. She took a mouthful, then gave one to the snake. It ate from the spoon.'

'Father!'

'I waited till it had gone, then asked the woman looking after her to fetch the child in.'

'Was it a king cobra?' Russel asks.

'They wouldn't eat porridge!' Grandpa sounds scandalised. He is good, Russel realises, at making you feel very silly. 'I had to dismiss the woman. You took that badly, Rosamund.'

'I remember someone going away.' His mum is staring at a small black statue on a shelf behind Grandpa.

'Russel might care to see the Snake Centre tomorrow. We could go to Mamallapuram after, if you like.'

'Mamallapuram?'

'You enjoyed it as a child, Rosamund. Mahabalipuram, one of the great architectural achievements of early India. Cave temples and a famous temple on the beach.'

'Rings a faint . . .'

'We shall depart early. Breakfast at six-thirty.'

'Fine, Father.'

His grandpa stands up.

'Don't go outside, Russel. They say they have seen a leopard. I don't believe it myself. But there are snakes.'

'Where can I email?'

He must tell Zoe he can't go out at night because of leopards and snakes. About the mongoose. And the tsunami.

'Tomorrow, you may use the computer in my study. I am working now. I suggest you sleep. Good night.'

'You OK in your alcove?' whispers his mum.

'I'm cool, man.' She looks strange.

'You OK, Mum?'

She smiles.

'I'm cool.'

Sunday 26 March, New York, 8.00 p.m.; Monday 27 March, 6.30 a.m., India

'We're on Mercer and Eighth,' Anka heard Helen explain on the phone. 'The doorman's called Pablo.'

'Who is?' said Anka.

'Guy in my class.' They had only been here three months, but already Helen had an American voice.

'Take old shoes off floor? Pink trainers. Please?'

'Doh, Mum! Gary won't, like, *mind.*'

Anka remembered Helen wearing those shoes in the village, at Christmas, in the snow.

'*Sretan Bozic,*' she said, laughing. Happy Christmas! So stupid, that she had been afraid to tell about Helen.

She had seen the village new through Helen's eyes. The Serbian army had pulled down many churches but theirs had been rebuilt so it looked good. The new priest had blessed them, they ate Christmas Eve bread and talked all night, watching the candles burn, her mother with her hand on Helen. Helen had decorated the tree with red dough hearts and lit extra candles for Anka's dead father and brothers. Quietly, by herself, Anka had lit two more for Tyler and Tess. All the flames had sparkled together in little mirrors hanging on the tree.

Helen laughed too.

'*Sretan Bozic!*' She carried her shoes away, one in each hand like a milkmaid balancing pails. Thank you, Helen, for making it easy to live in this city. Thank you, songs. Thank you love, that gave her the songs.

You could have a good love for a bad person. And anyway, he hadn't been all bad. He'd asked her to rescue him. Maybe he'd meant it, at first. He was so used to meaning things at the beginning. But he couldn't see it through.

All that lying. He must have felt so lonely.

'OK, Mom? Nice and clean now?'

The buzzer went. Gary, whoever he was, had arrived.

They are driving past bright green paddy, bright red earth and humpy cows. One cow has two little calf legs flopping out of her hump. The hoofs stir slightly as the cow walks like they're trying to get out.

'What's *that*?'

His grandpa turns to look.

'She was probably a twin. The other stuck to her in the womb.'

Bansi turns in through gates labelled 'Chooramaya Reptile Research Centre'.

'I am scientific advisor on their king cobra breeding programme. The old name for king cobra, Russel, was Hamadryad. Spirit of the Forest.'

A man in a check shirt put his hands together, like praying.

'*Namaste.*'

'*Namaste,*' said his mum, doing it back.

'Gopan runs the centre. Gopan, my daughter. From England.'

Russel feels his grandpa's hand on his shoulder, pushing him forward.

'My grandson, Russel.'

Gopan takes them into a building with a row of mesh cages like a zoo. In each is a tarry mound of sleeping snake. In one, a giant snake rears, opening its hood. Russel has seen photos of king cobras on the net but the real thing is bigger than he'd imagined. He goes closer. Mum puts a hand on his arm.

'This is not a spitting cobra, Rosamund,' says Grandpa. 'Russel is quite safe.'

Outside again, they pass boys sitting under a tree, tossing gleaming brown things from one bucket to another. Maybe insects?

'The poison-gatherers. They are harvesting the venom glands to make an antidote for scorpion stings.'

They walk on to an enclosure, look over a wall into a pit and see two men, several coiled snakes and a row of jars.

'Today is venom extraction day. Once a week, we milk snakes we catch in the fields. After a month, we let them go and catch new ones. That's how we manufacture antivenin.'

'You set poisonous snakes free again?'

'This is their home. They keep down vermin.'

One man tips over a jar. A snake covered in pale papery flutters flows onto the sand. The guy puts a stick under it and hoicks it up by the tail.

'A krait.'

'Like the one that bit Richard?'

'A different species. It is disorientated because it is shedding its skin.'

The man puts the snake down, it curls into a silvery heap and tucks its head under its coils. The guy fixes a wine glass on a post, stretches white stuff over the top and picks up another snake, a yellow one. He holds this too by the tail, with a stick under its neck, and points it at the glass, grasping the head between thumb and finger. The snake stares and opens a hood. There are spectacle marks on the back like a face. The real eyes are black, and look as if they're concentrating well hard. The mouth opens suddenly and the front teeth sink into the rubbery lid. Gold jism dribbles down inside the glass. The guy carries the snake to a tipped-over jar, it slips in and he ties a cloth over the top.

'Don't they get bitten?'

'They are Irula, the People from the Dark. They say they have been catching snakes for thousands of years. Certainly since the emergence of the snakeskin industry. They learn to handle them as babies. We get a few bites. Not many.'

Back in the jeep, they drive beside a blue sea which looks like it never heard of waves. It dazzles so it hurts to look.

'Does it hurt, being bitten?'

Bansi laughs.

'With a cobra,' his grandpa says, 'yes.'

'Have you been bitten?'

'So often that I am allergic to antidotes.'

'What'd happen if you were?'

'I'd probably die.'

'I didn't realise,' says Mum quietly.

'Did you enjoy Buxa, Rosamund?' Russel knows, somehow, that Grandpa dares to talk to her now she's actually said something. He

325

knows Mum's scared. But Grandpa is too. Like with Bono or Kaa, he feels he knows this without anything being said.

'Beautiful.' Russel waits for Mum to say about the snake she stepped on. She doesn't.

'Do many people die?' he asks after a moment.

'Yes, Russel, if they don't receive antivenin. Ten thousand deaths a year in India, from snakebite. That's why our Centre is important.'

They stop at a sandy beach beside a huge building, a monstrous upside-down beaker of brown sugar covered in wriggly carvings.

'This was a pilgrimage site in the seventh century,' says his grandpa as they get out.

'Welcome to Lord Shiva's temple,' says a guard, a skinny man with a silver tooth. 'The old name was Seven Pagodas. Once there were seven temples, not only one. So beautiful that the gods were jealous and covered them with sea.'

'The coastline has receded since the tsunami,' Grandpa says. 'People have indeed found structures that had been concealed by the sea.'

'What happened in the tsunami?' Mum asks.

'I was showing the temple to schoolchildren,' says the guard. 'We came back here, to the gate. I saw the wave – and we ran. Lord Shiva saved us. If we had stayed by his temple five minutes more, we would have drowned.'

Russel remembers running up the platform, seeing the doors close. He still dreams about that guy mouthing SORRY.

'No one died?' asks Grandpa.

'An old woman. She sold peanuts under that tree.' The guard points to a little tree on the sand.

They walk on past a row of stone bulls.

'Nandi, Shiva's mount,' says Grandpa.

'I remember.' Mum sounds excited. 'I wanted to climb them and you wouldn't let me.'

Birds flick in and out of carvings on the temple. Russel feels his grandpa watching him look at them.

'Would you care to walk in forest nearby, Russel? It's degraded forest but we might see something.'

'I'll stay here,' says Mum quickly.

'Bansi will come back with the jeep. He will be here if you need him. Stay out of the sun, Rosamund.'

The trees are higher than any Russel has ever seen. Poles of sunlight jut through chinks in the leaf-roof. Here, at last, is where he's always wanted to be.

He doesn't believe that just world thing now. It's not true that bad things only happen to bad people. The old woman selling peanuts could have been good. And the guy who tried to keep the doors open on the train. Sometimes he dreams it's Dad mouthing 'Sorry' as the doors close.

The noise of Bansi's jeep fades and he hears a needly whistle. His grandpa loops binoculars round his neck and points to the canopy.

'Look for a blue-black bird. That's the Malabar Whistling Thrush. They call it the Whistling Schoolboy.'

There it is, glinting like someone has poured blue salt over its back. With these binoculars, Russel sees a mosquito on the edge of its eye.

'Did you get the book I sent you, Russel?'

'Yeah. Thanks.' Wind shirrs in the leaves. 'I couldn't email, I didn't know . . .'

'That's all right, Russel . . .'

Their voices have overlapped. They break off at the same time, like animals that have accidentally come too close.

'You are honoured. Something that usually stays hidden is having a look at you.'

In the leaves above, Russel sees a face like a maroon egg with eyes. Then chocolate doll's glove paws, and a tail hanging like the string for the bathroom light in Irena's house

'A Malabar Giant Squirrel.'

It leaps from the branch. The tail trails behind like the string of a kite.

'Flying!'

'No.' His grandpa laughs. Uncertainly, like he's not used to sharing something funny. Russel knows what it's like, pushing people

327

away. 'We do have flying squirrels. This one's merely jumping.' He touches Russel's shoulder.

'You had a bad time, Russel, I gather. I telephoned your house the day of the bombs, to see if you were safe.'

'When?'

'Early afternoon.'

Russel remembers the phone ringing in the empty house.

'Would you care, next week, to make an expedition to pristine rainforest?'

'Cool.' Russel pauses. 'Thanks, Grandpa.'

The sea is blue yoghurt with a silver skin. What was it like when the tsunami hung over here, blocking out the sky, and crashed down till this temple was all underwater?

Fifteen months ago. Rosamund shivers. She never realised. All her life there's been so much she hasn't let herself think.

It's a shock how the same Father is. Still bossy, still stiff. The same clipped, timid-aggressive pop at the front of each word, same magenta veins down his nose, same wary tight mouth like something considering you from a cave. Same judging voice which says you never do anything right.

Russel seems to have taken him in his stride. But for her, there's too much to unravel. She'd thought Tyler being gone would make it easier to face Father, but everything between them feels like soiled knitting that she doesn't want to touch. Did he really wait coolly for a four-year-old to finish spooning porridge to a cobra? Did it cross his mind that it'd solve a few problems if the cobra finished *her* off instead?

Scott would say she mustn't think like that.

It is evening. Father is knocking at the door of her room.

'Rosamund,' he says, not opening it. 'A telephone call.'

She opens the door. He stays in the unlit passage.

'You will remember the telephone is in the study. Dinner is in fifteen minutes.'

Is it coldness or gaucheness? It's not her fault but feels as though it is. She remembers this feeling; it made her who she is. Made her yearn for male authority while knowing male authority was secretly terrified and would always disappoint. Whatever it is that Father emanates, it poisoned her then as surely, and maybe as innocently, as the snake that bit Richard.

But maybe none of what she felt about Father is really his fault. It just grew between them, father and daughter, like weeds in a ruined house.

The study smells as it always did, of books, dust and piano. Father used to play after she'd gone to bed. She remembers hiding under the piano once, smelling ivory and, she imagined, ebony. The breath of fatheriness.

She picks up the phone.

'Yes?'

'Just checking you're safe.'

'Oh, Scott, I was going to ring. Hadn't screwed up courage to ask if I could.'

'All OK?'

'Fine.'

He laughs at the word. So does she. Did she ever laugh in this room? Simply hearing Scott's voice lessens the power of the past.

'Boy OK?'

'Think so. They seem to take to each other.'

'Going to ask your dad about . . .?'

'I'll try. You all right?'

'Fine.' He pauses. 'Been using the tripod you gave me for my birthday.'

'Does it work OK?' She looks up. There's a gecko on the ceiling exactly like the one she used to watch when Father lectured her. Something here stopped her being who she was meant to be. This was where her jungle self grew, armouring her in shadows.

'Works a treat.'

Silence rustles between them down the wire, or airwaves, or whatever joins London to her childhood home.

'Take care, love,' he says.

'And you.'

She puts the phone down, feeling warm. There is the armchair where Father used to sit, to read to her and say what she'd done wrong.

In the other armchair she sees a ghostly little girl in shorts and a pink T-shirt, fingering brass studs on the arms, picking at the crumbly hairs of fraying leather round them, like a scab. A child for whom the most fraught thing is proximity. Who wears silence round her neck like garlic to ward off witches. A child who feels guilty without knowing why, afraid to understand how angry and alone she really feels. Hair the colour of ripe apricots tumbles round her face, which is shut in an owlish frown.

Rosamund is very sorry for her. But, like the jasmine that smothered those camellias, she's got to go.

'C'n I email tonight?' asks Russel at supper. He hasn't realised yet that everything to do with Father is fenced by unspoken prohibition.

'Do you wish me to show you how the machine operates?' says Father, to Rosamund's surprise.

'I'll know.'

'It contains all my data.'

'It's cool, Grandpa. I'm OK with IT.'

'Very well.'

Russel goes out.

'Would you care for beer, Rosamund?'

'Thank you.'

Govind pours them beer and the ceiling fan clanks as if about to crush them. Rosamund remembers being afraid of that too. What a scaredy-cat she'd been.

They sit opposite each other, the white cloth between. She never asked why it was squishy. Maybe she never let herself wonder what lay under anything. She looks at the black dancing god behind Father and remembers the moment by St Paul's, with Scott, when she felt that Tyler space being cleared inside her.

'Lord of the Dance,' she says. 'I remember your Shiva.'

'It is twelfth-century work, Rosamund. I bought it when we came here as a memorial to your mother. With money she inherited from her aunt.'

Her mouth is dry. Was that Browne professor right? She had found him repellent, yet for seventeen years she has believed everything he said.

'What really happened, when mother died? Professor Browne said—'

'You met Vic Browne?' His voice is sharp, like a beak.

'He was our examiner at college. He said there was a student living with you then. Vanona.'

'A refugee from Czechoslovakia. One of the philosophers at my college asked if she could lodge with us in return for help with the baby. With you.'

There is a crab inside her, pincering.

'Vic Browne was your mother's age, ten years younger than myself. I was busy in the laboratory. Vic took her punting, and to many events. Even a rock concert, I believe. It was 1969.'

'Was that the summer of love?' Maybe not. And anyway, would Father have cared?

'You did not stop crying. You did not like Vanona. One evening, I made clear I did not wish Daphne to go to a college ball with Vic and he took Vanona instead. Daphne and I had words. She accused me of – many things.'

'Sounds as if she should have been accusing him.'

'Next morning, she said she was going shopping in London and bugger the lot of us. Those were her words.'

'Professor Browne said she threw herself under a train.'

'Vic said *that*?' The white cloth between them burns her eyes. She feels sucked in, as if she were a vacuum and the air whirling round the clattery propeller is rushing round inside her. She daren't look at Father. Is she afraid of him, or for him? 'That was very wrong. The inquest made clear it was death by misadventure. The Cambridge platform was crowded, a previous train had been cancelled. Witnesses saw Daphne look in her handbag as the train came. The crowd surged and a student stumbled against her. They discovered later he was drunk. Someone pulled him back but Daphne fell under the train.'

'Why didn't you tell me?'

331

'I wanted to save you knowing that she – she was cut to pieces.'
Was that a secret properly kept, lovingly not told?
'I was so scared of you.' She didn't mean to say that. She's
breached the most basic taboo of all. She feels like a princess watching her father go out, from the city walls, to an enemy she has
summoned herself by accident.

Or is this terrible feeling of prohibition and taboo only in her
mind, not his?

'I am sorry, Rosamund. We – make mistakes.'

Silence. Except for the fan's relentless wrenching.

'Daphne adored you. She was looking forward to choosing you a
doll in Hamley's.' There is heat behind her eyes, like steam. 'People
said Vanona looked like Audrey Hepburn. She used to go round
the house in a nightshirt. I found it irritating. Daphne, I think, felt
threatened.'

'Professor Browne said you were having an affair with Vanona.
That's – that's why I gave up my degree.'

She watches the pulse jump in Father's throat.

'Vic was reckless,' he says finally, as if the words hurt, 'with
snakes and with people. And sometimes he could be – malicious.' He
takes a sip of beer. 'I loved your mother deeply, Rosamund. She
never needed to feel threatened by *any* woman.' His voice trembles.
'Daphne was the most beautiful, the warmest person . . . She was the
only— I miss her every day. I marvelled at how she moved. So different from myself.'

Rosamund feels something beginning to mend. Maybe he'd
longed for his daughter to be direct as he couldn't be. And she had
not been able to.

'Every day, for thirty-six years, I have blamed myself for what
happened.'

Inside him, she sees a long dark wound. It is not for her to heal,
but she might help. Russel might, too.

'For a long time, you were inconsolable. No one could do anything with you.'

'If I'd been different, Father, it might have been easier for you.'

'I am very glad, Rosamund, you are here now.'

She feels as if all her life she has been trying to tune a car radio whose electronics she never understood, and after years of chaotic squawk has suddenly hit a pure band of music. Slowly she raises her glass. After a moment he raises his, too.

Tuesday 11 April, Chennai, Tamil Nadu, 7.00 a.m.

'We won't take risks, Rosamund.' Father puts a box of mineral water bottles in his jeep. They are going to the Western Ghats for four days.

'Long sleeves in the forest, promise?' She looks at Russel. 'And a cap.'

'Doh, Mum . . .'

'*Yes.* Leeches, mosquitoes, skin cancer . . .' But Father will make sure Russel dresses properly. He is taking his grandson to the field as he never succeeded in taking his daughter.

She watches the car vanish in a rosy nimbus of dust and skips back to the bungalow. Seeing Russel deal with Father so easily has scotched that solitary, angry little girl for ever. Now she's going to have fun. Two friends of Richard's, Girish and Shanta, are coming to take her to Chennai bazaar.

Inside, there's a smell on the air like lavender. Govind must be trying a new floor polish. She goes into her room and sees something on the bed. It is Father's Shiva, with a note.

My dear Rosamund, I bought this with your mother's
money. It is yours now. With my best wishes for your future
happiness. Your loving father, Tobias Kellar.

She sits down on the bed and takes the little iron hoop in her hands. God knows how valuable it is. He has given her the most precious thing he has. Maybe he always did, and she was just bad at being given to. It wasn't her fault but it wasn't his either – why didn't she see that long ago?

Shiva stares up at her, his face still and smooth, his locks swinging out in the dance, and a snake swinging with them from one of his arms.

She imagines Scott's face looking at this, in that considering way he has. Maybe next time she comes, he'll come too.

Tuesday 11 April, Western Ghats, Karnataka, 4.00 p.m.

Russel stands with the binoculars beside his grandpa on a riverbank. The trees are so close the only sky he can see is above the stream. Thin leaves underfoot are like albino flames. The stream has a rock in it, with a crack along the top.

His grandpa points to a long snake swimming in a series of dark S's towards that rock. The water surface glints round it like coins.

'A king cobra, Russel. Thirteen feet. Probably male. He is heading for that rock. I've seen them basking there.' The snake slides vertically out of the water, up the rock face. 'There's another there already.' The crack at the top bunches into coils. A head winds up. Sideways, its neck looks thin as paper.

The new snake puts its head up over the rock and meets two steady eyes. Two hoods flare like black flowers opening.

'If that's another male, you're going to see one of the most extraordinary sights in nature. People used to think it was a mating dance. It is really males wrestling. This is the mating season and males are competing for females.'

The snakes sway back, forth and around, like two long-gloved hands belonging to the same person.

'They're exactly the same.'

'I think the one there first is fatter and bigger, don't you?' Two tongues flick in and out. 'They are immune to each other's venom. They have to win by physics, not chemistry.' Suddenly the bigger snake twists round the other and dashes it to the ground like rolling a Rizla. 'He's trying to wrestle him down.'

The new snake wriggles free and rears up. They go back to their swaying routine. Through the lenses, Russel sees smooth grey plates on each cheek and two mouths pursed like they are whistling in a mirror.

Another lunge and sudden twist. They roll again, trying to force each other's neck and head to earth.

334

'The bigger one has eaten more. If he wins, he will impregnate the females and his stronger genes will be perpetuated.' The intruder turns and pours like spilt petrol across the rock and down into the water. 'He's had enough.'

It's swimming right towards where they're standing. Grandpa's hand closes hard over Russel's shoulder.

'Bring your arm down, *very* gradually. If you're not comfortable, move slowly until you are, then freeze. Absolutely still. Like a statue.'

The snake has reached the bank. It must be just below. The forest has stopped about them. The only sound is a ripple.

'Most of what they see is movement.' Grandpa's voice is gentle but his hand is gripping Russel's shoulder-bone like iron. They see the snake's head coming over the bank. It stops and stares. Pearly rose-gold eyes with huge black centres look into Russel's soul. Its tongue flicks out.

Russel's nose itches. He wants to sneeze, to run, to be anywhere but here. He wants to be only here ever, all his life. He feels like Grandpa is holding him up, they are the same height but Grandpa seems to him stronger, like a tree.

Amazing, that Grandpa phoned the house that day.

Suddenly the snake has a hood and is streaming over the ground towards them, longer than Dad was tall, twice as long maybe. Longer than his bedroom in the old house. And it's coming straight for them, well not straight, curving side to side. He couldn't run even if he wanted to, Grandpa is holding him like a vice and anyway the snake's much too fast. How can it move like that, its head so high they can see its yellow throat and the great black body behind zooming over the earth?

Then suddenly it stops like Grandpa had told it to. Its head is right by Grandpa's ankle, so close they could touch it. Its body is huge, fat and black and stretches for miles. All down it are white slashes like the Nike swoosh logo.

Everything's still, even the trees. He isn't breathing and he's sure Grandpa isn't either. Only the snake's tongue moves. It pulses in and out a couple of times like it's licking the air in two directions.

But those cool eyes aren't looking at them now. It has new plans.

Russel sees it checking things out behind them. Slowly, it starts flowing on again. The hood has shrunk to just a faint cupping round the head. Inch by slow inch it passes Grandpa's shoe.

Russel turns his eyes and then, infinitely slowly, his head. He watches it go. Grandpa must be doing the same. When the head has disappeared in undergrowth behind, the tail tip flicks over Grandpa's toe, kind of saying goodbye. Then it's gone. He hears Grandpa sigh. He breathes again himself.

The sun slips a fraction lower in the sky. If they turned their heads they would see the other snake, the victor, still reared up to watch its rival go. And a transient ray, almost horizontal in the slide towards sundown, turning its yellow throat to gold.

But no one can see everything. Russel feels Grandpa's fingers relax. The hand on his shoulder is not a grip any more. In fact, it feels like a hug.

Russel looks up. From behind those glasses his grandfather's eyes, with that funny dark rim around the green, meet his. They are filled with tears.

'Well, Russel. You have met, face to face, one of the lords of life.'

TIGERS IN RED WEATHER

Ruth Padel

When Ruth Padel saw an advert for a cheap break to India, she decided to visit what she had always wanted to see: tropical jungle and a wildlife sanctuary. Her impromptu trip was the start of a remarkable two-year journey in search of that most elusive and beautiful animal: the tiger. Armed with her granny's opera glasses and a pair of Tunisian trainers, she set off across Asia to ask the question: can the tiger be saved from extinction in the wild?

Plunging into leech-infested jungles, she tracks tigers by jeep, by elephant and on foot, from Bangladesh to Bhutan, from China to far-east Russia. The result is a unique blend of natural history, travel literature and memoir, and an intimate portrait of an animal we have loved and feared almost to destruction.

'Thrilling and surprising . . . her prose has an intense, lush quality . . . She has an adventurer's intrepid spirit and a poet's eye for detail and ear for dialogue'
Sunday Telegraph

'This is not only a superb portrait of Asian tiger country, but also of the fears and longings that the tiger creates in human hearts'
Helen Dunmore

978-0-349-11698-3

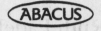

To buy any of our books and to find out
more about Abacus and Little, Brown, our authors
and titles, as well as events and book clubs,
visit our website

www.littlebrown.co.uk

and follow us on Twitter

@AbacusBooks
@LittleBrownUK

To order any Abacus titles p & p free in the UK,
please contact our mail order supplier on:

+ 44 (0)1832 737525

Customers not based in the UK should contact
the same number for appropriate postage
and packing costs.